"Jane Goodger delivers a spectacular debut novel that readers will cherish for its realistic emotional intensity."
—*Affaire de Coeur*

"What are you doing?" Maggie squeaked out as Carter roughly pulled her toward him. One hand swept around her waist, the other was lost amid her damp curls at the base of her neck.

"I'm seeing if you have amnesia, dear wife," he said, bringing his hard mouth down on hers. Maggie struggled against him, shocked at his behavior. She pushed against him with all her might while locking one leg behind his ankles. Stunned, Carter stumbled back, his arms flailing as he lost his balance. He let out a grunt as he landed heavily on his bottom side, his expression one of disbelief.

Maggie was shaking with anger as she stomped away and up to her room. Carter continued to sit on the floor, legs splayed. She had rejected him—as he thought she would. He had to admit, though he loathed himself for the thought, that a small part of him had hoped that she really was a different person because of the amnesia. Because from the moment he saw her, Carter had been wildly attracted to her. She simply was a gorgeous creature.

When There Is Hope

~

Jane Goodger

St. Martin's Paperbacks

WHEN THERE IS HOPE

Copyright © 1996 by Jane Goodger.

ISBN: 0-312-95860-9

Printed in the United States of America

St. Martin's Paperbacks edition / June 1996

10 9 8 7 6 5 4 3 2 1

To Bob Scherman, whose big heart and generosity
are boundless.
And to Karen Levin, my first critic, first fan,
and first friend.
Thanks to both for your help.

When There Is Hope

~ *Prologue* ~

S usan looked down at her rounded belly and smiled as she felt her baby move. She shook her head, still not believing that her body could produce a living human being. Amazing.

"Look how big I am," she yelled to her husband, who was leaning over their bathroom sink shaving. Steve stopped the buzzing razor just long enough to spread his arms wide to indicate her size and said, "Huge!" Rather than get angry, Susan smiled again. It seemed she was always smiling these days, no matter how sick she felt or how many trips to the bathroom she had to make to relieve her demanding bladder. After more than two years of trying to get pregnant, and thinking she never would, she had been overjoyed the first morning she flew to the toilet and threw up.

She'd rushed back to the bedroom after giving her mouth a quick rinse and shaken Steve awake. "Steve. I just threw up!" she said as if announcing she'd just won the lottery. Steve had looked at her groggily, and said, "Just don't give whatever you've got to me."

"Steve," she'd said, exasperated. "I think I'm pregnant." Steve was clearly skeptical.

"You've thought you were pregnant every month since we started trying."

Susan had given him a scowl. A week later she was still throwing up and a home pregnancy test and a blood test had confirmed her belief. And ever since then, she smiled constantly. She was driving Steve insane, even though he secretly enjoyed her obsession with the baby. Now, five months later, he viewed her growing belly with as much enthusiasm as his wife. How couldn't he be happy with a wife that grinned even as she emptied her stomach into the toilet? Even her friends, who had gone through morning sickness and knew its misery, were clearly disgusted by her good cheer.

This morning, she had put on a maternity T-shirt and shorts and was rushing about to get ready for her monthly visit to her obstetrician. Brushing her long, straight blonde hair, she said, "Too bad you can't come with me to my appointment. You work too hard. I should talk to your boss and give him a piece of my mind." It was a running joke between them that Susan would confront Steve's boss and plead her husband's case.

"I wish I could come, too," he said, clearly meaning it. Steve's strong sense of responsibility had only become more apparent since they knew they were going to have a baby. "I know," Susan said, giving him a sloppy kiss on his cheek. "I've got to get going. Call me when you're ready to leave work and I can start supper. 'Bye."

" 'Bye," he said.

"Say 'bye to Daddy," Susan said, holding her hand on either side of her stomach. She jiggled up and down and said, " 'Bye, Daddy," in a high-pitched voice. She laughed at her own silliness and at Steve's embarrassment over his crazy wife. But he relented and patted her slightly rounded belly and said, "Good-bye, my baby."

The drive to Providence was only about a half hour down Interstate 95, an easy drive on a Saturday. Susan hummed along with the radio, at times singing at the top of her lungs to one of her favorite songs by the

Three Non Blondes. The song had just ended when she noticed a tractor-trailer truck coming up behind her in the high-speed lane whose driver was obviously in a hurry. She turned on her blinker and stepped on the gas so she could pass a Volvo station wagon on her right to get out of the truck's way.

"Okay, guy," Susan said, slightly irritated by the driver's impatience. "I'll move over as soon as I can."

The truck driver was being a jerk, flashing his lights and coming what looked like just inches from her Saturn's bumper. Suddenly, a black Trans Am cut across three lanes and slammed into the Volvo, which careened toward Susan's car. Her stomach lurched in fear and her grip on the wheel tightened painfully as she swerved to the left, realizing the Jersey barrier was just inches away. She almost steered clear of the accident, but made the horrific mistake of slamming on the brakes. The truck driver behind her, seemingly surrounded by cars spinning out of control, could not stop in time and his truck literally rolled up the back of the Saturn. Squealing tires, grating metal, and screams filled Susan's head. "My baby. God, don't let my baby get hurt," she thought, before a terrible emptiness engulfed her and all went black.

Susan never woke up. Her car, with her inside, was crushed beneath the truck and wedged against the Volvo and the white concrete barrier. The highway was strangely silent when the last tire screeched against the steaming asphalt. In the other lane, all eyes looked with horror at the little car that had literally been run over by the truck. The drivers who drove safely southward knew with a certainty, as they slowed down to gape at the spectacle, that whoever was in that little red car had died.

Susan felt no pain, just the horrible realization that she was dead as she floated away from the accident. Desperately, she felt her abdomen for her baby, looking down with awful detachment at the twisted metal that was once her car.

She felt the beginnings of the calm that only the dead feel, but then there was something else. A yearning, a sadness that is almost never present in the souls that drift up to heaven. The yearning grew stronger the farther she floated away from the gruesome wreck until she was overwhelmed by it, perplexing those angels who watched from above. And when she began the frantic and impossible struggle to return to her ruined body, agitated beyond anything they had ever seen, they began whispering quickly among themselves. Clearly, they had a rare case here. They put their heads together until one gave a shout of triumph that came out as a resounding clap of thunder to those living souls below.

She was perfect. She was just what they had been waiting for all these years. She, of the thousands of candidates put before them, would be able to get the job done. With a questioning look to God, who gave a satisfied and pleased nod, the decision was made. Susan Butler could right the wrong a bumbling angel had made more than one hundred years before.

The funeral had been pure hell, but coming home was worse. Steve had walked around like a zombie during the two days before the funeral, numbed by grief. But despite the pain, he still had not come to grips with the fact that he was alone, that Susan was gone, that their baby would never live.

And now, in their apartment with so many reminders of Susan in every room, it was almost as if she would be home any minute, carrying a bag of groceries and groaning about her aching back. Her tattered sneakers still lay in the living room where she had kicked them off carelessly three days before. Steve didn't want to pick them up, to store them in the closet. Because he knew once picked up, they would never lay messily in the living room again. What had once been an irritation now brought tears of longing to his eyes. The reminders were everywhere and would eventually have to all be put away. Just not now. He needed those reminders, needed to know that Susan existed, and still did, in his broken heart.

Steve loosened his tie and took off his dark blue suit jacket, telling himself he would never bring himself to wear that somber suit again. He had just slumped down into his easy chair when the doorbell rang. He squeezed his eyes shut in an effort to gather the energy to walk to the door and open it. It was probably a friend who wanted to see if he was okay. He could not bear another "I'm so sorry." He just could not. He knew his friends and family meant well, and grieved themselves, but he wanted more than anything else to be left alone, to lose himself in his sadness. Just for a little while. When the doorbell rang again, he heaved himself up. He was surprised to find a complete stranger standing in the doorway, a young man wearing an expensive-looking suit and carrying a briefcase. A lawyer, perhaps.

"Steven Butler? Oh, my god," the man appeared quite stunned, but quickly collected himself. "I am so sorry to disturb you at this awkward time. I read about the accident in the *Journal.* I've always hated those damned tractor-trailers. My name is Robert Fisher from Tillman, Bancroft, Bancroft and Schuler. I am here on a matter of some importance. And mystery, actually. May I come in?"

"This isn't the best time," Steve said, but stepped aside, allowing the man to enter. He led him to the living room, where Steve sat heavily in his chair, not even attempting to hide his weariness. The man sat on the couch, snapped open his oversized briefcase, and brought out a thick leather packet, which he handed over to Steve. He looked at the thick package with little interest then brought his attention back to the young lawyer.

"I have to confess to you, that despite the circumstances, I am glad to have been the one to deliver this to you. That packet has become quite the legend in our office. You see, an elderly woman named Margaret Johnsbury brought that into our offices sixty years ago with a request that it be delivered to Steve Butler at this address on this date. To be honest, I didn't think such a person existed, but then the accident and the packet clicked together, so to speak."

"What is this?" Steve said, holding the leather packet, his curiosity finally piqued.

"That's just it. We have no idea. We were given very specific instructions, and part of that was that no one was to open the packet except Steven Butler. You."

"You say this woman brought it to your offices sixty years ago? And instructed at that time for it to be delivered to me now? That's impossible. It doesn't make sense. I don't know any Johnsburys." Steve creased his brow in concentration trying to think. "No. No one."

"The only way to find out is to open the packet," the lawyer said, obviously hoping he would do so in his presence.

Steve obliged, unbuttoned the leather carrying case, and withdrew a thick packet of individual letters tied together in a brittle red ribbon. He fished around inside the packet and withdrew a single envelope with the words, "Open First" scrawled on it. Steve opened the letter, taking out two sheets of paper with impossibly familiar handwriting on them. He read the first few sentences, growing very still. His eyes, against his will, filled with tears.

"I'm sorry, Mr. Fisher. But I really need to be alone right now. I know you are curious. I'll fill you in someday. Just not today."

"Of course, I understand." But clearly, Mr. Fisher

was disappointed. The mystery would continue, at least for a time, and the crew back at the office would be disappointed as well. "I'll show myself out," he said, when it became clear that Steve was already engrossed reading that tantalizing letter.

Steve couldn't believe what he held in his hand. It was like a gift from God. The letter was from Susan.

Steve,
    I know right now you are devastated, believing me dead and lost to you forever. In a way, I suppose I am. What I am about to tell you will be difficult to believe, but I know you know me enough to realize that it is the truth and no cruel joke. I agonized over whether to send this packet to you, and in the end, I thought it could be a great comfort. It is me, Susan, although I'm sure you already recognized my chicken scratch. I am an old lady now, but I still think of you with love and our brief time together as one of my happiest. The strangest thing happened to me after the accident on 95. Somebody up there decided I shouldn't die. But as you probably know (but don't like to think about) my body was unrecyclable, to be rather graphic. It was irreparably damaged. So, somebody up in heaven decided I should live, but in another's body. Unfortunately, they chose this horrible woman from the 1800s. I know they had their reasons, and everything, in the end, turned out for the good.
    Over the years, I've written you letters, always with the idea that someday I would send them to you. I pray that this packet gets through to you. I tried to pick a law firm that will be still around in your time. The poor people in that office thought I was an eccentric old fool. I'm just eccentric, though, and after all I've been through I definitely

deserve a little craziness. I've had a good life, I've been happy, for the most part, though it was hell in the beginning, let me tell you. Isn't this strange? I'm sure it's stranger for you than for me. By now, for me, this is all natural. I've enclosed some stock certificates that I took out in your name, which I think are still redeemable. They should make you rich, rich, rich. Aren't I nice? The most important thing, though, are my letters. My life.

Your loving wife,
Susan

~ *Chapter 1* ~

*. . . The first few days were the worst. I was so
confused and hurt. . . .*

S usan felt as if there was something inside her head
chopping away. When she opened her eyes, it was
worse, the pain sharpened, intensified, a white light slic-
ing through her skull. She felt strange, as if her body
were wrapped in a thick, wet blanket.

"Margaret. Open your eyes. Margaret." A man's
voice close to her ear, a hand on her arm. There were
other voices, muffled, more distant. Was the man calling
her Margaret? She opened her eyes to see, but pain
exploded in her head so she quickly closed them. Susan
had never hurt so much or felt so . . . odd. She tried to
think past the pain, past the confusion, but she could
not. Trying not to move, for moving caused her head to
explode, Susan tried to determine what was happening
to her. The accident, she remembered the accident, the
Trans Am, the Volvo, the truck. Then . . . Susan
moaned as the horror of what had happened to her became clear. She had died. Then why did she feel alive?
Surely heaven would not hurt so much, would not leave
her feeling so confused.

Moving her hand, she felt cold, damp grass. That had
to be wrong, didn't it? She should still be in her man-
gled car, or at least on the hot, gritty asphalt of Inter-

state 95. Why should she feel so cold? It had been a scorching summer day when she'd left her apartment.

"Cold." She said that single word, the only word that seemed to come to her.

"Someone get a blanket," a man's deep baritone shouted.

Dimly, Susan could hear voices of others who had apparently gathered around her while a hand gently shook her, but it hurt so much to even think about what had happened to her and who was trying to rouse her. She felt something heavy being draped over her. A blanket that smelled of hay and horses.

"Jesus, look at her head," a man said, his voice higher than the first.

"Head . . . hurts." Susan tried to say more but the effort was simply too much.

Then, like a wave crashing over her, she heard voices, all talking on top of each other, but somehow making sense. The voices tumbled into her brain with a roar that deafened everything around her. Susan wanted to scream at the voices, to tell them to go more slowly, to stop the roaring in her head. Though tumbling atop each other, she was somehow able to understand each message sent to her. In the back of her tortured mind, she realized she was not actually hearing these voices, but simply knew what they were saying. And what they were saying was so unbelievable, so horrifying, Susan shook her head, causing another rush of pain.

She was dimly aware of someone trying to calm her, but she continued thrashing her head back and forth as if to stop the voices that continued to invade her mind. But despite her attempts to silence them, their message made it through and it was understood.

Susan knew with blinding certainty that she had died, and her unborn baby had died with her, in that crash on I-95. Her body was dead but her soul was alive and in the body of another woman. She knew that this woman was not pregnant, and that, although she was living the other woman's pain, Susan—her mind and soul—would live on. For some reason, once the voices had completed their message, she did not feel frightened or even surprised. Strange. She knew she should feel something more than this odd calm, but did not. The voices had somehow soothed her even though they told her something so horrific it should drive her mad. She should be scared enough to scream, but she felt just a bit confused and nauseous. The voices stopped, but Susan felt a soothing stroking sensation on her head . . . no, in her head. It was like a feather lightly touching her, brushing away the confusion, the agony of their message. Susan put her hand up to her head, where it hurt the most, and felt sticky blood. A lot of it. She opened her eyes.

"I'm hurt," she told the man who hovered over her. She could not make out his features, for the sun was at his back, putting him in silhouette.

"I think you'd better call 911," she said, noticing her voice sounded strange to her ears, deeper, throatier, as if she had a cold. "I'm hurt pretty bad." She was about to tell them about the baby, how she was afraid for the baby, when she remembered there was no baby. This woman was empty. And she started to cry, letting out a grief so violent, that the people looking down at her were startled and immediately tried to calm her.

Susan cried for her baby, for herself, for the husband she would never see again, for her life. Although the voices were there, soothing her, they did nothing to stop this wrenching emptiness, as if they somehow knew this purging was necessary for her sanity. Susan wished she could stop the body-wracking sobs, because crying only intensified the pain in her head. Even as she sobbed, she could feel the voices intensifying, calming her.

"What's she crying like that for?" asked a woman, who could not hide that she was irritated more than concerned. "I suppose it hurts," said a man. "At least she's not unconscious anymore. When we first came upon her, it looked like she was . . ."

"Enough!" From the man closest to her. "We've got to get her to the house."

As she felt herself being lifted by the man, who grunted with the exertion, she also felt that awful, wrenching sadness fade away, replaced by an odd sense of exhilaration. Chemical imbalance, Susan thought as she bounced happily along in the man's arms. The pain in her head was still intense, but at least she was on a chemical high. Someone in heaven was looking after her, she thought.

"I think I can walk," she told the man. "And I don't think you can carry me too much farther anyway." The man gave her a sharp look and Susan looked at him for the first time. Handsome. Very handsome. Dark, wavy hair, gray eyes—her favorite combination. But right now he had a deep scowl, his face was red from carrying her and his lips were compressed so tight it was hard to see what their shape was.

"Really. Put me down. I'll lean on you, but this is ridiculous," she said. Susan had always been independent and she was not about to start being coddled now.

He let just her legs down, but kept his right arm along her back, giving her support. When her legs hit the grass, she felt a little shaky, a little lightheaded too, and regretted immediately her demand to be let down. "Just let me get my bearings," she said, looking up at the handsome man. He seemed to spin before her as she tried to focus her eyes and she held out her hand to steady herself.

"You cannot walk," the man said sternly, gripping her arm. The world stopped spinning and Susan stared at the imposing man in front of her who had apparently taken charge. He wore a long brown coat, white shirt, and fitted brown pants that were tucked into shining black riding boots. He looked like something out of the

1800s. Glancing back at the people milling about, she noted with some bewilderment that all the people were dressed in period costumes. She looked down at her own attire and realized that she, too, was wearing a long burgundy gown beneath a heavy cloaklike thing that damply clung to her. She wrinkled her brow, which just made her head hurt more.

Looking back at the man, she raised her brows in surprise. "Wow, you're tall," she said without thinking. Susan was close to six feet tall and she was used to looking at all but the tallest men eye-to-eye. Why, this man must be close to seven feet tall, she thought with some wonderment. Then she realized what the problem was.

"You're not tall. I'm short!" she said with wonder. And I'm a bit chubby, she added to herself, patting her stomach and thighs that she could feel through the layers of cloth that reached her feet. "I'm going to have to start running again," she said, absently. The man was now looking at her as if she had two heads. Then he looked back at his party to see if anyone else had heard her. He looked relieved that they hovered around the horse Margaret had been riding when she took the fall. The horse had broken its leg and would have to be destroyed, he thought with regret.

Following his eyes, Susan asked, "What's wrong with the horse?" The beautiful chestnut mare stood fifty yards away but was surrounded by a small group of people who were examining one of its legs.

The man's eyes turned to ice. "It broke its leg. I told you not to jump her. I told you she wasn't ready. She will have to be destroyed."

"Oh, no. No," Susan said. Her head was pounding, pounding and she was aware she was slurring her words. "Can't you fix it? She's beautiful. Oh, the poor thing. That's horrible. I never understood why horses had to be destroyed. They fix people's legs and even dogs' legs. Why not horses?"

"You've got to be kidding. You know better, Margaret. And don't pretend sympathy. Have you forgotten who you are talking to?" He looked at her with something close to disgust and . . . hatred?

"But I didn't do anything," Susan said without thinking. Everything seemed so far away. The man's face wavered in front of her and she had an odd floating sensation. "That must have been Margaret, whoever she is. I just got here." Why was this man calling her Margaret? Margaret must be her, the woman whose body she was in. This is too bizarre, Susan thought idly, but her head hurt so much, she didn't much care. Susan knew she would have to be careful about what she said until she figured out how to get out of this mess. She tried to force herself to concentrate, but the effort was too much.

Hearing the woman before him deny that she'd had anything to do with the horse's injury apparently infuriated the man. The look he gave her was one of profound disbelief. Grabbing her left arm rather roughly, he forced her to walk beside him much faster than Susan wanted to, or even could manage in the full-length dress that tangled around her feet. He led her off the hard, lumpy grass and onto a dirt track that was smooth, but she felt odd in this little chubby body and her head continued to pound and her eyes to blur, so she found herself stumbling and dragging her feet. To their left were woods, the trees bare of leaves. To their right was a field, the tall grass shivering in a cold breeze. Although Susan left her house on a searingly hot August day, she got the feeling it was late winter in this world, wherever it was. The air was sharp, but had a fecund smell, as if things were again beginning to grow. And she also knew they were very close to the sea, for the familiar clean, salty smell was strong. As they turned a bend, Susan got her first glimpse of a huge house that was nestled behind high shrubbery. Dozens of windows glowed a weak yellow in the coming twilight, but as Susan tried to capture more details of the house, her eyes lost focus once again.

"Is that where we're going?" she asked. Her head pounded and she suddenly felt sick. "I don't think I can make it that far without resting. This body is in rough shape and I don't feel so hot."

He stopped, placed a hand against her forehead, and said, "No, you don't seem to be feverish."

"That's not what I meant. I meant I feel sick. Bad. I feel funny. I . . ." She threw up, then fainted.

Carter Johnsbury caught his wife as she slumped to the dirt. The knock on her head was making her act strangely, he thought. He would have expected Margaret to rant and rave and blame him for not training the horse properly. She was too goddamn cheerful considering what had just happened. He didn't like it and wondered what game she was playing. As he carried her toward Rose Brier, he looked down at her slack face. She was starting to look old and she was only twenty-five, he thought. The alcohol, the late nights, the . . . indulgences she never seemed to refuse were catching up with her. The face he fell in love with when he was twenty-two was gone, replaced by a harsh parody of that countenance. But he was not fool enough to think she had changed in other ways. She was just as vile at nineteen as she was at twenty-five, except then Carter had been young, blinded by a pretty face with a pretty pout.

He had known nothing about the real Margaret, nothing about what was inside her, when he proposed a year after they'd met. He was filled with self-loathing to realize just how gullible he had been. In his more charitable moments, Carter knew that few men would have been able to see through the charming, well-bred young woman Margaret had presented herself to be. No, he'd told himself more than once, she had not changed after the marriage. She had just shown her true colors and these were gray and murky brown. Holding her, he was taken back to the last time he had made love to her—their wedding night.

It had been a beautiful day, their wedding day, the sun bright in a cloudless sky and Margaret, serene and lovely in a midnight-blue wedding gown with cream-colored Irish lace. Carter, who had treated her with near reverence, had been anticipating their wedding night for months. He had decided it was important that when they finally consummated their love, it would be for the first time on their wedding night. And Margaret, acting demure and coquettish, had agreed, but had subtly tortured Carter with innuendo, heated gazes, and scandalous dress.

Six years later, Carter still felt a rush of rage and shame when he recalled his wedding night. Although more than experienced with women, Carter was as nervous as a virgin that night, shaking as he caressed his new wife. He tried to go slow, to bring his inexperienced bride to her release, but his restraint abandoned him in a flood of lust and love. He needn't have bothered. Carter, flushed and satisfied, had gazed down at his wife expecting to see a shy smile, maybe tears, anything but what met his eyes.

"I knew it," she had said, looking petulant, her arms crossed over her heavy breasts. "I knew you were as green as new grass."

Carter was at first confused, then he realized what she was about. She was no virgin. Hardly. She was experienced enough to know that he had lost his head and callow enough to remark on it. Embarrassed, ashamed, and very angry, he stupidly had choked out, "You weren't a virgin."

She'd started to laugh. "Of course not. But if you'd known that, would you have married me?"

"I don't know. I might have," he'd said, inwardly cringing to hear the emotion in his voice.

"Well, it doesn't matter now. The marriage is consummated, so they say. I'm going to sleep now," she'd said casually. Carter had looked at her, confused, hurt, wondering at the change in his beautiful Margaret. She'd laughed again.

"Oh, Carter, really. Don't look at me that way. You're a big boy. We all know what marriage is about. Business. My grandfather, through me, made a business arrangement, so to speak. I know you had yourself convinced that you were in love with me, but that's not the way of it, don't you see? Oh, Carter. Don't look so sad." And she'd patted his arm. "Go to bed now, you'll realize how silly all this is in the morning."

Carter had gotten up, dazed. His heart felt like a piece of lead in his chest, drumming out slow, lazy beats. He looked at her, and desired her, but that night his love died to be replaced by a festering hatred that Margaret had only fueled with her numerous and tawdry affairs. Over the years, he learned the sordid story of her deceit. Before he had met her, Margaret had been nothing more than a little tramp, spreading her legs for just about any man who would have her. Her parents died when she was just fifteen, leaving her in the care of a negligent governess who spent more time gossiping with the household staff than teaching her ward proper behavior. When her grandfather caught her with one of the gardeners when she was seventeen, he gave her an ultimatum: Find a respectable man to marry or her fortune would be cut off. So that is what she did.

After their disastrous wedding night, it was just sex between Mr. and Mrs. Johnsbury and only when Carter could not resist one of her seductive games. The last time they'd lain together sweating and spent was four years ago. He'd been so disgusted with himself, so filled

with loathing for her and that smug little smile that
played on her pretty lips, that he did not know whether
he wanted to kill himself or her.

In the end, he just ignored her. They appeared together socially, to keep up appearances, but few people
were fooled. Theirs was no loving relationship, not even
a grudging friendship. How it hurt to see his friends
marry, have children, be happy, knowing he would never
have that for himself. He was bitter, but he had convinced himself long ago that he was as happy as he was
ever going to be with his life.

The only solace he had was his work. Thank God for
that, he'd thought more than once. Unlike many of his
friends whose fathers still held the purse strings and had
little to do with the family fortune, Carter had been
head of the family for seven years. He owned three textile mills in Rhode Island and a carriage factory in Con-
necticut, as well as an interest in many other lucrative
ventures. He could do without a happy family life. Lots
of men did.

Without warning, the image of his brother, Charles,
and his wife and two children leaped into his head.
Charles had been the lucky one, surrounded by a loving
wife and adoring children. Just thinking about his
brother, who he loved more than his own life, made his
heart wrench—not with jealousy, but with longing. If
not for his family, Carter realized, he would have been
far lonelier and far more bitter than he was.

Carter's arms were aching by the time he reached the
house. Bruce McGrath met him at the door. The burly
Irishman was butler, protector, friend and a man who
had a fierce loyalty and deep respect for his employer.
He took Carter's burden without comment, raising his
eyebrows just a tad when he saw the blood on Margaret's head.

"She fell from the horse," he said, transferring her
limp body to his butler and friend. "It had to be de-

stroyed." And for a moment, just a moment, McGrath wasn't sure whether Carter had meant the horse or his wife.

The two men had an odd relationship. In many ways, he was the only man Carter felt he could talk to about his troubles. Carter held no prejudice against McGrath's Irishness and trusted him with his life. The two often pulled down whiskey together, but there still was a distance between the two, a pulling away by Bruce, who was always more aware of the employer-employee relationship than Carter was.

Bruce, followed by Carter, brought Margaret to her room and deposited her on her bed with as much emotion as if he had dumped a sack of flour, then he left the room. She tossed her head of dark curls and moaned as she again opened her eyes. The man from the field was standing back, his arms crossed as he looked down with no emotion.

"I fainted," she said. She looked around, taking in the frills, the gaudy colors, the gold-trimmed pink furniture. "I don't mean to be critical, but this is the ugliest room I've ever seen in my life," she said, with her characteristic bluntness. "And stop looking at me like I'm crazy every time I open my mouth."

"Margaret, you've suffered a blow to the head and obviously it's affecting you. I am simply reacting to an overwrought wife."

"Wife!" My God, Susan thought, this is worse than I imagined.

~ Chapter 2 ~

. . . It turns out I was married to a man named Carter Johnsbury. He was completely awful to me. . . .

She was shocked at first, then forced herself to calm down. Oh no, she thought, I'm married. This was just too much. Cursing the powers that had for some reason only they knew sent her back to earth, she forced herself to breathe normally, to think clearly. She would simply explain to this brute what had happened to her.

"What's your name?" And at his look, she quickly explained. "I don't know who you are. I've never seen you before. Let me explain. I am not Margaret. I am Susan. I died and came into her body, I guess. I don't know all the mechanics of it. No one explained it to me, you see. But I do know what's going on. I do know that I am not Margaret and I don't know who you are, except that you say you're my husband and I've got to assume you wouldn't lie about that. What is your name?"

"Carter," he said automatically, a distracted, disbelieving look on his face. Then, as if catching himself with his guard down, his scowl returned. "And you damn well know that's my name. I don't know what you're trying to pull here, Margaret, but I'm not going to fall for any more of your manipulations. I'm sick and tired of it. I'm sick and tired of you."

Susan looked at him with a look of utter patience that Carter found even more irritating than her normal rant-ing. "So, Carter, I can gather from all that, that you and I don't have the best relationship in the world." Her head felt as if it were splitting in two, but she felt she needed to talk to this man, her husband. Her husband. Jesus, Mary, and Joseph.

"But if you insist on calling me Margaret, let's make it Maggie. Margaret sounds so . . . proper and stiff. So, from now on it's Maggie. I'll make that concession since I'm going to be stuck here. At least I think I will be."

She was just about to ask why everyone was dressed in costumes when a knock at the door stopped Maggie from saying any more. A man who obviously was a doctor walked in after Carter's curt, "Come in."

"She claims she doesn't know who I am. She claims she doesn't even know who she is," Carter announced to Dr. Armstrong as he walked toward the newly named Maggie. He was a trim, youngish man with a smooth face, receding hairline, and neat mustache. His eyes were kind and intelligent and Maggie felt instantly calmed by his doctorly manner.

"Mrs. Johnsbury. Let's take a look at you," he said, leaning over her, his eyes on the gash in her head. But why did they bring a doctor to her? Shouldn't she be on the way to the hospital? "This is a nasty-looking injury. How are you feeling? Any nausea? Have you vomited?"

"She vomited and fainted about thirty minutes ago," Carter answered for her, ignoring Maggie's affronted look.

Dr. Armstrong felt around her wound gingerly, for even the slightest pressure caused Maggie to wince and once her eyes rolled back into her head briefly.

"Her skull has been fractured," he told Carter.

"Hello. I'm the patient here. You can talk to me," she said in a singsong voice. "Shouldn't I be in a hospital? Haven't you called an ambulance? I think I have a concussion."

Both men looked at her in surprise. Something was

very strange here, Maggie/Susan thought. The doctor was dressed in old-fashioned clothes, too, and he was carrying the type of big black doctor's bag she had only seen in the movies. Suddenly it dawned on her what was happening.

"What year is this?" she asked, afraid to hear the answer, her heart beating painfully in her chest.

"Why, it's 1888," Dr. Armstrong supplied, looking at Maggie with renewed interest. She let out a small groan. Things were much worse than she suspected, and just as she was about to panic, the soothing voices returned and she knew nothing but calm acceptance.

Maggie repeated the date slowly as if trying to remember some significance about it. After the Civil War, before the Blizzard of '98. She suddenly wished she had paid more attention to her American history classes. "You don't know what year it is? Hmmm. Mrs. Johnsbury, have you and I ever met?" the doctor asked.

"No. And I never met him either," Maggie said, pointing to her husband, wincing at the pain that simple gesture brought. "But I already explained everything to, uh, Carter?" she said, testing the name. To which Carter rolled his eyes in disbelief.

Dr. Armstrong ignored her and, after carefully cleaning her wound, began preparing a needle and thread.

"I need stitches?" Maggie asked, eyeing the needle suspiciously. "Has that thing been sterilized?" Maggie slurred, just before she slipped into the welcoming blackness.

When Dr. Armstrong was done, he motioned for Carter to follow him.

"Spunky, isn't she?" Dr. Armstrong said, chuckling. He got right to the point. "It's a very serious injury, Mr. Johnsbury. Very. In fact, I don't know what's holding her head together," he said, shaking his head. "She could have died. In fact, she should have died. While she appears to be out of danger, head injuries are tricky things." He looked at the younger man's face to gauge a reaction. There was none. "For the first twenty-four hours, someone has to stay by her bedside almost constantly. Right now, she's unconscious, and her breathing sounds regular, but I fear she may slip into a coma. If she does, I don't know if she will wake up. Do you understand what I am saying to you, Mr. Johnsbury? I've always believed it is best to be blunt. There is a very real possibility your wife could die."

Carter gave a curt nod.

"The next two days are critical. I expect some swelling, a fever. I must be frank with you. I've never seen anyone live with such an injury. It's remarkable she is still conscious. If she should go into a coma, I would call a priest. I would call any family." The doctor, obviously uncomfortable having to give such an unfavorable prognosis, searched the younger man's face for some sort of emotion—anything that showed this news meant something to him. He might as well been talking about the condition of a plow horse, he thought, for all the reaction he was getting from this cold man.

"As for her memory, it appears she has amnesia, not uncommon with this type of injury. I'm sure you've heard of the condition, but it can be frustrating when it's encountered for both the patient and the people around her. If she lives, I suggest you have patience with her. There are always sanitariums I can recommend. In most cases, though, memory returns within hours or even days. But there are rare cases it does not. I'll stay for a few hours, then you or someone else can take over."

Carter listened impassively to the doctor. And although he showed no outward emotion, the prognosis did affect him. More than he cared to admit. Years of hating, apparently, were not enough to cover all the tender feelings he had once felt for his wife.

But to the doctor, he said, "I have business I must attend to in two days. If she lives, I'll be leaving then. I expect you to continue your care of her. Good day, doctor."

For the next four days, Maggie slipped in and out of consciousness. Every time she opened her eyes, she was looking at another person, none of whom she recognized, except Dr. Armstrong, who gingerly changed her dressings. On the fifth day she woke up after a natural sleep and felt almost normal. Stretching until her muscles quivered, Maggie felt a sudden rush of panic when she finally looked around the room. My God, it's true, she thought. It wasn't a dream. Again, that soothing, those calming voices covered her like a warm, flannel blanket.

She gave her surroundings a cautious perusal. She was alone—that was one thing to be grateful for. Sun streamed through large windows on each side of her bed, laying bright golden rectangles on an Oriental rug that appeared to cover most of the floor in the vast bedroom. She sat up slowly, fearing that her head would begin pounding again, but, thankfully, felt no pain. Bringing her knees up, she rested her arms on them and was startled when she realized those arms were not her own. As Susan, her arms were golden, with hair so blonde it was hardly noticeable until it turned white in the summer sun. These arms were smaller, more delicate, and were lightly covered with much darker hair. With a feeling of dread, she remembered she was now in a new body. How odd. As she looked down, some of her dark curls fell forward. Another surprise. She lifted her hand, watching closely as she did as if watching someone else's hand, and felt the softness of those curls. With her hands, she explored her face, wincing when she touched her wound. She was still swollen and it had obviously not healed completely. She had the urge to look at herself, to see the face that would now look back at her through the mirror, for God knew how long.

Swinging her legs over the bed, she nearly sprawled onto the floor when she tried to step down. Used to long legs, she had forgotten that her new body was much smaller and did not stop to think that the distance between the bed and the floor would have changed. Susan/ Maggie had never felt so strange. It was as if everything in the world had gotten larger, taller. Bureaus, once as tall as her hip, now rose to her ribcage. She swept the long cotton gown she wore out of the way and looked down at her feet, her tiny little feet, and almost laughed. Finally, she could fit into those cute little shoes she had always coveted and always looked ridiculous on her size tens. Except in this century, she didn't know if there were cute shoes.

Padding over the soft carpet, Maggie walked toward a beautiful cherry-wood full-length mirror stationed against one pink and gold wallpapered wall. There she stood. Long, curling brown hair, deep brown eyes, nice mouth, little nose, a slight double chin. The blow to her head marred her forehead and on one side of her face was a hideous yellowing bruise. Her body was hidden by a cotton night thing that buttoned up her neck, ending with scratchy lace under her chin. She lifted the gown to see the body underneath, and grimaced. Big breasts, big stomach, big thighs. Dark thatch of hair. Susan had been so proud of her body. Long, lithe, toned, golden. She had worked hard; she had been one of those women all other women loathe, an athletic woman who ran daily and loved every minute of it.

She looked at her breasts with the detachment of a doctor examining a patient. Big, but nicely shaped, the dark pink tips puckering in reaction to the cold morning air. Although she had always insisted she liked her small, pert breasts, she'd always secretly wanted a more voluptuous figure. Well, I've got it now, she thought. I wonder for how long?

Maggie walked closer to the polished mirror and

studied the face closer. It was a completely unappealing face, she decided. Puffy, unhealthy, pasty—the face of a person who abused life and her body. The face, her face now, was smooth, and Maggie tried to guess how old this woman was. She creased her forehead in concentration trying to recall how much that man had told her. . . .

That man! "My God, she's married. I mean, I'm married. Oh, God!"

She desperately tried to recall something about that scowling man who had half-carried her to this house. She prayed quickly and fervently she would not have to sleep with him, a complete stranger. What possible excuse could she give for rejecting him? She was married to him, after all, and if she was meant to live here for a while, she couldn't act too coldly toward him. Another feeling of dread washed over her. She closed her eyes and tried to picture his face. The image of dark gray eyes, angry and cold, flashed into her mind. The only positive thing she could think of was that at least he was handsome. That she remembered. Devastatingly handsome, even when he was angry. Maggie bit her lip so hard it hurt, a bitter reminder that she was indeed inhabiting the body of a woman whom she knew nothing about. What year was it again? The doctor had said 1888—a time she knew next to nothing about, except that women were repressed and mistreated. Certainly her angels would not have put her with an abusive man. Obviously Carter and Margaret had money, she thought, looking about the richly, if gaudily, appointed room.

Maggie was still studying her face, trying to get used to the idea that it was hers, when a gray woman walked into the room. Gray. That was her color, what she wore, her hair, her eyes, her skin. Gray.

"Hello," Maggie said quietly.

"Oh. Mrs. Johnsbury. I'm so sorry. I didn't see you

there. You're up. How good," she said, as she quickly straightened her skirt and made an attempt to tame the springy gray nest. Maggie was embarrassed by the woman's obvious discomfort.

"That's okay. I'm feeling fine and I just woke up. I am starved, though," she said, realizing that she was, indeed, very hungry. "Could you show me where the kitchen is?" Maggie asked. The woman went from looking mortified to looking suspicious.

"I'll have Becky bring your breakfast in here," the woman said slowly, as if talking to a dimwit. "You always eat breakfast in bed, Ma'am."

Maggie thought about what it would be like to eat breakfast in bed. It would be messy and uncomfortable, she couldn't help thinking.

"From now on I think I'll take my breakfast wherever Carter does," she said, not knowing where one took breakfast in the 1880s.

"He takes it in his room, Ma'am," she said.

"Oh. His room. Well, then." Maggie was at a loss.

"How about in the breakfast room?" the woman asked, obviously uncomfortable with making a suggestion. She almost looked as if Maggie were about to strike her for daring to be so forward.

"The breakfast room. Of course," Maggie said, adding under her breath, "I hope there's a lunch room and a dinner room."

The maid, she learned her name was Stella, helped her into a huge, low-cut gown she called a day dress after putting on what seemed like endless layers of underclothes. Maggie could not help but giggle at the ridiculous drawers that looked like thin cotton pants. And she looked with horror at the corset Stella insisted on wrapping around her resistant body. Maggie felt very uncomfortable being dressed by a strange woman, but Stella was so matter-of-fact, she put her at ease. She still had the feeling that she was someone else, that Stella was dressing another body. Maggie, with the left side of her face still hideously bruised, felt not only ugly but obscene in a dress that exposed what looked to Maggie like huge mounds of white flesh when she peered in the mirror.

"Don't I have anything a little more, um, modest?" Maggie asked, clearly mortified by the display.

"Let's see." Stella now seemed to be taking the little changes in her mistress in stride. She began flipping through dress after dress, creating a small cloud of perfume as she did. Maggie, her nose wrinkling, stood behind her, making sure she didn't miss any that looked— or smelled—promising. She passed by one pretty thing, but Stella quickly shook her head. "The cut's too small," she said diplomatically. In the end, Maggie wore the dress she had on with a light shawl over shoulders pinned together with a large broach.

"I look like an old lady now, but at least I'm decent," she said, looking up at her reflection in the mirror. She started when she saw her image before realizing that she was looking at herself. Holding a small hand to her heart, Maggie took a couple of deep breaths to calm her nerves. "This is too weird," she said under her breath.

"I beg pardon, Ma'am?"

"Oh. Nothing."

Although her stomach was rumbling, Maggie's curiosity over where she was overtook her as they walked out the bedroom door and into a hallway with gleaming wood floors. "Stella, I'm afraid the knock on my head rattled me a bit. I wonder, if you don't mind, if you could give me a quick tour of the house."

Stella's eyes widened slightly in surprise, but clearing her throat, she took over the role of tour guide describing the house in quick, terse sentences. She felt distinctly uncomfortable showing her mistress a house she had lived in on and off all her life as if she had never stepped inside.

"This way, Ma'am." And so began the tour of what Maggie came to believe was the most beautiful house she had ever seen.

To the right, the hall seemed to stretch forever toward a large octangular window that let in golden light, which faded to muted yellow where Maggie and Stella stood. Charming fluted glass lamps were hung outside each heavy dark door on walls painted eggshell white. Dark moldings, in the same rich wood as the floor, bordered the ceilings and doors. Maggie let out a sound of delight when she discovered the delicate lamps were fueled by gas. Stella stood back and watched Maggie as she lifted the glass globe and examined the lamp as if she had never seen such a contraption. She turned the little handle to hear the hiss of gas escaping, smiling at the sound. Looking up, Maggie immediately saw her error. A woman of the 1880s would not be fascinated by a gas lamp, she realized.

"They're beautiful," she said, trying to justify her intense interest in what was likely a common wall lamp.

After giving her mistress a hard stare, Stella jerked her hand toward the series of rooms. "These are mostly bedrooms. Most are empty."

"Which is my"—she swallowed heavily—"husband's?" Steve's laughing face, not Carter Johnsbury's, flashed vividly before her and a sudden and devastating grief assaulted her so powerfully that she had to rest a hand against the doorjamb to keep from swaying. Just as quickly Steve's face faded in her mind until it was muted and untouchable—a memory the mind could no longer grasp. It was as if the angels had passed a soft brush over her brain, gently painting over Steve's memory. Maggie brought a hand up to massage her head and winced as she touched her wound.

"Are you all right, Ma'am?" Stella said, the concern real.

Maggie brightened and flashed a smile she almost felt. "Yes, Stella. I'm fine."

"Mr. Johnsbury's room is at the far end of the hall facing the bay, as your room does," Stella said.

"The bay?" Maggie instantly turned back into her room and gazed out the window. There before her delighted eyes was the amazing deep blue of a large body of water dotted by large chunks of melting ice. Seagulls hovered over the water, looking for a meal, and two sailboats, their sails a stark white against the deep blue, dotted the bay as they maneuvered around the ice floes.

"It's so beautiful," she said, sighing. Maggie loved the water, its calm, its danger, its ever-changing face. She closed her eyes and shook her head. So far, this place was the solidification of one of her favorite fantasies—a mansion by the sea in a time and place where everything was simpler, more peaceful. She'd been angry with her angels, but now she thought she'd better give them another chance. Perhaps they knew what they were doing after all.

Looking back at Stella who hovered uncertainly by the door, Maggie said, "What is it?"

"What is what, Ma'am?"

"The water out there, what is it?"

Stella was clearly still confused over her mistress's memory loss. "Why, it's Narragansett Bay, Ma'am. You're looking at the West Passage. That land there is Conanicut Island, Jamestown."

"I'm home!" Maggie said, swinging her gaze back to the window. She must be in Newport. In a grand old house in Newport. Wow. Maggie craned her neck looking north up the bay as far as she could see. "There's no bridge," she whispered. The bridge wouldn't be built for years, she reminded herself. "I can't wait to tell Ste—" She stopped. She could not tell Steve this. Steve wouldn't even be alive. Hell, his grandfather would not even be alive. Suddenly Maggie felt overwhelmingly lonely.

"Show me the rest of the house, Stella." Her enthusiasm had been doused like the flame in a pretty gas wall lamp.

Used to living in three- or four-room apartments, Maggie was quickly overwhelmed by the enormity of the house. She learned it was named Rose Brier, that it was completed twenty years earlier just as the Civil War was ending. It had twenty-four rooms, more than half of them bedrooms, a library, nursery, separate servants' quarters, a huge dining room that was often converted into a small ballroom. Most of the rooms were not wallpapered, giving the house a casual air despite its elegance. The dark wood floors, wainscoting, and trim were constant throughout the house.

After forgoing a look at the bedrooms, Maggie wanted to see the main floor. A large curving staircase with a sweeping banister in smooth, polished mahogany led down to what appeared to be a large entry hall. Maggie could see several rooms leading off the hall, all large and airy, all richly carpeted.

"There are three parlors—east, west, and main. This is the main parlor," Stella said, indicating a charmingly feminine room with a white marble fireplace and delicate-looking upholstered furniture.

Stella moved on to the next room but hesitated at the closed double doors. Spotting Mrs. Brimble, the housekeeper, she marched over to the woman and spoke quietly for a few moments before turning back and opening the doors. Maggie gave her a curious look, but the maid did not explain her little tête-à-tête with the formidable-looking woman.

"Who is that?"

"Mrs. Brimble, the housekeeper."

"Is she important?"

Again Stella found herself staring at disbelief at her mistress. "She runs the household with a firm hand. Mr. Johnsbury likes things just so, and Mrs. Brimble makes sure things are just as Mr. Johnsbury likes."

Maggie shifted her gaze from Stella to what she was informed was the library. Maggie's face instantly brightened seeing the towering walls chock-full of thick, leather-bound volumes. It was the kind of room she had only seen in photographs or while touring historical homes. Maggie breathed in deep, savoring the wonderful smell that only a room filled with books can produce. A massive desk faced a large leather couch, which backed a set of towering windows. If not for those windows, it would have been a dark, morose room, Maggie thought. But the muted light softened the masculine lines of the furniture and made it a room that welcomed a visitor. "This is my room," Maggie said to herself.

"This is Mr. Johnsbury's room," Stella said.

"His room? I don't understand."

Stella appeared a bit flustered by Maggie's question. "Er, I mean, no one else comes in here."

"You mean me. I don't come in here. But why? It's a wonderful room."

Stella's answer was an uncertain shrug.

"Okay. What's next?"

Stella led Maggie to a cavernous room, the formal dining room with a ceiling that soared two stories high. A bank of windows on one side reached clear to the ceiling and enormous deep blue drapes covered all but the center two panes. While large, the gleaming dining table took up only a small portion of the room.

"This is often converted into a ballroom," Stella volunteered.

"It's lovely." Intimidating was probably a better word. Maggie's stomach rumbled, reminding her she hadn't eaten any solid food in days. Patting her stomach, she said, "I think it's time to feed me. I'll explore the rest of the house on my own."

Stella led her to the breakfast room, a small sunlit room with a bay window overlooking what appeared to be a garden, still brown this early in the season. Maggie sat in a cushioned chair waiting as gray-uniformed maids, all wearing little white caps with their hair tucked underneath, brought in dish after dish and laid them on the table in front of her. It was enough to feed ten people. Eggs—scrambled, poached, and hard-boiled— pastries, bread, fruit, steak, and sausage. Maggie looked at the nearest maid and said, "Who else will be joining me?"

"Why, no one, Mrs. Johnsbury," she said. Again that confused look she was getting used to seeing on everyone's face.

"What is your name?" Maggie asked, shocked to see the stricken look in the maid's eyes.

"Betty, Ma'am," she squeaked out.

"I'd like to talk to the cook, please, Betty," she said, as offhandedly as she could. The maid breathed a sigh of what Maggie thought was relief. She would have to go gently, she thought. She didn't want them all to think she was some sort of a dragon, after all. When the maid turned as if to go fetch the offending cook, Maggie startled Betty again by following her to the kitchen. And what a kitchen it was—a cavernous, wondrous place, with bustling people in gray and white uniforms, sun streaming through a large bank of windows, happy chatter, pots and pans clanging, steam billowing from a huge pot, shoes scuffling on a gleaming slate floor. It smelled like fresh-baked bread, clean, homey. Maggie had to smile. But her smile faltered when she saw the reaction of the servants when they caught a glimpse of her standing at the double swinging door. It was as if someone yelled "Freeze!" That was how quickly the bustle and chatter died.

One woman, obviously in charge of the massive kitchen, took a large fortifying breath and walked toward her as if she were walking toward an executioner. Proud, slightly afraid, with a bit of stubbornness thrown in for good measure, the woman wiped her hands on a rumpled white apron. "Yes, Mrs. Johnsbury."

As if her words were some sort of "on" switch, everyone in the kitchen resumed their activity, but it was with a subdued, somber air. Maggie knew it was because of her. She had to remind herself that they were reacting to Margaret coming in to the kitchen, that their reaction had nothing to do with her. Nothing, she told herself, feeling very uncomfortable knowing that the servants disliked her as much as her husband did. Until that moment, she didn't realize just what sort of situation she was in. She was a different woman; Susan was gone. The only thing she could do was show these people that Margaret had changed, and that would be the most difficult thing she had ever done.

"I . . . ," she began, faltering. She closed her eyes, gathered her resolve. "From now on, I'll eat in the breakfast room at seven o'clock. I'll eat toast, unbuttered, fruit, juice, and coffee. That's all I'll need. I do appreciate the wonderful food you all cooked up for me. Honestly. But there is enough there for a whole family, and it's such a waste with so many people going hungry, don't you think?"

Maggie didn't know if there were homeless people in Newport in 1888, but she was sure there were hungry people. Somewhere. "And we don't have a big family. Do . . . we?" Maggie said, trying to sound nonchalant, as if she knew the answer, but failed miserably. The sudden horrifying notion that there might be children in this house that belonged to her who she did not know came upon her when she thought of how much food had been prepared. Stella hadn't mentioned children and had not shown her any children's rooms. But she was still unsure.

The cook blinked at her. Twice. "It was just for you, Ma'am. Very good, Ma'am," she said businesslike in a heavy Irish brogue. And Maggie left the kitchen and made her way back to the breakfast room to face the food that no one would eat. Maggie forced herself to eat a piece of toast that had been soaked in butter. And a strawberry. But she couldn't force another bite down.

Still feeling a bit blue, Maggie decided to go outside and search for a quiet corner where she could think, for God knew she had a lot to think about. Pulling the shawl about her, Maggie walked into the small garden off the breakfast room and sat on a cold marble bench. It was chilly outside, but the fresh air cleared Maggie's head and the strong sun lifted her indomitable spirit.

The plants, still brown and withered from winter, looked so ordinary, she thought. Birds sang, flitting from branch to branch. A squirrel, still fluffy with its winter coat, scratched up a tree, some edible prize in its mouth. Life, all around her was life. And she was alive when she should be dead. Was that not a miracle? Was this not something to be joyous about? Maggie was glad to be alive, glad to be sitting on a bench on a sunny day. But she was also frightened, thinking of all she did not know and all that was yet to come. Her angels had explained many things to her, but they had left far too many holes that Maggie would be left to fill in herself. She knew next to nothing of this woman whose body she occupied, and she knew even less about the man who was her husband. The little of this life she did know was daunting.

She wrote a mental list of the things that were going to cause her problems: People appeared to be afraid of Margaret. Her husband clearly disliked her. She had no inkling of what type of person Margaret had been, but the little information she had led her to believe she was not at all nice. She did not know how to dress, how to act in this century. She had no friends, no one to confide in, no one to relate to.

She silently raged at the people or angels or things that sent her to this century. Would she just have to hope they knew what they were doing? Maybe they were just bored and thought it would be fun to watch a 1990s woman flounder in the age of regression. In frustration, Maggie rested her chin on her hand and scowled at the ordinariness of everything around her. Why was she here? Why was she saved? Certainly this could not be a common occurrence or else the world would be overrun by confused people claiming amnesia.

Then it hit her, the shining truth, a lightning bolt sent from heaven. It hit with a force that would have knocked her down had she not already been sitting.

"My baby," she said, unconsciously bringing a hand to her stomach. "They're going to give me back my baby." Anyone watching her would have thought Maggie was looking at the face of God, her face was so bright and shining. A smile touched her lips and tears flooded her eyes, so great was her joy. The feeling lasted just a moment, but it was long enough to convince Maggie that she now knew at least part of the reason why she had been sent to this place. She had an uneasy feeling her angels had not told her the full story, but she was so overjoyed thinking about her child, she pushed away any negative thoughts. She smiled stupidly.

But when she thought what having a baby would mean—making love to Carter, she frowned. Carter hated her and she was completely indifferent to him. He was a total stranger. She decided her first priority was to become friends with her husband. Whether he liked it or not.

~ *Chapter 3* ~

. . . Everyone here hated me. Of course, that was completely understandable. But, oh, how it hurt. . . .

Her plans were momentarily put off when she discovered from a very stiff-sounding Mrs. Brimble that Mr. Johnsbury was not in residence and would not be returning for at least a month and probably longer. Maggie was unsure how to take the news. Part of her was relieved that she could slowly get used to living in a different century without the distraction of Carter's brooding figure, but part of her was in a hurry to start her new life.

Maggie decided to explore her new world. The house was lovely, the kind of place she had always dreamed of living in, rich, elegant, and somehow rustic with its dark hardwood floors and mahogany-trimmed doorways, windows, and walls. Maggie ran her fingers along the smooth wood furniture, the type of which she had only seen in museums and antique shops in the past. She had always loved this old stuff, and she almost smiled when she realized this rich furniture was all new stuff. Someone, the staff, she supposed, had placed flower arrangements throughout the house on tables that gleamed from polishing. Imagine, she was living in a house where other people did all the cooking, all the cleaning . . . all the work. A woman's dream, she thought, smiling.

She walked in the dining room, her footsteps echoing

from the parquet wood floor to the ceiling high above her. For the first time she noticed French doors that led out to a whitewashed porch, its ceiling painted a blue-green. Maggie was drawn to the windows, and let out a gasp. There before her, beyond a long lawn that dipped to a stone wall, was that blue, blue water of Narragansett Bay. She could see Jamestown in the distance, a gray-green dusky coast partially obscured by haze. She swept open the French doors, and was blasted by salty air, clean, fresh, sharp. A large steamship cut through the water in the distance, breaking up ice chunks on its way. Maggie stood there, hypnotized by the view. She still couldn't believe she was living here, for her dream had always been to live on the water, and here she was, breathing in this scent, this view.

Standing there, she remembered how beautiful the view was from her bedroom. Maggie lifted her skirts— probably higher than society allowed, she thought fleetingly, and ran up the curving staircase, her hand on the smooth banister. When she got to her room, she was instantly assaulted by the gaudy colors after being in rooms so simply elegant. But when she made her way to those windows that stood like sentinels on either side of her massive bed, she saw that blue, that healing blue. Like the windows below, these opened like doors onto a balcony. She walked out, breathing the air again. Maggie didn't know how long she stood there, arms wrapped around her to fend off the chilly breeze, before she heard a voice.

"Mrs. Johnsbury," Stella said, "Dr. Armstrong is here."

Maggie said to let him in to see her, and met him walking into her room. "I don't think you should be out of bed, never mind outdoors in this cold." Maggie smiled at his concerned expression.

"Hello, Doctor."

"You remember me?" he asked.

"Of course."

Maggie sat on the edge of her bed while Dr. Armstrong looked at her injury.

"Any headache? Dizziness? Nausea?"

"Nope."

"Remarkable," Dr. Armstrong said, mostly to himself. "Follow my finger without turning your head."

And Maggie's brown eyes easily followed his long finger as it moved from side to side.

"You're sure you have no ache? No dizziness?" he asked, clearly baffled by her quick recovery. "When Stella told me you were up and about, I didn't believe her. Do you have any idea how seriously you were hurt, Mrs. Johnsbury?"

"I have a pretty good idea," Maggie said, her voice laced heavily with laughter. She added silently, "So serious, you're talking to a dead woman."

"Well, I see no reason to keep you in bed," Dr. Armstrong said, although he was clearly uncomfortable making this decision. "But if you have any pain, any reoccurrence of dizziness, it's back you go and send for me . . ."

"Yes, Doctor."

"Now. Your memory. Has it returned?"

"Not a bit," Maggie said lightly. Dr. Armstrong quirked an eyebrow at her total lack of concern. In the cases he'd seen—and they were much milder cases—the patient was typically depressed and confused and wanted desperately to know who they were. Still, he felt the need to reassure his patient.

"It should return, Mrs. Johnsbury. It usually does."

"I don't think so, Doctor. But I'm really not worried about it. I don't think they are memories I really want to have anyway." She'd meant to reassure him, but that odd way of explaining it disturbed him instead.

Tilting her head, she said, "Do you know how old I am, Doctor?"

Dr. Armstrong smiled kindly and thought how horrible it would be to not know your name, not know your age. But this woman appeared to be dealing with this trauma amazingly well.

"I believe you are twenty-five."

"Really? I look like hell," Maggie said, getting up to look in the mirror. She still felt as if she were looking at a stranger.

Dr. Armstrong chuckled after he got over his mild shock at hearing a lady curse.

After Dr. Armstrong left, she realized that what she had told the good doctor was not entirely true. She did want and need to know about the past and the only way she could find out was through people who knew Margaret.

If anyone knew Margaret, it had to be sharp-eyed Stella. But she knew the maid was a bit terrified of her, something that made Maggie feel as uncomfortable around her as Stella apparently felt around Maggie. She arranged to meet with her later that day.

Maggie frowned as she looked at Stella, who was obviously not used to sitting down and having a chat with her mistress. She sat in a high-backed chair so close to the edge it looked as if she were about to teeter off. Her thin hands were clenched together in her lap, her face was pale and had taken on the gray tint of her drab uniform. Maggie took a seat in a matching chair near Stella, momentarily wrestling with the mounds of material that seemed to flutter up whenever she sat down.

"Stella. You know about my head injury," Maggie started gently. Stella's small white cap that covered her unruly gray hair bobbed up and down as if attached to a spring. Maggie sighed.

"And you know that I don't remember anything. Not you, not Mr. Johnsbury, and not even myself." Stella's eyes got wide and Maggie thought she detected a look of disbelief.

"It's true. I know it sounds unbelievable, but it's true. Now you must know that I am not crazy, I simply have lost my memory," she said, wondering at the ignorance about mental health of nineteenth-century people. She remembered reading horror stories about perfectly sane women who were committed to asylums by rich husbands who wanted them out of their hair. She had no idea what was known or not known about amnesia, something she had decided to claim rather than convince people Margaret had actually died. In fact, the little she knew about memory loss she'd learned in cheesy movies and melodramatic soap operas.

"Stella." The woman winced! She tried to continue as gently as possible, all the time cursing Margaret, who obviously had been a tyrant. "I need to know some things about myself. First, the easy things. Do I have any children?"

After recovering from her shock at the question, Stella told her she did not.

"Are my parents alive?"

"You have only a grandfather that I know of, Ma'am."

"No brothers? No sisters?"

"No, Ma'am. You do have a mother-in-law, a brother-in-law and his wife. Oh, and a niece and nephew."

Maggie let out a sigh of relief. She would have very little immediate family to deal with.

Now the tough part, Maggie said to herself. "I can tell by your reaction, by the other workers' reactions, well, even by my husband's reaction, that I used to be, uh, difficult."

Stella looked stricken as her cheeks flushed a scarlet red, but her lips remained compressed and as gray as the rest of her. "I . . . Mrs. Johnsbury, no one believes . . ."

Maggie interrupted. "Stella, I'm not stupid and I'm not blind. It is obvious that something is very wrong in this house and I have a very clear feeling that that something is me. I don't feel responsible or even guilty, because that person, that Mrs. Johnsbury, isn't me. I don't know her. I have no memory that she existed. But I exist and I can sense that she was not well liked. Now. Please, Stella, I need your help." She leaned forward, her eyes direct and honest and Stella found herself drawn to her.

"I need you to tell me what she, er, I was like. Tell me some of the worst things I did and to whom. I need to know, Stella. It's awful knowing people hate me and not knowing why. Maybe if I know why, I can change the way they feel."

"Mrs. Johnsbury. You must know that what you're asking is very difficult for me," she said carefully, her face lined with worry. "I'm sorry, but I don't think I can," Stella said, her voice shaking slightly, making Maggie want to weep. What kind of monster had Margaret been? No one could have been that bad. How could she even begin to tear down the barriers she'd erected unless she knew why and where they stood?

"Just answer me this, Stella. Suppose I wanted to change. Suppose I did change, suddenly becoming a friendly, warm person. How would people react?"

Stella took a long time to answer as she weighed whether honesty was worth her job. She pursed her lips and drew her eyebrows together and said, "Mrs. Johnsbury, my pardon, but no one would believe it. No one. They'd think you were playing a game, a mean game. I'm sorry to say it, I am. But it's the truth. You can fire me if you want." She sat up straight and lifted her chin.

Maggie wanted to cry, and looked so dejected, Stella actually felt sympathy for her mistress before she reminded herself of her employer's many sins against not only her but all the servants at Rose Brier. And most of all, she reminded herself, of her sins against Mr. Johnsbury. He was no saint himself, but he was a good, fair man who did not deserve such treatment.

"What if . . . what if it was to last for months. What if I really had changed," Maggie said, fearing she sounded pathetic.

"Well. Maybe. Maybe then. But people, they have long memories, Mrs. Johnsbury," Stella said more strongly, her confidence growing since her employer had not ranted and raved and thrown her out on her ear. After sitting in uncomfortable silence as Maggie gazed out the window, Stella said, "Is that all?"

"Oh, yes. You can go, Stella. And thank you." The older woman paused at hearing the "Thank you," then left Maggie alone.

"Why have you done this to me? Was I such a bad person?" she whispered to those angels who had sent her here. Her other life almost seemed like a dream that was fading more every day. For a moment she did, indeed, wonder whether she was crazy, that she had somehow dreamt that other life. After all, head injuries were tricky things. Perhaps she was under some delusion, living some fantasy. Perhaps she really was Margaret. She sighed a sigh that should not come from one so young, as if the world's worries were her own. No, she thought. Her old life was not a dream. She could still sing Beatles' songs, and knew who all the twentieth-century presidents were. She really was Susan, who the saints or angels or maybe God even, had given another chance at life. It just was not the life she would have chosen, that's all, she thought. Usually she could lighten her load by thinking of people who had it worse. But what, she thought, could be worse than what she had gone through in the past two weeks? She had died, lost her baby, her husband, been reborn into another woman, suffered a concussion, and found herself a piranha in the midst of her new world. Maggie looked around the elegant room, with its high molded ceiling,

sparkling chandelier, and rich Oriental carpet and felt
lonelier than she ever had in her life. She could talk to
no one about this. Who would believe her? She knew
she had already taken a chance by telling Carter, and
only God knew if he believed her. She prayed he did, for
the only other conclusion he could make was that she
had gone mad. She shuddered at the thought as if the
room had suddenly grown cold.

All her life as Susan, when an obstacle presented itself, she fought to overcome it. She was the kind of
woman who was daunted by nothing, the kind who
would try anything once, just to say she'd done it. And,
she was a person who never let life overwhelm her, remaining so cheerful in the face of trouble, her friends
and family had often been amazed. She'd not let this
strangely impossible event deter her from having a good
life, she thought fiercely. She mustn't sit still and allow
this other woman's problems to squash her. The helpless feeling that threatened her happiness disappeared
when Maggie decided to take charge of the only thing
she could here—herself. Maggie decided to do what
she'd always done when she felt blue—she would exercise.

Maggie stood up, cheered by her resolve to get this
1880s body into 1990s shape. Looking down at the
dress, cinched so tight she could hardly breathe, she
realized that the corset and the dress would be the first
to go—at least if she wanted to work up a sweat without
killing herself. She knew from her own investigations
that Margaret had nothing in her wardrobe that would
remotely be suitable for a good workout, but with all
those dresses, she sure had enough material to make a
pair of shorts and a shirt. Maggie found herself smiling
for the first time since she entered this life.

Enlisting Stella to gather up the materials she would
need, Maggie set about selecting which dress would be
sacrificed. She picked one of the most daring, garish

things in her wardrobe and, with a certain amount of glee, ripped the seam up to the waist. Within two hours, she had fashioned herself a pair of ill-fitting, oversized red shorts, cut to the knees as a modest concession to the times, and a simple pullover shirt. She used some leftover material to tie her thick dark curls back. Looking in the full-length mirror at the shorts that were a bit uneven and the shirt that fit like a potato sack, Maggie said to herself, "I won't win any fashion contest, but at least I won't be tripping over myself."

She was about to set out when she realized she had nothing to wear on her feet. Certainly she could not wear those torture devices she had been wearing. After some thought, she decided to run barefoot along the shore, despite the cold. By the time she had stretched Margaret's unused muscles, dusk was approaching, Maggie's favorite time to run. After another quick look in the mirror, with a grimace for the yellowing bruise that still marred her forehead, Maggie headed out of the house, ignoring the wide-gaped stares of the servants.

She'd had little time to explore the grounds of Rose Brier and now wished she had spent the day outside. She walked around the huge wood-shingled house, the cool green grass prickling at the bottom of her feet, to search for a way down to the beach. It was colder out than it had looked from inside the house, but she knew she'd warm up soon enough. The bay shimmered gold as the sun sank over Narragansett across the water and the sails on the few working skiffs that glided across the calm water glowed a burnished red-gold. Seagulls floated in the air searching for an evening meal, crying out to each other, screaming when their catch was threatened by a marauder.

Not far from shore, an ice floe bobbed in the water, carrying what appeared to be several gray dogs. Maggie squinted her eyes to see the dogs better, praying the

poor little animals would make it safely to shore. It was
then she realized she was looking at a small group of
seals enjoying a free ride on the ice. Her smile at the
discovery almost immediately became wistful, for she
knew that the seals would all but disappear from Narragansett Bay in the coming years. Again, without thinking, she gave herself a mental reminder to tell Steve
about the seals. Maggie breathed in the salty-fishy air
and images of her and Steve rushed into her head, for
the two had spent endless days by the water digging
clams and fishing for stripers and blues. Maggie waited
for the pain that she was sure would follow such a memory, but there was nothing but that strange calm, that
odd serenity she felt when she first came to be here.

She closed her eyes and tried to bring Steve's image
forward, suddenly wondering why she did not miss her
husband, why she did not mourn him. It was as if he had
somehow become a fond memory and nothing else, and
Maggie realized that her angels had somehow blocked
the pain so that she would be free. A part of her was
angry, for she wanted to remember Steve, wanted to
miss him desperately. But she knew she could not live a
life here mourning the life she once had. Her angels had
let her grieve in those first heart-wrenching moments
and now she must carry on.

Maggie followed a stone wall that ran along the
bluff's edge until she came to an opening that happily
led to a stairway dropping to the beach. She walked
down the steep but sturdy wooden steps to the beach
below and began running in the soft sand. She quickly
tired, as her leg muscles labored to keep pace with Maggie's ambition, for this body had probably not done anything more strenuous than walk up and down stairs or
climb in and out of bed. When she was gasping for
breath, her lungs aching from the sharply cold air, she
walked until she felt rested and ran some more, ignoring
a sharp cramp in her side.

Trudging up the steep stairs after her run, Maggie dripped with sweat and felt lightheaded and shaky. But she also felt better about herself than before her run. She was finally doing something to change her predicament. "To hell with everyone else," she said to herself, swiping a shaking hand across her forehead to lift her wet curls from her face. "I'll just please myself."

And that is what Maggie did over the next several weeks. She refused to wear the restricting corset, but soon her dresses were loose enough so she really didn't need it anyway. At first it was difficult to convince the cook that she did not require a mountain of food and five different courses each meal, but she finally got her way. Rich sauces were served in a gravy boat and mostly went ignored, butter was left on a small plate by the bread, fish and chicken replaced red meat. To their way of thinking, Mrs. Johnsbury was trying to starve herself to death, a fact that many in the kitchen met with glee more than concern.

Maggie's pallid complexion got a glow from walking in the sun along the shore. A few freckles appeared on her nose and her arms were getting a bit golden, but otherwise Maggie felt just as she looked—healthier. She certainly felt that way. The sluggishness Maggie felt a month ago was gone, her face had lost its sick puffiness, her hair was clean and shining. Even her teeth, which Maggie felt Margaret had neglected terribly, were beginning to whiten from the tooth powder she was using.

Maggie almost felt she was on a glorious vacation with nothing to do but bask in the sun, take endless walks along the beach, and read from Rose Brier's expansive library long into the night. This life isn't so bad after all, Maggie half convinced herself. The inconveniences of living in a time without electricity, phone, or television had not touched Maggie. She loved the soft light of the gas lamps, she had no one to telephone, and she had never watched much television anyway. She bathed daily, which was a task for servants, but not for her. Any guilt she felt about ordering a daily bath so she could wash her body and hair were quickly forgotten when she sank deep into the large copper tub that had become a fixture in her room. Newer homes, Maggie learned, were being constructed with plumbing, but Rose Brier's servants regrettably had to deal with a home built in a time before central plumbing by lugging bucketfuls of hot steamy water from the dumbwaiter in the hall to her room. And so the days passed, with Maggie following a routine that left her fit and content.

But in the back of her mind—and not so far back as all that—she knew Carter would return and would have to be dealt with. It had become even more clear that Carter and his wife were not a happy couple. Not a single letter or telegram had arrived from her husband in the weeks he'd been gone. She'd sneaked into Carter's room to try to get a feel for the stranger who was her husband, and although she'd been fascinated by the old-fashioned clothing hanging in the tall wardrobe, nothing in the masculinely appointed room told her much about him. Since thinking about her husband's imminent return was just about the only unpleasant thought during these blissful and relaxing days, Maggie pushed it away.

Each day, Maggie studied the newspaper, trying to find out from the narrow columns and tiny print what life was like outside Rose Brier. Although she tried to be interested in the national and state news, she found herself instead gazing at the advertisements and social tidbits. Reports of police raids on beer halls were the most interesting. The prohibition movement, which Maggie had always associated with the Roaring Twenties, had a strong foundation in 1888. She laughed when she read about one ingenious man who hid barrels of beer under his house and ran a tap through an ordinary faucet in his house. He got caught when the police sniffed the strong beer smell coming from the faucet. Almost every day brought news of beer busts from illegal halls and women's temperance groups meeting to plot the end of liquor sales. Knowing how it all turned out made the stories even more fun to read.

The servants could not understand Maggie's sudden fascination with the newspaper, and often looked at her askance when she chuckled over an ordinary item in the *Evening Bulletin*. But the newspaper was Maggie's best friend—it told her what the clothing styles were, that sarsparilla cured nearly every complaint known to man. It told her that people were horrified by violent death, but just as fascinated by it as ever. It told her what people did for fun and she found herself longing to attend the Newport Opera House when Minnie Diltney of the New York Metropolitan Opera House was set to perform. The newspaper, more than anything, was proof that she was not living in a dream, that this was real.

She was becoming comfortable in her new life. The house, once intimidating, had become home. Once in a while, she would still startle herself when she caught her reflection in the mirror seeing a stranger looking back at her. But as the weeks passed, Maggie became used to the pretty brunette who gazed back at her. She was also getting more comfortable with a household of servants around her. At first she had felt awkward and guilty asking one of the maids to do something for her. It wasn't until she realized they felt affronted when she did something for herself that they normally did, that she began letting them do their jobs. The first time she'd made her bed and saw the look at one of the maid's faces was the last time she attended to that chore herself. Maggie was unsure how she was supposed to act, so she decided to simply be herself. And that, more than anything, had the servants of Rose Brier completely confused.

Maggie could have no idea that her activities were
causing a stir in the Rose Brier household, but the mistress's strange activities were all the servants could talk
about. Half believed she had gone mad, half thought
she still suffered from the knock on her head, but all
agreed Mrs. Johnsbury was acting a bit queerly. They
just did not know yet whether this was a change for the
good or for the bad. Rose Brier had always been a tense
place at which to work, for Mrs. Johnsbury was often
flying into a tirade over the smallest slight—a cheese
sauce that was too thin, a wilted flower, a fingerprint on
a gleaming table. She had fired maids for offenses as
small as spilling a bit of wine. Most of the time, Mr.
Johnsbury managed to rehire the offending servant
without the mistress finding out, for she would have forgotten the incident by the next day thanks to too much
wine.

But other times, it was as if the house meant nothing
to her; she gave no concerns for decorating it—except
for her hideous bedroom—or for devising menus—except she liked her food rich and in large quantities. She
knew few of the servants' names and that was the way
the servants liked it had they been asked. It was this
unpredictability that made it so difficult for the servants
to keep their mistress happy.

And now, they were seeing yet another version of
Mrs. Johnsbury. She was a version who was happy with
everything, who took much less care of her appearance,
but appeared somehow more elegant. She knew all the
servants' names. She ate most of what was placed before
her, and complained only if it was something she had
explicitly said she did not want. It was a polite complaint
at that. She only occasionally had a drink of wine and
had completely changed her diet. One maid even spied
her taking the crispy, golden-brown skin off her chicken
when everyone knew that was the best part. No one
knew what to make of her wanderings, her strange "run-

ning" clothes, as she called them. What she was running from or to, no one knew. Of all the servants, Stella watched her the most closely, all the time remembering her tense conversation in the east parlor more than a month ago. Neither had mentioned the conversation since then, but Stella had remembered every word.

"Suppose I wanted to change. Suppose I did change, suddenly becoming a friendly, warm person. How would people react?" she'd said. Well, by all appearances, Mrs. Johnsbury had indeed changed. And the servants were reacting much like Stella had predicted. They didn't believe it was a change, just the mistress acting a bit queerly. They still walked on eggshells, awaiting the storm that was sure to come after this unprecedented calm.

Oh, there were subtle differences like a parlor maid humming or a bit of laughter heard from the kitchen. The whole house was less . . . subdued. But no one, not even Stella, believed the change was permanent. Something would happen to set her off. No one could change that dramatically. No one. Oh, it was a good act, all right. But it was just that. An act, Stella told herself. But in the back of her mind, there was a niggling doubt that she shook away whenever it reached the front. Someone so evil could not become so good overnight, she told herself, no matter how hard they were knocked on the head.

As interesting as it was just watching the mistress, everyone was waiting to see what happened when Mr. Johnsbury came home and saw his sprightly wife skipping down to the beach or curled up on a couch in his library for the sole purpose of reading a book. It simply boggled the mind.

As it turned out, Carter arrived home on an early evening in May, more than two months after he'd left, when Maggie was out on her daily run. She could go much

farther now and found she could sprint up the stairs
from the beach. Even she was surprised at how much
weight she'd lost and how quickly she had managed to
get Margaret's soft body into shape. Good food, running, and stomach crunches were her salvation, she'd
thought happily more than once. To her critical eye, she
still had a lot more work, but she felt good about herself
and had found the optimism she thought she had lost.

Carter was not in a good mood when he arrived. Although he accomplished a great deal on this trip, he was
greatly disturbed by recent events. For the past six
months, several of his suppliers had suffered grievous
losses and he now suspected that the losses were not
random. The first incident, which Carter had written off
as an unfortunate accident, occurred when a shipment
of raw cotton was burned in the hold of a ship as it
awaited removal. At the time, the incident was attrib-
uted to a drunken mate who brought a whore on board
for a little diversion and left a lit cigar burning. Two of
his mills were forced to slow production for several
days. And although that single loss was not significant,
the culmination of similar losses was beginning to dip
severely into profits.

Shipments burned, trains were robbed or delayed because of damaged rails, and warehouses destroyed all
the time. But it was becoming apparent that the only
shipments, the only warehouses being destroyed, were
those holding the raw materials that kept the Johnsbury
mills operating. It was a disturbing conclusion, and one
that Carter was forced to consider, despite the initial
skepticism he felt.

He'd spent the two months he'd been away systematically assessing each shipment lost and each mill, in an
attempt to determine exactly what his losses were as a
result of each incident. The total damage was stagger-
ing, and Carter was becoming gravely concerned. His
accountant, a genius with numbers, gave him the grim

news that if such losses continued, he would be forced to severely cut back production or close some mills entirely. An accomplished businessman, Carter was baffled that such damage had been done in such a short time and angry at himself for not noticing the pattern more quickly.

Armed with enough proof to convince even the biggest skeptic, Carter visited his brother Charles to discuss the problem. Standing behind his massive oak desk that dominated his modest office in his three-story Providence brownstone, Charles at first began a casual perusal of the documents Carter had placed before him. As the minutes went by, however, Charles' eyebrows rose higher and higher.

"My God, man, it looks like you're being sabotaged," Charles said. "And in a very ingenious way," he added, allowing some admiration to slip into his voice for the mastermind behind what must have been a complicated scheme.

"We're obviously not dealing with common thugs," Carter agreed. "If it were direct sabotage, I've a feeling it would be much easier to solve this mystery. As it is, I've no idea where to start."

"Well, the first step is to think of who hates you—or me—enough to want to destroy us," Charles said, and he shivered involuntarily at the thought.

"I've thought of that," Carter said gravely. "We've both made our enemies over the years, but I cannot fathom a hatred this deep. A fired employee wouldn't have the means nor the inclination for this kind of systematic destruction. A competitor wouldn't go after all my holdings. Why hurt my carriage works if your target is the cotton business? It doesn't make sense," Carter said. The two brothers looked at each other in shared bafflement.

"What about hiring a private detective," Charles suggested.

"I've thought of that, but I wanted to put this before you before taking any action. And I don't want word of our difficulties to get out. I thought, perhaps, you could make this a personal project," Carter said, and was pleased to see a broad smile appear on his brother's face. Charles did not have a head for business, but with his law degree, he had a fine head for legal and investigative matters and a large penchant for adventure.

"Brother, it would be my pleasure to find the scoundrel behind this mess," he said, slapping his brother on his back.

"It had better be quick. If this continues much longer, I'll be faced with closing down some of the mills," Carter said, letting just how worried he was come through for the first time.

"It can't be all that bad," Charles said. He had never seen his big brother so at a loss before. It was decidedly an unusual and disturbing sight.

"Let's just resolve this quickly," Carter had said.

With the feeling at least something was being done to resolve the problem, Carter was able to head home with a certain feeling of accomplishment. The thought of going home was never a completely pleasant one for Carter, especially if he knew Margaret was in residence. There would be no children to come running and throw themselves into his arms. There would be no loving wife to gently welcome him home with a kiss, and later there would be no lovemaking. But, still, he loved Rose Brier, loved looking out at the sea, loved breathing in that clean air and feeling the salty mist on his face. It filled him with peace when everything else in his life wore him down. He had thought fleetingly of Margaret and wondered whether her so-called amnesia had gone. He hoped she had given up this ruse and had gone about her life. If so, chances were she would not be home since she loathed Rose Brier as much as he loved it. As his carriage turned up the shell-covered drive and Rose Brier came into view, he felt the tension in the back of his neck begin to fade. It was good, despite everything, to be home.

Bruce McGrath, who had accompanied Carter, brought in Carter's bags and was making his way upstairs when the two heard a woman shouting. She seemed to be saying, although the words made little sense, "is neck and neck with her opponent as they head to the finish line. It looks like Maggie Johnsbury is once again going to capture the gold! The crowd goes wild! Yaaaaa."

Maggie, her hair in a pony tail, her face dripping sweat, stopped abruptly at the door when she realized she had an audience during her little Olympic drama. She leaned against the doorjamb, huffing and puffing, but smiling broadly in her embarrassment. "I just won the gold medal in the hundred-yard dash," she explained to her husband and his butler. Wiping her hand across her forehead she said, "What a good run, but I'm sweating like a piglet! Welcome home, Carter. Hello, Bruce," she said, glad she remembered his name. Maggie was so exhilarated from her run, she did not have time to get nervous about seeing her husband for the first time in months.

Carter would have laughed at the expression on Mr. McGrath's face if he had not had a similar expression on his own.

"Margaret?" Carter asked, even though he knew the vision he was looking at had to be her. Yet, it couldn't be her. Standing before him was a beautiful, slender woman with sparkling brown eyes and an impish grin playing about her mouth. Her complexion was rosy and shined with beads of sweat that ran from her damp curls down her face. It was the young face he fell in love with and was the face he had quickly grown to despise.

"That's Maggie, remember?" she said, smiling and lifting her eyebrows. For some reason, Maggie's heart began racing with more than just the strain of her four-mile run. Seeing Carter again so unexpectedly caught her off guard. She had forgotten how handsome he was, but if she had forgotten how clearly he disliked her she was reminded by the dark scowl on his face. Her heart thumped with fear as much as any other emotion.

"Maggie." Carter was clearly at a loss for words. "You look . . . different," he said, announcing the obvious.

"Yes, I guess I do. I started running and I don't eat all that fattening food they throw at me here."

Carter seemed to give himself a mental shake, as if recalling where he was and who he was looking at.

"What in God's green Earth are you wearing? You're practically naked. My God, Margaret, I know you got knocked on your head, but certainly you can't think your . . . outfit is appropriate. You're dressed like a whore. Worse than a whore," he amended.

Maggie just pursed her lips and looked down at her ugly shirt and shorts. "It's a running outfit. You don't expect me to run wearing a dress, do you? Don't answer that," she said quickly when he started to interrupt. "I'm sure you would expect me to wear a dress to run. But I won't. If you don't like what I'm wearing right now, don't look. I only wear it to run, anyway. I don't run around all day like this. Don't be such a prude. Ugh, what a century."

Carter stood silently for a while, then said, "I'm sending for Dr. Armstrong."

"What?" Maggie said, exasperated. "There's nothing wrong with me. I've never felt better. Look at me, Carter. I'm not the same old Margaret. I'm new and improved." She spread her arms out and flashed him that same bright smile that Carter was quickly growing to hate.

"You've gone mad," he said with a coldness that actually made Maggie shiver. She suddenly became serious, seeing that her biggest fear—that Carter would think her crazy—might be coming true.

~ *Chapter 4* ~

. . . Carter thought I was crazy, and frankly, I'm amazed I held onto my sanity for as long as I did. . . .

"Carter, I'm not crazy, just sensible," Maggie said, forcing her tone to be light. "I obviously needed to lose some weight and exercise is good for that. I couldn't run in a dress so I made this outfit. I know it seems odd, but it made perfect sense at the time."

"It's obscene," Carter said, dragging his cold gaze from her sandy bare feet, up to slender legs, to the sack-of-a-blouse that hung awkwardly on her slim frame. His distaste for her was almost a tangible thing and Maggie suddenly felt as if she were naked. But she resolved to not let him stop one of the few things that had given her any happiness in the past two months.

"If it makes you happy, I'll only run in the dark so no one can see me." Before he could voice his objection, she made to turn and go upstairs. "Now, I'll go up and dress in something more appropriate and then we can have dinner. But I have to warn you, nothing fits anymore so my old gowns look a bit dowdy."

Carter seemed momentarily appeased, if not still suspicious. "Why didn't you order more dresses?" he demanded.

"Order more? I don't know how," Maggie said, turning back toward him. There weren't any Macy's or JCPenneys nearby, for certain. Even if Maggie knew where to go, she would not know what to do when she got there. She suspected that Margaret had not routinely bought clothes "off the rack" and wasn't even sure whether there was a "rack" in 1888.

To that, Carter let out a huge laugh, a laugh of disbelief, but it was still a laugh. It was the first time she saw Carter look anything that resembled happy. He looked stunningly handsome and years younger. The smile didn't last.

"I'm sure Stella will explain it to you," he said dryly, becoming serious again. For the moment, he would forgo arguing about what she was wearing and turned to what he really was interested in. "Are you trying to tell me that you remember nothing? The doctor said some memory might come back."

Maggie knew then that Carter had not believed her story about dying and entering Margaret's body. She wasn't surprised, but it would have made her life—and her mission—much easier. But she stubbornly pulled him aside and in a whisper said, "I don't really have amnesia. I told you what happened. Don't you remember?"

Carter looked momentarily surprised. "You don't intend continuing with this fairy tale you've concocted. My dear Margaret," he said, as if she were anything but dear, "it is difficult enough for me to believe this total amnesia bit you insist on playing, so don't expect me to believe that other hogwash." His gray eyes turned stormy, his mouth was pressed into a harsh line.

Maggie was incredulous. Not only did this husband of hers not believe the truth—which, if she were honest, was understandable—he did not believe the doctor's diagnosis. This was not going well; this was not the scene she had played in her mind over and over since she decided to make the best of her life here. They were supposed to have talked calmly, ending the conversation with a handshake, making a vow that each would try to make this new life work. And in the best moments of the fantasy, Carter had believed that she was not Margaret. The problem was, she realized, that everyone else was still living their old life and saw her as Margaret the Evil, not as Maggie the Good. Frustration turned to anger, at this stubborn, cold man, at her situation, at her inability to make people believe the truth about herself.

"Believe what you want, then," she said, letting her temper get the best of her when she saw that Mr. McGrath was out of earshot. "If you want to be miserable the rest of your life, be miserable. But I plan to be happy. I know this is hard to believe. But as far as I can tell, I'm stuck here. I know she's been a royal bitch for years. But that was Margaret; that was a different person. I'm going to prove to you that Margaret is dead. But I'm alive and I'm not going to let you ruin my life the way she ruined yours."

Maggie was so angry that tears welled up in her eyes, something she hated, but happened every time she lost her temper. When she looked at Carter with her blurry vision, she knew she had made a mistake insisting Margaret was dead and talking about her in the third person. Because Carter no longer looked as angry as he looked cautious—the way a person looks at someone whose gone over the edge. She forced the panic down and took a fortifying breath and lied the biggest lie she'd ever told.

"I'm sorry," she said, her voice trembling a bit, to her utter disgust. "This has all been so upsetting, getting hurt, the amnesia. I haven't been . . . myself," and Maggie held back a bit of hysterical laughter at the truth of that statement. "I do remember a discussion with Dr. Armstrong," she lied, looking all innocent with her eyes shimmering with tears. And almost against his will, Carter listened. "After you left, I told Dr. Armstrong about a strange dream I had that I'd died and came back as someone new. The dream was so real, I guess I convinced myself it was real. He said that was normal for amnesia patients, that they are willing to believe almost anything but what has really happened. I was in and out of consciousness, and just forgot that it was a dream, um, and now that you reminded me of how silly that other story was, how ridiculous and impossible, I know that it was just a dream." She ended the little speech on a wistful note.

Maggie may have saved herself from being committed to an asylum, but she might as well have thrown her credibility over the cliff and into the ocean below for Carter continued to look skeptical. "So now you're saying it is amnesia. Were you also dreaming that no memory has returned?" Carter said in a nasty tone.

"No. The amnesia is real, Carter," Maggie said, her voice sounding hollow to her ears. "I still don't remember a thing. I still have no memory of you."

"Let's just see about that," Carter said, advancing toward her, taking Maggie by complete surprise.

"What are you doing?" she squeaked out as Carter roughly pulled her toward him. She put both arms across her chest like a shield as his hands gripped her shoulders, his fingers digging into her muscles. One hand swept around her waist, the other was lost amid her damp curls at the base of her neck.

"I'm seeing if you really have amnesia, dear wife," he said, bringing his hard mouth down on hers. Maggie struggled against him, shocked at his behavior—Carter, though cold and unapproachable, hardly seemed the type to take his revenge out this way. She dragged her mouth away and pushed against him with all her might while locking one leg behind Carter's ankles. Stunned by her action and her strength, Carter stumbled back, his arms flailing as he lost his balance. He let out a grunt as he landed heavily on his bottom side, his expression one of disbelief that he should be on the floor looking up at his angry wife.

"Don't you ever pull that kind of crap with me again, Carter. If you want a kiss, ask for it. Nicely. Don't you ever force me, you coward." Maggie was shaking with anger as she stomped away and up to her room as Carter continued to sit on the floor, legs splayed. He pulled one leg up and rested an elbow on his knee and shook his head. He'd expected Margaret to coldly endure the kiss and perhaps haughtily slap his face. Or maybe throw in his face that his touch was nothing like her current lover's, as she had done in the distant past. What had she said? "Don't pull that crap with me?" Where had she heard that kind of language? Carter continued shaking his head as he got up rubbing his sore derrière. He was as baffled by her behavior as by his own reaction to her. It had been years since he had felt anything more for Margaret than dislike. But in the brief moment he'd held her, he had been startled by how good she felt in his arms, how well she fit. He had also been surprised by the rush of lust that had driven him to such uncharacteristic behavior—especially where Margaret was concerned. He'd grown hard the moment he touched her warm, soft mouth, like some kind of a green youth. His reaction disgusted himself so much he quickly convinced himself he deserved to be thrown to the floor.

And where did she get the strength to not only shove him off, but to drive him to the ground? Certainly, he had been caught off guard, but he never would have believed such a little body could pack such punch. But the bottom line was that she had rejected him—as he thought she would. She had been a bit out of character, but the result was the same. He had to admit, though he loathed himself for the thought, that a small part of him had hoped that Margaret was not acting, that she really was a different person because of the amnesia. Because from the moment he saw her panting and sweating at the door with that ridiculous smile on her face, Carter had been wildly attracted to her. She simply was a gorgeous creature.

It was only in the last three years, when alcohol, food, and endless long nights had taken their toll that he had completely lost his desire for her. Before that, he had relied on his hatred for her to keep him out of her bed. He hoped that hatred was enough now, as well, for he hadn't felt such an all-consuming need since he was nineteen. He dragged a hand through his thick black hair in anger, at himself as much as at Margaret, and headed up the stairs to his room.

At dinnertime, Maggie furtively entered the dining room, agonizing over the loud rustle her skirts made, only to find herself alone in the room softly lit by the gas chandelier. "Coward," she said aloud as she marched to her seat.

"Who are you talking to, Margaret?" came a rumble from behind her. Maggie was so startled she let out a little squeak. Her hand on her heart, she turned to face her husband, who stood by a window, half hidden in the shadows by a wingback chair.

"You scared the sh . . . sugar out of me," she quickly amended. She'd never realized just how much she swore in her other life until she made an attempt to stop cursing. In the hours since her unpleasant confrontation with Carter, she had resolved to start again. As unpleasant a man as he was, she could not help but think there had to be some redeeming quality to the man other than his good looks. It was too early to give up on her dream and she was not entirely convinced that this odd marriage was completely doomed. Smiling at the shadowy figure, she attempted a smile. "Please call me Maggie. I've asked you that before."

"Maggie sounds like a maid," Carter said with finality.

"Margaret sounds like a bitch," Maggie said, pleased to see Carter's shocked expression.

"Then Margaret it is."

"Ahh. Witty tonight, are we? I suppose that is better than your sarcasm. You are much too grumpy for a man your age," Maggie said, grinning. "How old are you anyway? I'd guess thirty."

"I'm twenty-nine, as you know."

Maggie ignored the "as you know" part and asked, "And how long have we been married?"

"Six glorious years." He sounded bored.

"And were we ever in love during these six glorious years?" Maggie said, maintaining the light tone of the conversation.

"One of us was," he said, and he immediately cursed himself. Although it was said offhandedly, Maggie thought she detected a slight and brief change in his expression, but it was gone too quickly for her to decipher.

"It must have been me," she pronounced, "because you're much too serious for anything as frivolous as love."

Carter looked at her as if he were surprised by her response. "As far as I know, Margaret, the only person you've ever loved has been yourself." Carter could not keep the bitterness out of his voice. Maggie, not wanting the evening to turn sour, persisted in keeping the conversation at a less morose level.

"Then you loved me!" she said as if discovering the answer to a complex question. Maggie sobered as she quickly decided to confront Carter with her past. "But you don't anymore. Because Margaret, er, I mean, I did things, awful things, to you, to everyone. Is that right?"

"You remember, then." It was said coldly, without emotion.

"No. But I can tell how you feel. I can tell you hate me and that the servants are afraid of me. And I can tell

I don't have many friends since no one has come to call since the accident. Carter," she said, to bring his attention back to her when his gaze focused on the night's blackness outside the window, "do you think it's possible to start over? To pretend that I am a new person? I know I am not the person you married. I've changed. Can't you see that?"

Carter's face could have been carved from stone for all the warmth his gaze held when he finally did turn to her. He was disgusted with himself when he realized her words affected him, but he squashed any tender feelings that began to beat through his heart.

"It's too late for this. There is nothing left of this marriage. My God, how much do you think a man can forgive? And I am not a forgiving man. You should know that."

"But I don't know that, Carter," Maggie said, walking closer to his position near the window until only the chair stood between them. "I don't know anything about what I was or what I did. That's the whole point. Everyone hates me and I don't know why!"

"Then I'll tell you why." His voice was hard. "You have flaunted your lovers, abused the servants, lied, drunk yourself into stupors. Should I go on? Should I tell you about the men you've seduced, the families you've torn apart, the lies you've told? You want the truth? You insinuated in public once that a man, a good man, had shared your bed. It was a lie. I knew it, you knew it, and God knows the poor man knew it. But his wife, his fragile, loving wife didn't know you for the vile thing you are. She hung herself. Her four-year-old son found her." Carter's voice was rough with emotion as he told the horrible story. Carter's speech was interrupted by the appearance of a maid carrying in part of the night's fare. She quickly assessed the situation, her eyes wide when she saw Carter's look, and made a quick retreat, before Carter continued.

"You dared attend the funeral, dared to approach the widower with your false tears, begging for forgiveness. You are a consummate actress, Margaret, but even you failed to stir the crowd that day. I found out later that your grandfather had ordered that pathetic apology in a desperate attempt to save your tenuous place in society. That is only one story. Only one. Certainly the worst, but there are others. Shall I go on?" His hands gripped the top of the chair so tightly, his fingers disappeared into the fabric and Maggie wondered if he imagined her throat beneath his hands. She unconsciously raised a shaking hand to her collar.

"I only have to look at you sometimes and feel physically ill that I once wanted you in my bed, that I once . . . felt anything for you. And you think you can come to me with a pretty pout and a pitiful story and convince me that you don't remember a thing? That you've changed? It's a grand game, Margaret, not a bad scheme. But I don't believe a word of it and no one else will either."

Maggie was stunned. In all her imaginings, she had never painted a picture of Margaret quite as ghastly as the truth. The only thing she could think of to say was, "Then why are we still married?"

Carter's face turned into an ugly sneer. "Divorce is out of the question. Rose Brier is yours and I don't want to lose it. For that, for Rose Brier, I'll put up with your vicious behavior as long as you don't hurt another living soul. We've discussed this before, and I'm through talking. As a matter of fact, I think I've lost my appetite, as well. Good night, Margaret," he said and began walking from the room.

Maggie slumped into the chair as if the weight of all he told her pushed her down. "That's Maggie," she yelled over to his retreating back. She held her tears back until Carter had left the room. After an initial rush of self-pity, Maggie quickly got ahold of herself and once again assessed her situation. Things were certainly more grim than she had originally thought, but it was not hopeless. Not yet. Tomorrow things would look brighter; they always did. After all, what Carter said just did not make sense. What possible motive could Margaret have for pretending to have amnesia? It just did not make sense, and she intended to convince Carter of at least this, if not the total truth of her situation. Maggie just hoped her eternal optimism was not setting her up for a horrible fall.

Still burning with anger, Carter headed to his retreat, his book-lined library, the one room in the house that soothed his soul. The rich Oriental carpeting, soft gas light, and mahogany paneling had an immediate effect on his temper. After downing a quick brandy, Carter poured another and sipped slowly, thinking about the scene in the dining room. Talking about the past brought the fury he thought he had put away back to the surface as if the events had just happened. The woman still had the capacity to infuriate him. He did not know what he would do if Margaret continued her charade, but he doubted she would, now that he'd told her he'd seen through the act. He refused to believe, to have hope, that Margaret had changed. It was unfathomable, he told himself, feeling the brandy begin to do its job as it burned a trail down to his empty stomach.

"Hell, I'd better eat something before I end up three sheets to the wind," he said aloud.

He wandered to the kitchen where the cook and her helpers were still cleaning up. Poking his head through one of the double swinging doors, he grinned at Mrs. O'Brien, who greeted him with a smile of her own.

"It's good to see you, it is, Mr. Johnsbury. We've had no cookin' to do to speak of with the Missus not eatin' hardly enough to feed a wee bird. I just sent up a tray to her now, not that I have any hope that half of it will be touched. I hear your stomach rumblin' from here so why don't I just fix you up a plate of what you missed earlier." She paused as if allowing Carter the chance to explain the scene in the dining room. When he didn't, she continued her prattle.

"Got some fine baked ham for you tonight, with sweet potatoes and some split pea soup." As she talked, she piled a dish high and scooped the thick soup into a bowl. She placed everything on a tray and handed it to Carter—it was something she'd done before when he came in late or something interrupted his meal as had happened this evening.

"I and my stomach thank you, Mrs. O'Brien. Good night. I'll be dreaming of you tonight," Carter teased, saying the last in an imitation of her own brogue. She threw a dish towel at him, yelling, "Oh, you," as he made his escape. He carried the tray into the library and ate his meal at his desk. Alone.

The next day, Maggie rose before the sun, before most of the servants, even, as was her habit, and stretched her sore muscles. Morning was her favorite time of day. The silence of the bay was a panacea to her, a time before the gulls' loud cackling, before the wind kicked up the surf. It was a time for fine mists and the silent stalking of ghostly white egrets. As she had for several weeks, now, Maggie padded barefoot to the kitchen wearing a thick, forest-green robe over a thin cotton shift. As she waited for her coffee to perk on the coal-burning stove, she gazed outside, watching the first light tint the sky a rosy hue as the stars blinked out one by one. It would be a beautiful sunrise.

Maggie poured a bit of rich cream into the steaming black liquid and walked outside to sit on the porch to watch the day begin. The sun, softened by hazy clouds that clung to the horizon, made the whole world look approachable and kind. Maggie's face was a study of serenity and beauty when Carter happened to look out a nearby window. He sucked in his breath when he saw her, unable to believe something so beautiful could be so vicious. He again reminded himself of his wife's misdeeds so he would not be intoxicated by her beauty. But like a drug that cannot be resisted, Carter was drawn to Maggie, against his will and cursing his weakness.

"You're up early," he said, his voice low and rumbling like distant thunder. Maggie was aware of Carter's presence long before he announced himself, so she was not startled by the sound of his voice.

"I love the morning. I sit out here every day to watch the sun come up. It's so peaceful here," she said, letting out a long sigh as she continued gazing at the scene. "I love this place."

Carter said nothing, but he again found himself confused by Margaret's behavior. He had never seen her up before eleven o'clock in the morning in all their years together. And he had never known her before to gaze longingly at anything other than her own reflection. As far as loving Rose Brier, that, too, was something he'd never heard pass her lips. For some inexplicable reason, her words made the anger he'd felt last night come rushing back. The comments she'd just made, spoken so casually, sounded like calculated manipulation to his ears.

Not getting a response, Maggie turned her head to look at Carter. His hair was still bed-messy, his gray eyes dark and sleepy. He wore a casual pair of pants and a shirt, untucked and open at the neck. He was so handsome, Maggie ached inside, and then found herself startled by her physical reaction to a man who she not only did not know well, but disliked her intensely. As her gaze went back to his face, she found herself confronted by steely eyes that already Maggie knew meant he was angry. She quickly turned away, inwardly cringing, and feeling a rush of anxiety that bordered on fear. What possibly could have made him angry this time? she wondered.

"You hate Rose Brier. It's too quiet. It bores you. You hate this drafty house. You only come here when it's absolutely necessary and now you're trying to tell me that you love it here?" Carter had started off softly, with a menacing tone, but ended at a near shout. He appeared to have finished, but demanded, "And since when do you get up at the crack of dawn? What the hell is going on here?" He said the last more to himself than to Maggie.

Maggie smiled, and smiled wider when she saw Carter's scowl grow deeper. "Amnesia," she said, drawing out each syllable in a way that clearly said she did not believe that to be the reason.

"Amnesia," he echoed, still frowning.

Maggie let out a sigh. "Okay. Amnesia it is." Maggie smiled, her cheeks dimpling, her brown eyes turning to half moons. "I'm going to get dressed now, then I'm going for a walk on the beach before breakfast. Do you want to come?"

Looking as if he could not believe he heard her right, Carter shook his head. "My brother is coming to visit. With Patricia and my mother. Feel free to go to the city." Carter turned as if to go but was interrupted.

"Why would I want to go to the city? And what city?" she asked.

"Surely it won't come as a surprise to you that you dislike my family and they completely and passionately reciprocate those feelings. In fact, I can't believe you're still here. You seem to be completely recovered. Do run along to New York," he said with biting sarcasm.

"Oh." Maggie pursed her lips and thought about what she should do. "I think I'll stay and meet them," she said. Carter angrily swiped a hand through his mussed-up hair and swallowed the rage that swept through him. Clenching his fists and asking God for control, he said,

"I don't think that would be a good idea, Margaret. When I said you could leave, it wasn't a suggestion. I never thought for a moment that you would want to stay, number one. And, number two, now that you've decided to 'meet' my family, I am forbidding it. They do not have the patience with you that I do." Maggie stifled a bitter laugh at the thought that Carter had been displaying "patience" with her. "I am demanding that you leave. You have put them through enough without subjecting them to your confused state of mind. I won't have it."

Maggie was in the midst of controlling her own temper. "This is my house, is it not?" she said coldly, surprised at her bravery. Something about this man brought out a tough side to her that she had not known existed until now. Maybe before meeting this infuriatingly cold man she had not needed that toughness.

Carter's head snapped up, his eyes burning with the anger he could no longer hide. Maggie refused to be intimidated by his look. She was a strong woman on a noble mission and would not be deterred by a stubborn man.

"Since this is my house," she said as haughtily as she could, "I choose to stay here. I promise you I will do nothing to make your family feel unwelcome and I hope you will do nothing to make me feel unwelcome." Maggie stalked past Carter, her cheeks burning with anger. Every obstacle was more difficult than the last, she thought as she thumped up the stairs to her room. Again she cursed those angels who sent her here to live with such a difficult man in such an impossible situation. She must have led a worse life than she thought if this was her punishment. Flinging off her robe, she kicked at the crumpled garment, sending it sailing across her room.

"You can't beat me, Carter Johnsbury," she said, aloud. "I have nothing to lose. Nothing."

~ *Chapter 5* ~

. . . I met Carter's family for the first time, just a few months after I arrived. I was scared to death (pardon the pun). . . .

The remainder of the day, Maggie avoided the library, the place where Carter had decided to hole up. The library was one of Maggie's havens and his presence there upset her routine. She was tempted several times to just barge in and curl up on the couch like she had done every day for the past month and read until her eyes hurt. She was in the middle of *A Tale of Two Cities,* one of several classics she'd never had the time to read before but now planned to relish. But even with the book beckoning, she had to admit the thought of confronting Carter right now was not a pleasant one. She was in her room sulking when Stella interrupted her.

"Mr. Johnsbury suggested you should go into town this week and order some dresses for yourself. I took the liberty to send Tommy off with a note to the seamstress, if you don't mind, and scheduled us an appointment for Wednesday." Maggie was slightly taken aback that her husband would worry about her wardrobe, but the next bit of news imparted by Stella explained his concern.

"I don't suppose you remember there's to be a small ball here Saturday evening?" Stella asked.

The news shook Maggie more than she wanted to

admit. "No, I didn't remember. Thank you, Stella. How many people will be attending?" She nearly gasped when Stella calmly informed her that nearly a hundred people would be attending the affair, an event held each year to celebrate Carter's mother's birthday. It was bad enough she would be faced with meeting her in-laws for the first time tomorrow; now she was forced with the prospect of meeting a horde of people who would know her, probably dislike her, and who would all be strangers to her.

Maggie had been nicely secluded at Rose Brier for the past two months. So much so that she could almost pretend that she had not been thrust back in time but was experiencing a quaintly old-fashioned vacation. It wasn't that Maggie was deluding herself into believing that she truly was not living in 1888, but she had become pleasantly complacent about her predicament. The arrival of Carter and now the news of the ball was forcing Maggie to confront reality—she was a 1990s woman who was completely ignorant about life in the nineteenth century. Carter's horrified reaction to her running outfit was a glaring example of how little Maggie knew about her current situation. She certainly knew that the short pants and oversized shirt were a bit shocking for these people, but she had not anticipated the violent opposition to what she thought was a perfectly decent outfit.

Amnesia could explain away many things, she reasoned, but she would have to be careful about her dress in public, her penchant for swearing, and even her aggressive demeanor. Having grown up believing she could be and do whatever she wanted, that her opinions were not only respected but solicited, Maggie suspected she would be forced to bite her tongue or face the wrath of shocked men and women. She had a feeling that she would be shocking quite a few people, for Maggie had never been very successful at biting her tongue.

To her surprise, Maggie was even a bit frightened by the idea of going into town and leaving Rose Brier behind for her visit to the seamstress. Everything here was finally familiar, but the outside world was as foreign to her as if she were on another planet. Why could nothing be easy, Maggie wondered, clenching her fists in the folds of her skirt so Stella could not see her trepidation.

"You'll come with me to the seamstress? I may need some help with some of the selections," Maggie said.

"Of course, Mrs. Johnsbury," Stella said, allowing one eyebrow to lift at the thought of assisting her mistress with selections. Stella had accompanied Mrs. Johnsbury on many trips to the seamstress, and never had she been asked for her opinion on anything. She had sat in the front room, usually chatting with one of the workers or another maid, and waited interminably for the selections to be complete. Although most of Mrs. Johnsbury's dresses were created in New York, she frequently bought dresses in Newport as well, mostly because of Madame Dumont, whose Parisian name and skill drew society's elite. Madame Dumont had often in her diplomatic way tried to steer Mrs. Johnsbury away from some of the color and style selections she seemed to gravitate toward. Oh, they were rich and they were expensive and very stylish, but they never seemed to look quite the same on the page as they did when they were on Mrs. Johnsbury's back.

After Stella left, Maggie was plagued with doubts. The more she thought about the coming party, the more worried she got. As much as it went against her grain to comply with the absurdities and niceties that she could only guess at, she told herself she should try. It could only make the event easier to get through and after all, it appeared she was here to stay. Everything seemed so silly, so unnecessary—especially since she knew much of what these woman felt was vital would be deemed worthless in a few short decades. As painful as it was,

Maggie knew she would have to at least try to conform. There was so much to learn and, if she were truthful, it was a bit overwhelming. She had always been so sure of herself, so confident, and now Maggie found herself unsure of almost everything.

She let out a sigh strong enough to nearly blow out the lamp she had lit to brighten her gloomy room. After the brilliant sunrise, it had quickly clouded up and had rained all day. The grayness of the day reflected her mood. For the first time since her "voyage" back in time, she longed for an electric light, central heat, and a long, hot shower. She glared at the lamp, flickering from some hidden draft, as if it were the cause of all her problems. She suddenly felt restricted by her long gown, even though it was several sizes too big. She stripped out if it as she walked to her bureau, where she yanked out her running clothes.

"So much for following society's rules," she said to herself with a grim smile.

By the time she'd slipped on the poorly made outfit, she was already smiling in spite of the rain that splattered like grease sizzling in a pan against her window. Outside, with rain soaking her clothes and dripping into her eyes, she ran farther and faster than at any other time, as if she could run away from all her troubles. The sand, wet and compact, sprayed behind her in little clumps as she made her way down the beach toward the distant rocks that jutted out into the bay, blocking her way. When she reached the rocks, shiny and slippery from the rain and covered with tiny periwinkles, she plopped down on the sand, her back against a boulder, her face lifted to the sky. Sometimes she even amazed herself at her ability to rebound from misery.

Heaving herself up, she wiped the sand off her buttocks and slapped her hands together to brush the tiny grains from her palms and headed back to Rose Brier at a much more relaxed pace, stopping now and again to

stare pensively out at the bay. The house, crouched on
the bluff, blended into the bleak sky but its windows
were lit, a beacon of hope to Maggie's soul. Her run had
cheered her, but had done nothing to take away her
nervousness about meeting Carter's family. She wasn't
sure how she should act. She suspected Carter had told
them about her amnesia and his doubts about her having the affliction. Wiping the wet hair that streamed into
her eyes impatiently away, Maggie decided to just be
herself, to pretend she was in her old home and she was
welcoming guests. She would try, anyway, she told herself.

The next day, Maggie had just finished lunch, a huge
baked potato stuffed with broccoli—the kitchen was
getting used to her odd requests—when a commotion in
the front of the house drew her inside from her balcony.
Carter's family had arrived. Swallowing her nervousness, Maggie gave her reflection a quick check, practiced a smile that turned into a grimace, and headed
down to the front foyer. As she started down the steps,
she heard the happy sounds of the reunion above the
rustle of her skirts. Maggie was never more aware of
feeling like an outsider in this world as she gazed down
at the scene below. This would not be easy, she thought.
No, not at all. She was not a part of the happy family
scene that met her eyes: Carter lifting up his three-year-
old nephew as he bent to give his mother a kiss. A man,
who Maggie quickly identified as Carter's brother, held
a newborn in his arms, while his wife smiled broadly by
his side. Maggie stood there, three-quarters of the way
down the curving staircase, her hands unconsciously
twisting her skirt, waiting for someone to notice her.
And when they did, she wished they hadn't.

"What is she doing here?" It was said with unmasked
hostility by Carter's sister-in-law. All eyes, none of them
friendly, turned to Maggie standing miserably on the

staircase. She felt her already-hot face grow warmer under their scrutiny but mentally fortified herself with silent encouragement.

"I live here," she said, smiling at the four scowls cast her way. Maggie walked down the remainder of the steps, keeping a pleasant smile plastered on her face while her insides twisted and turned. But the smile became real when she looked at the infant in Carter's brother's arms. Forgetting herself, forgetting that Carter's family only knew her as Margaret, Maggie immediately went to get a closer look at the sleeping baby, pulling back a soft blanket that partially covered its face. Carter's sister-in-law thrust herself between Maggie and the baby, and took it from her husband's arms in a manner that was clearly protective.

"Don't you touch my baby," she said. If she hadn't looked so clearly frightened, Maggie would have been angered. Instead, she was hurt.

"I . . . I just wanted to look. I would never hurt her." She looked at Carter for some backing, but his eyes held nothing but concern for his sister-in-law and the babe. "Oh, come on. Margaret was rotten, but even she wouldn't hurt a baby, would she?" When she realized she had slipped once again and was talking about herself in the third person, she whispered, "Damn" to herself.

At their looks of confusion, Maggie said, "Didn't Carter tell you?" They continued to look blank.

"Margaret insists she has amnesia and quite conveniently has no memory of any of us, nor of any of her own misdeeds," Carter said in a way that clearly told his family he did not believe a word of it.

Maggie put her hands on her hips, and gave her husband a scowl. "Carter doesn't believe it, but it's true. Confirmed by Dr. Armstrong. And please call me Maggie. It is what I prefer," Maggie said stubbornly. The family looked at each other, gauging their reactions to Carter's announcement.

"So, you don't know any of us," said Carter's mother, looking shrewdly at her daughter-in-law. If Maggie felt intimidated by Carter, she felt doubly so about his mother. She oozed class, with her soft, gray hair piled artfully on top of her head. Her intelligent steel gray eyes, so much like her oldest son's, held no warmth for Maggie as they gazed at her with an intensity that made Maggie decidedly uncomfortable.

"I realize it is difficult to believe," Maggie said when she could find her voice. "But it is true. And I plan to prove to you, to all of you, that I have changed." The sister-in-law gave an unladylike snort of disbelief while Carter's brother rolled his eyes dramatically, showing his opinion. But Carter's mother continued to examine her as if she were judging the cut and quality of a suit of clothes.

"Well, then, Carter, perhaps you should introduce her to your family," his mother said in a tone that allowed no argument. Maggie gave her a small, grateful smile, which the older woman chose to ignore. It would not be so easy to win over this woman.

Carter made a sound of exasperation, but complied with his mother's wishes. With exaggerated formality, he began. "Margaret, please meet my mother, your mother-in-law, Kathryn Johnsbury; my brother, Charles; his wife, Patricia, and their two children, Reginald and Lily." Unsure whether to shake hands, Maggie simply nodded to the adults. But when introduced to Reginald, Maggie bent slightly and formally offered her hand. "Nice to meet you, Reggie," she said, smiling at the towheaded little boy. Reggie hesitated at first, then thrust a little hand into Maggie's and solemnly shook it. "Good grip," Maggie said, sounding impressed. And Reggie's face bloomed into a huge smile. She then turned to Lily, still asleep and oblivious to the adults around her. Patricia reluctantly showed Maggie the baby, a perfect little cherub with ruddy velvet cheeks and a little bow mouth.

"Hello, Lily, pleased to meet you," Maggie said, taking her thumb and forefinger and shaking the infant's little hand, which automatically curled around Maggie's fingers. Against her will, her eyes flooded with tears as she thought about her own baby, who had died with her that awful day. She swallowed heavily, mortified that she might cry, and when she lifted her head, her eyes betrayed her only a little. Patricia's wary look turned to one of disbelief when she noticed her sister-in-law's teary eyes.

Maggie straightened and after a few moments of awkward silence, said, "I'll leave you all to visit and I guess I'll see you tonight at dinner."

"My family and I will be dining out this evening," Carter said, making it clear Maggie was not invited.

Maggie lifted her head up with a jerk, and though she tried to shield how much those words hurt, Carter saw the pain in her eyes. "Oh. Then I guess I'll see you tomorrow at breakfast," she said with forced cheerfulness.

He could not believe what he saw nor what he felt when he looked into her eyes. A feeling of shame washed over Carter and his cheeks turned red with it. But Maggie had already turned away and was heading back up the stairs.

"Why do I suddenly feel like a heel?" he asked his family after she had gone.

"You've got to be kidding me," Charles said, clearly exasperated. "She knows, and you know, that she would not be welcomed at the Crandalls'. I can't even imagine you'd consider such a thing. Carter, don't tell me you're going soft on me. Don't you dare let that woman get to you. Do I have to remind you about . . . ?"

Carter cut off his brother's speech by lifting his hand

as if warding off an attack. "I know, brother, I know more than any of you, believe me." But his eyes, as if they had a will of their own, looked up the staircase where his wife had retreated.

Patience, patience, Maggie told herself over and over as she paced back and forth in her room. Patience had never been one of her virtues and the task facing her was moving at such a very maddeningly slow pace. She told herself she must remember how difficult it was for people who knew Margaret to believe she had changed. But Maggie had never had difficulty making friends; she had never had to work at it. How long would it take if she were to let time take its course? How long before Carter looked at her with anything but contempt? How long before she could call someone—anyone—friend?

"Oh, stop feeling sorry for yourself," she said aloud. But, oh, this was far more difficult than she had ever imagined and it seemed there was no easy solution. She plopped down onto her bed and wriggled until she had sunk into the feather mattress. Her grandmother had always told her to follow her heart. But just now, her heart wanted love more than anything else, to feel love and to give it. She never realized how empty life could be to have no one and for no one to have her.

"Oh, woe is me," Maggie said dramatically, and then giggled. If she could just distance herself to everything and everyone and sit back and enjoy this experience. She had always thought it would be fun to go back in time and live another era. She'd always pictured herself wearing flowing gowns and dancing at balls. Well, here she was and all she could do was complain, she chastised herself silently. At least she hadn't come back poor. Being poor in the 1800s would have been much, much worse, she knew. Maggie had been here less than three months, and she was already tiring of the struggle. Why couldn't her guardian angels have put her in a body with fewer problems, she thought, gazing up at the filmy pink canopy that covered her bed. Maggie was still thinking about her dilemma when she fell asleep.

She woke the next morning before the sun showed its face and her first sight was two saucer-shaped, impossibly blue eyes peaking over the thick mattress. Maggie smiled at the little boy. "Good morning, Reggie," she said softly, fearing she'd frighten him away.

"G'morning. No one else is up."

"It's awfully early for most people. But I'm a morning person and I guess you are, too," Maggie said, pulling her legs over the edge of the bed.

"I'm a morning person, too," Reggie echoed. Maggie smiled at the sleep-rumpled little boy who had obviously dressed himself—his sweater was on inside out and his pants appeared to be misbuttoned.

"C'mere and let me fix you up a bit," Maggie said, reaching for the bottom of his sweater. "You almost got it right." He automatically reached up over his head making it easier for Maggie to lift the sweater off. As she repaired his appearance, she said, "Do you know what morning people do?" He shook his head as it popped through the sweater's head hole.

"Morning people watch the sun come up. Would you like to join me? I'll make you a hot cocoa, if I can find the stuff," she said. Throwing one of Margaret's voluminous gowns over her nightgown and grabbing a down comforter from the bed, the two trouped down to the kitchen, still dark and cool. Maggie set Reggie up on a counter while she made coffee. She smiled to see him swing his legs back and forth like she used to do when she was a child watching her mother.

"Now, if I can just find the cocoa . . . ," Maggie said as she rummaged in the pantry. "Ah, here it is," she said triumphantly, holding up a tin of Baker's Breakfast Cocoa. She dipped a finger into the powder and made a face. "Yuck. I think I better add some sugar to this. I'm not sure this will work, but I'll give it a try, okay?"

The result was a hot, brown, lumpy liquid that Maggie looked at skeptically when it was finished. But she smiled after taking a tiny sip. "Not bad, if you don't mind the lumps," she said, helping the boy from the table and handing him the steaming mug.

"I don't mind," he said.

"I didn't think you would, being a morning person and all. Morning people are almost always cheerful," she said, smiling down.

"Sometimes I get mad," Reggie offered as he followed Maggie out the door, carefully holding the mug so no liquid would spill.

Maggie spread the blanket onto the porch steps, sat down and motioned for Reggie to sit beside her. She then took the blanket and wrapped them both up in it to protect them from the early-morning chill. The two sat silently, their slurping sips the only sound that broke the stillness as the sky became rose-tinged and seagulls began slowly circling the sky.

"Do you see those seagulls?" Maggie said in a low voice.

"Yes." Reggie's eyes were round with wonder and excitement.

"They're looking for their breakfast. If we're lucky, maybe we'll see one find a quahog or a crab. It's low tide, so it's easier for 'em to find food," Maggie explained. It wasn't long before they were rewarded with the sight of a seagull carrying a large clam in its beak. Maggie pointed excitedly to the bird and put a finger to her mouth to keep the anxious little boy quiet.

To their delight, the bird flew above their heads and dropped its prize on Rose Brier's roof with a loud crack. The wounded quahog tumbled down and landed on the soft grass with a thump, its insides oozing out.

"Why'd it do . . . ?" Reggie started.

"Shhhh. You'll find out, but you've got to be very, very quiet," Maggie said dramatically.

The seagull swooped down to the quahog and began pulling out the soft clam meat as another bird swooped and cried noisily in a half-hearted attempt to scare the triumphant seagull away. Reggie could not help his delight and giggled loudly at the birds' antics. The little boy tried to stifle his giggles with one pudgy hand, but the startled bird grabbed what it could before taking flight. He was immediately repentant.

"I'm sorry. I scared him off," Reggie said, looking adorably mournful.

"Oh, it's okay. He was done with his breakfast anyway. Can you sound like a seagull?" Maggie said, to take his mind off his error. "I can. Listen." And Maggie attempted to make the screeching sound of a seagull, much to Reggie's delight. When he stopped giggling over Maggie's horrid imitation, he tried to mimic the bird's loud cry but ended up laughing at his own attempt. The two were laughing so hard, they ended up rolling off the porch, clutching their sides, and laughed all the harder when they found themselves on the dewy grass looking up into the sky. It was at that moment Patricia chose to arrive at the scene, having frantically looked for her three-year-old son all over the house. To find him wrapped in the arms of the woman she detested most—and to be giggling with delight—caused her to pause before rushing to her son's aid.

Maggie pushed herself onto her elbows and while still trying to contain her laughter, said, "Hello, Patricia. Reggie and I were just getting better acquainted."

"Mommy!" the little boy shouted as he rushed to fling himself into her skirts. "We was looking at seagulls and we saw one eat a quahog right in front of us and it ate it raw and then we tried to sound like a seagull and started laughing and we fell off the porch. It was fun," he said without taking a breath.

Maggie got up, grabbed the blanket, soggy from the morning's dew, and approached Patricia cautiously. She was fully aware that the woman did not like her and she was not sure what she would say.

"I'm glad you had fun, Reginald. Now go in the house and find your father. We were worried about you when we couldn't find you in your room. You shouldn't really sneak off, honey," she said kindly, putting a graceful hand on her son's blond head.

"It was okay, Mom. I was with Aunt Maggie," the little boy said with such innocence that it made Maggie's heart ache.

Patricia looked up, her eyes turning hard. "That's fine, but we were still worried. Now that we know where you were, everything's fine. Now, go find your father and explain everything to him."

When the little boy was gone, Maggie started up the stairs, only to be stopped by a hand on her arm.

"You never play with children, Margaret," Patricia said, still giving Maggie that intense gaze with her dark, hazel eyes.

"Apparently I never did a lot of things," she answered. Patricia turned to go back into the house. "I don't want you near my son," she said. "He doesn't understand anything. But I do, Margaret. You won't win me so easily. Or Charles, either."

~ Chapter 6 ~

*. . . My first attempt at fitting into this society was
a complete disaster. I wish you were there, Steve, to
lend a hand. I sure could have used it. . . .*

Maggie looked in the mirror once again, still unable
to believe the image that stared back at her. Stella
had piled her dark curls on top of her head, artfully
letting some fall, creating a soft yet intricate coiffure.
The dress she had asked Madame Dumont to create so
quickly was a stunning design that molded gently to her
body in a way no man would fail to notice, but without
overt sexiness. The bodice dipped low, without revealing
too much, and her breasts were two creamy mounds just
hinted at above the clinging fabric. But even that modest amount of flesh caused Maggie, who was not used to
such exposure, to blush. She looked almost virginal, a
thought that caused a giggle to bubble up. The color of
the gown, a soft gray-rose, was subdued yet elegant and
the cut made her hard-earned tiny waist appear ridiculously small—especially with the aid of the corset Stella
politely, but sternly, requested she wear.

"You look beautiful, Mrs. Johnsbury," Stella offered,
sounding matter-of-fact.

And Maggie, staring at her reflection as if she was
staring at a stranger, said, "I do, don't I?" It was said
quietly without conceit, but with wonder, and Stella
smiled. "Yes, you do," she said softly.

The woman in the reflection looked beautifully se-

rene, but the real woman was a wreck. Her palms, damn
them, were sweaty; her stomach was doing loop-de-
loops. She was about to descend into a large crowd of
people she did not know, but who, unfortunately, knew
her—or at least thought they did.

"How late can I go down without people saying something," Maggie said, opening up her bedroom door to
hear the muffled rumble of voices from downstairs. It
was obvious most of the guests were here and any further delay would mark Maggie for the coward she was.
Maggie had no idea what awaited her. She was somewhat disappointed that Carter had not bothered to stop
by and see her this evening, but not surprised. He and
his family had managed to avoid her for most of their
stay thus far, except at the infrequent meal they shared.
Stella took out a little watch she constantly stored in her
skirt pocket and gave a slight frown.

"If I were you, Ma'am, I'd go down as soon as possible," Stella said.

Maggie took a deep and quivering breath. Grimacing
a bit, she said, "Wish me luck," and walked out the
door.

Stella smiled and shook her head. Almost against her
will, she was starting to take to the lass. She'd waited for
her mistress to slip, to revert back to her old self; she'd
watched her when Maggie did not know she was looking. But in the past two months, she'd seen nothing,
nothing to dislike about the mistress she'd once loathed.

Their trip to the dressmaker, normally a harrowing
experience with Mrs. Johnsbury screaming and fighting
with Madame Dumont about designs and colors, was
almost enjoyable. The shop was nearly empty when they
arrived, as dress-buying was not typically done in May,
and Mrs. Johnsbury dragged Stella with her to help pick
out patterns and materials. If Madame Dumont was surprised, she did not show it, that cool one, and she
quickly took over—something she would not have dared

just a few months before. Although seeking their opinions graciously, Mrs. Johnsbury picked out beautiful, intricate gowns, if not a bit too modest for Madame Dumont's liking.

"My dear, with that figure, you must show a bit more, no? You work hard, you looking beautiful, so we let the world know," the French seamstress said while pointing out other designs in her thick books. "These come straight from Paris; only two months old now, they are the latest. You must pick one of these, please. It will look so lovely. I have one here, already made. Look. Only small alteration and it will fit beautifully," Madame urged.

Stella could barely disguise her mirth at the seamstress urging her mistress to be *more* risqué. In the past, the arguments had been much different, with Madame trying to lure the plump Mrs. Johnsbury into more subdued designs than she would have picked. The result of this needling would be shouts of outrage from Mrs. Johnsbury and quick apologies and flattery from Madame.

Maggie bit her lip and agreed to buy one of the more revealing gowns—the one she wore that evening. Stella's mind kept running over the past few days as she straightened up her mistress's rooms and turned down her covers. If the way she had acted in the dress shop was telling, then the story Bruce had confided to her was downright unbelievable. Maggie had approached Carter's right-hand man so that he might teach her to dance. Dance, of all things. Bruce had obviously been charmed, much to his chagrin, by the new Mrs. Johnsbury. He'd felt guilty, as if by teaching her to dance, he was somehow being disloyal to Mr. Johnsbury, and it was for this reason he sought Stella's counsel. But it soon became apparent that Mrs. Johnsbury, even if she'd been the most consummate actor, could not possibly have danced as badly as she had on purpose.

"She was two left feet, she was," Bruce had told Stella. "But after about an hour, she caught on. But only the waltz. She were hopeless with anything complicated. And I'm not the best dancer myself, truth be known. I'm telling you, Stella, and I never thought I'd hear myself say these words, but that Mrs. Johnsbury is a lovely woman. She was polite and kind and patient. I don't mind telling you I was practically quaking when she asked me, and I'm no coward, as you know. She does take on when miffed." Stella had nodded in agreement.

"Others have noticed the change too," Stella had confided in a whisper, bringing up her hand to further muffle her words. "But they're all afraid she's playing a trick. I'm still not sure myself. I got to agree with you, though, Mr. McGrath." And she proceeded to tell him about the trip to the dressmaker. The two were interrupted by a scowling Carter, and they quickly changed the subject to one more acceptable.

"Yes, yes, a fine polish on that floor, Stella. Mrs. Brimble does an excellent job directing the staff, I agree."

Carter had looked at the two suspiciously, then had gone on his way. The two had parted without saying more.

Stella smiled at the memory and then mentally chastised herself for daydreaming when there was work to be done. Perhaps later she would sneak down and get the full report from the kitchen staff.

Maggie paused on the stairs, desperately looking through the crowd for a familiar face. When that failed, she looked for a friendly one. What she saw made her quake. It was obvious that she was seen, but it was just as obvious she was not welcome. The cold stares, the whispers behind gloved hands, the shaking heads were enough to tell Maggie that she was in for one of the most difficult nights of her life. "Dammit, this is my house," Maggie said fiercely to herself. She plastered what she hoped was an elegant smile on her face and tried, as gracefully as possible, to walk down the curving staircase without getting atangle in her new dress.

To her relief, she saw Carter approaching the stairs and was not even dissuaded when she took in the expression on his face. He looked up at her blankly, his body held stiffly erect, as if he were one of those Buckingham Palace guards who never smiled. He looked impossibly handsome, she thought, wearing that black suit and plain white shirt, with his short hair slicked back for the occasion. She almost made it to the bottom of the stairs, when she tripped on her dress, the darned thing. She only stumbled a little, just enough so that she was forced to grip the banister to catch her balance. Good-natured as always, Maggie smiled at her own clumsiness. Her smile died when she again looked up at Carter. For the first time in her life, she understood the expression "if looks could kill." So fierce was his expression—no, so fierce were his eyes—that Maggie nearly swayed. But his eyes softened when he saw her stricken look and heard—and smelled—her breathy, "Carter, what's wrong?" When he saw her stumble, Carter's stomach clenched, fully believing that his wife was once more going to make a drunken fool of herself and of him. And although he knew he had every right to suspect she had been drinking, he felt ashamed of his thoughts when he smelled nothing but sweetness when she spoke.

"Nothing's wrong," he said. And looking at him, Maggie knew that whatever had been bothering him was no longer. She was just about to relax, when he said in her ear, "You're on your own, here, Margaret. I just want you to know that. You're not welcome here. I just ask you to behave yourself."

He walked away, leaving Maggie staring in bewilderment at his back. She felt like a child abandoned in a crowded street, staring panic-stricken at the disappearing back of a parent. It didn't take long before Maggie realized she was being completely ignored as she walked among the perfume-clouded crowd. Conversations stopped as she walked by various groups and started after she'd passed. Maggie would have thought herself paranoid if it hadn't all been so comically obvious. More than once she heard the affronted, "What is she doing here?" and Maggie felt like shouting, "I live here. This is my home!" But tonight she felt like a stranger, and an unwanted one at that.

Carter, for all his vow to ignore his wife, could not seem to stop himself from seeking her out with his eyes. He told himself he was just checking up on her, but he knew the real reason. His wife, damn her, had never looked more beautiful. His heart had nearly stopped when he saw her descending the stairs. His face never showed it, but he was drawn against his will toward her beauty, cursing himself for every step he took. When he saw her stumble, he was able to snap back to reality—and the reality was he was married to a drunken bitch and a slut. But his world was turned again on end when he realized she'd stumbled from clumsiness, not drink. And that smile, that damned charming little smile. Where had that come from?

Now, he watched her without realizing he was doing it. She held her head erect, but her cheeks were flushed and her eyes showed something he refused to believe was there: stark fear. He watched as group after group ignored her and watched as her mouth, which seemed frozen in a slight smile, began to tremble just a little. He watched as she settled near a wall taking in the crowd, looking bored. But her hands were clutched so tight in front of her, her knuckles were white. "Good," he said to himself. But he did not feel good. He felt like he wanted to take her in his arms and lead her out onto the dance floor and claim this beautiful woman as his. Then he watched as Curtis Rensworth, a rake with a reputation for sleeping with other men's wives, including his own, strolled up casually to Margaret. And he watched as she beamed a smile to him.

"I'm an idiot," Carter said aloud.

"Did you just call me an idiot?" his brother, who had just come upon Carter, asked good-naturedly.

"Hmmmm?" Carter gathered himself together. "No. I'm an idiot, brother." And he turned his full attention to Charles.

Maggie smiled at the young man who walked toward her with such purpose. Finally, a friendly face, she thought. It wasn't long, though, before Maggie guessed that this man had been more than friends with Margaret.

"You look edible, dear Margaret," the man said softly. He was handsome, but Maggie could predict what he would look like in a few short years. His face, she thought, had a puffy, soft look of someone who rarely had to think about anything more taxing than where the next party was. His belly had just begun to fold over his waistline.

"Do I?" Maggie said, trying to sound bored. She did not want to be downright rude to the first person who had spoken to her all night but she found herself mildly repulsed by him.

"Mmmm. I'm surprised, pleasantly so, to find you among this crowd. What a boring lot," he said, sweeping his dull brown eyes over the crowd. "Why aren't you in New York? You told me you were only going to stay at Rose Brier a short time. I was expecting you in New York."

"Why does everyone want me in New York?" asked Maggie, laughing a bit.

"Well, I don't know about everyone. But I, for one, am exceedingly glad you are here, Margaret. I have to admit, though, this is the last place I thought I'd find

you. And I have been looking, my dear. It is a bore here,
but we can make our own fun, hmmmm?" he said, leaning closer suggestively. Maggie, who wasn't remotely attracted to the man, decided to set him straight.

"Look. You obviously haven't heard, but I got a serious knock on the head a few weeks back and lost my
memory. I honestly don't remember you. But I do remember I'm married, so if you're suggesting what I
think you're suggesting, then stop. I'm not interested."

"What!? Lost your memory?" The man looked genu-
inely confused by her tone, and slightly angry, then he
started laughing. "You can't be serious!" When he saw
that she appeared to be very serious, he immediately
believed he'd caught onto her game.

"Well, then, allow me to introduce myself. I am Curtis
Rensworth. And I find it hard to believe that you've
forgotten me, but as you apparently have, I suppose I
should fill you in." He moved even closer to her so that
no one nearby could overhear. Maggie, who was pressed
against the wall, could not move away without shoving
him out of the way, so she decided to stay put for the
moment and suffer his attention rather than make a
scene.

"You and I have done the most wicked things together." He went on to describe, in most explicit terms
and to Maggie's complete disgust, what they had done.

Maggie was no prude and was not aware that had any
other lady been whispered to in such a way, they would
have either fainted or immediately slapped the offending man. Her lack of reaction only served to encourage
Rensworth, who never for a moment believed her "lost
memory" story, and was thoroughly enjoying her new
game of seduction. But when he secreted his hand up to
brush her breast, Maggie had had enough. "I think you
should stop," she said as sternly as possible without
shouting. But the cad just smiled and brushed his hand
against her again. She did what she would have done

when she was Susan. She brought up her knee as hard as she could, landing it where she meant to.

Curtis Rensworth doubled over, too much in pain to as much as let out a yelp. He fell to the floor, clutching his crotch, and began moaning. Maggie was so furious, she did not even see the shocked faces that had gathered around her until she nearly stumbled into Carter.

"Next time you have a party, cross that pig off your guest list," she said loudly, not caring about the little crowd who looked at her as if she had done wrong. Bruce appeared and bent over Curtis Rensworth to assess the damage done. When he stood, his mouth was grim, but his eyes were laughing. Pulling Carter aside as Maggie tagged along, he quietly told his employer what had transpired, or as much as he had seen.

"It seems that Mr. Rensworth got out of hand with the Missus and she dealt him a knee where it means the most," Bruce said, obviously trying not to laugh aloud.

"I doubt Rensworth tried anything that hadn't been tried—and welcomed—before," Carter said coldly, still seeing in his mind Maggie's face laughing up into Rensworth's. It had just been one more scene in a lifetime of Margaret's scenes.

"What?" Maggie said, her face a mask of disbelief. "You're taking that jerk's side? He molests me, practically in the middle of the room, and you take his side? You've got to be kidding me."

"Please spare me the theatrics, Margaret. You've had your little scene. Now end it," Carter said, his eyes so cold, Maggie shivered. And to the crowd, Carter said with casual charm, "I apologize for the, er, excitement. And to you, Curtis. The dancing will soon start, if you will all go into the ballroom."

The crowd stood still for a moment while Carter held his breath, wondering whether they would head for the front door instead. But his neighbor and friend, Samuel Penders, one of the most respected men in the city, led

the way to the ballroom and soon everyone else followed. Curtis Rensworth gingerly picked himself up
with the reluctant help of Bruce. The injured man gave
Maggie a scathing look that was far more frightening
than anything Carter had ever sent her way. It was a
look of pure hatred.

Maggie, who was unsure of what to do, was left standing with Bruce, shaking her head in stunned disbelief
that somehow she had been to blame for what had transpired. Welcome to 1888, she thought with bitterness.
"Bruce, I didn't overreact. That man was awful. He was
way out of line. Why is everyone taking his side?" Maggie said, feeling her throat constrict. She swallowed, refusing to let her emotions show. She found she was
second-guessing herself. Maybe the touch on her breast
wasn't deliberate? No. She was certain it had been. Had
she overreacted? Maybe.

"Mrs. Johnsbury. I saw what happened. You did
right," Bruce said, a bit shyly. Maggie managed a tentative smile.

Despite Bruce's welcome support, Maggie knew
Carter did not believe her, and if she were honest, she
knew her husband had good reason to doubt her word.
Swallowing her pride, she realized that in Carter's eyes
he was completely justified for taking that man's side
against hers. When had Margaret ever spurned someone's advances? What she knew of Margaret told her
she was the type of woman who would make a scene,
then lie about the reason for it.

Watching the crowd file into the ballroom where the
dancing would soon begin, Maggie resolved to try to put
the ugly incident behind her and attempt to salvage
something of the evening. After Carter finished the
traditional first dance with his mother, Bruce had told
her that Carter would then dance with her, as she was
the official hostess of the party. She took a deep breath

and once again found herself fortifying herself as if for an enemy.

Maggie was almost to the ballroom when she heard the orchestra begin. She hurried her steps, so she could watch her husband dance with his mother. Working her way through the crowd that had gathered to watch mother and son, Maggie smiled as she spotted the two whirling gracefully around the dance floor. The two danced effortlessly together and Maggie felt her stomach churn to think about her clumsy attempts at the waltz with Bruce. When the music stopped, Maggie took a deep breath in a vain attempt to calm her frayed nerves and waited for Carter to approach. But Carter had chosen to dance with another woman. Fine. Next dance, Maggie thought, thinking that perhaps Bruce had been mistaken about the tradition. But Carter had yet another woman on his arm as the third dance began and he disappeared from the floor for the fourth and fifth dances. He reappeared for the seventh with a young woman who appeared to be about to suffocate in a frothy yellow gown.

It soon became glaringly apparent to Maggie that Carter Johnsbury had no intention of dancing with her, a fact that was well marked by the crowd looking on. A direct cut by one's husband was almost unheard of. Many knew that the Johnsburys were not a happy pair, but Carter had always at least kept up appearances. Tongues were wagging in delight. Even Maggie knew there was some significance to Carter's snub, but she had no idea how much. It did not take long, however, to realize that Carter's snub in a sense gave them all permission to do the same. Where before they simply ignored her, now they turned their backs to her.

Bruce looked on, his heart breaking for the girl, and he vowed he'd stand up for her to Carter, even if it cost him his job. He could not fathom why his employer was taking such a harsh stance. Carter was not a cruel man, not even a mean one. And yet now, when his wife was kinder and gentler than she had ever been, when she looked more beautiful than the day they'd met, he was crushing her. Bruce shook his head in confusion. Aye, he'd talk to Carter, all right. He spied Stella peeking into the ballroom from the hallway and moved toward her. After telling her the whole story, Stella was as confused as Bruce.

"I'm supporting you, if you need it, Bruce McGrath," Stella said, realizing her stance could cost her the position she'd worked so hard to gain.

If Maggie had known Bruce and Stella were plotting for her, she would have been heartened, but instead, she felt lost and depressed. This was not the grand night she'd been expecting. She'd pictured herself dancing in Carter's arms, and even went so far to conjure up a romantic moment between the two. Despite his singularly disagreeable personality, he was a fantastic-looking man and a woman would have to be numb not to be attracted to him. She'd told herself again and again not to create such fantasies for herself, for she would always be disappointed. But she'd done it again, and here she was, disappointed—again.

Maggie walked out on the porch, determined to hide from the ball for at least an hour or so. She hadn't the courage nor the acting ability to tough this one out. She had no idea people could be so cruel. And Carter. What a man to get stuck with! She did not know him well, but Maggie had felt he was a good man—a good man wronged. But tonight he had proven himself to be petty and mean.

"I don't deserve this, you know," Maggie said to her angels. "I'm sure you thought this was a good idea, but it's not turning out that way." She felt tears well up in her eyes and she dashed them angrily away. The soft "ssshhh ssshhh" of the waves coming to shore soothed Maggie. It was a bit chilly on the porch, but she did not care. She sat on a bench situated close to the house hidden from anyone who might look outside. She hugged her knees and closed her eyes, leaning her head against the cool stone chimney. Maggie sat there for long minutes until she was startled by the French doors opening. Holding her breath and praying she would not be discovered, she watched as a portly old fellow lit up a cigar. He took just a few puffs before carefully grinding it against the railing, and, tucking it safely back into a breast pocket, he walked back into the house. Maggie was just starting to breathe normally after that close call, when the door, to her chagrin, opened again. This time, the figure that stepped onto the porch caused her heart to stop. Curtis Rensworth walked out massaging his injured manhood. He too lit up a cigar, but unlike the portly man who never turned toward Maggie, Curtis Rensworth did.

"Hello," he said in a singsong voice when he spotted her skirts shimmering in the moonlight. "And who is hiding from the crush this evening? A lost lady?" But when he recognized Maggie, his pleasant smile contorted into an angry mask. "You. You little bitch. Who the hell do you think you are embarrassing me like that? What the hell is going on? Don't you love me anymore?" He gritted this last out with sarcasm.

"I . . . I . . . didn't mean to hurt you. Okay, I did mean to hurt you. But you were out of hand. You know you were," Maggie said, trying to sound rational.

"I didn't do anything I haven't done a hundred times before and you haven't loved a hundred times before, as your husband so nicely and accurately pointed out, you lying bitch." He was so close she could smell his whiskey-and-cigar-tainted breath, making her want to gag. He tossed his cigar away, took her jaw in a steel grip and shoved her head roughly against the stone chimney. Maggie cried out in pain. She tried hitting him, but he caught first one hand and then the other, holding both in one large paw.

"Stop it. I'm sorry I hurt you. I just reacted, I'm sorry." She was trying to appease a man who obviously was close to losing control. Crazily she thought she should not cry out, that somehow she would be blamed for this as well. The bravado that came upon her in the ballroom had flown. She was alone with an angry man who was much stronger and more vicious than he looked.

"I'm sorry," he mimicked, shoving her head harder against the stone causing her to cry out again. Maggie felt blood trickle down her scalp and her vision momentarily blurred. "I'll make you sorry. You've no idea what I can do." He pressed his legs against hers so that the bench dug into her calves painfully. Maggie tried to jerk her head away but his grip was like a vise. She relaxed suddenly in an attempt to throw him off guard, but he took that as a sign she was giving in. With a grunt of triumph, he brought his mouth down savagely on hers. Maggie renewed her struggles and managed to get one hand free, which she used to grab a handful of his hair. Rensworth used his free hand to grab her arm and he thrust it hard against the wall. Maggie's scream of pain and outrage was cut short—almost before it got out—as his mouth brutally came down on hers again. All Maggie could think of was, "This cannot happen to me. This cannot happen with one hundred people just a few feet away." She begged those angels, those hated angels to help her, but all she heard was her own muffled screams and Rensworth's harsh breathing.

It did not take a lecture from Bruce McGrath or even his mother's surprisingly scornful looks to make Carter realize he had done his worst—even Margaret had not deserved to be cut by her husband at such an affair. He had taken a private quarrel and made it public and that was unforgivable. And to top it all off, he quickly realized he had been wrong to blame Margaret for that scene. He could not understand what was wrong with him. He was acting like the worst kind of brute. And he was acting like a jealous man, something he refused to believe he was. For a jealous man cared. Before Bruce could corner him, Carter sought out his friend to ask his counsel.

Once they were privately ensconced in the library, Carter held up his hand in an attempt to stop the deluge of criticism his friend was about to pour over him. Brushing back his hair with his hand in a distracted way, he saw an expression in the burly Irishman's face he'd never seen directed at him—angry scorn.

"She didn't deserve it, sir." Bruce could hardly contain himself, so he clenched his fists to relieve some of the pressure and Carter eyed him warily.

"You're not thinking of hitting me, are you, Bruce?" Carter said, almost awed by the thought.

Bruce looked down at his beefy mitts as if they were not his own and he purposefully unfurled them. "I'd not hit you, Carter, you know that," he said, with just a bit of apology in his gruff voice. "But if you ever deserved a thrashing, it's now. If there's one thing a lass must depend on, it's to have her man defend her. Now, I'm not saying that she's an angel. I know that better than any man alive, saving yourself. She's dealt you more than a good man could withstand. But she's still the mistress of this house and should not be molested in it. I saw what happened and I saw that Rensworth got what he deserved."

"I know," Carter said, miserably.

"Aye, you know," Bruce said, as if he did not believe him.

"I've got to set things right," Carter said, almost to himself.

"Then ask her to dance. But make sure it's a waltz.

The lass has got two left feet for anything else." Bruce saw the surprise on his friend's face. "I had to teach her to dance. She didn't know how and she wanted to be able to dance with you tonight," Bruce said, his voice hard and accusing.

"Margaret knows how to dance," Carter said flatly.

"Let's see if you think that when you come back from the floor," Bruce said, allowing a bit of humor to enter his voice.

Carter's search began in the house: in the ballroom, the connecting rooms, the kitchen. The door man hadn't seen her, so he knew she hadn't been to the second floor. Then Carter remembered all the times lately he'd seen her sitting on the porch gazing off to the bay and he knew where he'd find his wife. He went outside and began making his way around the house. It was dark, but the lights from the house lit up the porch and most of the lawn. He had just about circled the house when he heard voices, immediately recognizing them as a man and a woman. He almost turned around then, disgusted he had even bothered to feel guilty about snubbing his wife, when he heard a muffled scream.

What he saw when he reached the spot where the scream had come from filled him with a murderous rage. Later, he would not know what kept him from beating Curtis Rensworth to death, nor what caused him to want him dead. Because God knew when he first saw Rensworth nearly on top of his wife, mauling her with her desperately fighting, he wanted to kill him. Carter pulled him off with superhuman strength and set about pummeling his face and body with a flurry of punches. He did not know how long the punches went on, but Margaret's shouts finally reached his consciousness and Curtis Rensworth's bloodied face registered in his mind. By the time he stopped, Bruce McGrath was beside him, trying to pull him off, and his brother was rushing off the porch.

"What's going on?" his brother asked, immediately coming to the wrong conclusion, that his brother had come upon a tryst and had vented his anger. "Is she at it again?"

Carter's punch would have met with his brother's face if he hadn't worn himself out on Rensworth. Charles easily ducked out of the way, and took his big brother in a bear hug to steady him. "Whoa, there, Carter. It's not me you're angry at."

Carter pulled firmly away, and chucking his brother not so gently in the head, he gave him an apologetic, lopsided grin. "My wife is not at fault here. Not here, not inside." He said it loud enough for the ears of the small crowd that had, for the second time in one night, gathered around to gaze at Curtis Rensworth lying on the ground.

Carter walked slowly to where Maggie still stood. She trembled slightly, and as he noticed her bruised lips, he felt that awful anger well up in him again.

"Are you injured?" he asked, choking the words out. She looked up at him with those huge brown eyes so filled with pain and he felt an almost undeniable urge to take her in his arms. And Maggie, seeing the concern etched in his face, the first real tenderness he had shown her, wanted nothing more than to be held by him. But neither moved. She simply shook her head and said, "I'm all right. Just some bruises, I think." Her voice shook, betraying the fact that she was deeply affected by the incident.

Hearing her trembling voice was nearly Carter's undoing. He brought a hand up and, resisting the terrible need to caress her bruised lips with his fingertips, instead took a silken strand of her hair that curled by her ear. Maggie closed her eyes and let out a shaking breath. When she opened them Carter had stepped back. "I was wrong earlier. I'm sorry," he managed gruffly.

"I know." She made a lopsided attempt at a smile, all she could manage with her bruised lips. Bruce watched silently, thinking that Mrs. Johnsbury had overnight turned into a saint. Where did such understanding come from? he wondered.

Stella was suddenly by her side, acting like a mother hen. Maggie was surprised by her concern and her overt way of demonstrating it. All at once, Maggie felt exhausted and leaned on the older woman as she was led back into the house. The crowd, silent now, parted for the two women.

Carter faced his guests for the second time that night. "Again, I must apologize. This time to my wife and to you all. I'm afraid this party is over. I'm sure you are all grateful for the wonderful gossip that will come out of this evening," Carter said frankly, and many in the crowd chuckled their appreciation. "Good night to you all. I cannot guarantee such an interesting evening the next time, but I hope you will all agree to grace this home again in the future."

~ *Chapter 7* ~

. . . It all seems like so long ago, but I still get the chills when I think of Curtis Rensworth. . . .

After the guests had either all departed or, those who lived too far away had made their way to their rooms, Carter took refuge in the library. That is where his brother found him, brandy glass dangling forgotten in a hand drooped over the arm of a massive leather chair. Charles poured himself a drink and took a long pull from the glass before settling himself in a matching chair by the hearth. The two brothers sat in silence, both knowing that the other wanted to talk, but both also seemingly unwilling to begin what could be a painful conversation.

Finally, Charles' patience ran out. "What, on God's green earth, is going on in this house?" he demanded. Carter's only reaction was to bring the brandy glass lazily up to his lips for a small sip. Only then did he speak.

"I have no idea. I'm as confused as everyone else seems to be. I leave a wife, lazy and miserable as the day is long, to go to our mills. And I come back to the creature you saw tonight. Why she is here in the first place, I don't know. You know how she hates Newport. Which is just as well since everyone here hates her. Or hated her. Jesus. I come back and it's 'Mrs. Johnsbury said this' and 'Mrs. Johnsbury did that' and it's not complaining their doing but praising her."

"And look at her. She's beautiful," he nearly shouted. Then softly, so that Charles could barely make out the words, "So goddamn beautiful."

"And she's not drinking?"

"Not that I've seen. The most she's had is a glass of wine with dinner. I think she had two one night, but the second was left half full."

"Do you think just stopping has made the change?" Charles offered, but he clearly did not believe that to be the case.

"No. It's more than that. She's . . . different." Carter was clearly disgusted with this revelation.

"She's not so different, Carter. She's the same woman who cuckolded you, more than once, too. The same woman who caused Patricia's miscarriage," Charles said, letting emotion get the best of him. Patricia had miscarried after a particularly ugly confrontation with Margaret about her indiscretions and the embarrassment they were causing the family. Charles, and particularly Patricia, had blamed Margaret for the miscarriage that occurred later that same night.

"Jesus, Charles. Not that again. You can't blame Margaret even for that," Carter said, wearily. "I'm not blind to her faults. But Margaret at her worst isn't a complete monster. And now . . ."

"Now what? Now all it takes is a pretty face and you're ready to ignore years of misery? You know what she's capable of, Carter. I don't have to lecture you on your wife's trangressions."

"You're right. You don't."

"Ah. I can see I stepped over it, didn't I, brother? Hell. What a night. I'm done in," Charles said, getting up and heading for the door.

"Charlie," Carter said, stopping his brother before he left the room. "Thanks." His brother grunted in response.

Carter sat in the library for long minutes after his

brother left, thinking, thinking. How was it Margaret could touch his heart in mere days when he had held her in nothing but contempt for years? Was he that susceptible to her loveliness? No. It was her eyes. For years they had been dull, bland, held nothing. No passion, no humor, no joy. Now they sparkled when she teased, shot daggers when she was angry, and looked so mournful when she was sad. Hell, she looked sad tonight. He brought a hand up to rub his forehead as if he could erase the thoughts that plagued him. For so long he knew where things stood. His life held no joy, but it held no conflict, either. Aw, Maggie, he thought, don't do this to me. I just can't take any more.

As Carter was heading toward his room, he was surprised to see Stella coming from his wife's bedroom. "How is she?" he asked, walking down the hall a bit.

"Oh, she'll live, sir. But she got a bit more hurt than we all thought." At Carter's stricken look, one she noted with satisfaction, she quickly continued.

"Nothing like that, sir. The animal apparently cracked her head against the wall a few times. There was some blood, but not much. She'll have an egg and a big headache in the morning, that's for sure. Her neck's bruised, her jaw and arms, too, and you saw her mouth. The brute," she spit out. "I don't think anything's serious enough to call the doctor. If she'd hit her head in the same spot as before, I would have called you right away. But I've doctored worse myself." Stella hesitated before saying, "This has upset her, sir. More than she is letting on."

Carter felt as if his heart were being squeezed. He wanted to go to her, but could not go to her.

"Thank you, Stella." And as he walked away, Stella shook her head, thinking that this house had been sad long enough. More than long enough.

* * *

As Stella had predicted, Maggie did indeed have an egg
and a splitting headache the next morning. "I feel like I
drank a bottle of cheap wine," Maggie moaned to Stella
when she awoke early the next morning.

"Today should be the worst of it, Ma'am," Stella said
matter-of-factly. Stella took a deep breath as if trying to
decide whether to say something of importance. She apparently made her decision when she said, "Mr. Johnsbury asked about you last night. And twice this morning.
I told him the extent of your injuries." Maggie's only
reaction was to raise one speculative eyebrow.

When Stella closed the door behind her after leaving
Mrs. Johnsbury to mull that casually imparted information, the maid pressed her hands, folded as if in prayer,
to her mouth. And smiled.

Maggie lay in bed the entire day nursing her head and
other injuries. Carter did not visit, but she thought she
recognized his voice muffled outside her door more
than once. And one time, she thought he might have
stopped outside her door, as if deciding whether or not
to knock. As she stared at the shadow outside, she wondered if she should shout for him to come in, but just
the thought of raising her voice made her head ache all
the more. Then, miffed, she decided that if he was too
much a coward to come see her, the heck with him.

Maggie tried to keep the image of Rensworth out of
her head, but time and time again she saw his face,
contorted in anger and lust, looming over her. She felt
his rough hands squeezing her breasts, she smelled his
fetid breath. "I will not cry, I will not cry," she chanted
to herself. But she did. The tears fell silently as Maggie
lay there, her head turned to one side so she couldn't
feel the lump on the back of her skull. When she closed
her eyes, the images returned, so she tried to keep her
eyes open.

Unlike that last time Maggie had hit her head this
time the healing process progressed at a much more

normal, albeit slow, rate. She rarely slept and when she did, she awoke from a nightmare in which she was being chased by Rensworth through a well-dressed crowd. One by one, the people simply turned their backs when she asked for help. The dream ended just as he was about to reach her.

After two days in bed, Maggie lamented whether she would ever have a clear head and enough energy to begin her daily beach runs again. Running would soothe her, she knew. She could think of nothing else that would clear her mind of the assault. Certainly laying about in bed was not the answer.

She was bored and tired from sleepless nights and more than a little bit bothered that Carter had not visited her even once. The only joy she got was two visits by Reggie, who looked at her with wide-eyed surprise to see her abed at noontime.

"When can you come out to play?" he asked time and again. And Maggie would explain that there was nothing more she wanted to do than to go play with her little nephew. She read to him a bit each time he sneaked in, for he knew his mother did not approve of his visits, but that did little to break the monotony.

After three days abed, Maggie had had enough and, with Stella's assistance, dressed and went down for breakfast. She felt weak and unsteady, and her head continued to pound. No one was about, and she was told Carter and his family had left for an early sail to Rocky Point and would not be back for several hours.

She was disappointed that she had been unable to go, for she was more than curious to know what the amusement park on Warwick's rocky shores was like in the 1880s. The Rocky Point she knew was a tacky, gaudy place where teenagers with lacquered hair went on first dates. But she was even more disappointed that no one had bothered to ask her along, even if she did not feel up to it. Maggie sullenly picked at her food. It was another long day and she was in a deep, dreamless sleep before the sailors returned.

When Carter felt he was cured from these odd tender feelings he was having for his wife—feelings that continued to anger and baffle him—he decided it was time to return to his daily routine. His family had been a shield for him, a way to avoid a confrontation with Margaret. At first he'd felt guilty as hell for not going to see her, but as the days passed, he convinced himself they were better off without another ugly encounter. A subtle hint to his brother and the next day his family was ready to depart. They had stayed longer than intended, and were anxious to return home. Charles had been at first a bit confused by Carter's sudden desire for sailing, picnicking, and visiting neighbors, all at the crack of dawn. He'd wake up his sleepy son and wife and, with apologies and shrugs, describe Carter's latest desire for adventure.

But when he realized he had not seen his sister-in-law for three days straight, even after she had apparently recovered, he quickly deduced his brother was trying to avoid his wife. The reason for this avoidance was still a mystery and Charles was content to let Carter explain in his own good time. He realized he was walking on sensitive ground here. But these early-morning ventures were getting a bit tiresome, so when Carter hinted he should return to work, Charles jumped eagerly at the opportunity to let his brother do so. Carter was too distracted to notice his brother's unusual enthusiasm to leave Rose Brier or his mother's knowing look.

For his part, Carter found that absence made the heart grow harder. He knew himself well enough to know that if he saw Margaret the morning after the ball, hurt and dispirited and needing comfort, he was through. He was that close to giving in to his damned heart then, and that scared the hell out of him. So after nearly a week of recounting in his head every evil act Margaret had done to him, he felt himself prepared to see his wife and feel nothing more than contempt once again.

Maggie was left a bit perplexed by this abandonment. She had begun her walks on the beach once again and by the end of the week her daily jogs. She was healing her heart as well as her body. The big house seemed always empty and Maggie walked about it as if lost. She missed Reggie, who after the first couple of days had not returned to her room. To her disgust, she found herself purposefully avoiding her in-laws, as much as they apparently were avoiding her. It was a test of sorts, to see who would give in first, and Maggie was not about to give in. When she'd hear their carriage pull in, she would dash upstairs or down the walk to the beach until she was sure they had all disappeared into their own rooms. It would have been hysterically funny if Maggie had not been so terribly lonely. And yet she could not gather up the courage to confront anyone—especially not Carter. This made her wonder where her gumption had flown. It was one of the oddest weeks of her life, one spent living in the same house with five other people and yet never seeing them.

When Stella came to tell her Carter's family was leaving, she was finally stirred to action and her lethargy deserted her like smoke being swept by a breeze. She ran out the door just as her in-laws were stepping up into their carriage that had been pulled in front of the house. Reggie poked a head out and saw her standing on the porch and he squiggled past his mother, hopped off the carriage—no small feat for such a young lad— and flew into his aunt's arms.

"Aunt Maggie. I thought you were gone!" the little boy shouted. "I thought I wouldn't get to say good-bye."

"Well, I'm right here, Reggie. I missed you," Maggie

said, giving the boy a mighty squeeze. "Who's the best hugger?"

"You are," the boy supplied by rote.

"No, you are," Maggie said in practiced reply. "Now, have a good trip. I'll see you soon, I'm sure."

"When?" he demanded.

"Soon, you hound," and she ruffled his blond head, so silky beneath her hand. He ran just as fast to the carriage as he had run from it, shirt tails flopping, having happily completed his mission. Charles' expression was hard to discern—it held a look of a man who has lost a tennis match and is not upset, knowing the better player won. Patricia, though, shot only daggers at Maggie and made a big show of helping her son aboard the carriage as if he were running from a pack of rabid dogs.

As the carriage pulled away, Maggie's eyes misted, for she knew she would miss her nephew. It hit her hard that the only person in this world who loved her had just left.

Carter had watched the scene with forced detachment. If he had been honest with himself, he would have admitted defeat then and there. The minute Reggie flew from the carriage and leaped into Maggie's welcoming arms, he was done. The child obviously loved his wife, unconditionally. And his wife—this beautiful wispy thing standing on the porch with tears in her eyes—made his heart ache so he had to look away. Had he become so weak that with one look he was beaten? he thought. No, dammit. He'd been taken in before. He'd had it thrown in his face. Carter clenched his jaw in an effort to give himself fortitude, and by the time Maggie turned to him, all she saw was the same harsh look she'd been seeing since the fall from the horse all those weeks before.

"Very touching scene, my dear. But I'm sure you know that the rest of us are not as gullible as a three-year-old," Carter said, his voice dripping with disdain.

He turned abruptly to walk away, but Maggie stopped him with her words. "That's not fair, Carter. You've no idea how I feel. You've no idea who I am or what I am, so you can keep your sick opinions to yourself from now on. I plan to be pleasant. I expect you to be pleasant back," Maggie spat, so angry she wanted to slap her arrogant husband's face. She was sick of being disliked, sick of trying, trying.

Carter was stunned by her words and he whirled about to face her.

"And another thing, you stupid, stupid man. You don't deserve it, but I'm going to be nice to you. I'm going to be so nice, it will drive you crazy. So you can keep up the scorn and the dirty looks and you can try to ignore me and avoid me but it's not going to work. I'm here to stay, God curse me, so I'm going to be happy if it kills me. And you know what just might happen? You might find yourself being happy, God forbid. Your life, this life, is pathetic. You have been only existing, and I understand why, but from now on, Mr. Johnsbury, things are going to change." Maggie had run out of things to say, having just lanced free words that had been festering just beneath the surface for days.

"Are you finished?" Carter managed to say coldly.

"No. I'm not finished. I've just begun."

"I don't know what you hope to accomplish with little scenes like this," Carter said. "You call me stupid. But Margaret, when it comes to you, I am not stupid. I have studied you like a scholar, which is not a very difficult task. There aren't a lot of layers," Carter sneered.

"Do you always revert to put-downs when you're angry?" Maggie asked, pretending to be bored with the conversation.

"This discussion is over," Carter said with finality.

"Oh no you don't," Maggie said, grabbing his arm and spinning him around. She almost laughed at the expression on Carter's face. Instead, she smiled. She could not help herself—his expression of surprise was so comical. And Carter, against his will—and God knew he had a will of steel—found himself fighting back a smile of his own. He could stop his mirth from moving to his lips, but his eyes, those stormy gray eyes, could not hide it.

And seeing that, Maggie beamed a real smile at him, nearly taking his breath away. They smiled at each other foolishly for a few moments, but suddenly, Maggie became serious.

"Why are you trying so hard to hate me?" she asked quietly. Nothing she could have said could have had a greater effect on Carter. It felt as if his heart stopped, then sat heavily in his chest. His gray eyes held a look of defeat.

"There's so much ugliness between us, Margaret. So much history. Too much." There it was, laid out and exposed in quiet words.

"So that's it. No more trying. You're giving up?"

"I gave up on you, on us, a long time ago."

Maggie felt like crying at his honesty.

"I just want you to think about this, Carter. I know you don't believe the amnesia, and God knows you don't believe the other story. Think, Carter. What possible reason could I have for trying to make you love me again? What could be my motive?"

"If that's what you're trying to do, Margaret, you're doomed to fail." But her question would nag at him for weeks.

She let Carter walk away this time, but said to herself, "I haven't given up. After all, we've only just met."

I'm going crazy, Maggie thought as she trooped down to the beach later that day, oblivious to the beauty around her so gloomy were her thoughts. Her angels had deserted her, it seemed, and she knew she was going to have to tackle this all on her own. Whatever those angels' job was, it was apparently over. She grew uneasy as she thought about the strong sense they had not told her everything. They could have explained things a bit better, she thought with disgust. Maggie spent long moments thinking about her predicament. She had come to terms with the fact that she was in this century to stay and that the reason for her rebirth had something to do with her baby. Hers and *Carter's* baby. But damned if she knew why those angels had selected such a miserable life for her to enter. Was she here for her own good or for Carter's? To her way of thinking, Carter was getting all the benefits out of this deal. He lost a bitching, manipulative, cheating, slovenly wife and was getting a cheerful, happy, agreeable wife. Maggie lost a wonderful, loving, and understanding husband, and instead ended up with a miserable, overbearing boor. It wasn't fair.

She stood by the water's edge, her skirts whipping around her legs in the stiff breeze, making it difficult for her to stand in one place. Maggie let her gaze wander up to the grand house perched on the bluff, and, for the first time, it did not look inviting. It was more than the dark clouds broiling up behind the massive home casting it in shadows that left her feeling morose.

"You're alone, Maggie," she said aloud. To her disgust, she again found herself fighting back tears. She swiped them away with the heels of her hands and dried her hands on her skirt. "I'm just feeling sorry for myself. Again," she thought aloud.

Nothing made sense. People died every day and were not thrown back in time, babies died in car wrecks, husbands left behind families. Surely there must be a larger reason. Surely . . . She inhaled sharply, her eyes growing round, then narrowing as the seed of suspicion grew. She was not worth saving, no more than the thousands of perfectly nice people who died every day. She refused to believe it was a whim. God was a lot of things, but she

did not believe He was whimsical. There could only be
two reasons why she was sent back. Either it was not her
time . . . Or it had not been Margaret's time.

And since Maggie found herself thrust back in time,
she had a strong suspicion that somehow a mistake had
been made and had never been resolved. It made sense,
she thought, biting her knuckle. Did heaven have
grander plans for Margaret? She was such a nasty
woman, how could heaven have thought Margaret more
worthy than the uncountable good people who died every day? It seemed like an awful lot of trouble to go
through. How big a mistake could it have been to kill off
such a miserable human being?

Oh, my God, Maggie thought, as the realization hit
her. *The baby.* Could it be? Was it in the grand scheme
that Carter and Margaret, despite everything that had
been between them, were to have had a child and somehow a mistake was made and Margaret had died before
her time? Could such a mistake have happened?

Yes.

The answer came to her as if dancing on the wind.
The voice was frightening in its silent strength and she
knew it was not the chattering of her angels she heard,
but someone much, much higher up.

Maggie gazed up into the sky fearfully expecting to
see God up there pointing an angry finger at her. Had
she imagined it? She looked down at her shaking hands
and let out a puff of air she had unknowingly been holding. Oh, Lord, Maggie thought to herself, everything
now made such perfect sense.

She could imagine the conversation with Carter. "So,
God and I were having a little discussion and He was
saying we ought to have a kid. Whaddya say we get
naked and do a little skin dance?" She smiled miserably,
knowing that her mission had taken on a new, awesome
level. And she wondered, holding back a shudder, what
would happen if she failed.

Bruce looked down at Maggie, standing so still, wavering against the gusty wind. He could hear her skirt snap in the breeze from his vantage point on the bluff. Sweet, sweet Maggie, he allowed himself to think. Who would dare not love this little beauty. If he weren't such a loyal man, he'd try to steal her for himself. But Bruce knew he could not do that to his friend Carter, no matter if he deserved it for being so blind. Bruce was a little amazed at the thoughts that were plaguing him, for it was not so long ago he was cursing the woman himself. But his place was not to lecture Carter, although God knew he'd done enough of that. Bruce was a proud man, but he knew what he was. He was a glorified butler, no more, no less. Somehow none of that mattered to Maggie. She never looked down on him, or patronized him. "Watch your heart, Brucey," he told himself. He loved Carter like a brother and would never hurt him, but damn if he would let him hurt Maggie. He knew more than she did how strange their burgeoning friendship was, how forbidden by society's unwritten but well-known rules. But, then, Maggie was special.

Maggie was oblivious to Bruce's perusal, but would have been heartened to know she had a secret ally. As Maggie headed to the wooden steps that led up to Rose Brier, Bruce moved back from the bluff, keeping hidden, but watched her make her way up the stairway. She was going more slowly than usual. Poor Maggie, he thought, she deserves to be happy. A drop of rain snapped him out of his reverie, and dragging his eyes away, he went back inside.

Bang!

Carter cast an irritated eye at the ceiling and wondered how much more the ceiling could take before it came crashing down upon his head. But when he heard another crash, then the telltale scream of his wife, he blanched. Out of breath, he reached her door only to find her tangled up in the heavy gold and pink drapes that, along with the heavy hardware, had come crashing down upon her. The dust was still whirling about her, diluting the brilliant sunlight that now streamed through the multipaned windows, when he came upon her. Seeing that she was fine—more than fine, she was laughing—Carter leaned up against the doorjamb, arms crossed. Damn, she looked absolutely adorable. And absolutely desirable.

"You said I could redecorate. Remember?" Maggie said, waving a hand in a futile attempt to clear the dust around her.

"But I don't recall any mention of tearing the house down." His eyes took in the general mayhem about the room. He noted with satisfaction that a painting of cherubs he particularly loathed was obviously the source of one of those bangs that had disturbed him. Maggie held out a hand looking for help up, and Carter, without thinking, obliged. He heaved as if he were lifting a full-grown man and she shot up—and into—his chest with a "woomf" as the air got knocked out of her lungs.

God, it felt like hitting a stone wall, Maggie thought. Putting a hand on his chest to steady herself, she felt his muscled chest, his beating heart, beneath his crisp white shirt. Maggie felt heat rush to her face and a telltale tingling in her breasts. The feelings were completely and totally unexpected and hit her with such force, she backed away as if Carter had turned into a flame.

Carter was not blind, nor immune, to her reaction. He could not quite believe what he was seeing. Her eyes showed her want, her lips were parted as she brought up a trembling hand to tuck a stray curl behind her ear. It took all his will not to draw her back into his arms. And, like always, his surge of desire turned into a surge of anger. For Margaret had never reacted to him like this before. It had always been so much more . . . staged.

As if Margaret were acting like she should but did not truly feel the emotions or passion she displayed.

"Sorry," Maggie said, still blushing. She turned away and made a show of gathering up the curtains to hide her embarrassment.

"You act as if you've never touched me before." Carter cursed himself even as he said the words. Why call attention to their obvious attraction to each other when he had no intention of acting on it?

Maggie whirled around to look at him, the dust swirling with her, framing her in a golden light. Carter had to remind himself to breathe.

"Well, if I have, I've forgotten." She tried to say it lightly, but it came across as an invitation. Their eyes met, troubled brown eyes, stormy gray. Maggie saw the lust in her husband's eyes and nearly panicked. She was not ready for this, she thought.

To change the subject as quickly as possible, Maggie said, "Don't you want to know what I'm planning for this room?"

He smiled, a smile that told her the question had a double meaning. But he said nothing, grateful for the switch in topics. God knew, one look at a particular part of his body would have told her just how that contact and their suggestive conversation, brief as it was, had affected him.

"I'm redecorating. I'm getting rid of this hideous furniture. I'm painting the walls pale green with a white trim. It should really lighten it, don't you think? The bed's got to go. Too ornate. I want something simple, mahogany would be a nice contrast to the light colors. Eyelet covering, white lace curtains. Or panels, maybe. It's too dark in here. I want to bring the bay into this room."

Carter watched her, caught up with the picture she was drawing of the room, captivated by her enthusiasm. It would be beautiful.

"And what will you do with that painting? It cost a pretty penny."

Maggie wrinkled her nose at the gilded-frame painting of cherubs floating above a garden of pink roses. It was just too much. Not wanting to insult Carter's taste, in case he had picked out the painting, Maggie suggested it might look good in his own room. She laughed aloud at his horrified expression.

"Then how about the trash? It can always use some bright colors to offset the drab potato peels."

"You picked out that painting, Margaret. You had to have it. Pray God, why has your taste in artwork changed so drastically. I am not complaining, mind you, I'm just curious."

Maggie gave him a look of pure impatience. "Let's just say the knock on my head knocked some taste into it."

When Carter left, Maggie let out a deep sigh of relief. It had been a long time since she had reacted so strongly to a man's simple touch—if ever. She did not want to make love to Carter before they even liked each other. Nothing would be accomplished by pure animal mating, she thought. Though she knew she could get a baby by him that way, the thought of making love for the sole purpose of getting pregnant was somewhat distasteful, even if she had God's sanction. She had never been promiscuous and had never slept with a man she did not love. Then again, even with her husband when she was Susan, she hadn't felt this . . . pure lust.

"I'm such a vamp." She smiled at the image. For now, this vamp had to clean this room, she told herself. Most of the work would have to be done professionally, but for now she wanted to get rid of the items that were particularly offensive. There were only a few pieces of furniture she wanted to keep. Most of it was too heavy, too ornate for her tastes. One piece she wanted to keep and move to a more visible part of the room was a lovely cherrywood secretary. It was a delicate and simple piece that had nearly been hidden by a highback chair. Maggie brought it out and placed it by one of the windows, caressing the wood in appreciation of the craftsmanship that went into the piece. She tried to lift the lid, but found it locked. She'd have to ask Stella where she kept the key later. It wasn't as if she needed to write letters to anyone, she thought, allowing herself a bit of pity. Maybe someday. After all, she'd only been here three months. For now she would have to be content with the friendship of a three-year-old boy.

"Come on, Maggie girl. You vowed no more feeling sorry for yourself. It's all getting a bit boring," she chastised herself.

~ Chapter 8 ~

*. . . Do you remember when we first met, Steve? I've
learned some new tricks since then. . . .*

M aggie began her assault on her husband the very
next day. Get him when he's weak, she thought,
and smiled when she remembered that heated exchange
in her bedroom the day before. Her husband desired
her, and that was one step further away from the look of
distaste he'd thrown her way the previous weeks. She
entered the library as if she belonged there as much as
Carter did, walking with determination over to the shelf
where she had abandoned the thin volume of *A Tale of
Two Cities* weeks before. Carter stopped writing mid-
word and silently watched his wife march to the book-
case that covered an entire wall of the library. Expecting
her to take her book elsewhere, he tried to ignore her
and began writing again. But his head snapped up and
he threw his pen into the inkwell with a little splash
when she sat Indian-style, her legs hidden beneath her
voluminous skirts, on the leather sofa directly across
from him.

"What do you think you're doing?"

Maggie looked up as if surprised to see Carter there,
and holding up the book, said, "I'm knitting you a
sweater." She smiled, pleased with her joke. Carter
frowned.

"I'm trying to work."

"Oh. Does my turning pages disturb you?" Maggie asked, all innocence.

"Your presence disturbs me. Please leave."

"Nope. I'm here to stay. I read here before you came back and I intend to read here again. This is my room as much as it is yours. I like it here. It's peaceful. I promise I won't disturb you." She opened the book and pretended to read.

"You're already disturbing me," Carter said, swiping a hand through his dark waves. He glared at her in what Maggie thought was an attempt to look menacing. She smiled.

"You're not intimidating me with that face, so cut it out."

Carter let out a curse underneath his breath and, with a great show of patience, picked up his pen again. An obvious attempt to ignore her. Maggie smiled at her husband, his head bent over the letter, a look of concentration on his face as he tried to continue writing. He was such a handsome man.

Maggie read for about an hour, occasionally gazing at Carter as he scratched out his business writings with a fountain pen, before getting up to stretch. The couch was placed in front of a large window where the sun had just begun to come through. She walked into the sunlight, basking in the warmth, unaware that Carter's eyes were burning into her. She put her hands at the small of her back and arched backwards, letting out a small groan as her muscles stretched. Carter shifted uncomfortably in his chair, clenching his teeth to stop himself from saying anything to her. His body had instantly reacted when she arched her back, for she looked like a seductive nymph standing in the sunlight, her hair backlit, making it look soft and touchable. Her whole body looked goddamn touchable.

Maggie turned before Carter could look down and

their eyes met. "What time is it?" she asked, completely unaware of the effect she'd had on him.

Carter quickly gathered his thoughts and brought out his pocket watch. "Eleven."

"Why don't we eat lunch at noon. I'll go tell Mrs. O'Brien what to prepare. I usually go for a nice long walk on the beach after lunch. Would you like to come?"

He heaved a sigh. "What are you doing, Margaret?"

"That's Maggie."

"Maggie. What are you doing?"

Maggie tilted her head to the side with a look of impatience. "I'm inviting you to go for a walk on the beach with your wife."

"No. Thank you," Carter spit out.

"Fine with me," Maggie said, and smiled that smile that Carter found so infuriatingly charming.

When Maggie had left the room on her mission to plan lunch, Carter propped his elbows on his desk and rested his head in his hands. "Ignore, ignore," he said to himself as if saying a prayer. And he conjured up a vision of his wife naked in bed with Norris Batchley, a man whose only attribute was that he was rich. It was the only time he had actually discovered his wedded wife in such a compromising position, but it sufficed to strengthen his resolve against this vixen who was trying to burrow her way into his heart. Batchley was a bear of a man with as much hair on his back and buttocks as on his chest. His body had overcompensated for his baldness, Carter had always thought.

By the time Maggie returned to her place on the couch, he did not see this slight little thing wearing a lemon-yellow, puffy-sleeved blouse and a slimming brown skirt, but a sweating, naked, inebriated woman in the arms of Norris Batchley. There. He felt better now.

When the maid brought in their lunch on a large silver tray, Maggie dragged a small wingback chair to

Carter's desk and sat down. Carter just stared at her, his jaw clenched. The nymph was back. Ignore, ignore.

"That's okay, Sally, I'll serve. You go ahead. And thanks," Maggie said, smiling at the young woman.

"Yes, Mrs. Johnsbury. Be sure to ring the bell if you need anything more," Sally said, smiling shyly.

"I certainly will, but everything looks just fine."

Carter watched this unusual—no, this impossible—exchange with interest. Margaret knew the maid's name. She said, "Thank you." The maid, this Sally, this shy, young, freckled girl, had actually had a conversation with his wife. What the hell was going on here? Ignore, ignore.

Maggie leaned over the broad mahogany desk, unaware that in doing so the material on her modest blouse stretched tightly across her breasts, and gave Carter his plate. Then she proceeded to load it up with diced cold chicken, steaming rice, and cold herbed potatoes. Onto her plate, she put the same, but in smaller portions.

"This is my own recipe. Actually, I saw it on *Oprah Winfrey* once . . . er . . . anyway, it's good even though it looks plain." She picked up a piece of chicken on her three-pronged fork, and put the morsel in her mouth. Closing her eyes, she let out a little moan of pleasure at its taste. "Mmmmm. That's good," Maggie said.

"I think this is not a good idea," Carter said, his voice sounding oddly strained. He had not been able to take his eyes off her mouth as it opened for the small piece of chicken, as it closed over the fork, as it turned upward in a pleased smile. But his undoing was that little moan of pleasure. He was, quite simply, in pain with his need.

Maggie was flabbergasted. "What? I can't eat lunch with you? That's absurd."

Yes, it was, Carter agreed silently. Why the hell

couldn't he control himself? He detested this woman. She had not had this effect on him since . . . hell, she had never had this effect on him. He stabbed a fork into a piece of chicken in an effort to rid himself of his thoughts, and jammed it into his mouth.

"Good?"

"Good."

Maggie smiled to herself. She was beginning to see the effect she was having on her husband, saw that he fought it with every cell of his being, and was quite enjoying herself. Because it was apparent he was losing this battle. Desire was one thing, love quite another, she reminded herself to keep her expectations down.

After lunch was cleared away, Maggie walked around the library idly, but stopped when she reached the beautiful Victrola that graced a side table. She had discovered the record player weeks ago, but had been unable to locate any records. Giving the crank a couple of lazy turns, she turned to Carter to find his eyes on her, a look of annoyance on his face.

"Where are the records?"

Carter jerked his head. "In that cabinet."

Maggie smiled. "I never thought to look there. May I?"

A heavy sigh. "I am working."

"Oh, just one. I've never heard a Victrola," she said, walking over to the cabinet and grabbing the first record. Pulling it from its sleeve as she walked back to the Victrola, Maggie marveled at the thickness and weight of the disk. Carter put his pen down, giving up the pretense of working and watched his wife gently place the record on the player.

"How many times do I have to crank this thing?"

"About ten."

As she cranked, the turntable began to spin. Bending slightly, she rested the pin on the record as if placing an egg on shards of glass. When the tinny sounds of music came out of the gramophone, Maggie laughed in delight.

"This is wonderful," Maggie said, clearly enjoying the moment.

Carter could not help but smile at her childlike pleasure in the music. When the player slowed, distorting the music, Maggie made to crank it up once again.

"I really do have work to do," Carter called over, feeling like a cranky old man.

Maggie lay a hand upon the record, stopping it, and put it in its sleeve. Walking over to place it back in the cabinet, she announced she was going to the beach and invited him along. He declined.

So set the pattern of the days ahead. As the days grew warmer, and May closed in on June, Maggie spent more and more time in the library, slowly torturing her husband, many times without even realizing that she did so. She would grill him on what he was doing and learned more and more about the vast businesses he controlled. Maggie could tell there had been some trouble, but Carter was silent on what the matter was. It was a good day when she got him to smile, a triumph if he let out a chuckle. But most days, to Maggie's growing impatience, Carter was simply a coldly handsome man and she wondered whether even she could crack through his icy barricade. She wondered if God were getting impatient.

She was beginning to grow tired of constantly reminding herself that Margaret's path of destruction was deeply cut. She'd been in this world nearly four months, now, and it felt like a lifetime. The house's staff had grown accustomed to her, she thought, and were no longer skittish. She could walk into the kitchen and the chatter would continue. She was a common sight in that sunny, cavernous room, at times just stopping by to grab a bit of fruit and talk to Mrs. O'Brien about Ireland and her immigration to the United States. Maggie still did not feel a part of this century, and so wanted to learn as much as she could, as if studying a bit of history. After some suspicion, Mrs. O'Brien opened up to Maggie, for it was not in her nature to dislike people, no matter what their past. But there remained just a hint of caution, for Mrs. O'Brein was first and foremost loyal to Mr. Johnsbury and so always held a bit of herself in reserve.

The servants still talked about the old Mrs. Johnsbury. They still were not sure what to make of this cheerful, pleasant woman that had somehow replaced their old nemesis. But the memories of the tantrums, the firings, and the outrageous demands were slipping further and further into the part of the brain relegated to lore. Servants hired in recent months refused to believe such tales, for Mrs. Johnsbury was nothing like the woman they described in discreet whispers.

Maggie continued her daily runs in the late afternoon, avoiding Carter when she wore her running clothes because of his stern looks of disapproval. She had made three different outfits, all dismal attempts, but they suited her purpose. Maggie ran down the wooden steps one day, only to draw up short. There on the beach were several people, strolling along, wearing the bright colors of summer. The women wore huge straw hats and pastel-colored dresses, while the men wore tan pants and white cotton sweaters. Maggie, giving her clothes a quick assessment, felt naked in comparison to the elegant couples. Crouching down, she squeezed underneath a railing, and hid behind a seaspray rosebush with its spiny branches and ever-flowering pink buds. The prickers dug into her back and head and pulled at her hair, but she ignored the slight pain. She could hear their laughter as they strolled along, two women side by side, and two men trailing behind, both smoking pipes. The women walked, arms linked, chatting animatedly and Maggie felt the first pangs of jealousy over that easy friendship. She thought of friends she'd left behind, friends who thought she was long dead, friends who would not be born for another seventy years. Crouching there, hiding, Maggie felt tears of loneliness threaten. She let them come.

After the quartet had passed, she trudged up the stairs to return to the house. She'd have to start running in the dark, for no one outside this household would take for granted that Mrs. Johnsbury liked to run along the shore wearing almost nothing.

"Hello, Mrs. Johnsbury." It was Bruce.

"Oh, Bruce. Hello." She gave him a tired smile. Maggie paused on the lawn and looked down at the beach where the two couples walked. "There were people on the beach today."

"Must be the Browning sisters and their beaus," Bruce said, craning his neck to look at the shoreline. He noticed her red-rimmed eyes and her wet and spiky eyelashes, but said nothing. "You'll start to see more and more people on the beach now that the summer season's starting. The Brownings are almost always the first to arrive."

"I'd forgotten that Newport was mostly a summer place," Maggie said, not realizing she spoke in the past tense. "Why do we stay here all year?"

"You normally don't."

"I'm usually in New York. That's right. But Carter stays here all the time?"

"He mostly stays here, but at times goes to New York and also stays with his mother in Providence when he has business there. But in summer, he's here."

Maggie looked up at the big Irishman, a crease between her eyebrows, her eyes wary and still tinged with sadness.

"Bruce, if Rose Brier belongs to me, why does Carter love it so. I mean, I understand why. It's lovely here. But it seems to go deeper than that."

"Aw, Mrs. Johnsbury, that's something I can't tell you. I'm sorry." But at Maggie's look of dejection, Bruce decided to tell her, after all. Something about her touched him, as if there were a sadness in her that a mere smile could not wipe away despite her seeming cheerfulness. He wondered if Carter had noticed it, or only saw the wicked woman she used to be.

"You didn't always own Rose Brier. It was built by Mr. Johnsbury's grandfather, who lost it in a gambling debt to your grandfather. It was a fair game, so they say, but it rankles just the same."

Maggie was stunned. It explained some of Carter's ill feelings and why he felt so strongly about Rose Brier. It would have been his, this house he loved so. No wonder he refused to divorce Margaret.

"So. He married Marg . . . er . . . me for Rose Brier."

Bruce looked surprised at her conclusion. "Carter loved you, Mrs. Johnsbury, before he even knew who you were or that you were connected to Rose Brier. The names were not the same, your grandfather's and your maiden name. He loved you."

"Oh."

She turned her head to look at the bay, feeling tears threatening again, and Bruce found himself wanting to give comfort. He did not move. It would not have been right.

"Thank you, Bruce." Loved. Past tense. Well, that was certainly understandable, she told herself. Then why did it hurt so much? Because you're falling in love with your husband, Maggie girl. That's why.

Carter had gotten used to having Maggie in the library each day. His prayer, "ignore, ignore," seemed to have been answered. Much of it had to do with the intensity of his work. He had gone over the numbers a hundred times, it seemed, in an effort to juggle his assets so he could keep all his mills running at full capacity. There had been no more incidents and his brother was having little luck discovering who was behind the sabotage. But he could not comfort himself with the knowledge that for some reason the accidents had suddenly stopped and was becoming obsessed with the idea of finding the culprit.

He was going over a long string of figures when Maggie walked up behind him. She hovered there, not saying a word, until she pointed a delicate finger at one column.

"That should be a five," she said, pointing to a seven.

"Margaret, mind your own business, please."

"Maggie. Fine. If you want it to be wrong."

Carter re-added the figures and discovered, to his disgust, that he had made a mistake. He changed the seven to a five without a word.

"Told you so."

Maggie leaned one elbow on the desk and rested her head on her hand. She had such an enchanting smile on her face, Carter found himself smiling back.

"Okay. Since when can you do figures?" Carter demanded, the smile still lingering on his lips. Lips that Maggie just could not take her eyes off.

"Since grammar school," she said without thinking. She was completely distracted by Carter's mouth. Their heads were just inches apart, one move by either one, and they'd be kissing, she thought. And they both knew it. Their smiles faded. The air grew thick, and they both seemed to have difficulty drawing oxygen into their lungs. One move, Maggie thought, one little inch closer . . . Maggie swallowed, suddenly losing her courage, and stood up. Carter looked down at his desk, the numbers swimming in his vision. He had wanted to kiss her. She had wanted that kiss, he knew. He stiffened when he felt her hand on his shoulder, but it was there fleetingly, just a caress as she walked behind him to return to the couch. She might as well have caressed all of him. He gritted his teeth. This simply could not go on, he told himself. He found himself walking around in a perpetual state of excitement. It was getting goddamn irritating, not to mention uncomfortable. If she was so hot on getting him into her bed he would oblige, he thought angrily. To hell with that vow he made all those years ago when he swore he would never touch her again. Then, it had been easy, for he'd hated Margaret. But now . . . now it was getting more and more difficult to conjure up those distasteful images of her. More and more difficult to deny what was inevitable.

Carter stood up with near violence. Maggie, who had gone back to her book in an attempt to cool her own frightening desire, looked up, startled. Carter walked over to the couch and planted a fist on each side of Maggie's head. She scrunched down into the leather, pushing her head back as far as it would go. Carter's expression was frightening in its intensity, and she was suddenly reminded of the expression on Rensworth's face when he crushed his thick wet lips against hers. Tears formed in her eyes and she began shaking uncontrollably at the memory.

"Carter, please don't," Maggie said, turning her head away from him.

Carter's expression immediately softened. "Maggie. I just want to kiss you," he said, bringing a hand up near her face. When she winced, it was if he'd been slapped himself. Oh, no, he'd not hurt her. He smiled when he realized how fierce he must have looked to her. He caressed her face, bringing his thumb over to soothe her trembling lips.

Maggie swallowed, ashamed of her reaction.

"I'm sorry. You frightened me. You looked so angry coming over here. All I could think of was . . . that man." She relaxed when she looked into his face and saw nothing but gentleness. Taking a deep breath, she said, "You can kiss me if you want. In fact, please do."

Damn Rensworth to hell, Carter thought as he gazed down at his beautiful wife. His wife who had just asked him for a kiss. He lowered his head slowly. Maggie waited. Their lips touched, a soft brush, hardly felt at all. Carter kept his hand on the side of her head; his thumb caressed one soft cheek, and brought her closer for another kiss, this one harder, more intimate. He slanted his head, opening his mouth and she opened hers willingly, accepting his tongue, matching it stroke for stroke. Maggie brought her hands up to clutch at his shirt and he put one knee onto the sofa, which gave a leathery squeak as he did. It felt so good, Maggie thought, to have a man kiss her so, to have this man kiss her so. She let out a contented sound and he groaned in response, his kisses becoming more urgent. His hand lowered to caress her neck and the bit of skin exposed on her chest above her cotton blouse. Soft, gentle caresses. She felt so good, he thought. He couldn't believe this willing little thing was Margaret. No. Maggie. This willing little thing, clinging to him, moaning softly into his mouth, was Maggie. He pulled away to gaze down into her face. Maggie smiled sleepily at him, completely done away by his kisses.

That smile. It was completely unlike those smug, triumphant smiles Margaret used to give him, but it was enough of a reminder to Carter to crush his desire instantly. It suddenly occurred to him what he was doing. Kissing his wife! Jesus, man, get a grip on yourself. He thrust himself away from the couch as violently as he had gotten up from his desk.

"You!" he shouted, pointing an accusing finger at her. "You are to stay out of this room. Do you understand me? If you come back, I will physically remove you, do you understand?"

Maggie sat back, still reeling from those kisses, and

crossed her arms over her chest. "Didn't you like the way I kissed?"

"I liked it too goddamn much," he said before he could stop himself. "Maybe you've forgotten—and I'm sure you will claim you have—but we don't like each other, Margaret. We can't stand to be in the same room. You do not love me. I do not love you. We loathe each other, remember?"

"I don't loathe you, Carter," Maggie said simply, trying not to get angry.

"I will not tell you again. Do not come back."

"Why? Because you can't control yourself? Because you find yourself looking at me and wanting me? What's so horrible about that? After all, you are my husband. And it wasn't as if it were unpleasant. We both enjoyed kissing. And that's all it was. We didn't make love, not that that would have been so bad," and she put in as an afterthought, "Although I'm not quite ready for that."

"Not ready? Oh, you were ready, Margaret. You'll spread your legs at the blink of an eye. Even for me, it seems."

"Oh. Not fair. Maybe you haven't noticed, but I haven't left this house in months. I haven't so much as spoken to a soul other than you and the staff." Maggie hadn't felt this frustrated in her life. "I can't do this anymore. I can't be Suzy Happy Face all the time. I can't. You think your life's miserable? My life's miserable. I saw some people walking down the beach the other day and started to cry. To cry! Because I'm lonely and all I have for company is you, you lout. You're a hoot, oh, what fun we have. I haven't laughed so much in years," Maggie said, her voice tinged heavily with sarcasm. She wasn't finished.

"All you do is feel sorry for yourself and complain about what a rotten wife and rotten life you have. Open your eyes, bucko, and tell me how rotten your wife has been in the past five months. Name one thing I've done.

One. I'm sick of trying to make you l— . . . oh just forget it. You'll be begging for me to come back into this library. Begging. And then I'll say no. Pigheaded, stupid, liver-lilied, selfish . . ." and the names continued as Maggie stalked out the door and slammed it.

Before Carter could close his mouth, which had opened in stunned surprise at the beginning of Maggie's tirade, the door swung open again.

"And the name's MAGGIE!" She jumped up and down at each syllable of her name screaming so loud her throat hurt. Bang! The door slammed again.

Carter stood there, stunned, for several seconds, then slumped down into his chair. Then he started to laugh. And laugh. And laugh. What the hell was he going to do?

He ended up doing something he was sure he'd regret. He invited her back.

Two days went by before Carter saw Maggie again. The first day, he entered his office at nine o'clock as usual. No Maggie. He was not surprised, and he pretended he was pleased. But his eyes were constantly going to the couch, which continued to be empty. It seemed very empty, indeed. And every time the door opened after a timid knock by a servant, his heart hammered in his chest hoping it was Maggie. He might tell himself he wanted her out of his life, but his heart knew better.

He missed her happy chatter. He missed her smile, the way she sat so unladylike on the couch, the way she'd read to him parts of the book she found amusing or interesting, the way the sun looked on her hair. He missed her. Period.

So when on the third day she marched into the library without a look in his direction and without a word of greeting, he found himself ridiculously pleased.

Maggie had stopped being angry about three hours after their fight. She never could remain angry with anyone no matter how hard she tried. She reminded herself how pigheaded, how cold her husband was. Then she remembered those kisses, those wonderfully intoxicating kisses, and her anger would melt away like ice on an August day. She stayed away for two days just to let him stew for a while, then headed to the library.

She was sure he would say something. And that's all she needed to bridge the gap between them and get them talking again. Maggie, her heart beating like a rabbit running from prey, blindly grabbed the first book she saw and turned around to head for the door. She was just a few feet away, her hand outstretched to grab the doorknob, her heart plummeting in disappointment, when she heard, "Maggie."

Her back was to Carter when she stopped, and she could not help but smile. But when she turned to him, she had an expression of cold indifference on her face. "Yes?"

Carter found himself fighting back a smile. He admired her spunk, her back stiff with indignation, the haughty angle she held her head.

"You may read in here," he said as if giving an edict. "In fact. Please do." He unconsciously echoed the words she'd used when asking for a kiss. But she recognized them, and smiled a cool smile.

"Since you're begging, I suppose I will relent." Maggie, with utmost grace, walked over to the couch. She then jumped up, turned in midair, and landed in her place sitting Indian style. Adjusting her skirts daintily, she picked up her book and pretended deep interest. Carter was charmed.

"I was not begging." There was laughter in his voice.

"Oh, yes, Carter. There was just a hint of begging. And also a bit of apology. Which I accept."

"I am not apologizing." His smile widened.

Maggie laughed. "Oh, all this was worth it, Carter, just to see that smile. You really are very handsome. But only when you smile." Carter laughed aloud, shaking his head.

After that, they slipped into comfortable silence. But both would send secret glances when the other was not looking.

A week later, Maggie returned from her daily walk on the beach, grateful she had not seen another soul in the midday heat, and found a letter addressed to Carter on a little table in the front hall. The letter would not normally have attracted Maggie's notice but this one was in a fancy, sculpted envelope and reeked of perfume. Picking it up and holding out in front of her as if it were a bit of rotted fruit, Maggie brought the letter into the library and tossed it under Carter's nose.

He immediately blushed.

Okay, Maggie, she told herself, it might not mean a thing, that blush, but her heart sank to her belly. When he casually put the missive aside, Maggie said, "Who's that from? It stinks."

Letting out a sigh, Carter picked it up. Taking a wickedly sharp letter opener, he carefully opened the envelope. He'd known what the letter was the moment the heavy scent hit his nostrils. "It's an invitation."

"So I assumed. To what? A bedroom?"

Carter laughed. "Don't tell me you're jealous!"

"My husband gets an invitation soaked in perfume and I'm not supposed to wonder what it is?"

He felt a rush of satisfaction when he realized she was, indeed, jealous. And he felt the need to put her at ease immediately.

"It's an invitation to the First Ball. You know, the Brownings throw the summer's first event. Mrs. Browning thinks it's the height of style to send out scented envelopes. Every year it's a different, and I think a more pungent, scent." He held out the invitation so Maggie could read it for herself.

"Mr. and Mrs. Robert A. Browning III request the

presence of Mr. Carter A. Johnsbury at their home for
the First Ball, Saturday evening, eight o'clock, June fif-
teenth, eighteen hundred and eighty-eight."

"Mr. Carter A. Johnsbury," Maggie read aloud. She
looked up at Carter, trying to hide the disappointment
in her brown eyes. She really should not want to go, not
after the disaster they had at their little event. But she
did feel disappointed. Carter shifted uncomfortably in
his chair. He knew what the glaring omission meant,
and he understood it. No one in polite company invited
Margaret Johnsbury to their home. No one. To his surprise, Carter felt angry over the omission, when all he
should feel was relief. Maggie sat across from him, looking at him with those whiskey-brown eyes and his heart
clenched a little. She deserved it, he reminded himself
cruelly. Then why did he want to take her in his arms?
Why did he suddenly want to go against society and
present his wife at the ball?

"I guess I understand. But at some point, they're going to have to come around. I can't sit here for the rest
of my life and let the world pass me by just because of
the past. You're going to go?"

"I always do."

Maggie stood up, hugging her arms around herself
and walked over to the windows, which were open to let
in the sweet summer air. Would it always be this way?
she wondered. She could tell herself she did not need to
go to balls, that she did not want to go. But she did. Her
loneliness was pressing down harder and harder, and
the thought of a lifetime without a single friend was
most depressing. It would only be livable if she could fill
her life up with a family. But even that, for now, was
impossible. Maggie was lost in her thoughts, and did not
hear Carter come up behind her.

He had watched her for several moments before giving in to the urge to comfort her. He stole up behind
her and gently put a hand over each of hers. She imme-

diately stiffened then just as quickly relaxed, leaning back against Carter's chest. He tucked his head over her shoulder and brought his arms around her. They stood that way, loving the feel of each other's bodies, the simple nearness of two beings, for several moments.

"I understand, Carter, but I can't help feeling a little bit sorry for myself. I just wish everything could be different, you know."

"I know."

She turned and pressed her head into his chest, breathing in his scent, feeling safe in his arms. "There. All better." She looked up into his face and smiled. She gave him a quick kiss and pulled away, the smile still on her lips. That smile nearly took his breath away.

"I'm going to see how Mrs. O'Brien is doing with dinner," Maggie said. She felt like she wanted to get away, away from Carter's intense gaze, away from his desire, which showed so naked on his face. Desire was not love. And love would have brought her to that ball.

~ Chapter 9 ~

. . . To this day, I don't know what possessed me to seek Carter out, but I'm glad I did. . . .

Maggie had a plan. She was going to spy on the ball. The Brownings' mansion was just four houses down on the beach but set so far back it was not visible from the sandy stretch. A series of stone stairs, which Maggie had never been up, led up to the wide lawn of the Browning estate. It wasn't that she was spying on Carter—well, she was—but she convinced herself she was bursting with curiosity about Newport society. If she was completely honest, which she refused to be, she was very curious about how Carter would act. Would he dance? With whom? Would he be surrounded by women, or would he be in the center of male companions? Sneaking up to the mansion under the cover of darkness held a huge appeal for Maggie, who was in desperate need of some excitement. The odd chance she might get discovered just added to the appeal. She decided she'd later change into one of her running outfits so she would have an easier time traversing the stairs and running down the beach after her little mission.

The night of the ball, Maggie waited downstairs for Carter to appear in his formal wear. When he did appear, she again wished she were going along, if simply to protect him from all the women who were certain to flock to his side the moment he entered the house.

Carter walked down the stairs, adjusting his cuffs and noted, with some guilt, Maggie's scowl.

"You look handsome," she said as if angry with him.

"Sorry." He smiled.

She let out an unladylike snort. Maggie felt downright dowdy standing next to Carter in his perfectly fitted formal wear. As Carter gave himself one more look in a small mirror placed by the door for just that purpose, Maggie gave him a look of disgust.

Noting her expression he said, "You don't expect me to go to a formal ball wearing my usual attire, do you?"

"Oh don't be so full of yourself. You don't look that good," Maggie lied.

Carter stood awkwardly at the door, not knowing what to say, but suddenly feeling like a heel to be leaving Maggie standing at the door waving good-bye. She should be with him tonight, he thought, not for the first time since the invitation came. Just as quickly, he cast those thoughts away, for he knew it was impossible—as impossible as it would be for Mrs. O'Brien to attend the Brownings' ball. If their small event was any indication, his wife would not be a welcome guest—especially not to the socially conscious Brownings. Why was it getting more and more difficult to remember Margaret as a manipulative witch who had no place in polite society? Carter wondered. It had never bothered him before when Margaret's name was pointedly omitted from invitations. In fact, he never had given the omission a second thought. It was simply understood among his circle in the past several years that Margaret was not to be included. On the rare occasion when the two had to appear together, they had simply arrived and left together. Other than that, the two had little contact. Now, after four years of living separate lives, he felt awkward leaving her behind. And if he were completely honest, he actually wanted her along. What the hell.

"Well, good night." He wanted to kiss her good night.

"Have a good time." She wanted a good-night kiss.

But Carter turned and left without another word.

Maggie closed the door slowly after watching him jump into his carriage. As soon as she did, a wicked smile came upon her lips, and she ran up the stairs lifting up her skirts obscenely high. She changed into her darkest running outfit. Now all she had to do was wait a little while then take off down the beach. She rubbed her hands together in anticipation of the adventure.

It was a balmy night, unusually warm for June. The air was still and the cicadas and crickets sang a chorus that nearly blotted out the sound of the waves coming ashore. Barefoot, Maggie walked along the cool grass, her feet getting wet in the dew and collecting blades between her toes. The lawn had been cut just that day and the air was thick with the smell of newly cut grass. She stood at the stone wall looking out at the bay, shimmering under a quarter moon. The water was molten silver, it was so calm. Maggie was thankful for the semidark night, for when the moon was full it was bright enough to cast shadows under the trees and would have made her mission more difficult.

Maggie walked along the shore, letting the water run up to her ankles. It felt bathwater-warm because her feet were so cold. She had only walked a short distance when she heard the first strains of music and the sounds of laughter from the Brownings. Sound traveled amazingly well near the water, so when Maggie reached the first set of stone stairs, she tried to wipe the sand off her feet even though she was fairly certain no one could hear the sandy scraping her feet made as she walked up the steps.

The stone steps were connected by little walkways in a zigzag pattern up the steep bluff. The last stairway was bordered by a stone wall that was about as tall as Maggie and ended with two large stone pillars that acted as an entryway onto the Brownings' lawn. The mansion, a huge, sprawling, two-story white stone structure, was brightly lit by chandeliers, lamps, and candles. A set of Japanese lanterns had been strung along a broad marble patio built about three feet above the lawn, the candles inside flickering in the slight breeze. A few people strolled along the patio; a couple leaned against the stone railing and appeared to be looking directly at Maggie. She stopped, panicked, before she realized that although she could see them clearly, they would not be able to see her in the shadows of the stone pillars.

Maggie stood there for nearly an hour, reluctant to leave her relatively safe hiding spot. She listened to the orchestra, tapped her foot, and kept her gaze riveted on the people who passed by the windows or stepped out onto the patio. Darn, no Carter. Where was that man? She could be honest with herself now. The sole reason she had sneaked out to the Brownings was to spy on Carter. She had not had a glimpse of Carter yet, and was about to give up, when he walked out to the patio and leaned up against the railing. Her heart gave a mighty leap at the sight of him strolling alone toward the end of the patio.

It did not take long for Maggie to formulate a plan. Keeping close to the woods that bordered the lawn, Maggie made her way silently toward the patio. Feeling a bit silly, but having the best time in ages, Maggie stopped about six yards from where Carter stood. No one was near him, so Maggie took a chance.

"Carter," she said in a harsh whisper. No reaction.

"Carter."

His head snapped up and he cocked his head as if listening. "What the devil?"

"No, Carter. It's me. Maggie." He straightened up, a look of disbelief on his face. Then a look of worry as he realized that only something very serious could have brought Margaret sneaking to the ball.

When Maggie saw him coming toward her, she

walked back along the woods toward the beach steps, afraid they might be discovered. Carter half ran to where she stood waiting for him.

"Margaret. What's wrong?" Carter said, gripping her arms. Maggie had no idea what to say and simply stared back at him dumbfounded for a few seconds. "Maggie, has something happened?"

Then she got inspired.

"Are you going to be late tonight?"

"What?"

She repeated her question.

"You came all the way out here and spirited me away to ask me that? Yes. I am going to be quite late. Good night." When he made to turn, Maggie stopped him. "Carter. I didn't come all the way out here just to ask you that. I came to get my good-night kiss." She smiled, her teeth glowing in the darkness.

"Your good-night kiss." Carter repeated the words stupidly. Then he smiled. He simply could not help himself.

Before he could say another word, Maggie raised her arms and locked her hands behind his neck, stood on tip toe and gave her husband a kiss that was just one step beyond chaste. Carter automatically put his hands at her waist to draw her closer and was pleasantly shocked when his hands touched bare skin, exposed when she raised her arms. His grip on her waist tightened and he realized he would not be able to let her go after one little kiss.

"My God, what are you wearing?" he said against her lips.

Carter's hands felt delicious against her bare skin, Maggie thought. "It's one of my running outfits." And she kissed him again, soft lips against firm.

Carter moved his hands to her back, running his hands up and down, loving the feel of her soft skin beneath his palms. "This is all you wear when you run?"

"Well, I usually bind my breasts so . . ."

Carter crushed his lips against hers with a groan, pulling her tight against him. His tongue assaulted hers and she moaned in answer, tightening her grip on the back of his neck. He moved his hands down to her shorts, caressing her buttocks over the cloth, then, growing bolder, he slipped one hand beneath the drawstring waistband, molding her buttocks to his hand and bringing her even closer. She could feel his hardness, his need, and moved against him almost against her will. His hands moved up and down her body, as if he wanted to touch all of her at once, but was frustrated at only having two hands.

Carter's brain had gone numb the instant he touched her and all he had left was raging senses that wanted to touch, lick, taste. He would not think about what he was doing, for to think about it was to stop. And he could no more stop touching her than he could stop the rising tide. He was consumed by her, he was aflame. He was mouth and hands and hardness.

Maggie arched against him, loving the way he felt, knowing that he wanted her as much as she wanted him. It must be the summer air, she thought, that has drugged me and turned me into this wanton thing. She let out a little laugh.

Carter pulled back, fearing she was laughing at him.

"What's so funny," he said, his voice hard with passion and tinged with anger.

"You just feel so good. I didn't know you would feel so good," Maggie said dreamily, looking up into his face and stroking his muscled back. She moved her hands to his chest, and unbuttoning just two buttons, slipped one hand into his shirt so she could feel his chest. She opened the shirt a bit, and brought her mouth up to his chest and licked his skin, tasting him. "Mmmmm."

Carter thought his heart would surely burst at the touch of her tongue, and he thought it would stop when she brought her hands down to cup his buttocks in an imitation of his own caresses. Maggie tilted her head up for more kisses and Carter was happy to oblige. He was consumed with his need for her and closer than he cared to admit to throwing her down on the ground and entering her without preamble.

Maggie was amazed at herself, for she was not usually an aggressive lover. But when Carter brought his hands up to skim her breasts, she felt like tearing off his clothes then her own. Carter pulled at her erect nipples with his thumb and forefinger sending shards of pleasure through Maggie. And when he lifted her shirt to take a taste, she had to bite back a screech of pleasure when the gentle suckling began.

"My God, Carter. What you do to me." Her voice was breathy and she felt like she'd just run three miles. Carter was just about to lower Maggie to the grass when a female voice called out.

"Carter? Are you out there?"

He froze, his mouth still on one swollen nipple, when the woman called his name again.

"Carter, darling. Is that you?" A woman, dressed in a peach-colored gown, was walking toward them. Carter immediately realized the woman could not see Maggie in the shadows and had spotted him only because his white collar shone like a beacon in the night.

"Go," he whispered harshly to Maggie, giving her a little shove in the direction of the stairs.

Maggie's heart nearly stopped when she realized the woman was advancing toward them. She quickly followed Carter's directions and hid behind the stone pillar, crouching down so that only the top of her head showed above the top step.

Maggie watched Carter turn toward the woman and take her into his arms. She reeled from the effect it had on her. Carter knew she was there, yet still greeted the woman with what appeared to be enthusiasm. Maggie was stunned by the impact, the pain of seeing another woman in Carter's arms. But what had she expected, after all? Her face burned with humiliation and hurt.

"Why are you hiding out here?" the woman cooed. She was beautiful. Tall, elegant, cultured. Maggie suddenly felt ridiculous and frumpy in her shorts and shirt.

"I thought I'd get some air," Carter said. His voice sounded hoarse.

"It's too chilly out here, Carter. You missed our dance and I am quite angry with you," she pouted as she caressed his back.

The woman suddenly raised her eyebrows in obvious delight. "Is this for me?" she asked, while laying a bold hand on Carter's crotch. Maggie wanted to vomit when she saw the woman's caress.

Maggie could not watch a second more. She turned and ran, not caring whether the woman heard her. She stumbled down one stair, landing on her knees, scraping them badly, but she did not stop running. By the time she reached the beach, tears were running down her face and blood down her legs.

"Damn him," she said to herself over and over as she ran toward Rose Brier. When she thought about what she could have witnessed had she not arrived before the woman did, fresh feelings of shame hit her. She tortured herself with images of Carter and that woman, that beautifully elegant creature.

She rested on the bottom steps that led up to Rose Brier. "Stupid, stupid, stupid." She slammed her fist against her thigh, angry with herself, angry with Carter. As she sat there, looking blindly out onto the water, she admitted to herself how much she loved her husband. The cad! But she loved him. That was certainly worse than desiring him. Love's flame was not extinguished so easy. And love hurt so much more.

* * *

When Carter realized Abigail had discovered him, his first thought was to protect Maggie. His body was still hard from their near lovemaking, his mind still reeling from what they had been doing, when Abigail came into his arms. He was painfully aware that Maggie was just steps away and just as aware what she would make of the scene she was witnessing. It took more self-control than he thought he had not to go running after her when he heard her tear off. And when he heard her small cry of pain as she fell, he winced as if feeling the hurt she felt.

Abigail, feigning fright over a prowler, clung to Carter.

"What was that?" she whispered.

"Probably just some kid spying on the adults," Carter had said as casually as possible. At least the noise had given him an excuse to take her hand away. He pretended to listen to the woman standing in front of him, but his ears were tuned to the beach. He thought he heard, though he could not be certain, the sound of Maggie sobbing as she ran.

Damn.

Carter took Abigail's arm and led her back into the ball. He'd have to make things right tomorrow.

When Carter awoke the next morning, hours later than usual, the memory of the night's passion had faded, and his jaundiced view of the world and of his wife had spirited away most of the guilt he'd felt. He began to manufacture ulterior motives for Maggie's visit where none existed. It was his last attempt at self-preservation, for he felt himself being drawn in closer and closer to his wife like a man caught in a whirlpool. He was losing his fight and that scared him. For what if . . . What if it was all a lie, after all. He was so close to believing that Margaret as he had known her was gone. And the more he believed, the more vulnerable he became. His heart could not survive another beating by Margaret.

Carter sat on the edge of his bed for many long minutes. He hated this feeling of uncertainty, of reading lies into every word, every action. He hated this hope that spread through him and warmed him like a long drink of brandy.

He decided to avoid Maggie, just for a couple of days. Coward, he thought.

Maggie awoke to bright sun shining through her windows. She opened her eyes, then immediately closed them. She did not want to face this day. Heaving herself up, she sat on the edge of the bed, rubbing her eyes, which felt sandy and swollen from the crying she'd done the night before. Maggie was not angry with Carter. If she had been, it would have been easy to get over. She was crushed. And the worst of it was that she suspected that had Carter known how she felt, he would not care. Any man would kiss a half-naked woman who literally threw herself at him, she told herself cruelly. She was not ugly. She had a pretty face. It was simple lust on his part, she thought.

"I'm nothing but a lovesick jerk," she said aloud.

She dreaded confronting Carter, fearing he'd treat her as before with indifference, with coldness. If he did, she'd cry, right then and there. And God knew she was sick to death of crying. How could she have let this happen? How could she fall in love with a man who hated her? Was she that needy? Was it because he was the only man around? No. Carter was charming and warm, intelligent and funny, and damn good-looking to boot. Her mother had always told her that people could not help who they fell in love with and Maggie had always thought that was so much hogwash. Now she knew it was true. For who in their right mind would allow themselves to fall in love with someone who hated you?

Eventually, she knew she'd have to see Carter. But not today. She wasn't ready today, she thought. Coward.

Carter left that day to visit his mother and brother. He left word with Bruce, who immediately knew something was awry, but decided, this once, not to pry.

It took Carter the better part of the day to reach Providence, taking first the crowded steamer *Eolus* from Newport to Wickford, then waiting for a train to Providence. When he finally arrived at the three-story brownstone on Benefit Street, his mind was numb from thinking, thinking.

His mother was surprised when her housekeeper informed her that her oldest son was paying a visit and was resting in the parlor.

"Carter, this is unexpected." She came upon her son, who was gazing blindly at the cold hearth. He sat uncomfortably on a wingback chair, leaning forward, an arm dangling over each knee. She knew her son and something was definitely wrong. Carter had not looked this unhappy since he realized his marriage was a sham. That had been a tough one for Kathryn to handle, for she loved her son and wanted nothing more than for him to be happy. Unfortunately, Carter had so little happiness and her heart ached for him as only a mother's heart can when one of her children is in pain.

Carter looked up at his mother and gave her a weak smile. "Yes. I wanted to get away from Rose Brier for a couple of days. And I wanted to talk to Charlie about the mills. He told you about the problems we've been having?"

"Yes." Kathryn Johnsbury gazed at her son and wondered if she should press him on the real reason for his visit. Carter met business problems head on, with assurance and cold calculation. The only thing that could put this forlorn expression on his face, no matter how he tried to hide it, was a matter of the heart. She ignored his attempt to talk about the mills and attacked the real problem directly.

"Is Margaret still at Rose Brier?"

"Maggie's still there." One graceful eyebrow gave a quirk when her son called his wife "Maggie."

"And does this visit have anything to do with your wife?"

Carter gave his mother a genuine smile this time and shook his head at her perception.

"I never could hide anything from you, Ma." Carter wiped a hand through his hair which told his mother even more about his mood. Her son was deeply troubled. Carter took a deep breath.

"Something has happened. I don't know how. I didn't want it to happen, Mother, you must know that."

Kathryn's concern grew. Good God, she thought, I hope he didn't hurt her, or, heaven forbid, kill her. But what he said next was almost worse.

"I . . . Oh, God help me, Ma . . . I love her." Now that the words were out, they lingered there as if they were visible in the air. Carter looked up at his mother, took in her shocked face, and laughed.

"It's as bad as all that?"

"Oh, Carter. How did this happen?" Kathryn's heart nearly broke at her son's words, at the light in his eyes. Margaret would hurt him, damn that witch. She always hurt him. Kathryn thought her son had learned, had finally come to grips with his life. She would have hoped for more happiness for her son, but anything was better than the heartache he was sure to have by loving Margaret.

"I can see you're not pleased with my announcement," he said ruefully. "Do you think I like it? Do you think I wanted this to happen? But she's changed. She . . . I don't know. You only saw her for those few days so you don't know. I've seen her every day for weeks. I know it's crazy. I hate myself. How do you think I feel?"

"I think you want it so bad you'd be willing to see anything. God knows you deserve love, Carter. But Margaret has no soul. She has no conscience. That woman is incapable of love."

Carter could not get angry with his mother, for everything she said was true. Or at least had been true.

"You saw her with Reginald. That was real."

"She can fake any emotion. I've seen her do it, don't forget. I don't know what she's after, but she's smart enough to know she can get to you through your niece and nephew."

"That's just the thing, Mother. What could be her motive?" And he remembered Maggie saying just those words. There was no motive that he could think of.

"I don't know, Carter. I just don't want to see you hurt. And she has already done that so many times."

"I know," he said, miserably. He hated this. Hated to feel. He almost wished for the days when he merely existed. For living like this was hell. He did not like feeling weak, had prided himself on his ability to look at the world through cold, objective eyes.

"Where's Charles?" he asked, changing the subject.

"He's off playing detective and loving every minute. Patricia is none too pleased with the assignment you gave him, you know. She's barely seen him in the last month."

"His last letter said he hadn't found anything. Is he working on anything good?"

"All I know is he received a message from Mr. McGrath and left that same day for Woonsocket. That was about four days ago. I haven't heard a word from him since, not that we expected to. You know how single-minded he can be. Are you going to wait for him?"

"I'll stay a couple of days." He was already anxious to return home. Now that he had said the words out loud, it did not seem so ludicrous. I love my wife, he thought, and smiled.

Kathryn saw that smile, that faraway look in her son's eyes, and felt nothing but fear.

When Maggie finally made her way downstairs, she was almost immediately informed by Mrs. Brimble that Carter had gone and was expected back within a week. Relief washed over her. Then anger. As much as she wanted to avoid a confrontation herself, she was a bit put off that Carter had acted so callously. He must have known she was upset. He obviously did not care.

She wandered to the library and walked behind Carter's desk, letting her fingers brush along the top of his green leather chair. The leather was smooth but cold beneath her hand. She noted with a small smile how neat his desk was, with nothing laying atop it, nothing out of place. Wandering over to the couch, she flopped down on it, the air hissing out of the cushions. I'm such a lovesick calf, she thought miserably. Maggie didn't know how long she lay there, staring at the molded tin ceiling. The beach held no attraction. She did not feel like running, did not feel like reading. She wanted Carter to come back so she could find out whether there was any hope. She'd thought there was. During those long, wonderful days in the library, the two had struck up a rapport, a friendship. They'd laughed and talked and, at least that once, kissed.

Remembering those kisses, Maggie was once again brought back to the Brownings' ball. Could someone kiss and touch her the way Carter had and not feel anything? It had seemed as if he was as affected as she. But perhaps he was not. Perhaps he responded to every woman that way. One thing was for certain, Maggie had never felt that way.

Three days after the Browning ball, Maggie was back to her old routine, her mood much improved. She simply could not dwell on the bad things in her life, even when she tried. Maggie shrugged her shoulders when she woke up and felt her old self. She was a cup-half-full person, she reasoned. No matter what happened, Carter desired her, and that would have to be enough, for now. There was nothing so wrong about having a gorgeous man with a drop-dead body wanting you in his bed, she told herself. Of course, it would be nice—no, wonderful—if Carter loved her. She would just have to resign herself to the fact that he might never feel that way.

"Who am I kidding?" she said aloud, looking at her reflection in the mirror. "It's got to be all or nothing." An uncharacteristic feeling of dread washed over her at her own words. All or nothing. All. Or nothing.

~ Chapter 10 ~

*. . . I suppose it was only fitting that it happened on
one of my walks down the beach. . . .*

It was a blustery warm day in late June. Clouds skidded across the sky chasing each other east. The bay
was choppy with white-capped waves, and only a few
brave sailors cut across the water, their skiffs leaning
heavily in the wind. Seagulls hovered, riding the breeze
as if they were suspended in the sky from a string. Maggie stood at the stone wall looking out at the water as
she did almost every day, loving the smell and feel of the
bay. Her hair was down, whipping behind her, the wind
plastering her dress against her body.

"Mind if I join you for your walk?"

Maggie turned around, startled by the familiar voice
and not quite believing her eyes. Carter stood just a few
feet away, looking at her quite oddly, his hands behind
his back, his bare feet planted in the cool grass.

Maggie's heart was doing double-time, but outwardly
she remained cool.

"Okay."

She began walking down the wooden steps, acutely
aware that for the first time Carter was trailing behind
her. She had meant to give him the silent treatment, but
she could not hold her tongue.

"Where've you been? With that woman?" Maggie

asked as casually as she could as she continued down the steps. Behind her Carter grinned.

When she reached the bottom of the steps, she turned around, raising an arm to shield her eyes from the afternoon sun.

"That woman is Mrs. Thornbrush. The Widow Thornbrush. At times she acts as if I were her possession. An opinion she shares alone, I might add. I won't tell you that our friendship has always been platonic in nature. But I will tell you that it has been that way for several months. Including the night of the Brownings' ball. I will not defend my past, Margaret."

"She seemed awfully nonplatonic that night," Maggie persisted.

"She was. I was not. I can't say I blame you for coming to the conclusion you did. She is a rather aggressive female. But nothing happened."

"You don't have to justify your actions to me, Carter," Maggie said, turning away.

Carter gently took her arm and turned her toward him. "You're wrong, Maggie. I do."

Maggie lifted her troubled gaze to his eyes and saw something indefinable.

"If you say so." But Carter heard the doubt.

Maggie turned and began walking down the beach. She believed Carter completely but didn't think there was any harm in keeping him a bit off-balance. For once she felt she was in control. Carter had come to her. It was all Maggie could do to stop from leaping and skipping like a silly girl, even though that was exactly what she felt like.

"Welcome to my famous walk down the beach. This is it. We walk, pick up interesting shells and rocks, throw them into the water. Maybe skip a flat stone or two. That's it. Nothing too exciting."

Maggie tucked the back of her skirt into her front waistband in a businesslike manner. At Carter's look of disapproval, she said, "If you're going to be part of this walk, you have to play by the rules. Roll up your pants."

"Maggie, I don't think you should walk around like that." Carter was enthralled by the sight of her naked legs, visible almost to her knees. Had she no sense of decorum? Had she no sense of what the sight of her was doing to him? Her hands were on her hips, the wind blew her hair away from her face except for two long wavy strands that cut a diagonal across her cheek to her mouth. When she spoke, the strands flew into her mouth as if trying to escape the wind and Maggie impatiently flung them away, only to have them return a moment later.

"If anyone else comes along, it's a very simple matter to make myself respectable again." She demonstrated by untucking the hem and letting it drop. "See? Now stop being such a prude." She brought her skirt back up. "You try walking in this wind with long skirts. It's impossible. I'll end up flat on my face."

Maggie walked to the water's edge, then began strolling along the shore where the sand was firm and walking was easier. Carter was soon by her side and Maggie looked approvingly at his exposed hairy calves. They walked in silence for several minutes, neither knowing quite what to say, but both very much aware that this seemingly casual walk meant something significant. They strolled, not touching, not talking until Maggie thought she'd go crazy from all the words boiling about her head that needed to be said.

Maggie stopped. She looked at Carter, afraid to say what she had to say, afraid her heart was on her sleeve. She was truly miserable.

Carter was simply happier than he could remember. He drank in the sight of Maggie, the curve of her breasts, her wind-whipped hair, her sunburned nose, the few freckles sprinkled on her cheeks. He'd never noticed those freckles before. On Maggie, they were beautiful. He felt drunk with it; he let the feeling wash over him, for he was so tired of trying to hide how he felt. He watched as she heaved a huge sigh, but he was oblivious to her misery. He was having too good a time.

"Carter. I've got to tell you something. This is very difficult for me." The slight smile that had curved his lips faltered and he went very still at the seriousness of her tone.

Maggie bit the side of her lip, then forged ahead.

"When I saw you with that woman, I can't explain to you what that did to me. I'm sure you would never understand it. But it hurt. A lot. I know it will be hard for you to believe, but I was really floored," she said, slipping into modern jargon. But the meaning was clear to Carter. He was elated.

"I realize you cannot love me. I realize you probably don't even like me. And I know you probably don't believe that I care. But I do. More than I want to, knowing how you feel. I understand how you feel, really I do."

"And how do I feel, Maggie?" he asked quietly.

"I know you desire me." Maggie flushed as she said the words. "But you also hate me." Maggie's throat closed up and, to her horror, her eyes filled with tears.

"You are right, Maggie, I do desire you. Very much so." Carter put a hand on each of Maggie's upper arms. "But I do not hate you. I want to hate you, but I do not."

"Yes you do," Maggie argued.

Carter answered with a quick, hard kiss. He lifted his mouth away and pressed her cheek to his. "Believe what you will of me, but I do not hate you. I do not." He dragged his lips across her cheek and held her head between his hands, tilting it up so she was looking into his eyes. His expression became fierce.

"I'm afraid of what I feel for you, Maggie. So help me God, if you are playing me for a fool, you will regret it. I cannot play games. I will not. Tell me. Now, Maggie.

Swear to me that this is real. Swear to me." He shook her head a little, but his grip was not painful.

Maggie closed her eyes and two tears escaped. "Carter, I swear to you, Carter." She swallowed, afraid to say the words. She opened her eyes and looked into his smoldering gray ones. "I love you. I could never hurt you. I swear."

Pure joy washed over Carter at her words. He wanted so much to believe her. He brought his mouth down hard onto hers, wrapping his arms around her so tight, Maggie could scarcely breathe, but it felt wonderful. He ended the kiss, but kept his hold on her and Maggie squeezed back just as tightly. He had not told her he loved her, but Maggie felt sure he did. Her heart nearly broke when he pleaded with her not to hurt him. She knew what it cost a man like Carter to lay his heart out to her.

"Make love to me, Carter." He looked down at her with a smile she had never seen before—a smile with nothing behind it but happiness.

"Come on." He grabbed her hand and pulled her toward the wooden steps. Maggie ran along beside him, full of anticipation, laughing like a young girl. They ran up the steps like two children, racing each other to the top. And when they reached Rose Brier's lawn, they both assumed an air of dignity, when neither looked anything but dignified with sand on their toes, wind-mussed hair, and naked legs. They looked at each other and laughed some more.

Then, as if they were thieves, they sneaked inside trying not to be spotted by any of the servants. Carter led Maggie to his room, never letting go of her hand. He felt like a teenager about to experience the mysteries of the bedroom for the first time. Once inside, Carter grabbed Maggie pulled her into his arms and kicked the door shut with one sand-covered foot.

They undressed each other as if in a frenzy to touch

naked skin, kissing and touching after each article of clothing was cast aside. Carter was on fire and almost in pain with his need. He could not touch her enough, he could not stop kissing her soft mouth. He could not believe he was acting this way.

Maggie never felt such urgency, and knew she was ready to accept her husband, something that was immediately confirmed when Carter put a hand between her legs to stroke her most sensitive spot. She moaned as she pressed her mouth against his lightly furred chest, too moved by his caresses to do more than rest her head against him. He moved one hand to her breast, and lifting one soft mound up to his mouth, drew a taut nipple in to be stroked by his tongue. Maggie sucked in her breath from the pleasure of it and let out a shaky sigh.

"You have no idea how good that feels," she said, breathless.

Maggie moved her hand down, down, and finally touched his silken hardness, moving her hand up and down the shaft. Carter hissed out his breath and took her hand, stopping her.

"Oh, I think I do," he ground out.

In answer, Maggie moved her body seductively against Carter and tenderly bit his neck while letting out a playful little animal sound.

"Wench."

Carter lifted her up and threw her down into the middle of his huge featherbed, playfully diving on top of her. Suddenly serious, he buried his hands in her hair on each side of her head and gave her a long, deep kiss. He brought his head up so he could gaze down at her. It was as if he kept reassuring himself that the woman beneath him, the woman who set him afire, was actually his wife.

Maggie brought her hands up and caressed each side of his face, a gesture meant to ease the frown that formed on his face as he looked down at her. She touched his mouth to erase that frown and smiled when those sensual lips curved up.

"That's better. No frowning allowed when naked in bed." His smile broadened and his desire grew. He kissed and stroked and suckled as Maggie writhed beneath him, trying to answer his caresses with her own.

He moved his hands over her as if memorizing her body, stopping when he came to her knees, still showing the injury when she fell escaping the Brownings' ball. "I'm sorry you were hurt," he said, kissing each knee with more tenderness than he realized he had.

"I'm all better now," Maggie said, a mischievous smile on her lovely face as she drew him upward to kiss him.

When neither could stand the waiting any longer, Carter positioned himself between her legs and Maggie brought her knees up to hold her husband to her. He entered her tightness slowly as if savoring each moment.

"So good. You feel so good," Carter said harshly against her mouth before bringing his head down so he could sample one hard nipple.

Maggie arched against him, unable to believe how right he felt inside her. He began moving more quickly and Maggie, close to her pinnacle, urged him on by bringing her hands to his muscled buttocks. Her body was enveloped by the release and she cried out in joy as she felt herself convulse around his hardness. The moment Carter felt her contract, he was lost. He drove again and again, losing himself in her warmth, her tightness, until he, too, found his release.

They lay together, catching their breaths, feeling sweat trickle between their bodies, lightly caressing, for several minutes. When Carter finally withdrew and lay on his back, Maggie turned with him, laying half over him, trying to stay near. She lifted her head and sneaked a look at her husband, trying to gauge his mood. Now that the passion was over, she was afraid he would regret their lovemaking.

Carter was doing just that. Years of abuse could not be wiped away in a few blissful moments and he felt that old twisting in the pit of his stomach. He gazed at the ceiling, feeling his naked wife snuggle against him and felt almost nothing but fear. Then he turned his head slightly to find Maggie staring at him, her face etched with worry. 'She cannot hide her emotions like she used to.' The thought came to him unbidden.

When Carter turned his head toward her, Maggie's hear` wrenched. For she saw not love, but a bleakness in his eyes that could only mean he regretted what they had just done. Maggie leaned over to kiss his frown away.

"I don't expect you to feel the way I do, Carter, but the least you could do after good sex is smile."

"Good sex? Good God, Maggie, where do you come up with these things?"

"If I told you, you would not believe me," she said, giving Carter another quick kiss, and his frown returned.

"I love you, you stupid man. But if you choose not to believe me, that's your tough luck." She peppered his face with tiny kisses until she heard the rumble of laughter.

"That's better."

Carter refused to give in to this little imp. "Kisses aren't going to make everything go away, Margaret." Maggie tensed at the use of her proper name. "But they're a good start," he said. He surprised her by enveloping her in an embrace and kissing her soundly. The playful kiss soon turned into passion and once again they were lost beneath a sea of desire.

For four days, Maggie and Carter enjoyed each other in and out of bed. They created a little island for themselves where nothing existed but the two of them. Carter, for the first time in years, put aside his business and did nothing but have fun. They went on picnics, dug for clams, took long walks on the beach, and had lazy hours in bed that almost always led to a frenzy of love-making that left them both breathless. The rest of the world could have gone away, and they would not have noticed it, so captivated were they with each other.

Carter managed to throw away any doubts about Maggie. As each day passed, he became more and more relaxed, he smiled easily, and he stopped veiling his emotions behind steel gray eyes. Once in a while he'd find himself amazed at the turn of his life, but he stopped waiting for the dream to end.

Maggie could not remember being so happy, so content. Forgotten were the tears, the frustration she'd felt when she first arrived here. She imagined her angels and God were quite pleased with her. In retrospect, five months did not seem all that long to have convinced Carter she had changed. She basked in his love. Carter had a way of making her feel completely desired. When she was in a room, he could not take his eyes off her. When he was near, he could not keep his hands off of her. A single touch from her was often all it took for him to grab her hand and lead her posthaste to his bedroom. Maggie's own room had become nothing more than a large, well-decorated closet. She loved sleeping beside this man, who seemed so large and masculine.

Their carefree days ended the day a telegram came from Charles.

Maggie and Carter, both golden tan from their days on the beach, were eating a lunch of lobster and crab when Bruce walked into the room, a telegram in his hand. He'd returned from helping Charles' investigation just two days before with no news about the sabotage.

"This just came from your brother, Mr. Johnsbury."

Carter read the short message quickly and cursed.

"Carter. What's wrong?" He held out the telegram for Maggie to read: HERNDON STREET MILL DESTROYED IN FIRE/NO ONE HURT/REQUEST YOU COME IMMEDIATELY/ CHARLES.

Maggie's brown eyes grew round with concern. "Thank God no one got hurt," she said.

"Yes, that's one consolation. Maggie, if you'll excuse me, I must talk with Bruce." Carter was all business, and Maggie knew their blissful days, at least for now, were over.

"Goddamn it!" Carter said once Maggie had gone. "They've gone too far now. I was afraid this would happen."

Bruce jerked his head in agreement. "It looks like they're turning their sights directly toward you. And gettin' bolder to boot. I'll go pack a few things and have the stable ready the horses."

"No, Bruce, I want you to stay here. If they're brave enough to go after my mills, they might be brave enough to come after Rose Brier. I'd feel better leaving if you were here."

"To protect Mrs. Johnsbury," Bruce guessed.

Carter swallowed hard. He did not know if he liked this feeling of fear that washed over him at the thought of Maggie being in danger. But the best way to protect her was to find out who or what was behind these attacks.

"Yes. To protect her," he admitted, giving his friend a lopsided grin. "Who would have thought it."

"Well, I for one was wondering when you were going to open your stubborn eyes and look at your wife," Bruce said, feeling bold.

Carter held up his hand to stem the lecture that Bruce was about to give, and for once, Bruce shut his mouth. But he was smiling.

Bruce was not the only one in the Rose Brier household that noticed the Johnsburys had apparently reconciled their differences. In the kitchen and in the servants' quarters, all gossip had surrounded the couple. Whenever they heard the unbelievable sound of Mr. Johnsbury laughing, eyes would meet and knowing smiles would form. Even the stiff Mrs. Brimble had to smile at the couple's antics.

That first night when they had asked for their dinner to be served in Mr. Johnsbury's bedroom, the news had traveled faster than the wind on the bay during a Nor'easter. A maid would lean to another, and she would fly off to tell another, until the entire household was abuzz with the news that the couple were finally experiencing some wedded bliss.

The more romantic of them would gaze longingly up at the ceiling and sigh. The more practical of them thanked God the tension that had surrounded the household like an unrelenting fog for years was finally dissipating. But in front of the Johnsburys, not one servant acted as if anything special were happening. Behind closed doors, however, Mrs. Johnsbury's sneeze was reported by one maid, and Mr. Johnsbury's 'God bless you' by another. Stella found herself in the pleasant position of being 'in the know.' Most of the staff had always been a bit standoffish with Stella since she spent much of her time with Mrs. Johnsbury and Mrs. Johnsbury had spent much of her time in New York. When the two arrived at Rose Brier, they were met with apprehension. The two were difficult to separate since they were always seen as a pair.

Now that Mrs. Johnsbury had redeemed herself in the eyes of the staff, so had Stella. And Stella found she liked being the expert on Mrs. Johnsbury. Once quite reticent about spreading gossip, Stella had become quite proliferate and glowed under the attention she was receiving. She was very discreet about it all, prefacing almost everything she said with, "Don't repeat this as it wouldn't be right, but, did you know the Mister and

Missus spent the entire day playing chess?" or "Don't repeat this as it wouldn't be right, but, did you know the Mister insisted the Missus wear a particular dress last night? He never cared before, you know."

It was all great fun. The members of the staff that remembered the old days, the fights, the cold politeness, were surrounded by newer servants who were hungry for any new tidbit. The little drama going on right under their noses was better than anything they could see at the Newport Playhouse. And so when Carter left that buzzing hive without so much as a by-your-leave and with an extremely serious look on his face, the servants were in a frenzy to find out the latest. Bruce remained silent. He'd had enough of gossip and ignored his co-workers thinly veiled attempts to find out what had happened. His duty now was to protect, to remain silent, for anyone and everyone was a suspect. That mill fire had come too close to home for comfort.

With Carter gone, the house seemed an instantly empty and lonely place for Maggie. She wondered how she had possibly filled up her days when he was gone before. Nothing seemed as much fun alone as it had in the past four days. She moped about all day, unaware of the servants' questioning looks. Carter said he would be gone about a week, but he had no real idea when he would return. He had held her a long time before leaving, almost as if his going would somehow make what they'd shared in the past few days disappear.

"I'll miss you," Maggie said, tilting her head back for a kiss. He obliged with a hard, searing kiss that left them both breathless.

"You should go away more often," she joked. He hugged her tighter in reply. He could not shake this feeling that his Maggie girl would be gone when he returned, that something would happen. This kind of happiness scared the hell out of him and he simply could not accept it without feeling dread. Maggie sensed his reluctance to leave. "When you come home, I'm going to fling myself in your arms so hard I'll knock you over. And I don't care how embarrassed you get or who is watching at the time."

"You'd better," he said, giving her another hard, quick kiss.

For two days, Maggie wandered about, idly picking up a book for a few minutes, then putting it down. She was in the library, when Bruce knocked and entered carrying an envelope.

"This came for you."

"Oh. Is it from Carter?" She grabbed the letter and ripped it open. Her smile turned into a frown as she read the cryptic note.

I must see you. Meet at the P, Thursday, at noon.
Do not disappoint me again. —C

Maggie handed the strange note over to Bruce. "I have no idea what it means or who sent it. This is the third note I've been handed from this mysterious 'C.' Are you sure it's for me?"

Bruce studied the note and nodded. "The envelope has your name on it: Margaret Johnsbury. I don't like the tone of this. It sounds rather ominous to me," he said, thinking aloud. Seeing Maggie's expression, he immediately sought to reassure her. "But it could be nothing but an old friend you haven't been to see."

Maggie immediately knew what he was getting at. "You mean it could be an old lover," she said bluntly. Bruce blushed, his ruddy face growing redder.

"You don't remember anyone . . ." Again embarrassment caused Bruce to redden.

Maggie ignored his discomfort. "The only 'C' I know is Carter and this certainly isn't from him, the handwriting is completely different. But it could be a last name. It says to meet this person Thursday. That's two days from now. I say let's just ignore it. If I don't show up, perhaps the person will send me a more explicit note or show up in person."

"I don't want to just ignore it, Mrs. Johnsbury, just in case this person means you some kind of harm. But you may be right. We may be able to do nothing more than wait to see if this person tries to contact you again. This does concern me, though."

"This person must know us socially, although I don't know why they bothered being so mysterious about identifying themselves."

Mr. McGrath cleared his throat, clearly uncomfortable talking about Mrs. Johnsbury's indiscretions so publicly. "Perhaps this person was concerned that the letter could get into the wrong hands. And, you see, they were right to be cautious," he said, waving the note in his hand.

The two were lost in thought for a time. "We should try to figure out who and where this meeting is to take place. Once that's done, I can go to the meeting with you close by and we can figure out what all this mystery is about."

"I don't think that would be prudent, Mrs. Johnsbury."

"Why not? It's the only way we can get to the bottom of this."

"I'm afraid Mr. Johnsbury would be very angry with me if I allowed you to put yourself in danger. And very angry with you."

"Yes. I suppose you're right."

Bruce relaxed.

"Here's an idea. We'll figure out what the note means, then you go and see who is waiting for me. That would accomplish our goal and I would be kept far from danger. How's that sound?"

"That's reasonable. But it means we will first have to determine not only what 'P' is but where it is. It could be anywhere. 'P' could mean Providence, or a park, or a pond, for that matter. We don't even know if the meeting spot is in this state. Whoever it is gave you two days for travel. I'd say it's impossible."

"You're right. Darn." Maggie knew Bruce was right, but the note nagged at her. *C. C.* Maggie paled so quickly Bruce thought surely she would faint. And indeed, Maggie had never felt so close to losing consciousness from simple fear.

"Oh, my God." Maggie whispered the words and felt light-headed with fear.

"Mrs. Johnsbury, what is it?"

"Curtis Rensworth. The note must be from Curtis Rensworth."

∼ *Chapter 11* ∼

. . . The fire was devastating. It was one of the worst times for us, in more ways than one. . . .

C arter was still a mile from the mill when he caught the first hint of the acrid smell of the burned mill. When the building finally came into view, Carter stopped his horse in the middle of the street, unable to believe what he saw. Nothing was left but the mill's tower and one blackened brick wall. The mill, which once covered an entire city block, had caved in on itself, its middle a pile of smoking rubble. Several people were still walking about with buckets pouring water on hot spots causing little puffs of dark gray smoke, thick with ashes, to erupt from the debris.

A man with blackened face walked purposefully toward Carter and was within just a few feet from him before he realized the man was Charles.

"Pretty sight, eh, brother? When I get my hands on the man who did this, I swear to God, Carter, I will not be responsible for what I do," Charles said, his voice thick with emotion and scratchy from the smoke.

Charles' face looked as if he had purposefully blackened it with the charred wood. His eyes, red-rimmed from the irritating smoke, told Carter about the fruitless hours he and scores of others had spent trying to salvage something of the mill.

"Chief O'Connell is certain it was set. You can still

smell the kerosene the bastard used. I got here about two hours after it was reported. When I left the house, I could see the smoke all the way from Benefit Street and I knew it was lost. That's when I sent the telegram. They tried their damnedest, but after a while it was no use and we just let it burn."

"Thank God it was a Sunday. At least we know whoever it is has some decency. My God, when I think about what could have happened."

Carter was as close to tears as he'd been in his adult life as he gazed at the destruction. This mill was more than bricks and mortar and a way to fill his pockets. It was the most modern mill of its type, trumpeted in the press as a revolution in textile production. He'd put blood and sweat into this project, and whoever was behind its destruction certainly had a good inkling just what this mill meant to him. Three stories high, with a tower that reached seventy feet, it was one of the tallest structures in the city. The tower now stood as a sad memorial to Carter's dreams. The two men stared silently as the last of the firefighters worked to douse the hot spots. A few walls remained partially standing, and equipment, charred and ruined, lay amid the debris like so many skeletons.

It was Monday morning, more than twelve hours after the fire was set, and many of the mill workers who would have normally reported to work came anyway to view the destruction. They met in small groups, whispering, as people do during a funeral or wake. And in a way, this was a funeral. Their jobs and way of life had gone up in flames along with the mill. They stared hollow-eyed at the building where they had once made their living.

"They've been coming and going all morning," Charles said, nodding toward another group. "A few have expressed their condolences. They haven't asked, but I know they want you to tell them whether we'll be rebuilding. Whether they'll have jobs if you do."

Carter tilted his head up to the sky, a brilliant blue that seemed out of place this sad day. When he was nineteen years old, he'd taken over the family business. With his father dead and his brother only sixteen, it had been left to him to take care of business. And he'd done it. He'd fine-tuned what his father had started and doubled the family's fortune in just five years. It had been hard work, but he had been driven and single-minded. The thought of starting over was daunting, but it must be done. It would be difficult, for the months of sabotage had chipped away at profits. But his creditors had always had confidence in him and there would be no difficulty financing the mill's rebirth.

Carter looked at the workers, many of whom had helped the firefighters try to douse the fire. Instead of saving the structure, they had been forced to watch the city's premier mill and their jobs be consumed.

"May I have your attention, please," Carter shouted at the people milling about. "As many of you know, I am Carter Johnsbury, owner of this mill. Or what's left of it." Carter smiled grimly and a few in the crowd chuckled. "I pledge to you that this mill, within six months, will be rebuilt and your jobs will be returned."

A shout rose up among the workers.

"In the meantime, I will try to accommodate as many of you as possible in our other mills. Wages will not be what they were here, but they should hold you over until the mill is completed. If you have any questions, please see Mr. Kraft. I cannot tell you how badly I feel that this will hurt you financially. This is a great blow to us all. But we will rebound, of that I am sure. I want to thank those of you who tried valiantly to save this mill. I am touched and honored to have such loyal employees."

More cheers followed. They had heard what they came to hear, what they were desperate to hear.

To his brother, Carter said, "We must act as quickly as possible. I do not want my creditors to believe that we are in any financial trouble."

"Are we?"

"You know as much as I do. Since the accidents have stopped, we have done quite well. Orders have increased as has production. We've set aside most of those profits in an attempt to develop a cache of money in order to avoid ever coming that close to financial ruin again. That money will be used toward the new mill. I'm sure the bank will finance the remainder. We are not poor, brother, but any further incidents will prove, shall I say, troubling. We must catch the bastard behind this."

Carter looked at the mill again, a deep rage building inside him. "Bruce tells me you found nothing new." Carter picked up a brick and threw it as hard as he could against one crumbling wall, giving into the anger that consumed him.

"I think it's time to go to the authorities and tell them what we have," Carter said. "And I think it's time we hired guards for our mills. And perhaps even for our homes."

"They wouldn't dare."

"I didn't think they'd dare do this. Did you? This has got to be a personal vendetta. But for the life of me, I cannot think of a person who hates me enough."

Charles was afraid to say the one name that came to mind. For there was only one person who did loathe Carter, one person who had the financial wherewithal to pay some culprit to do the dirty work.

"Well . . ." He could not bring himself to say it.

"You have an idea, brother? Spit it out. We have to look at every possibility, no matter how absurd it might seem."

"You're not going to like it, but the only person I know who hates you is . . ." Charles stopped again and his brother gave him a look of exasperation. "Margaret."

Carter's reaction was not what Charles expected. Carter let out a laugh. "No. Not Margaret." He was sure of it. Margaret loved him, he had no doubt. For the first time ever he was secure and happy with his marriage. Maggie was his joy, his life, and he could not and would not believe she was behind anything so sinister.

"Mother told me that you and Margaret have, er, come to terms?"

"More than that, little brother. More than that." But he did not elaborate.

Like his mother, Charles was afraid for Carter, especially when he saw the expression on his face when they talked about Margaret. His eyes softened, a slight smile curved his lips.

Carter interrupted his thoughts. "Have you had any sleep in the last two days? I thought not. You should go home, Charles. I'll take over for now and stop by later today. Go home to your family. I'm going to meet with the bank today, with an architect, and suppliers as well if I can fit them all in. I also plan to talk to the police about this matter. I brought all the documentation with me. I'll see you this evening. Tell Mother I should be home late. Try not to let her worry. And don't you dare mention your ridiculous suspicions to Mother. The next thing I know she'll be sending the constable to Rose Brier to throw Maggie in shackles." Charles grunted in reply. The thought had crossed his mind, truth be known.

The rest of the day was spent in the bank. Word of Carter Johnsbury's financial troubles were a grave concern for the bank's president, Mr. Waynewright. While Carter showed a hefty balance, the rumors that surrounded Johnsbury holdings were troubling. So Carter had more difficulty than he would have thought securing a loan to rebuild the mill. It was only when he threatened to take his business elsewhere that Mr. Waynewright, a plump, bespectacled man, suddenly became solicitous and apologetic. His appearance as a benevolent, jolly man was deceptive, and Carter knew it. Waynewright was a shrewd businessman, who kept his ear to the ground of the financial world. It was more than disturbing to have such a man question his ability to pay back what was a relatively small loan.

"I realize you have been a good customer, Mr. Johnsbury, and I'm not saying that you're not good for the loan. I am confident that you are. But, as you and I both know, it sometimes only take rumors for creditors to demand full and instant payment. And that is a possibility we must consider given the recent production of your mills."

"The recent production of my mills has been exemplary, Mr. Waynewright," Carter said coldly. "I will acknowledge a slowdown in early winter, but we are working to resolve the matter. As for the mill, once it is rebuilt, I have no fear we will be able to repay the loan in a matter of months." Carter was unused to haggling over money, and was one step away from walking out of Mr. Waynewright's office.

"I am sure you are right. And I apologize if I indicated any doubt in your business abilities, Mr. Johnsbury. As I said before, I am aware you are a valued customer. But I must look after my own interests as well. I'm sure you understand."

"I do understand, Mr. Waynewright. And I thank you for your time."

Carter left the meeting feeling a bit bewildered. He did not think that the slight trouble he had with his mills following the accidents was common knowledge in financial circles. That meant someone was doing more than attacking supplies and his own holdings. Someone was also attacking his business reputation. Carter almost found that the most disturbing event of all. But it was a development that might make it easier to discover who was behind the incidents. After all, he had many friends in the business world, any one of whom would be happy to tell him who had been spreading nasty rumors. Only a handful of people knew he had been hurt by those accidents, and among that handful was the person responsible. A quick look at his pocket watch told him it was too late to meet with the police. That would have to wait until tomorrow.

The next few days were spent with architects, city planners, and the chief of police, who, while interested in the arson, could only offer to look into the matter, leaving Carter frustrated. He worked furiously to get all the loose ends tied up quickly so he could go home to Rose Brier and to Maggie. Any stay would be brief, for the new mill would likely dominate his attention for the next several months. Just thinking of Maggie walking alone on the beach was enough for him to cut meetings short with uncharacteristic bluntness.

Finally, business was complete and Carter was joyfully contemplating the trip home. He was walking toward the train station, when a hand dropped on his shoulder.

"Carter, my boy. What brings you to town?"

It was Maggie's grandfather, a tall, imposing man with a white handlebar mustache, distinguished sideburns, and a full head of shockingly white hair. At sixty-five, Jonathan Edwards was an impressive-looking man. He was also a man Carter admired and liked. Even during the long, unhappy years with Margaret, Carter had always gotten along with her grandfather, even if he had thought the old man too soft on his wayward charge.

"Jonathan, how are you?" Carter said, warmly shaking the older man's hand. "You've heard about the mill fire? Yes, well, that's the business I've been on for about the past week. But I was on my way home."

"Yes, that was awful business, awful. Any idea how it happened? The paper said arson."

"That's what we suspect. The police are investigating, but I don't know how successful they'll be. They more or less told me it was near impossible to solve arson cases without a witness. But we're rebuilding and this shouldn't set us back too far."

"Good, good. Listen, I've just gotten in from New York, hotter than the dickens, that city, and I've got a meeting in a few minutes. I'd like to talk longer with you," he said, wiping a handkerchief against his wet forehead. "I'm glad to be near the sea again, though it's not much cooler, by God. Perhaps I'll stop by and visit Rose Brier. By the way, I looked for Margaret in New York and the house is closed up. Looks almost abandoned except for that old coot Barnsworth. I swear he's going senile and he's a younger man than me. He didn't recognize me and met me at the door with an old flintlock pistol, if you can believe it. You wouldn't happen to know where my granddaughter is."

Carter couldn't help himself. He smiled. "She's at Rose Brier."

"Rose Brier? Still? My God, I think that girl finally took me seriously."

Carter was still smiling, but something about what Jonathan said sent a slight tremor of fear through him. "Seriously? What do you mean?"

"Well, Carter, let me ask you this. How has Margaret been lately?"

Carter looked at the old man curiously. "To be honest, Jonathan, she's been like a different woman. We're getting along quite well."

"Well, I'll be damned. Looks like she finally got the message then," Jonathan said, obviously pleased with the news.

But Carter's heart stopped in his throat and his stomach gave a sickening twist. "What do you mean?" He tried to say it lightly, as if he did not care what the old man said. His eyes grew cold, although his lips still held a stiff smile that was becoming more and more difficult to maintain.

"Well, as long as you two are getting along now, I suppose it won't do any harm in telling you. Some time ago, I gave Margaret a little lecture. I am not as blind to her faults as you may think, you know, young man. I saw what she was doing to others, what she was doing to you. And I must say, I was beginning to get a bit embarrassed by her indiscretions. I thought it was time for it to stop. You know Margaret inherits a huge trust fund on her thirtieth birthday, and the rest when I die. Though I've still got plenty of years left, God willing. I was desperate for her to act, well, more in keeping with her station. So I threatened to withdraw her trust fund and inheritance unless she became a good wife. I know I shouldn't have meddled, and in retrospect, I'm not sure if what I did was right or if I would have truly followed through with my threat. Anyway, I told her to go to Rose Brier and make things right. At first she ranted and raved. Oh, you should have seen her. Then again, I'm sure you can imagine. I left for Europe shortly after, never truly thinking she'd come through. Well, she's surprised me again."

With every innocent word the older man spoke, Carter's heart grew more and more cold. He had to remind himself to breathe, he had to consciously tell himself to keep a stunned look off his face. The only evidence that Jonathan's words were ripping him apart was the clenched fists, hidden behind his back, squeezed so hard, his arms began to shake. But that smile remained, cold and horrible. Jonathan was too pleased with himself to notice that the happy young man in front of him was slowly dying to be replaced by a bitter, hard, cynical shell.

"Your little plan apparently worked," Carter managed to say. He was even surprised how casual he sounded, how normal.

"You're not angry, are you, Carter? I was only doing what I thought was best. The end justifies the means sometimes, my boy." He slapped the younger man companionably on his back.

"Yes. She's been the perfect little wife." The perfect little liar. The perfect little whore, selling her body for her trust fund.

Jonathan took out his pocket watch and said, "I'm late for that meeting, but I'll drop by Rose Brier sometime soon. I hope I haven't upset you, boy."

Jonathan already regretted telling Carter the truth and he mentally gave himself a kick for being so callous. He liked the young man, and had always felt he deserved better than his wayward granddaughter. Jonathan loved Margaret, almost to a fault, and he could not help but think that so many of the decisions he'd forced on her, for her own good, were wrong. He was a man of business, not one to give in to softer emotions. He knew he had a duty to Margaret and when she began to stray as a teenager he came to the conclusion a fine man would straighten her out. He gave no thought to what he was doing to Carter, only that he was helping Margaret. This latest scheme was a pitiful attempt to right a wrong. He never truly thought it would work, and if he were honest, he was a bit disappointed that it was only the threat of losing her fortune that caused Margaret to act the good wife.

"I'm going to be quite busy with the new mill, Jonathan, but feel free to stop by. I'm sure Margaret would like to see you," Carter said, his voice sounding strangely detached. Jonathan gave him a worried look, then chalked up his concern to an overactive imagination.

Carter walked to the train station blindly as if someone were leading him and he had no control over where he went. Her words came back to him: "Think, Carter. What possible reason could I have for trying to make you love me again? What could be my motive?" Well, now he knew.

He made the trip home the same way, not thinking, mind blank, body straight and stiff. But when he turned up the familiar curving drive and saw Rose Brier standing in the distance, he reined in and stared. No warm feeling washed over him. No sense of calm. He tortured himself by thinking about what the homecoming could have been, should have been, with his Maggie throwing herself in his arms, just as she'd promised so prettily. He spit to rid himself of that pathetic, lying image. There was no Maggie. As he sat there, looking at Rose Brier, the rage he'd been suppressing during the long ride began to build at an alarming rate. It was rage against himself for being so foolishly gullible, against Jonathan for crushing his dream, but mostly against the woman who called herself Maggie. The woman who had found his heart only to rip it to shreds with her malicious lies. God, how he loathed that woman. He took a long and shuddering breath, shaking his head in a vain attempt to rid himself of the all-consuming anger. Then he clicked his heels against his horse and rode slowly up the drive.

Maggie was sitting in the library when she heard the crunch of horse hooves on the drive pass the house and head toward the stables. She flew to the window, her heart hammering madly in her chest, hoping she'd see the familiar figure of her husband. Just as she was running to the door, Bruce popped his head in the library and announced that, indeed, Carter was home. Bruce smiled at the brilliantly happy face that greeted his news. Maggie flew to the front door, pausing just two seconds to catch her image in the hallway mirror. Patting her curls ineffectually, she heaved open the door and began running to the stables to make good on her promise to greet her husband by flinging herself in his arms. She had missed him more than she thought possible and her heart felt as if it would explode with love at the thought of seeing him again, holding him again.

Maggie was still running toward the stable when Carter walked out of the building, head down. He heard her running and jerked his head up. Maggie's heart wrenched when she saw his face, and she stumbled to a stop still a few feet away. Something was terribly wrong.

"Carter, what's wrong?" Maggie asked, feeling an unexplained sense of dread. She took a couple of tentative steps toward him, but it was as if his eyes alone were pushing her away. He did not speak.

"Oh, Carter, please tell me. What's happened?"

Carter looked at her as if she were an offensive bit of rotted fish. He was pleased to find that the sight of her, as lovely as she was, did nothing but fill him with renewed rage. The tears he saw fall down her lovely cheeks only produced a sneer.

"I had a nice chat with your grandfather, Margaret. That's all you need to know." Carter strode by her, making an obvious effort to avoid her outstretched hand, and headed toward the house. Maggie stood still, bewildered and hurt, tears falling unheeded.

"Carter. Please. I don't know what's happening. Please." She began to run after him, but he ignored her. She'd never felt this desperate, this lost. "Please, Carter, tell me what's wrong. Talk to me. Please. I love you."

Carter stopped as if he had struck a wall. He turned toward her, his face filled with hatred. "Don't you ever say that to me again. Do you hear me? Not ever."

With that, he continued on into the house, slamming the door behind him.

Maggie stood on the dusty walkway, oblivious to the bees buzzing around the bright pink roses swaying in a soft breeze, oblivious to the soothing sound of waves coming ashore. She sank down onto the steps, picked up her hem and wiped her face. It was obvious something in Margaret's past had once again reared its ugly head. But this time was different, she could tell, and Maggie felt nearly suffocated with despair. Carter, with all his scowls and heated looks, had never looked at her with such violent loathing.

What could her grandfather have said to Carter to change him so dramatically? Maggie felt certain that if she knew what the old man had told Carter, she could reason with him. Was there some horrible thing in Margaret's past that Carter had not known? It seemed unlikely that her grandfather would know something Carter did not.

She had been so looking forward to his homecoming. Sitting alone, forlorn on the front steps, was the last image she had conjured up. She had pictured her throwing herself in Carter's arms while he swooped her up with a resounding kiss. She had imagined smiles and words of love and gentle touches and not-so-gentle touches. Well, she had won him over before, she reminded herself, she could do it again. "I can do it," she said aloud, to make her resolve real. While her heart cried out for her to try, Maggie was not a stupid woman. And she now knew Carter well enough to realize that whatever had driven them apart this time went deeper, far deeper, than the pettiness, even the infidelity, of Margaret's past. Something had bruised Carter's soul and turned his heart to stone.

When Maggie went inside, her lashes still spiky from crying, the first person she saw, hovering outside a closed library door, was Bruce. The perplexed look on his face told Maggie that he was as confused as she about what was happening. At his questioning glance, Maggie said, "I don't know what happened, Bruce. He's terribly angry, and hurt, and I don't have a clue why."

Bruce looked at her skeptically. "There must be something."

"Oh, God. I wish I knew. You should have seen his

face when he saw me. I swear to you, Bruce, he looked as if he could kill me. As if he wanted to kill me. I don't know what to do. Yes I do. I have to find my grandfather. The only thing I know is that whatever set Carter off had something to do with something my grandfather told him."

"Your grandfather? Have you seen him lately?"

"No. I don't even know the man," Maggie said, so upset she did not stop to think how that would sound. "I know I haven't seen him since the accident and that was almost five months ago. I don't know where to begin looking. Do you?"

"I just know he travels a great deal."

Maggie rested an elbow on one arm crossed in front of her and tried to think. She must send letters to every house her grandfather owned asking him to come to Rose Brier, but she did not even know his addresses.

"Do you know where his houses are?"

Bruce gave her a long, hard look before saying, "I don't know, but I'm sure Mrs. Brimble has a complete list."

"Good. I'm going to write to him to find out what this is all about. I have a feeling Carter isn't about to volunteer any information, at least not to me, for a while."

The two looked at each other, then at the closed door. "Bruce. Carter—he confides in you at times, doesn't he?"

Bruce became cautious, his loyalty for his boss springing forward like so many ruffled feathers.

"I would never ask you to take sides. I know where your loyalties lie," Maggie said, correctly interpreting Bruce's stance. "But I can't stand this. I'm telling you, Bruce, I will not be able to endure this for long. I know myself well enough."

Her voice grew soft. "I love him, Bruce. And for a short time, I think he felt the same way, or very nearly so. If there's something I did to make him hate me this

way, I have to know. I have to try to make it right. I
don't think I can live with Carter hating me this way."
Having said it, the words even shocked Maggie. She had
not realized the depth of her love for her husband until
that moment.

Bruce said nothing, but his heart clenched tightly at
her words. He nodded, neither making a promise nor
denying her wish. In this matter, he would reserve judgment. Carter had been wrong before. But like Mrs.
Johnsbury, he also had never seen Carter's face so contorted with rage and pain. Whatever was hurting him, it
went deep. And wounds so deep are sometimes impossible to heal.

~ *Chapter 12* ~

. . . I was so helpless. Unable to act, unable to do anything but wait until the storm blew over. . . .

For three days, Carter holed up in the library, coming out only at night when he was sure no one was about. He drank himself silly in that darkened room, frightening the servants and nearly driving Maggie out of her mind with worry. He would only allow Bruce to bring him his meals, then would throw the bewildered man out almost immediately. Maggie spent her days near the door, hoping he would come out or ask for her. The entire household walked about on tiptoe, casting wary glances at the library door. But they avoided looking at Maggie, who for hours on end sat in an uncomfortable hall chair and listened to her husband moving about in the library.

After the first day, in which Carter must have flung every breakable item he could find into the fireplace, the room was fairly quiet, other than during periods of muffled shouting. Maggie cringed each time she heard him shout and each time he threw another item about the room. She almost barged into the library when she heard what must have been the beautiful Victrola being demolished, followed by record after record being smashed. Clearly, Carter was taking out on inanimate objects what he wanted to do to Maggie. The lump in her throat became a constant affliction and it seemed she was always on the verge of tears. She had never felt so hopeless, so unhappy.

"Please, God, my angels, Mother Mary. Please make Carter realize his mistake. Please make him know that I love him." She prayed silently, over and over until it became almost a chant in her head, until she could almost drown out the violent noises coming from within the library. She felt he picked that room to further torture her and himself. Memories flooded her of the two smiling at each other, of Carter's exasperation at her relentless pursuit, of his kisses. Those lazy days they'd shared had become a magical time in Maggie's mind, when they had become friends and laid the foundation for a love that Maggie had never known. Why, of all rooms, would he pick the one where they came to love each other?

Bruce was never far away so he could hear Carter bellow his name. He knew one of these times, Carter would sober up and need to talk. He watched Maggie flinch when an unexpected crash was heard; he saw her silent tears, her wretchedly sad eyes. And he wondered what she could have possibly done to destroy the man behind that closed door. Carter must be wrong. He must be.

Early on the third day, a ragged, scruffy, but sober Carter opened the library door and called Bruce inside. He remained inside the room so did not see Maggie sitting in her chair against the wall. Maggie would have leapt up, but Bruce shot her a warning look and she forced herself to remain seated.

Carter seated himself at his desk, aware of what he looked like and what he had put his friend through in the past few days. With hollow eyes, he stared at the fireplace, filled with the broken objects of his rage, while Bruce stood patiently in front of the desk after crunching over bits of broken records. With a little shake of his head, Carter brought his attention to Bruce and gave him a crooked smile. If Maggie's distress had touched him, seeing Carter this way broke Bruce's heart. He was acutely aware he was looking at a man who had lost a vital part of himself. There was no light in his dull gray eyes, no life, just hard, cold calculation, tinged with a bleakness that was quickly shuttered.

"I suppose you want to know what caused this little hiatus of mine." Carter held a hand up when Bruce made to disagree. "No. I know you're curious about what happened that could nearly drive me mad." He chuckled, a hard, humorless sound that brought a shiver to Bruce's spine.

"It was all about money. Money." Carter shook his head, as if still unable to believe it himself. After taking in Bruce's bewildered look, he continued.

"The little bitch was going to lose her trust and inheritance, as commanded by Jonathan, if she didn't act like the perfect wife. She did a pretty good job of it, didn't she? Fooled us all." Carter's eyes became suspiciously shiny, and Bruce swallowed hard seeing even a hint of tears in his friend's eyes. As quickly as they appeared, they were gone, pain masked by bitterness.

"I cannot imagine the kind of evil that must exist in a person for them to . . ." Carter could not finish, for he felt that rage he had felt since talking with Jonathan building again. What he wanted most, from now on, was to control his emotions, to feel nothing.

Bruce was not convinced, for to be so would be to admit he had also been taken in. After all, he was the one who had encouraged Carter to act on his feelings for Margaret. In what he'd convinced himself was brotherly love, he too had been sucked in by Margaret's charm, her seeming innocence. He had not known he was that gullible.

"Are you sure you understood her grandfather correctly?"

"Yes! Goddammit, don't you think I want it to be a

lie? But it all makes sense, doesn't it? Just think of the timing of it all. Margaret comes to Rose Brier, a place she has professed on many occasions to hate, in February. She avoids this place in the middle of summer, never mind in such a bleak part of the year. And what did she tell me? She tells me she's bored with New York. Suddenly bored with her friends, the opera, the theater. As if Rose Brier holds any excitement for someone like her. Now that I think back, I can't believe how I was taken in by the bitch."

Bruce creased his brow in thought. He, too, remembered Margaret's unexpected arrival. He tried to think back on that day, but remembered only sketchy details. What he remembered most was Carter's unhappiness at his wife's arrival. The only event that stood out in his mind was the accident.

"But she didn't really change until after the accident, if I remember," Bruce argued.

"It was the perfect scam, don't you see, Bruce? Pretend amnesia, pretend to become a 'new' woman? It makes me sick to think how her mind works. She did exactly what her grandfather told her to do. To the letter. And we've all paid for her duplicity. We've all paid for her little charade. I'm sure now that she knows we're on to her, she'll give up and go away. God help her if she doesn't."

"To think a woman could be capable of such evil," Bruce said, almost to himself. As much as he did not want to believe Mrs. Johnsbury could be so calculating, he realized he'd been duped and he felt a good dose of the anger that consumed Carter. "How did you stop yourself from throttling her?" he asked, letting anger get the best of him.

Carter gave him a sad smile. "I came in here, got drunk, threw things around. That's how I stopped myself. One thing that bitch is not worth is my hide in prison."

"What happens next?"

Carter let out a heavy sigh that gave some clue to Bruce that he still suffered. "I have a lot of work between the new mill and looking for the saboteur. It won't take long before I get back to my old routine."

Bruce knew that routine involved working sixteen hours a day, long periods away from Rose Brier, away from Margaret. For a time, the two were silent, each lost in his own thoughts. For Carter, the thought of the "old routine" was immensely depressing. He could not rid himself of the images of how happy he had been in the past few months, and especially those four impossibly blissful days when he had thought himself in love with his wife. Although he believed it now to all be a lie, he had never been happier in his life, those four days. The fact that it was all a lie made it hurt all the more, for he could not even enjoy those memories without feeling like a fool. His future looked bleak, indeed, and for the first time he wondered about his obsession with Rose Brier. If it were not for this house, he could be free, he could divorce Margaret and maybe find some happiness. It was not too late, he was still a young man, he told himself. But he knew in his heart, he could not give up what was his birthright. Margaret would go back to New York, and once again it would be become his haven, his home.

When the door to the library opened, Maggie stood, her heart in her throat. She relaxed slightly when she saw that Bruce came out alone, but almost fainted when Bruce turned toward her.

"Oh God, Bruce, no. No! Please tell me what's happening!" Maggie pleaded. Anyone hearing her anguish could also almost hear her heart breaking. Maggie could not believe the cold look on Bruce's face when he walked by her. He did not say a word. He did not have to. Maggie crumpled to the floor, sobbing.

In the library, Carter heard her. And he smiled.

* * *

Maggie lay abed staring at the ceiling. It was midday,
two weeks after Carter had come home. It was the worst
two weeks of her life—and that was saying a lot, she told
herself. Her grandfather had not responded to any of
the four letters she had immediately sent out. Where
was that man? she'd thought for the hundredth time.
She knew it would be foolish to even attempt to talk to
Carter until she knew where she stood.

So she had avoided seeing him—something that
turned out to be not that difficult since he left Rose
Brier almost immediately following his discussion with
Bruce, who also left the next day. It was apparent that
Bruce had confided at least something to the household
staff. It was clear their loyalties lay with Carter for they
were coldly polite to Maggie, their eyes filled with accusation. Even during her first days at Rose Brier Maggie
had not felt such an outcast.

As the days passed, Maggie found herself slipping
further and further away from the woman she had
been—happy, hopeful, and full of life. It was brutally
apparent she had no friends, no one to confide in. Even
Stella had lost what little warmth she had shown toward
her mistress.

Maggie still went for her runs on the beach, but now
only at night when the beach was deserted. During the
day, it was filled with strolling couples and playing children. Seeing others' happiness only made Maggie feel
all the more depressed.

Carter would come home for a few days at a time
then leave again. When he was home, he would spend
little time in the house, often attending picnics, lawn
parties, and dances at the Casino. Invitations would pile
up on the foyer table, all specifically addressed to Mr.
Johnsbury, and he attended a select few. Maggie came
to believe he was attending more social functions than
normal, just to get under her skin, to proclaim to her

and the world, "See? I don't need you. I'm fine by myself."

Maggie wrote more letters to her grandfather; all went unanswered and she was beginning to lose all hope that she could salvage her life here. Carter seemed to have rebounded quite nicely, she thought with some bitterness. Apparently she had miscalculated his feelings toward her by a great degree.

Although Maggie made a point of being out of the house when Carter was home, it was inevitable that they see each other. At first, they did not speak, with Maggie trying to communicate with only her eyes. Carter completely ignored her and when he found it absolutely necessary to communicate something to his wife, he did so through servants. Maggie felt she would go insane if this awful life continued. She had not had a conversation with another human being in weeks. On top of everything else, she was bored senseless.

It was that boredom, almost more than anything else, that drove her to her next mistake. She noted with some interest an envelope, an obvious invitation, that was stunningly addressed to both Mr. and Mrs. Carter Johnsbury. She opened it up to make sure there was no mistake. Yes. She was included. A small bit of hope stirred in Maggie's heart. Perhaps if she and Carter were to go to a ball, if Carter could see her talking with his friends, could see her looking beautiful in a new gown, then some of the ice around his heart would melt. Perhaps he would finally say what had gone so dreadfully wrong the day he had met her wandering grandfather.

It also dawned on her that her grandfather might also be invited to an event such as the one the Hellewells were throwing. She went into what she knew was an empty library where an imposing portrait of her grandfather dominated one wall. He was a handsome man with a distinguished mustache and sideburns and Maggie hoped he had not changed too much since the portrait was painted. Maggie was studying the painting intently and did not hear the soft footsteps muffled by thick carpet as Carter walked into the library.

Carter was surprised to find his wife in the library and amazed at her courage. Or her stupidity. Her curling hair was pulled back but allowed to flow in rivulets down her back, a simple but elegant style. "She's lost more weight," he thought idly, and then mentally chastised himself for the bit of niggling worry that touched him.

"What are you doing in here?" Carter felt a bit of satisfaction when Maggie jumped in surprise at his question.

"I was looking at my grandfather's portrait," Maggie said, matter-of-factly. "By the way, I've been invited to the Hellewells and I plan to go."

"No."

"Yes. I can go if I want. I was invited." Maggie felt ridiculously close to tears looking at Carter. He looked so handsome, but so tired. She did not dare think that his haggard appearance had anything to do with her. It was obvious he'd been working long hours on his mill and some other business that was a complete mystery to her. She wanted nothing more than to cradle his head against her and soothe his brow. But soothing a rattlesnake would have been easier, she knew.

"I am attending that ball. I have business to attend to there and must go. That means you cannot."

"I'm going if I have to go by myself."

"I'll make sure there is no carriage available."

"I'll walk."

"I'll make sure you cannot walk." His look was so frightening, his voice laced with so much menace, Maggie actually took a step back. But the fear was quickly replaced by anger.

"Are you so afraid to be in the same room with me? Are you afraid of me, Carter? Or of yourself?"

"Oh. I'm afraid for you, my dear." He almost looked as if he were enjoying this awful game, Maggie thought.

"Cut it out. I'm not afraid of you, Carter. If you were going to hurt me, you would have done so long ago. So stop these silly innuendoes."

Carter quirked an eyebrow, surprised at her perception. "Very well, go to the damn ball. We will arrive together and leave together. That is all. I am not close to the Hellewells, but they are important to my business affairs, and perhaps that is why they included you on the invitation. They simply didn't know any better."

~ *Chapter 13* ~

. . . I had to try something, Steve. What else could I do? I was losing him. . . .

This was a mistake, Maggie thought as they climbed down from their carriage. Hordes of people in the most gorgeous dress Maggie had ever seen strolled the grounds of the Hellewell estate in the soft, early evening light. Elegant, proper, and subdued, the Newport elite chatted and burbled laughter on a plush lawn that dropped gently to the shores of Narragansett Bay. Nothing so raucous as a guffaw here. Maggie was at a loss at how to act. Do women shake men's hands? Shake other women's hands? What about these ridiculous gloves—could she take them off? Should she take them off? This was going to be more difficult than she ever imagined. Carter was no help. He had not spoken a word to her since they climbed into the carriage. They had sat in uncomfortable silence the entire ten-minute trip.

Carter stared out the window at the dusty street, his gaze not wavering, his hard expression carved as if from stone. Maggie had attempted to make small talk, but the scathing look of hatred he had given her was as effective as a gag. She'd flushed miserably and gazed down at her hands, twisting the hated gloves in her lap, for the remainder of the ride.

Why did she think this was a good idea? She should be back at Rose Brier, she thought, then quickly chastised herself. Be brave, Maggie, this could be your last chance.

As they walked up a sweeping set of marble steps outside the Hellewell mansion, she involuntarily clutched at Carter's arm, causing him to turn his head downward—the scowl on his face gave Maggie no comfort and no courage to ask, once again, that he stay by her side during this ordeal. Oh, stupid, stupid, stupid idea.

"Margaret. Dear. You look lovely, but so thin," said a huge blonde with hair piled so high Maggie wondered how she didn't tilt under the weight. She felt briefly panicky when a laugh nearly erupted from her.

She was assaulted by a nauseatingly sweet perfume wafting from the blonde and could feel a headache beginning. She would never get used to this century's habit of limited washing and healthy doses of perfume. But what could be worse than the smell of an unwashed person? Perhaps the smell of perfume that failed to mask that smell. Breathe through the mouth, she reminded herself silently, breathe through the mouth.

When the blonde tower of hair saw Maggie's blank stare, she immediately affected a sympathetic look. "How's the head, dear, dear Margaret. We were all so worried." She patted her arm with sympathy and walked away. Obviously not one of Margaret's better friends, Maggie thought with a mental shrug. But at least word of her head injury and amnesia had begun to reach people. Carter had already drifted away, leaving her to smile stupidly at the people near her. Thank God no one was turning their backs to her. She stared fretfully at the back of Carter's head as he made his way through the crowd and Maggie could not help but again feel that overwhelming sadness that washed over her like an incoming tide since Carter's return.

She had gone over that devastating scene outside the stable again and again, wondering what it could possibly

have been that her grandfather said that had turned
Carter away from her. She smiled wistfully as she remembered those few precious days when everything had
seemed like it would turn out right. And now, it seemed
as if all she had worked for in the past months was for
naught. The summer was waning and Maggie could not
get over this nagging feeling that whatever she was sent
here to do should have been accomplished by now, that
her time was running short. She had to find her grandfather and ask him what he'd said, she thought as she
scanned the crowd for a man resembling the stern portrait in Rose Brier's library.

As she made her way through the crush of people, her
head beginning to ache in earnest from the overpowering scents surrounding her, the music from a small orchestra began in the ballroom. The French doors had
been left open to allow the cool breeze to filter in off
the bay. Oh thank God for that, for something to listen
to and a breeze to dilute the perfume.

She found a small chair against a huge potted fern,
and sat. This was all she wanted now, to soak in the
atmosphere of the place, to watch the flow of impossibly
beautiful gowns and hope that the old man had, indeed,
decided to attend the ball. Maggie could not help but
think how this ball could have been so different. She
would have been on Carter's arm, they would have
danced, they would have walked on the manicured lawn
as dusk fell, not caring that the dew was ruining their
shoes.

Sitting in that corner, watching the stiff-backed men
and the graceful women, was like watching an old
movie. Everyone seemed to know what part they played
as they laughed and fluttered eyelashes and delicate
fans. Maggie held one of those silly things in her own
gloved hand and hadn't the foggiest notion what to do
with it. Certainly no one was using them for their purpose as the breeze off the bay was making the ballroom

decidedly chilly. Still, her hands sweated and itched beneath her gloves and she longed to take them off, but as no one else had, Maggie decided to suffer. She fingered the small seed pearls on the back of her gloves nervously.

Once in a while she caught a glimpse of Carter, his dark head tilted downward so he could catch what his friends were saying. She'd never realized how much taller Carter was than other men, how he seemed to command attention. Now and then, he'd let go a laugh, throwing back his head, and Maggie smiled before she could catch herself. She would not smile for that man or because of that man, she told herself fiercely. How dare he have fun when she was sitting here miserable, loving him so while he ignored her so easily.

The seeds of a deep and abiding sadness had been planted the day Carter returned from Pawtucket. Maggie had been so happy to see him. She had missed him so much. And he had not even told her what had happened to change everything. This last, pathetic effort to be with him, to force him to see them as a couple, was doomed to fail, Maggie knew. Whatever it was between them could not be resolved by her alone. She must speak with her grandfather, but that man was impossible to pin down. A trail of letters from Maggie asking him to see her followed him about, unread.

She continued to watch as Carter was surrounded by three women she did not recognize. At least the Widow Thornbrush was not among them, she told herself as consolation. He seemed to be having fun, damn him. He seemed not even to wonder where his wife was.

Carter knew exactly where Maggie sat. He knew she was miserable and he was truly glad. Truly. He made a big show of flirting with as many women as he could, knowing that Maggie watched. He did not care that she watched. He did not care that she was miserable. He wanted her to suffer, to feel just a part of the humiliation he had been dealt by her duplicity. Although part of him feared another scene like that at his own ball all those months ago, he relished in the fact that no one approached her. Carter silently congratulated himself on how far he'd come in just a few short weeks. The pain he had felt in his heart, that made it feel as if it were dissolving inside him, had turned into a dull ache. He did not stop to consider that she was on his mind entirely too much, even if his thoughts were malevolent. He did not stop to consider that a man who did not care would not take so much care to notice his wife was sitting alone in a corner by a potted plant looking more forlorn than he'd ever seen her.

The past few weeks had been hellish for Carter, worse than he would have imagined. He mourned a woman that did not exist, and hated himself for every kind memory that forced itself upon him when he least expected it. Every woman, no matter how plain, no matter how obese or blonde or old, reminded him of Maggie. He would see an old woman wearing dark blue, and think, Maggie would look beautiful in that color. When he realized what he'd been thinking, he would tighten his jaw in anger. Why couldn't he get the damned woman out of his mind?

Carter had told no one but Bruce about what Margaret's grandfather had told him. He could not bear the look of sympathy his mother would be sure to give him, nor the 'I told you so' from his brother Charles. Work helped keep his mind off Maggie, but even there she stole into his day. The progress he made on the mill, the small accomplishments, the big problems—how many times had he thought, 'I wonder what Maggie would think?'

It did not help that Margaret remained at Rose Brier, that she continued to pretend to have no knowledge of her pact with her grandfather. Every time she looked at him with those brown eyes so filled with hurt and confusion, it affected him more than he cared to admit. Staying at Rose Brier was out of character for Margaret. And that alone was enough to disturb Carter.

As Maggie sat there, watching, she realized that had Margaret truly had friends, they would have surrounded her immediately, tried to jar some memory. And even though that would have been a futile exercise, at least it would have been interesting. But no one approached. And Maggie, despite her resolve to remain interested and cheerful, found her throat begin its now-familiar ache from unshed tears. She dug her fingernails into her palms, clenched her fists, and mentally scolded herself for being such a wimp. It seemed lately she was always fighting back tears.

Maggie forced herself to get up and wander about the room that was rapidly filling up with people who had lingered outside in the cool early-evening air. Dancing would begin soon and Maggie wanted to strike up a conversation with someone before it did.

She spotted a group not far away and could tell at least some of the people there knew her because they were looking at her with recognition. If Maggie had not been so nervous, she would have seen that the look on most of the women in the group was one of open hostility, not simple recognition.

"Hello," Maggie said, with what she hoped was a graceful smile on her lips. That smile, which took more courage than Maggie knew she had, remained there even as she realized she was not welcome. "It's a beautiful night. Cool and . . ."

"You have some nerve, Margaret Johnsbury, to show your face to me after . . ." The pretty brunette, her hair swept back elegantly, was so upset she could not continue. To Maggie's mortification, the young woman's eyes filled with tears. The other women huddled around her in a protective circle. "I'm sorry," Maggie managed to squeak out. "What ever I did, I'm sorry. I don't remember what I did, but it wasn't me." Upset as Maggie was, she realized how absurd that sounded.

A tall, elderly man, with sideburns stretching down his jaw, planted a firm hand on Maggie's upper arm and said, "I think these ladies could do without your company right now, Mrs. Johnsbury." Maggie looked up at the man and saw in his eyes the same thing she had seen in nearly everyone she had met—disgust, dislike, and distaste.

Against his will, Carter watched with intensity the scene over the heads of the small group he was standing with, his gray eyes darkening in anger when he saw the women snub Maggie. When Carter realized his reaction, he was shocked and disgusted with himself and he tried to ignore the twist his heart gave when he watched Maggie walk, back stiff with pride, from the women.

Trying to be brave, Maggie turned from the group after giving each woman a silent plea to understand. She might as well have been looking at statues, she knew. Walking away on wooden legs, Maggie swallowed back the tears that threatened, lifted her head, and slowly made her way back to the chair by the potted fern. She'd try again with another group, once she got her courage back, Maggie told herself. As much as she wanted to leave, she also hoped to see her grandfather and knew this was a chance to meet the man who seemed to have ruined her life.

It was only after the dancing started and Carter danced with four different women and had seen her sitting by the drooping fern but had not acknowledged her with even a nod that the first tear slipped down her cheek. Looking up to the ceiling, to hold the threatening tears at bay, she quickly decided to leave and never attend another ball. Margaret was not liked, not by her contemporaries, not by the servants, and certainly not by her husband. Heck, she didn't even like the lady herself. The path Margaret had cut for herself was too deep to be obliterated by this new woman calling herself Maggie. From their point of view, it was easy to understand. They could not see the new light in her, the kindness, the love. They would not let her close enough. If she could not convince Carter, who saw her every day and who once even thought himself in love with Margaret, the entire campaign was doomed.

Heaving a sigh and using her gloves to blot the corners of her eyes, she stood up and walked out of the Hellewells' mansion. A line of carriages three deep stood outside, the horses stamping impatiently while their drivers talked among themselves and tried to sneak a few nips from hidden flasks. Some appeared to have been more successful than others in this endeavor, if their loud laughter and back slaps were any indication. Real uninhibited laughter. She should have come back as a servant, instead of a blueblood, Maggie thought. At least it would have been more fun.

Maggie saw the Johnsbury carriage blocked in, the driver nowhere in sight. The need to go home overrode the need of a carriage, so she stubbornly decided to walk the two miles back to Rose Brier. As Maggie passed one driver, who quickly tried to conceal his flask, she said, "Can I have a swig?" and held out her gloved hand. While the poor gentleman was still debating the propriety of handing over his flask to a lady, she took the flask and downed a huge swallow. And didn't even wince. From the look on the face of the driver, Maggie quickly realized she had just captured an admirer.

Maggie was halfway home when the Johnsbury carriage with an angry Carter hanging out the window approached. Maggie kept walking, but said, "You didn't have to leave on my account. It was a mistake for me to go. You were right, but not for the reasons you thought. Go back. Have fun."

"Stop the carriage," Carter yelled to the driver. "Margaret. Get in. Now. Do you have any idea what you look like walking down the street in the dark like a common tramp?"

Maggie stopped walking. She was quaking inside but was not about to let him know. "Listen, Carter," she said, making an effort to make her voice soft. "Just go back and have fun. I don't want you to feel you have to come get me. I'm okay. I'm almost back to the Rose Brier. So . . ."

Carter's face was stone. "Get in the carriage. Now."

Maggie was not a woman of the 1880s. She was a woman of the 1990s who was bright enough to know that these people were simply a long way from understanding anything about independent women. But her 1990s ire was being tested.

"No." And she started walking. Carter could not have looked more surprised if she had slapped him.

"No? No?"

"No," she said lightly, even smiling a bit, as she continued to walk. She heard Carter telling the driver to wait and knew he was about to pursue her on foot. Maggie was suddenly glad of all those tortuous miles jogging down the beach under the moon. She took off running before Carter put a step on the street. Skirts hiked up, hair falling down, Maggie flew down the street, now muddy from a recent watering, energized on by a wonderful burst of adrenaline. But her body could not overcome the stays, pulled so tight she could barely fill her lungs, and the ten pounds of dress she was wearing, not to mention the flimsy shoes that were completely unsuitable to running, especially on slippery mud. Needless to say, Carter quickly caught up, snagging first a bit of her dress, then working his way up to her left arm. When Carter spun her around, the last thing he expected to see was a huge smile. Tears maybe, rigid anger almost certainly, but never a smile.

"You're quick! But let's race some time when I'm not wearing this ridiculous dress," she said, and laughed at his look. "Oh, Carter, you're a young man. Have a little fun. I'm so sick of all this dreariness."

That's about the time he smelled her breath. "Yes. It seems at least you've been having some fun." His expression went cold, his voice cutting. "A little too much to drink, Margaret?" He swept his hair back with his hand in an angry gesture Maggie had become used to. "Well, at least you left first."

It dawned on Maggie that Carter was not reacting to a wife whose breath smelled faintly of alcohol. He was reacting to years of a wife who got drunk, who was probably abusive when she was drunk, and whom he hated. This was something new. Maggie had not known Margaret indulged a bit too much and that it had apparently been a huge problem. Damn. And here she was with whiskey on her breath. She never should have indulged in that swig. When she remembered how triumphant she felt when she failed to gasp as the harsh liquor burned her throat, she wanted to curl up and die. For every step forward she took with Carter, it seemed she always managed to take two steps back.

"Oh, Carter, I didn't know. I'm sorry." Her eyes filled with remorse, but her expression had no effect on Carter that she could see. After all, drunks were often repentant. "Margaret drank, didn't she?"

He grabbed her by the shoulders, hands digging into her skin and shook her violently, shouting, "You're Margaret. Goddammit. You're Margaret. No more of this. No more." He stopped shaking her and let go so suddenly she stumbled. "No more, Margaret," he said, sounding defeated.

And because she was just a little bit mad at being manhandled in the street in front of the driver, she said, "My name is Maggie. I had just one sip. I am not drunk, although that's not such a bad idea. So you can just go to hell." She stalked off, biting her lip to stop the tears.

She had never felt so angry in her life. She was sick of this. Sick, sick to death.

Maggie walked home that night, seething, burning with anger at Carter, at the world, at those angels and their unrealistic mission. They had obviously picked the wrong woman. In the days that followed, the burning anger became a burning ache. She hated her life, herself, and she was beginning to hate Carter. How could this have happened? Maggie became enveloped by these new emotions. She had always been able to rebound from sadness. Perhaps it was because she had always been so happy, so cheerful, that made this so devastating to her. Maggie knew she was close to losing hope. And she reasoned that's what God was waiting for in this grand experiment. When all hope is lost, there is no point to living. Hope, not love, is what brought her here. Hope was all she had when she was leaving her ruined body on Interstate 95. And that hope, that things would get better, that Carter would love her, that she would have her baby, was all but gone. She had failed herself, she had failed God.

Despite trying valiantly to remain cheerful and keep busy, she began feeling more and more sad. Everything was dark and murky. She cried so much, her eyes were constantly gritty and sore. With nothing to look forward to, with no escape from the pain, Maggie began slipping further and further away from the happy, hopeful woman she had once been. She no longer cared that Carter did not love her. She no longer cared that she would not have her baby. She no longer cared whether she lived or died.

She slept longer and longer each day. Why get up early when there was no one to talk to, nothing to do that was interesting. And nothing was interesting.

Carter was never home. When he was he shut himself away either in the library or his own room. Some marriage, Maggie thought on more than one occasion. When Maggie finally got the courage and energy up to barge in on him in the library to invite him for a walk on the beach, he was in a meeting with several men all wearing expensive-looking suits. His look made her shrivel and made the men he was with shift uncomfortably in their seats. After a hasty apology for interrupting their meeting, she left the library and went up to her room for a nap, even though it was only ten in the morning.

She wanted to be alone. Completely alone. She did not want to see Carter, or Bruce, or Stella. She did not want to walk along the beach. Two days after walking into the library, Maggie told Stella to take a vacation.

"A vacation? You mean go on a holiday?" Stella was clearly flustered.

"Yes. Don't you have relatives you could visit? I'm sure they would love to see you. I will continue to pay you, of course."

"Pay me even though I'm not working? I've never heard of such a thing. Have I done something wrong, Mrs. Johnsbury?"

Maggie sighed, a bit exasperated. "This is a reward for your loyal service, Stella. It's a good thing. I'm giving you a holiday because you've done such a fine job. I think one month should be just about right. You've barely had any time off. Please accept this as it was intended."

A smile lit up Stella's face. She was so pleased, she failed to see Mrs. Johnsbury's eyes looked slightly odd, blank, and lifeless. "Well, I've got a brother in Boston I haven't seen in years. And nieces and nephews. Why thank you, Mrs. Johnsbury. Thank you."

"Please just have some fun, Stella. You deserve it. You may leave tomorrow if you wish." Maggie knew she would never see Stella again and was tempted to give the woman who had been so kind to her a hug. But she did not want anything to change her plans or her mind. She did not want any hope.

"Oh, and Stella, please assign one of the new young maids to cover for you. It will be good experience for them."

"Certainly, Mrs. Johnsbury. I think Betty will do just fine." Maggie nodded her approval at her choice. Betty was a silly, rather slow girl and would be no threat to Stella. Or Maggie.

Once Stella left, Maggie began a pattern of days that would continue for weeks. She rarely left her room. Most mornings just the thought of getting out of bed made her want to go back to sleep. Maggie lay for hours abed, recounting her time here, her old life, wishing, wishing that things were different but having no energy to try. For the first time in her life, she did not wash her hair, she did not wash her body. If she ate at all, it was little. She spent long hours on her balcony staring listlessly at the bay.

No one noticed Mrs. Johnsbury was not about, for no one much cared. Bruce was solidly in Mr. Johnsbury's corner. Carter was trying valiantly to ignore his wife and pretend she did not exist. He drove himself harder than ever before. He worked day and night on the new mill, trying to make some time to continue his own investigation into the accidents that had not recurred since the fire. He ignored the pain in his heart, refused to acknowledge why he sometimes caught himself staring at the empty couch across from him. When he reached for her in his bed at night and found nothing there, he told himself he was reaching for any female. When she failed to arrive for dinner, he was relieved, not curious. When he failed to see her at all, he assumed she had finally given up and returned to New York.

Maggie had, indeed, given up. But she had left for her own little world, a dark, bleary place where she waited,

waited for her angels to come and rescue her one final time.

Four weeks after the Hellewells' ball Carter saw a young servant leaving his wife's room. "Is Mrs. Johnsbury back, then?"

Betty, who had never spoken to the master of the house, was visibly flustered. "No, sir. I mean, yes, sir. I mean, she never left. She's been in her room."

Carter was confused. He had not seen his wife for nearly a month. "How long has she been in her room?"

"Since I started serving her. Since Stella left."

Carter shook his head in confusion. "And where has Stella gone?"

Betty twisted her apron in her hands. She was clearly almost too frightened to answer and Carter had no idea his fierce expression was scaring the little maid.

"Mrs. Johnsbury sent her on holiday, sir. Three weeks ago, sir. And Mrs. Johnsbury's been in her room ever since."

"Three weeks." My God. Maggie, who could not go a day without breathing in the sea air, had spent three weeks in her room? It did not make sense. Then a thought hit him. Margaret was on a binge. But even Margaret had never hid in her room for more than two or three days.

"Why wasn't I told?" he demanded of the poor girl. She was visibly quaking.

"Mrs. Johnsbury said she didn't want to be disturbed. She said she didn't want to see anyone or anyone to see her. She was very clear, sir."

"Is she sick?" he asked, trying to find out diplomatically whether his wife had indeed been drinking.

"No, sir. At least I don't think so. Most times she's just asleep. Or just laying there staring at the wall. I didn't think anything was wrong, sir. She never complained." Betty was almost beside herself with worry, mostly for herself. It had been her experience that many women of the upper classes "took to their bed."

"You've done nothing wrong," he said curtly. "Please stay here while I check on Mrs. Johnsbury."

She must be drinking, he thought. What other explanation could there possibly be? And he continued to think that as he looked into her room and saw the drapes pulled tight against the afternoon sun. Maggie lay on the bed, sheets twisted about her, her hair a matted mess on her pillow, her face pale, her eyes closed. Drunk.

Then he realized there was no sickening smell of stale alcohol. There were no dirty dishes or glasses or empty bottles.

"Margaret." A small mumble came from the bed. He stepped closer, frowning as he saw how thin she looked, how pale. The dark circles under her eyes were almost frightening. "Margaret," he said, giving her bony shoulder a shake. God, she felt so frail. "Maggie."

Maggie opened her eyes slowly, taking her time to focus, and registered just a little surprise to see Carter's concerned face gazing down at her. "Maggie, are you sick?"

"Sick?" she repeated as if she'd never heard the word before. "No. Just tired. I'm so tired, Carter. I just want to sleep. Go away." Carter leaned close to her but detected nothing on her breath but staleness. If she had not been drinking then why was she abed?

"But it's two o'clock in the afternoon. You should be up."

"Nope. Time to sleep." And she rolled over, pulling the pillow over her head. Carter stared at her for a full minute before running from the room. He nearly ran over Betty.

"How long has she been like that?" he demanded.

Betty, suddenly realizing she might somehow take the

blame for whatever was happening, looked up at Carter with dread. "How long?" he demanded again.

"Three weeks, like I said. She weren't sick, so I didn't think I should tell anyone. Though I got to say she hasn't been eatin' much, true enough. But I didn't think she was sick. Is she sick, sir? Oh, Lord help me, I didn't know. She just seemed so tired, so I just let her sleep."

Carter tried to think back at the last time he'd seen Maggie. "Jesus," he whispered when he recalled it was the day he met his attorneys about his mills. Now he remembered her pale face, the look of defeat as she turned to go out the door. "Draw a bath, put it in my room," he told Betty as he walked quietly into her room. He debated whether to send for a doctor.

"Maggie," he said. He had never been more afraid in his life. She looked like . . . like she was dying. "Time to get up."

"Sleep." That one word, muffled, barely spoken at all, ripped at Carter's heart. What was wrong with her? "We're going for a walk on the beach," he said, his throat constricting when he recalled his reaction when she had asked weeks ago if he'd wanted to join her. She had not asked again. For the life of him, he could not conjure up an angry thought for his wife as he stared at her frail body, he could not feel anything close to the hatred he had almost convinced himself he felt. Pulling her around, he was once again startled by how fragile she looked, how pale, almost like corpses he'd seen, and he shuddered.

"We're going to give you a bath, comb your hair, get you awake," he said, smoothing her matted hair away from her forehead. "Okay? Marg . . . Maggie? Sound good?" He heaved her up with ease, remembering the last time he had held her like this was a day they walked on the beach. She weighed almost nothing. He pulled her nightshirt off, sucking in his breath when he saw her ribs poking through her almost translucent flesh.

Wrapping her in a sheet, Carter carried her to his room where Betty was still drawing a bath. It was the first time Maggie had been in his room since they'd made love. When Carter lowered Maggie into the tub and dunked her head under the water, she finally rallied, sputtering and wiping water out of her eyes. "What the hell do you think you're doing? Leave me alone. Leave me alone. I just want to go to sleep. You've no right. You don't care. Just go away. I hate you."

"You were starting to stink," he said, deciding that coddling her wasn't going to work. He was immensely pleased to see her rally, but hid his pleasure with a frown.

"Me stink? You stink. This whole fucking century stinks, stinks, stinks. And you're the biggest stinkeroo in this whole backward place." The water had done its job. Maggie felt more awake than she had in weeks. She smiled an ugly smile up at Carter's startled face. "Ha! I shocked you. Ha! Now leave me alone."

Carter did not know what to make of her outburst, but decided to continue being stern. "Finish your bath and dress. After that we're going for a walk on the beach whether you like it or not."

"Fuck your walk," she shouted, loving saying the word, the feel of it, after months of deleting all her expletives. Maggie was angry. They should have let her alone. They should have let her die. A few more days and her plan would have been successful. But now she knew Carter would not let her die. Damn him.

~ *Chapter 14* ~

. . . It was a long time before I felt myself. . . .

Carter stormed out of the room and Maggie garnered enough energy to wash her body and her hair, but was startled at how weak she felt. She even shocked herself when she got up and caught her emaciated reflection in the mirror. Her ribs clearly showed, her stomach was not only flat, but hollow, her hips stuck out sharply, her eyes looked like great brown spheres in her gaunt face. Her examination was interrupted by Betty who came to help Maggie dress. She could not get over how weak she felt, how tired. She could barely get the energy to assist her maid to help her into her dress, never mind pulling a brush through wet and tangled hair. Betty was still struggling to smooth Maggie's hair when Carter returned to the room, and again pulled Betty aside. "I sent Timmy to get Dr. Armstrong. He should be here momentarily. Send him up when he arrives." Betty, still fearing she'd done something wrong, could only nod.

Carter turned his gaze to Maggie, who sat staring at him like a child staring at a hated vegetable. Her dress hung on her like a rag and her face was still deathly pale, but at least her eyes were more alive. He was distracted by Dr. Armstrong walking toward him.

"You were lucky. I was just down the street at the

Brownings taking care of the old lady's gout. How that poor woman suffers."

Carter gave the doctor a brief explanation of why he was sent for before leading him to Maggie.

"How are you feeling?" he asked, tilting her head toward him and gently feeling her jaw and neck.

"Sleepy," she said, her voice tinged with belligerence.

"Nothing else? Do you feel nausea, headaches, muscles sore, feverish, cramps?" She shook her head to each. "How's your appetite been? You look like you've lost quite a bit of weight."

"Oh. Not so good. I eat, but nothing seems good. It all tastes the same. I don't know. I know I've lost weight, so I guess I haven't been eating," she said listlessly. Maggie knew how she sounded, but could not garner enough energy to care. He nodded, and asked another list of questions. "When was the last time you left the house?"

"I don't know. A month ago?" she said, looking at Carter, who nodded in agreement.

"And when was the last time you left your room?" Dr. Armstrong asked.

"I don't know."

Carter interrupted. "The maid said three weeks. But I haven't seen her in about a month." Carter flushed at Dr. Armstrong's look of surprise.

"Other than tired, Mrs. Johnsbury, how do you feel?" Dr. Armstrong said, turning back to his patient.

"I know what's wrong with me. I've read articles on it. It's depression. I can't believe it because I'm usually so happy. But, lately, I just can't feel anything but sad. I just wish I wasn't here."

"Wish you weren't here?" the doctor asked kindly.

"I wish . . ." Her eyes filled with tears and she whispered, "I wish I was . . . dead." I wish I was in heaven with my baby, she thought silently as the tears fell slowly down her cheek.

Carter felt as if a hand had clutched his heart and squeezed tightly. His resolve to remain detached was being sorely tested. He'd had no idea she was so unhappy. Margaret got angry, not sad. He had never seen his wife cry for any reason other than to get something she wanted, or in the midst of a temper tantrum. And he wondered, suddenly, why he cared. He could no longer pretend that seeing Maggie so disconsolate had no effect on his heart. My God, she actually wanted to die rather than continue living as they had been in a state of undeclared war.

"Mr. Johnsbury, I need to speak to you," Dr. Armstrong said. He could not help but recall the last time he had treated Mrs. Johnsbury. She had been a robust, feisty woman who bore no resemblance to this ghostly waif sitting on the edge of the bed.

Normally, being ignored by the doctor would have incensed Maggie. She would have demanded that she be part of any discussion about her. But for some reason, she remained indifferent.

Outside the room, Dr. Armstrong looked up at Carter, pulling his bushy eyebrows together sternly.

"Your wife appears to be suffering from acute melancholia. This is not something to take lightly. I've seen women—and men—slowly kill themselves like this. It's baffling, I know. Has anything like this ever happened to your wife?"

"No." Carter did not even have to pause to think.

"Do you know of anything that would have spurred this episode on?"

"I . . . My wife and I are not on the best of terms. It's not unusual for us to ignore each other for long periods of time though we live in the same house. She's never cared, but that was before . . ." Carter looked the doctor in the eye as he struggled to explain his strained marriage.

"Back in February she changed after that fall from

the horse and claimed she lost all memory. She did seem different, almost a different person entirely." Carter stopped. Seemed a different person. He gave himself a mental shake as he remembered what Margaret had told him when she had first regained consciousness. That she was not Margaret at all, that she was someone who had entered Margaret's body. It had always seemed entirely too absurd to contemplate. It still did, he told himself firmly. Carter felt a bit of the old anger return, knowing now that the ridiculous story and the amnesia were part of her game.

"She was cheerful after the accident. More so than ever. She stopped drinking," Carter said, shocking himself by what he was saying. He didn't even realize until now just how much Margaret had changed after the fall. She'd gone above and beyond her grandfather's edict. She even demanded to be called by a different name. The look Carter gave Dr. Armstrong was one of complete bafflement and wonder.

"In fact, it got so I would get angry with her for being so goddamn cheerful. I never realized until now just how different she is," he said. How good an actress, he tormented himself by thinking.

"Is she more like her old self now, Mr. Johnsbury?" the doctor asked, even though he seemed to already know the answer.

"No. She's the same Maggie. Just . . . sad. Terribly sad."

The doctor gave Carter a kind smile. "Sometimes a bad blow to the head can have devastating effects. I originally diagnosed amnesia, for that's what it appeared to be. But head injuries are tricky business. Sometimes the changes after an accident such as your wife suffered are so dramatic it's as if the person that existed died leaving behind a new person. Has she shown any other signs of mental trauma, forgetfulness, sudden temper, headaches, anything?"

"No. She's been healthy and . . . normal. And you have not convinced me that those changes were due to her accident. I'm afraid I know that is not so." But still. It all came back to him—Maggie playing with his brother's children, rejecting a former lover because of her marriage (of all things), Maggie laughing at his scowls, and trying, day after day, to become part of his life. Maggie loving him.

"What can I do?" he asked, the pain at those happy memories constricting his throat, making his words come out harshly.

"Just get her back into the real world, for starts. Take things slowly, but keep a close eye on her. From what she said, it's unusual for her to feel this way, so perhaps it's a single event that set this melancholia off. Some people are constantly fighting these terrible feelings of doom. It's sad, really, and for their own protection they are often institutionalized. I wouldn't recommend that for your wife, however. At least not yet. I'll be back tomorrow and see how she is. I don't think there is anything physically wrong with her. But we need to get her eating. She's so weakened that it wouldn't take much for her to become gravely ill."

The doctor paused. "Mr. Johnsbury. Since you and your wife, as you said, are not on the best terms, is there anyone else she is close to who could help her through this difficult time?"

"No. No one."

"Then I suggest you try to be pleasant." At Carter's deepening scowl, the doctor added mercilessly, "unless you want her to die."

"Of course I don't want her to die. I . . ." My God, he'd almost said, "I love her." Did he? Certainly not. What kind of a fool was he? Stunned and distracted, Carter thanked the doctor and returned to his room to find Maggie.

She was sitting on the edge of his huge, mahogany

bed, wrapped in a sheet and looking terribly young and frail. Her mass of curling brown hair still hung limply about her, but it was clean and shining and her huge brown eyes were wide and clear, if not a bit wary.

Carter let out a tremendous sigh as he saw her eyes fill up with tears. When they spilled over, Carter found himself pulling her to him, holding his wife for the first time in weeks.

"I just felt so sad," she said, hiccuping slightly. "I just . . . gave up. I know what's wrong with me. I'm depressed, but I'll get over it. I've never stayed this sad for so long. I just don't understand it, Carter. I'm always so happy. But lately, I've just felt so . . . sad," she said, as tears fell slowly down her already-wet cheek. Maggie hated herself for sounding—and feeling—so weak.

Carter turned her head toward him with his index finger gently on her chin and bent his head for a gentle kiss. But Maggie turned her head away.

"Don't." It was too late for kisses. Kisses would not make the sadness go away. Carter watched as two bright red spots appeared on Maggie's pale cheeks. Maggie knew she was not ready to live just yet. Just as she knew now she would not die. But that thought brought no happiness, only a dull acceptance that her life would continue, day after day, with a certain sameness.

Carter held her for several minutes, stroking her hair, his heart aching. Against his better judgment, he buried his head in her hair and whispered harshly near her ear.

"Maggie. I don't know what's been happening. Please believe me when I tell you I never meant to hurt you. I didn't think you were capable of being hurt by me. Do you understand? I never would have pushed you away if I had thought this would be the result."

A month ago, Maggie would have been moved. She would have cried and flung herself into his arms. But too much time had passed, too much pain. Those days in her darkened room allowed the wound to fester until it spread like a cancer to her heart. His words, seemingly filled with emotion, meant no more to Maggie than the buzz of an irritating fly. Maggie did not know this man who was holding her so tight, whispering warmly into her ear. The man she knew pushed her away, despised her, humiliated her in public. That was the man Maggie saw, must see. For the only emotion she could allow herself to feel was anger. Anything else was too dangerous. To love meant to feel pain. Anger was healing. It made her feel alive and so that is what Maggie focused on sitting there next to her husband.

Maggie stood up quickly and almost fainted from the movement. She would have fallen had she not put a hand on the bedpost. Carter reached out to steady her, but she moved away, jerking the sheet around her tightly until she was standing unsteadily in the center of his room.

"Don't worry, Carter, I've decided not to die. You won't have that on your golden conscience." Maggie wrapped her arms about her and shivered. She could not stay at Rose Brier with its soothing shores and sunlit rooms.

"You said we have a place in New York?" Maggie asked.

Carter looked puzzled. "Yes."

"If you'll tell me where it is, that's where I intend to live."

"No."

Maggie stamped her foot with anger. "I'll find out where it is on my own, then." She turned in a huff and stalked out of the room, swaying only once, before reaching the hallway.

Carter immediately ordered the servants who knew the location of their New York brownstone to feign ignorance should Mrs. Johnsbury inquire as to its whereabouts. With little effort, Carter knew it would be a simple matter to keep his wife at Rose Brier indefi-

nitely. Or at least as long as it took to make her well and
to come to grips with these damn soft feelings that had
invaded his heart once again. Damn the woman, did she
have some sort of spell over him?

Maggie was nearly exhausted by the time she reached
her room, which had already been cleaned and aired out
by Rose Brier's efficient staff. Despite her weariness,
she resisted the strong urge to settle herself into the
inviting bed. Instead, she dragged a brush through her
still-damp hair, pulled it back with a ribbon, put on
some shoes, and went looking for the New York brownstone.

By the time she'd interviewed the third member of
the household staff, Maggie knew she'd been sabotaged.
The servants, including Mrs. Brimble, flushed hotly
while lying that they had no idea where the property
was—even though most had spent several seasons there.
Cajoling, begging, and demanding had little effect on
the servants, and Maggie was frustrated to learn that
Carter still was master of this household.

Maggie went to the library, hoping to find some clues
among the books, or perhaps in Carter's desk, but found
nothing. She stood in the middle of the room, a frown
on her face, arms crossed and fingertips drumming as
she tried to think where the address might be. Her fingertips stopped drumming. A huge and devious smile
spread over her face. Margaret's secretary. Surely she
would find some clue in that little desk.

Gripping the banister, Maggie heaved herself up the
curving staircase, flabbergasted at how much energy it
took to walk up the steps she once flew up. Once in her
room, Maggie went directly to the secretary. Moving a
pile of letters that had accumulated as she lay in her
month-long stupor, Maggie jiggled the desk cover in
vain. It was locked solid. She cursed herself for failing to
ask Stella about the key as she stared at the offending

piece of furniture. As much as she liked the piece, it would have to be sacrificed, she decided.

Grabbing a sharp letter opener, Maggie jabbed at the lock, gouging the wood around it, until it began to give. With a little shout of victory, the lock popped off and another piece fell off inside the desk with a small ping. If Maggie expected to see a pile of bundled letters, she was disappointed. Apparently, if Margaret received letters while in New York, she did not bring them with her to Rose Brier. Darn.

The only thing inside the desk was a single piece of paper with an old-fashioned delicate scrawl on it. Curious, Maggie began reading the page, but it made no sense. It appeared to be a list of companies, dates, and addresses. It looked like something Carter might have needed, although the writing was much more feminine than his bold strokes. Putting the paper aside, with a mental note to give it to Carter, Maggie turned her attention to the small pile of letters that had accumulated in the past month.

Maggie's indifference turned to stark fear when she realized who the letters were from. Without even opening them, Maggie backed away from the innocuous stack, as if they were a writhing pile of poisonous snakes. She stood in the middle of the room, trembling, before garnering enough courage to read the things. "They're just letters," she said aloud.

Putting off the inevitable, Maggie put them in order before reading them. When she was ready, she smoothed out the thin pile of five notes, all in the same handwriting, and picked up the first.

M—Why didn't you come to me. What is going on? Certainly you are not still angry. I must speak to you. I don't believe you understand how determined I am. —C

Each letter was more frightening than the next, each with a more desperate tone. By the time Maggie got to the third letter, she was trembling so badly she could not read the letter while it was in her hand. Putting it down, she read,

I can only think you mean to betray me. I will not be betrayed. It is too late to turn your back on me. You are very much mistaken if you believe that by ignoring me, you will be safe. If you will not come to me, I must go to you. And it will not be pleasant, my dear. Believe me.

Maggie let out a shaky breath and wiped the tears of fear that ran down her face as she read the cryptic note. The handwriting was more and more erratic as the letters progressed, fueling Maggie's fear that Curtis Rensworth did, indeed, intend to contact her. She was convinced the letters were from him. As much as she hated the thought of it, she knew she would have to show the letters to Carter. She had to admit that she alone could not handle someone like Rensworth and would need Carter's protection. Grabbing the packet of letters she went to look for Carter.

She found him still in his room. When she knocked, he called for her to come in and his face showed his surprise at seeing his wife at his door. Maggie simply held out the package of letters in one trembling hand and said, "Read these."

Carter had been spending the last long minutes trying to understand why Margaret would fall into such a state and why he should even care. Was there some doubt in his mind about what her grandfather told him? Was there a chance that it was truly amnesia and not the ultimatum that caused such a drastic change in his wife? If that were so, he was the biggest sort of cad. For the woman he'd left when he'd rushed off to fight the fire seemed to be a warm, loving woman—Maggie. He shook his head, bewildered as he found himself separating his wife, Margaret, with the new gentle beauty that his wife had become, Maggie. One thing he did know was seeing her hollow-eyed and frail tore at his heart no matter how hard he tried to shield it. The damn woman still got to him.

When she walked in the room, looking haunted and shaking from fear, his first inclination was to hold her, to soothe whatever it was making her tremble so. But she'd held her hand out straight, not coming close enough to make contact, holding her distance physically, as if she must to hold herself away emotionally.

Carter read the letters with growing concern and curiosity. By the time he'd finished, his mouth had gone white around the edges, the muscles of his jaw flexing in anger.

"Who are these from?"

"I'm not sure. I got three others asking me to meet this person—one when you were in Pawtucket. I showed it to Bruce, hoping he would know what it meant. I . . . I don't know why, but the only name that came to me, maybe because of the viciousness of the letters, is C-Curtis Rensworth."

Maggie suddenly felt weak and walked over to the bed, falling heavily upon it.

"You are asking me to believe you don't know who these letters are from? Whoever is writing them seems to be sure you will recognize the initial and the handwriting."

Maggie rolled her eyes. "Gee, Carter, I never thought of that. Why, let me see those letters again? I'm sure this time I'll know right away who they're from."

Her sarcasm was not lost on Carter, who clenched his jaw in frustration.

"Then that is what you're saying. You don't know. Or you won't tell."

Maggie closed her eyes, suddenly exhausted, suddenly wishing she'd had not decided to show the letters to Carter. With a note of defeat, Maggie said, "Give me the letters, Carter. I'm sure it has nothing to do with you. I'll handle it. Whoever it is will show their face eventually, then the mystery will be solved."

Carter gave her a hard look as if trying to read her mind, her soul. Suddenly the image of her earnest face, gazing up at him, swearing to him that she loved him, swearing that she was for real, crashed before him. He turned his head away from her, closing his eyes, as if unable to look at her. God, how he'd wanted to believe her. He still wanted to.

Still looking away, he forced himself to say her name: "Margaret. I'll take care of the letters, I'll take care of Rensworth, if that's who they are from."

Against her will, some of the anger she held toward him faded away and she cursed herself for her soft heart. Why could she not remain angry? she asked herself crossly. And she gave him a tentative smile. It felt awkward on her lips, foreign. At the sight of that shy smile, Carter felt healed. She has such power over me, he thought, a little put off by his reaction. He resolved to not let his wife see that vulnerability, just in case it was Margaret he was staring at instead of Maggie. He gave himself a mental shake at the craziness of that thought.

"Are you off to New York?"

Maggie looked startled, then she blushed slightly. "No. I guess not. None of the damn servants would tell me where we live anyway." She gave him an accusatory look, which he ignored.

"That's good, because my family usually spends the last two weeks of August here and . . ."

"You mean your brother and his wife and the kids?" Maggie said, light coming into her brown eyes. "Reggie?"

"Yes. If you're up to it. It's still one week away, but if you're not ready, I'll tell them to delay."

"Oh, no. I feel better already. Really, Carter." She knew she needed Reggie, that he would help her heal, give her a reason to continue in this world. She needed a reason more than anything. Then a sobering thought struck her. Patricia. The woman hated her and might scheme to keep Reggie away. Carter saw the abrupt change and asked what was wrong.

"It's Patricia. She doesn't appreciate my relationship with Reggie. If she keeps him away from me . . ." Maggie was suddenly, overwhelmingly depressed again. It came with such suddenness it frightened her beyond reason. My God, was she really ill?

"I'll talk to my brother. I promise." She looked so fragile at that moment, Carter would have promised her anything.

Maggie looked up at her husband, seeing his look of startled concern, and laughed. "I'm sorry, Carter. I guess a person can't just snap back into being well." She fidgeted with her hands on her lap, deeply embarrassed and by her own frailty.

"The doctor said it would take time." Carter was beside himself. Margaret had always been such a strong woman. She'd had only two weaknesses, wine and men, but even drunk she had never appeared emotionally fragile; rather, she'd been belligerent and hostile.

Maggie resolved to get well for Reggie. She resolved to take healing walks on the beach, to eat healthfully, to try to forge some kind of relationship with her husband—even if it was a grudging friendship. He seemed to be bending a bit, even if it was out of pity, she thought. That bit of hope that she thought had been lost in her darkened room had not died out completely. It was a tenacious thing, this hope, and it was already beginning to grow, much to Maggie's surprise.

She planned to hone that small bit of hope and remake her life. What else could she do?

Maggie reentered life slowly, taking small tentative steps to reclaim her place in the Rose Brier household. She dared not enter the library, which had become Carter's brooding domain. She had lost confidence in her ability to charm him and so stayed away.

Maggie's appearance shocked the household staff, especially Mrs. O'Brien, who had developed a soft spot for the girl. She had loyally stood by Mr. Johnsbury, but found herself pitying the younger woman. Mrs. Johnsbury had faded away to almost nothing! So when Maggie got the courage up to enter the kitchen, Mrs. O'Brien acted as if nothing had happened. She firmly believed that good food could solve most of life's problems. Oh, she was a bit more cool toward her, but not anywhere as standoffish as she had been when Mr. Johnsbury returned from the fire. A person would have to be a blind fool not to realize that the reason for Mrs. Johnsbury's appearance was that she was despondent over what had happened with Mr. Johnsbury.

Mrs. O'Brien took it upon herself to fatten Maggie up. For the first time in her life, Maggie shoveled all sorts of fatty, high-calorie foods into her mouth, much to the cook's delight. After only two days, Maggie's color improved markedly, thanks both to good eating and hours in the sun. Maggie's outlook on life improved with every passing day, until on the third day since Carter had dragged her protesting out of bed, she found it hard to believe she had actually contemplated dying.

She saw little of Carter, but when they did meet, he politely asked about her health. Maggie sighed, recalling their oh-so-polite conversation at supper the previous night.

"How are you feeling, Margaret" Carter asked, stabbing his fork into the tender lamb chop on his plate.

"Much better, thank you," Maggie said, after swallowing a mouthful of green beans.

"Good. Good."

"Yes."

At least they weren't shouting at each other, or worse, ignoring each other. Maggie suspected this was what their life had been like before she had come onto the scene. Two well-bred strangers dining together, chatting about inconsequential things. Talking for long minutes without revealing a thing.

Maggie was trying to convince herself that this was enough. It was not such a bad life. She had a beautiful home; a handsome, if cold, husband; plenty to eat; and occasional visits from her favorite nephew. It would have to be enough. It was more than many people had, Maggie told herself. But her arguments to herself fell flat. She had always been so . . . alive. Now she was just existing, just as Carter had done for years. What she needed was something to stir things up.

That's exactly what she got.

~ *Chapter 15* ~

. . . I had mixed feelings about meeting Margaret's grandfather. After all, he was to blame for much of what drove us apart. . . .

Jonathan Edwards heaved his tall frame out of his carriage and gazed fondly at Rose Brier. He had spent little time at the huge clapboard mansion. He'd never felt quite right about taking over the place after winning it in that fated card game, truth be known. Other than the huge portrait that he indulged himself with in the library, Jonathan Edwards had left no signature on this place. And that was fine with him.

With some trepidation, he walked up the front steps. He had finally received one of Margaret's letters and had been informed by his secretary that he had received several of the missives at each of his homes. From all appearances, his granddaughter was desperate to reach him. He feared he had said too much to Carter and now regretted more than ever confiding in the younger man.

Jonathan was met at the door by Mrs. Brimble, who officiously led him into the main parlor. He would have been more comfortable in the rustically furnished library, which was connected to the femininely appointed parlor, but he acquiesced to the housekeeper's decision. Next door in the library, Carter heard Jonathan's arrival clearly. The two rooms shared a door and a vent, which made eavesdropping not only possible but unavoidable. Carter was about to enter the parlor to greet the older man, but he stopped just as his hand reached for the crystal glass doorknob on the connecting door. Jonathan was almost certainly here to see his granddaughter, and Carter was more than curious about what the two would say to each other.

Maggie's stomach did tumblesaults when Mrs. Brimble informed her that her grandfather was waiting to speak to her in the formal parlor. 'Oh, God. This is it,' Maggie thought. 'I'm not ready for this.'

Jonathan turned toward the door when he heard it open and found himself blinking at the vision before him. She was a beautiful, lithe thing, a waist so tiny, he could have spanned it with his hands. This woman standing there looking so solemn could not be his granddaughter. She simply could not be. Margaret had always been a beauty, but she paled compared to the vision standing before him.

"Margaret? My God. Look at you. I can hardly believe my eyes. You look wonderful. If I didn't know any better, I would think you were an impostor. Are you sure you're my granddaughter?" The older man was teasing and Maggie inwardly winced at how close he had come to the truth. Her grandfather opened his arms, obviously expecting a hug, but Maggie balked and instead walked into the room and sat on the edge of a chair.

"Yes, I'm your granddaughter," she said, for she could not bring herself to say "I am Margaret." She paused. "You're Jonathan Edwards."

Carter, with his ear shamelessly pressed against the vent, raised his eyebrows in surprise, then creased them in puzzlement. Margaret was calling her grandfather by his given name? Margaret who spared no affection for the old man, who flung herself in his arms at each greeting, even when she was miffed at him? Who called him Grampy? Was she trying to fool the older man, too?

Jonathan was surprised that this cool beauty had

called him by name and was puzzled by her stiff reception. But for some unfathomable reason he couldn't quite discern, it seemed almost natural for her to do so. She wore a dark green skirt, cinched at the waist with a black velvet sash, and a high-necked, snowy white blouse with bell-like sleeves that fit snugly from her elbow to finely boned wrist. These were garments that Margaret would normally have wrinkled her nose at as being too staid.

Maggie sat uncomfortably beneath the old man's perusal, not knowing quite what to say. She felt badly for him, for he no doubt expected a much warmer greeting from his granddaughter. In a flash of sadness, she realized that his granddaughter had died and he had not only been denied the right to mourn her, but was confronted with a stranger in his granddaughter's body. Should she pretend to know the older man? Give him a warm hug? It wasn't in Maggie to do so. She'd just as soon tell him the truth than pretend to be someone she was not. That would be more cruel, she decided.

And so, she decided to tell the lie that was less painful—at least to Margaret's grandfather. Selfishly, she was more concerned about finding out what he had told Carter that had made him pull so violently away than she was about saving the old man's heart. Irrationally, she was a bit angry with the distinguished gentleman in front of her for ruining the fleeting bit of happiness she had had with her husband.

"You heard about the accident I had on the horse?" Maggie asked.

"Yes. I would have come right away, but Carter wrote that it was minor, that you were doing fine. You certainly look wonderful."

Maggie looked down and shook her head. Carter was insufferable. "Actually, I was less than fine. I have no recollection of anything that happened before the accident. I didn't know Carter, this house, even my own name when I woke up. The doctor said I have total amnesia."

Her grandfather looked suddenly gravely concerned and took several steps closer to his granddaughter. "But certainly that is a temporary condition. Certainly you remember me. I've known you your entire life. Are you telling me, dear, that you don't know me?"

"I don't know you. In fact, the only way I recognized you was from your portrait in the library," Maggie said gently.

"Then why were you trying to find me? My secretary told me a stack of letters has accumulated from you asking me to come see you." Her grandfather sat heavily in a chair opposite her, still studying her intently.

Maggie stared at her lap, not knowing what to say. After all these weeks of hoping he would come, a part of Maggie felt it was too late. That nothing she could say could convince Carter that she was not the manipulative person he thought she was. Her driving need to find out what her grandfather had told Carter had waned. Carter may have been acting more kind lately, but he was still cold—and Maggie had finally come to the conclusion that their relationship would remain cold. She had slipped into a kind of numbed existence, going through the motions of life, but not really living. Still, she was curious about what horrible thing Margaret had done to cut the fragile thread the two had tied in those love-filled four days.

"Carter and I . . ." How did she say that she had fallen in love with her own husband? "Carter and I had mended our differences. This was before he went away, before he saw you. Carter never truly believed I had amnesia, but I convinced him, mostly through dogged determination, that whatever I had been before the accident, everything had changed. We . . . I think we fell in love. At least I know I did." As Maggie said the words, memories came flooding back, and against her will, she began to feel, began to hope again that something could change between them. She leaned forward and looked intently at her grandfather with her solemn brown eyes.

"I need to know what you told Carter to make things change. I honestly don't believe at this point it will make any difference. But I need to know so I can understand just why Carter hates me so."

Jonathan squirmed uncomfortably. He'd known he should not have told Carter about that damned ultimatum. And now he was facing his granddaughter, whom he'd never seen looking so dejected. It was something in her eyes, or something lacking there, that pulled at his heart.

"If what you say is true, then I've inadvertently done more damage to the two of you than I thought possible."

"You don't believe me." She said it as a statement, almost an accusation.

"I can see you are not the granddaughter I talked to several months ago. A person would have to be blind not to see you have changed, and not simply your outward appearance." Jonathan stopped, realizing he had just convinced himself she was telling the truth. "Yes, I believe you, Margaret, and I cannot tell you how sad that makes me. For me and for you."

He heaved a huge sigh. "You said Carter does not believe you."

"No."

"Then now I understand. I'm afraid you are going to be angry with me. But please understand, my dear, I was only thinking of you. I truly did not intend for the rift between you and Carter to widen, as it apparently has. Oh, dear. This is difficult." He rubbed an index finger back and forth across his forehead as if hoping to brush away his troubled thoughts.

"Although I love you dearly, Margaret, you have always been a trial to me. I have been too soft, and that's my weakness. Last winter, I tried to set things right. You had gotten . . . to my thinking . . . out of control. You were becoming an, er, embarrassment." Jonathan was clearly uncomfortable talking this way about his beloved granddaughter.

"I tried to set things straight in my own way. I threatened to take away your trust fund and inheritance unless you came to Rose Brier and acted the good wife." He misread Maggie's shocked expression, and quickly explained.

"I didn't have a choice, my dear. You were flaunting your affairs, you were mistreating your husband, ignoring your heritage. And you refused to bear an heir," he choked out, turning a dull red. "It was simply too much. I had to do something."

Maggie was stricken, her eyes, dry for days, filled with tears. No wonder, she thought. No wonder he hates me.

"And you told Carter this?"

"I told him about my ultimatum, yes. You see, I thought you two had patched things up. I thought, well, I suppose I didn't think at all. I should never have told him about my plot."

Maggie leaned back in the chair, looking quite unladylike with her legs stretched out in front of her. But she was beyond caring what she looked like. She imagined what it would have been like to be Carter hearing Margaret's grandfather blithely explain how it came that his wife had changed. Their hold on each other was so new, so tentative, his fear that she was only playing with him so palpable, such news would have been devastating. It clearly had been.

"My dear, my dear. It cannot be that bad. Certainly it can be fixed." Jonathan rushed to her, seeing her pale, despondent face, and held her hands.

Maggie pulled her hands free, not caring that such a movement was slightly cruel to the older man. "It cannot be fixed. Don't you understand? Carter loved me. He finally trusted me. And then, just days later, he believed that all along all I wanted was money. To him it would seem all too believable, knowing our history together. To him it would be the ultimate betrayal. Don't you understand? He doesn't believe me. He doesn't believe that I am not Margaret, at least not the Margaret he remembers. And this proves the scam. Don't you see what this would do to him? He gave me his heart and now he thinks I've stepped on it."

Maggie was blinded by unshed tears, but when she blinked and drove the drops down her cheek, she finally took in Jonathan's stricken expression. "I'm sorry," she managed to say. "I know you meant well. I know you didn't know what was happening here. I don't blame you. There is no one to blame here. Except, maybe, Carter, for not having faith in me. For not believing in me." Maggie felt a small stab of anger about Carter's lack of faith, but of all people, she understood his reasons.

Now she knew and that knowledge only made her feel more hopeless. She had always clung to the hope, even to this day, that once she knew what Margaret's grandfather had told Carter, that she could somehow make things right. But not this. She could never convince Carter of her sincerity. He would only think she was once again trying to manipulate him.

And where did that leave her? Should she continue living in this house, side by side with the man she still loved but who despised her? Could she do that? Maggie thought again of her long days alone in her room and she fleetingly wished she had taken a more direct approach to dying. She shook her head to rid herself of that thought. No. She did not want to die. But she did not want to live this kind of life. She was still young. She had a trust and an inheritance coming to her. She would divorce Carter, let him have Rose Brier, as much as that would break her heart, and perhaps they could both find happiness. Maggie could not help thinking that her angels had other ideas for her when they sent her to this place, but perhaps even they did not know the obstacles that existed. Stupid angels, she thought.

She decided to voice her thoughts to the man who looked at her with such worry. Here was a man who loved her—or at least loved Margaret—unconditionally.

"I will grant Carter a divorce and give him Rose Brier. This house is the only reason we're still married anyway," Maggie said with conviction.

Maggie would not have believed it if she had not seen it with her own eyes. Jonathan's eyes, almost moist with tears, suddenly became hard, beaming icy shards her way. His mouth grew grim, the hands that had held hers so gently clenched into fists.

"No. I will disown you. You will receive no money from me. I will cut you off completely."

Maggie widened her eyes in shock at the older man's harsh tone. Then she gave a small shrug.

"That doesn't bother me," she said matter-of-factly when she recovered from his verbal attack. "I don't want your money, this house, this life. I want none of it. I only want some happiness and I know I can't get that here."

"I mean it, Margaret, you will get nothing. You will be completely cut off from society. You will be poor, Margaret. I'm sure you do not know what that means. Your friends will not help you and I'll make sure your lovers don't either."

"Friends? Lovers? Who the hell are you talking about? I don't have any friends and the only lover I've had since I've been here is my husband," Maggie said, letting her anger control her. "I'm a college graduate. I don't need you or Carter or anyone. In a fair divorce settlement, I should have enough to live on until I get a job."

"What the hell are you talking about?" Jonathan looked at her agape. He had never been so furious at his granddaughter in his life.

Maggie grimaced. Forgot the old amnesia story for a minute there, girl, she chastised herself. She would have to learn how to control her temper. Clearly, her degree in computer science would not only be invalid in 1888, it would be completely worthless.

In a more subdued tone, Maggie said, "I don't know what I'll do, but I'm sure something can be worked out. Carter, I'm sure, will be more than happy to be rid of me." Unexpectedly, she felt tears threaten. Damn, she still loved him.

"I will not allow you to disgrace the family, Margaret. Your mother, God rest her soul, always put her family before everything else. You would do well to follow her lead."

"I have no memory of that woman. I have no loyalty to the Edwards name. I'm sorry, truly I am. But you have no control over me. I am a grown woman. If Carter agrees to a divorce, and I'm sure he will, then we will divorce."

The old man's face grew pale. "You have no idea what you're saying. The disgrace . . ."

Maggie's patience was wearing thin. "Oh, for crying out loud. How much more scandalous can a divorce be compared to all the things I've supposedly already done? You say I will lose my friends and social standing. Well, as far as I can see, I have no friends and no social standing. I'd be doing everyone a favor, including myself, if I just disappear. I can't continue to live a lie. I can't continue to live in a house with a man I . . . I just can't do it."

"Then go back to living in New York. Go back to that old life, Margaret. You do have friends in New York, you have a life there. I never should have asked you to return to Rose Brier. I see that was a mistake now."

Jonathan was desperate to save something of what he, unwittingly, had torn apart. A divorce would close all doors for Margaret. He was sure she did not completely understand what such a scandal would do to her and the family name. For certainly if she understood, she would never consider such an idea.

Maggie did have an inkling of what a divorce would mean for an 1880s woman, but she did not care. All she wanted was a chance at life, and certainly that chance with Carter was gone. But could she truly leave Carter loving him the way she did? She did not know.

"New York is not an option. I know no one in New York."

"But all your friends . . ." Maggie stopped Jonathan with a hard look. "You're saying you don't remember your friends. Of course. Then you must stay here."

Maggie rolled her eyes in frustration. This man just would not give up!

"Okay. I'll stay until the first of the year. If nothing changes, I'm gone. That's as much as I'll give you."

Jonathan sighed, having won this first battle. Surely something would happen between now and January to change his granddaughter's mind. This ludicrous idea of getting a job when she had absolutely no skills, and, he hated to admit, was lazy as the day was long—where did she come up with such an absurd notion as that? In the coming months, he planned to point out to her the obvious flaws in such a plan. A divorce settlement would never keep her in the style she was accustomed to living. When she realized this, he knew Margaret would change her mind about this ridiculous plan.

"Agreed."

Maggie let out a puff of pent-up air. That was settled. For now. Remembering her role as hostess, Maggie asked if Jonathan could stay for an extended visit, but he declined, saying he had plans to visit old friends in the area he hadn't seen in years. "Newport's getting so crowded these days that some of the oldest families are beginning to avoid the place," he said.

Maggie could only smile, thinking about the bustling summer hot spot of the 1990s that made this Newport look almost rural. She led him to the door and gave him a brief hug. His genuine happiness at her affection tugged at her heart. He was not such a bad old gent, just a bit manipulative in a well-meaning way.

"I'm sure I'll see you soon, my dear."

Maggie leaned against the open door as the handsome carriage pulled away and down the curving drive lined with towering elms. She had five months left here and she wondered idly if she could bear it. How could she face Carter's cold gray eyes when her heart ached so. Her resolve to remain angry simply had not worked. Every time Carter walked into a room, her heart began slamming against her chest, and it certainly was not anger that was causing those palpitations. She was only fooling herself when she tried to convince herself that the man did not affect her. But that just made the thought of living in the same house as Carter all the more difficult. The feelings of hopelessness that seemed to overwhelm her for weeks had all but disappeared. Five more months at Rose Brier. She could simply get through them and then carry on with the rest of her life. Or she could try to convince Carter again. Allowing herself a crooked smile, Maggie hugged her arms around herself. She made up her mind just that quickly. Sighing, she shook her head in resignation.

She simply had no sense where that man was concerned.

Carter leaned his forehead against the smooth mahogany paneling, his fists clenched tightly on each side of his head. The conversation between Margaret and her grandfather had torn him apart, for it left him doubting. Again. Dammit, the woman sounded so sincere, so convincing when she talked about not remembering. It was not what he expected, it was the last thing he expected, to hear Margaret talk about how they had been in love. To hear her say she understood his anguish.

And when she said she would grant him a divorce and give him Rose Brier, he needed all his strength of will not to barge into the parlor and demand she take it back. He wanted to shout to her that he would never grant her a divorce. But then he stopped. What was he thinking? Her solution was almost too perfect, wasn't it? He would be rid of the woman he loathed and he could have Rose Brier. It was exactly what he had dreamed of. He could remarry, have a real life, a real family, his reputation only being slightly tarnished by the divorce. Then why did the idea fill him with only rage? Why did he want to shake her until she took it back? Why did it hurt so much to hear her talk so casually about leaving him?

Carter knew the answer, but he simply would not let the thought come forward. He refused to acknowledge that he still cared for her, that he still thought of her as Maggie. His Maggie. Seeing her so distraught that day he discovered her abed cracked the ice around his heart, and in the ensuing days the crack had widened a tiny bit each day. He was coolly polite outwardly, but he watched her surreptitiously for signs she was slipping back into the blackness that nearly destroyed her. He noticed the dark circles that marred her beautiful face, the dullness of her brown eyes, the tempting mouth that never seemed to smile. She had gained a little weight in the past few days, but she was still so painfully thin, so fragile.

Despite his softening, he had finally come to the conclusion in the days following her illness that his life would revert to what it had been before Margaret's fall from the horse—stiff politeness when they were alone and well-acted public performances. She had taken him for a fool, but she would not do it again. He had been comfortable knowing where things stood, almost relieved that this torment would end. He was willing to accept that he had once again been duped by Margaret, but he refused to believe it could happen again.

Now this, a visit from her grandfather, to shake his world yet again. Carter had listened with disbelief as she had told the older man about her amnesia. He'd smiled with satisfaction when it appeared as though the old man did not believe her. But then the old fool had changed his mind. He'd always been so blind when it came to Margaret, Carter told himself.

But the talk of divorce. Of forgoing her trust fund and inheritance—and Rose Brier—just to be free. That was taking the drama a bit too far, even for Margaret. The Margaret he knew would never have given up her inheritance, no matter what. She would never bluff about something so serious, for there was always a chance the old man would take her up on the idea. No, she would have needled and cajoled, she would have cried and lamented until her grandfather gave in. He'd seen her work her "charm" on the older man before. He'd never heard her talk so bluntly to Jonathan. Margaret had numerous flaws, but Carter knew she adored her grandfather. He was the only person on earth that Margaret truly loved. She never would have dared oppose him in such a manner.

Oh, Jesus, Carter thought, could it be she was telling the truth? He felt his stomach twist at the thought. He pulled his fists to the sides of his head and massaged his temples. Carter was being torn apart, half of him wanting to believe, desperate to believe that Margaret told her grandfather the truth. Hadn't she sounded despondent, hadn't she sounded sincere? But the other half of him, the cautious half, the part that had been hurt over and over and was still healing from what he thought was betrayal—that half shuddered at the thought of believing her.

Margaret had said she would remain for five months before leaving. If nothing changed. If. He smiled. He would give her another chance. He'd watch her, spend time with her, and make up his own mind.

Dammit, he thought, ignoring the sick twist in his gut, he just did not have a lick of sense when it came to that woman.

~ *Chapter 16* ~

. . . I cannot tell you how stubborn Carter is. It is almost beyond explanation. . . .

Carter had been looking for Maggie for fifteen frustrating minutes before he stumbled upon her in the kitchen—leaning up against a tall wood-block table, one hand tucked under her chin, the other holding a stalk of celery, which she was using to stress some point she was making with Mrs. O'Brien. The cook was held rapt by the amazing predictions Mrs. Johnsbury was making, all about the rich losing or selling off the huge mansions they were building off Bellevue Avenue. Someday, Mrs. Johnsbury said, they'd be nothing but extravagant museums in which ordinary people like herself could stroll about. Mrs. O'Brien noticed Mr. Johnsbury first, and cast him a guilty look, like that of a patriot consorting with the enemy.

Now that he had found her, Carter did not know quite what to say. He was still torn, still doubting, but he could not help admire Maggie's slim figure as she stood, an unreadable expression on her face. He watched as she swallowed heavily and almost smiled realizing his presence made her uncomfortable.

"What's this about the Bellevue crowd?" Carter asked, curious despite himself.

Maggie had long come to the conclusion that while the Johnsburys were well off, they were nothing compared to the Vanderbilts and the Astors, who were building great monuments to their wealth that they had the audacity to call summer cottages. The Johnsburys and their ilk had their own crowd and only rarely reached higher and attended what was deemed a more "significant" event. That the Johnsburys lived in Rhode Island almost full-time, that they lived in Newport for more than just the summer, and that Mr. Johnsbury actually worked for a living, put them in a separate class of rich.

"I was just making some predictions about Newport's ultra rich," Maggie said, a bit defensively. "Basically that their reign here will be short but well remembered."

Carter smiled. "You're probably right. I hope you didn't count us among the doomed."

"No, of course not. We are rich, but not in their category. At least I think so. I'd rather have a home like this, in this spot rather than on Bellevue. It's too visible there, too showy. I don't know how they stand it. It's like living in a glass bowl."

Carter agreed completely. "Perhaps I wouldn't want their lifestyle, but I wouldn't mind the money that allows them their lifestyle."

"I suppose." Carter studied her intensely, marking her reluctant tone.

"Are you saying you wouldn't want to be as wealthy as the Vanderbilts?" he asked, not bothering to hide his amazement.

"I'm saying that all the money in the world, the biggest mansion in the world, doesn't guarantee happiness." This conversation was getting a bit too serious, as far as Maggie was concerned. There was a decidedly hostile undercurrent to this seemingly innocuous conversation.

"Then what does bring happiness? Good works? Good food?"

Maggie almost said "Love," in an automatic rejoinder to his baiting, but stopped herself short.

"Apparently, you have no idea. That's why you're so miserable all the time."

"I'm not miserable," Carter said, quirking his eyebrow. "I'm quite happy. I have a lovely home, a challenging career. I have good friends and a loving family."

"Good for you," Maggie said under her breath, noting he had purposefully left her out of that list. For some reason, he was getting her angry, and she had a suspicion that was exactly what Carter was after. For his part, Carter had no idea why he was baiting her. All he knew was that he was enjoying himself.

"I'm sorry," Maggie said, obviously not. "I'm not with you when you attend all those social occasions of yours. The only Carter Johnsbury I see is one who rants and raves and throws things. The only Carter Johnsbury I see works so hard he falls asleep at his desk and grumbles to servants about the noise they make and scowls at the stable boy when he brings his horse one minute later than expected. That's the Carter Johnsbury I see."

"Why, Margaret, dear, I didn't know you cared." Some of her remarks hit home, and made Carter uncomfortable. He had been a cad lately, but he had her to blame, dammit.

"Everyone's noticed." Maggie could not help the sullen note that crept into her voice.

"Everyone?" Mrs. O'Brien, who had continued to hover nearby, suddenly blushed red from her neck to her ruffled cap. She immediately found that the floor needed a good sweeping and decided to attend to it herself.

"You are quite right, Margaret. I am not the happiest of men. Why don't you tell me why. Hmmm?"

Maggie looked up, surprised by the admission, but sensed a trap. How had the light banter turned into something heavy and heated?

"I don't think this is a discussion we should be having here." She hoped that would stop the conversation. She was wrong.

"Where should we go, then? Perhaps the library? You seem to like the library. Why don't you lounge on that big leather couch and let your dress creep up just a bit. Why don't you stand in front of the window and stretch oh so casually? Hmmm?" Carter grabbed her arm to lead her to the library, angry with Maggie and angry with himself. This was not what he had intended when he had sought her out.

"Carter, no. Stop." Maggie's eyes, to her disgust, had filled with tears at Carter's baiting. She was confused by his attack after days of cold politeness and she was still emotionally savaged by the meeting with Margaret's grandfather and her bleak days in her room.

Carter's heart wrenched, but he led her out of the kitchen to get away from the curious looks of the kitchen staff. He dropped her arm and let out a harsh breath through his nose, angrier with himself than Margaret. "Goddammit. I'm sorry, Margaret." It was not a very convincing apology.

Maggie, head turned away, tried to blink away the tears that fell silently. She could not help thinking that Carter believed she deserved such treatment. She cried tears of frustration, knowing that nothing would change in the next five months. These past few minutes had made that clearer than ever, that Carter was harboring deep anger toward her and was not even capable of carrying on a simple conversation without letting his animosity creep through.

"Stop crying," he said, none too gently, realizing he was handling this badly but too confused about his own feelings to do anything about it. "I mean it. What are you crying for, anyway?" Carter turned away. "Jesus, save me from a weeping woman."

"Oh don't you dare pull that 'weeping woman' crap

with me." Her eyes dried almost instantly. "You set out
to make me upset today and it worked. See?" Maggie
swiped at the tears tracking down her cheeks with a
rough, impatient hand. "Tears. Big man. You made a
woman cry. Happy now? So, we find out what makes
Carter Johnsbury happy after all."

Carter winced. What was wrong with him? And so he
became more gentle, ashamed that Maggie was right.
He was trying to upset her, and he did. The damn thing
of it was, he did not know why.

"I am sorry, Margaret. Seeing you cry does not make
me happy. I didn't plan to get into a fight. Look. I just
wanted to tell you about the party next week. About two
hundred people will be here, and I wanted to warn you
in case you wanted to leave."

Maggie sniffed, giving him a scowl in response to his
seemingly sincere apology, but grateful that he had
steered the conversation away from the personal. "Two
hundred? Here?"

"It's our annual summer affair. My mother is taking
care of all the details, something she professes to hate,
but I know she loves. She and my brother should be
here by the weekend."

"Two hundred." The small event held early in the
spring had brought about seventy-five people to Rose
Brier; the thought of more than twice that number to
contend with was daunting.

"If you want to leave, I understand. You haven't attended in years, anyway." Carter did not mean to, but
his voice had become coolly disinterested.

Maggie gave Carter a searching look, trying to gauge
from his expression what he wanted her to do. "Do you
want me to leave?"

Here it was, Carter thought. It came down to whatever he said, did it not? He could tell her to leave, and
that would be that. Or he could tell her to stay. She was
leaving it up to him, not even knowing that he was still

aching from the words she'd said to her grandfather the day before. Those words had given him hope. Hadn't he decided to give her another chance? Hadn't he?

Maggie took Carter's hesitation, his look of uncertainty to mean one thing. He wanted her to leave. She'd just have to explain to her grandfather; he would have to understand. As angry as she had been with Carter just moments ago, her heart cried out for him to ask her to stay. She had her answer and began to turn away.

"Stay. Of course, stay if you want." His words stopped her, almost brought a smile to her face. She looked into his eyes, trying to see . . . something. But Carter once again had mastered emotions that were getting more and more difficult to master.

"I'll think about it." And then she did smile, acknowledging the small victory. Carter felt a smile tug at his lips, allowing her that bit of triumph.

The discussion about leaving, brought up so abruptly, reminded her of Margaret's pact with her grandfather. Maggie had been debating since he left whether to let Carter know what the old man had told her. Until today, Carter had seemed too aloof, too cold, to bring up the subject. She wondered what his reaction would be, if he would scoff at her, or dismiss her, or tell her to leave immediately, that in five months nothing would change.

The past several days had been quite strange for Maggie, who was still recovering physically and emotionally to what she referred secretly to as her "dark month." Despite Carter's warmth the day he discovered her abed, he had quickly reverted to character, spending as little time in her company as possible. She might tell herself that is what she wanted, but Maggie was hurt by his emotional abandonment, although she told herself again and again she must try to understand. Margaret's grandfather may have explained why Carter was so deeply hurt, but even that knowledge did nothing to help her bridge the gap between husband and wife. But here had been an opening. Carter, for whatever reason, had broken down that emotional barrier he had erected by picking a fight. Not much of a break, Maggie thought ruefully, but it was a start. If she really wanted to make some inroads, she would have to punch a bigger hole through the cold brick wall surrounding her husband's heart.

"Let's talk." Maggie grabbed his arm, trying not to notice his muscles flexing beneath her hand, and led him to the main parlor. Carter followed, ignoring the jolt of electricity that shot through him at her touch. He suspected what she wanted to talk about and was not sure he was ready for such a discussion.

Once inside, Maggie closed the double doors and turned to face Carter, who stood awkwardly in the middle of the room. He looked so masculine standing amid all the delicate, feminine furnishings in the parlor. Maggie gave him a tentative smile.

"My grandfather came to visit two days ago." Carter inclined his head to indicate he knew. Maggie twisted her hands together nervously, then grabbed her skirts to stopped the nervous habit, making her appear even more unsure.

"He told me about the ultimatum." Having said it, Maggie let out a sigh of relief. Just saying those words seemed to open the floodgates, and she began to talk quickly, leaving no room for Carter to reply. Turning her back to Carter, fingering the back of a Windsor chair, she began.

"I know you won't believe me, but that was the first time I heard about the deal he made with . . . me. Now I know why you reacted the way you did and why you felt so betrayed and why you . . ." A heavy breath. "And why you don't . . . care for me anymore." Maggie turned, her brown eyes so big, so filled with pain. "I understand, Carter. Truly I do. But it hurts just the same knowing you don't believe me. That's a kind of betrayal, too, you know. I know you have far more reason to hate me, I know our history together has made it difficult for you to believe anything I say or do, but I swore to you once not to hurt you. And if there was anything I could have done to change what has happened I'd have done it. I know it's too late. But, anyway. I just wanted to let you know that . . ." Maggie stopped searching for the words. "I guess I just want you to know, whether you believe me or not, that I didn't break my promise to you."

Carter swept a hand through his thick hair and kept it behind his head, kneading the back of his neck. "I don't know what you want me to say."

Maggie felt her throat constrict, but this time she refused to give in to those damn tears. In a perfect world, Carter would have come to her and told her he believed her. He would have apologized for being so blind, that of course he knew she loved him, that of course he believed she never would hurt him intentionally. But he just stood there, kneading the back of his neck, his expression unreadable.

"I promised my grandfather I'd remain here until January. Then, if you agree, we can divorce." Maggie was amazed at her businesslike tone.

Carter continued to knead his neck and remained silent.

"I'll give you Rose Brier. Well, actually, I'll sell you Rose Brier since my grandfather said he'd cut off my inheritance and trust. That means I'll need some money. I'll just ask enough so I can live comfortably until I get back on my feet. I'll be out of your life, and you'll have Rose Brier." Maggie stopped, trying to read something in Carter's expression. She continued to talk, more to herself than to Carter, for it was as if he were no longer in the room. "We're both young enough to find some happiness. I can remarry. I'm still young enough to start a family, have babies . . . my baby."

Carter's head snapped up. "What did you say?"

Startled by his reaction, Maggie stammered, "I was just thinking aloud. I just said I could remarry. So could you."

"No. The other part. The part about babies."

"Oh." Maggie flushed with unexpected embarrassment. "I was just saying I'm still young enough to have a family."

Carter sat down heavily in the nearest chair, his elbows on his knees, his big hands drawn into fists against his forehead. He was lost in an ugly memory, a discussion he'd had with Margaret just weeks after they were married. Despite his disgust with himself and his hurt over her lack of virginity, for a time Carter had tried to make something of his marriage. Margaret had gone into the marriage bed willing enough, but was soon pleading a headache or other ailment each time he approached her. He had finally pleaded with her, saying that no children would come of the marriage if they did not make love.

"Of course not, silly," she had said. "Why do you think I am keeping you out of my bed? Do you think I want to become a fat cow like Elizabeth Windsor? You should see her now, sagging and pudgy. She used to have a figure better than mine. She actually held the little things to her breasts when they could have afforded a wet nurse. It was a disgusting display." Margaret had shivered delicately. She had then gone on to explain that a doctor, thinking he was assisting her in creating a family, told her about a woman's cycle. Just to be safe, Margaret extended the days he said were "safe" even more, just to be sure.

"But I want children," Carter had said. "That's part of being married."

"That's not part of being married to me," Margaret had said, punching a little fist into her pillow.

Ironically, despite her fears of losing her figure in

childbirth, she had quickly lost it to rich foods and too much wine, much to Carter's disgust and despair.

Carter shook his head slightly to escape that ugly memory and looked up at Maggie, who gazed at him worriedly. He gave her a crooked smile. "You told me you didn't want children, Margaret."

Maggie gave him a look that bordered on pity. "Oh, Carter. All I can say is, that wasn't me." Maggie clenched her fist in frustration, angry once again at Margaret. At every turn that woman was thwarting her. It was a good thing the earth was rid of her, but why in blazes had her angels decided to put her in Margaret's evil little body? Maggie paced, stomping back and forth, ignoring Carter's intense gaze. Goddamn that woman, she thought, realizing that He probably already had.

Carter made a steeple of his hands, rested his chin on two thumbs, and looked at his angry wife thoughtfully. Another puzzle piece had fit into place.

"Let's see where things stand in January," Carter said, and walked from the room.

His words stopped Maggie in her tracks. Hope sprung up before her newfound cynicism could stomp it down. Maggie clasped her hands together to suppress her happiness, but a broad smile erupted despite her good intentions. Hot damn!

"No one knows where Rensworth is," Bruce told Carter later that day. "He's disappeared."

"No one just disappears. But the fact that he cannot be found is mighty suspicious."

"That thought did cross my mind." Bruce had returned from a weeklong investigation into the whereabouts of Mr. Curtis Rensworth. In that time, no more mysterious letters had arrived at Rose Brier, and the man himself appeared to have disappeared. But the trip had not been without some gains.

"Our Mr. Rensworth had been accumulating some

debt," Bruce reported, glancing down at his notes. "And that may be the reason he's gone underground. But it could also be the reason he's been so persistent with Mrs. Johnsbury. Perhaps, if you'll excuse me, sir, he expects some sort of money from Mrs. Johnsbury. I did hear from more than one person that the two had been closer than we originally thought. Which makes me wonder why Mrs. Johnsbury didn't recognize his writing."

Bruce left that last hanging as an accusation. He had gotten angrier and angrier the more he thought about Mrs. Johnsbury's betrayal. He had not been at Rose Brier much in the past six weeks, and so had not seen Maggie. It was infinitely easier to feed his anger when he did not see her sad eyes looking at him.

"I don't believe she did recognize the writing, Bruce." He left it at that, no explanation. Bruce gave his employer a sharp look, but said nothing.

"Oh, and I do have proof that Rensworth did, indeed, write those letters." Bruce slapped three letters to creditors signed by Rensworth as proof. The writing, Carter noted, matched those of the notes sent to Margaret.

"Let's discuss what we know," Carter said, leaning back in his leather chair. "We know Rensworth and Margaret had some sort of relationship. I suspect they were lovers for quite some time. I have a strong notion Margaret helped finance the little weasel, but for some reason or other Margaret stopped payments. Rensworth could have been blackmailing Margaret, but I doubt it. I'm sure any money Margaret gave Rensworth was voluntary in nature, until fairly recently. Obviously they were not on good terms in May at the party, based on what happened there. We know that without Margaret, Rensworth has been unable to pay his creditors and that would explain the increasing desperation of his notes. Did I miss anything?"

"Well. We know that Margaret was lying when she

said she didn't know who the notes were from." Bruce was surprised Carter had not mentioned that very pertinent fact.

"I'm not so sure."

"What?" Bruce could not hide his surprise. "Did something happen here in the past few weeks? Have I missed something?"

"Everything is not as cut and dried as I first thought."

"Meaning?"

Carter gave his friend a thin smile. "I have some reason to believe we may have judged Margaret a bit too quickly. A bit too harshly."

Bruce gave Carter a look of pure disbelief. Was this not the man who locked himself in his library for three days because his wife had betrayed him? Had he not been told in no uncertain terms that Margaret's so-called personality change had been financially motivated?

"Carter, what the hell are you talking about?" Bruce rarely called him by his first name, preferring to keep a certain distance despite their being friends. That he had used his name and cursed in the same sentence was quite telling, Carter thought.

"Margaret's grandfather came to visit her and I happened to be in here when they were next door," he said, jabbing his thumb toward the door that connected to the parlor. "Let's just say that what I overheard bothered me. Apparently she didn't know about the ultimatum."

At Bruce's look of disbelief, Carter quickly explained.

"You had to have heard her. No one could act that well. She couldn't have known I was overhearing their every word."

"Why not? She's lived in this house, too, and would know the two rooms are hardly private. She knows you spend most of your time in this library. Why do you insist on doing this to yourself?" Bruce rarely spoke so frankly to Carter, but this affected him, too. He had been taken in by the girl, and he refused to believe that all the animosity he had been harboring toward her was ill spent. It had been difficult to convince him that Mrs. Johnsbury had duped them all, it would be even more difficult to convince him she was sincere.

"You didn't hear her," Carter said stubbornly, angry that Bruce would fertilize the seeds of doubt that had been planted by her grandfather. "She says she's leaving in January, she says she'll grant me a divorce, sell me Rose Brier, and go on her merry way."

"She won't do that, sir."

"I believe she will." Carter was getting impatient with Bruce. "As I said, you didn't hear her. You didn't see her when she was ill."

"Bah, you've grown soft," Bruce said with disgust. "I'll admit she got to me, and that's not an easy thing to do, let me tell you. But not again. Fool me once, sir, and I don't give you another chance. Before you go and lose your heart again, tell me one thing. When you first met her, when you asked her to be your wife, did you ever, for one moment, believe she could be the woman she turned out to be? Remember, Carter, she is a great actress, she's had a lot of practice. I, for one, refuse to be part of her audience."

"Jesus Christ." Carter angrily ran a hand through his hair. "You're probably right. I'm sure you're right. But I've given her until January. She has my word on it, Bruce, and I mean to stick by it."

"I understand, sir."

"So, it's 'sir' again, is it?"

"Yes, sir." But Bruce gave him a grin.

"I'm so damned confused, Bruce," Carter said, standing up to pour himself a small bit of brandy. He motioned for Bruce to help himself. "My brain is telling me one thing and my heart another."

"Your pardon, but are you sure it's your heart and not

some other part of your body that's dictating how you feel? Mrs. Johnsbury is a beautiful woman."

"Yes, she is. But she's been beautiful before and I've managed to resist her, er, charms. I don't know what it is that draws me to her. It used to be so easy to dislike her. Now, try as I will, I cannot hate her. And I've tried, believe me, Bruce."

"My God, you're in love with her."

"No." It was said with such force that the old saying "Me thinks thee protest overmuch" popped into Bruce's head. "That would mean I'm a complete fool. And trust me when I tell you this, Bruce, I am not."

Bruce gave a noncommittal grunt. "Do you want me to continue looking for Rensworth?"

"No. No other notes have come this week. Perhaps he's found another pigeon to pluck. Don't feel badly, Bruce, my brother hasn't had any better luck in his little investigation than you had with yours. I'm beginning to believe we'll never get to the bottom of the sabotage and the fire. Charles'll be here in a couple of days. Then the three of us should sit down and discuss whether to carry on."

Chapter 17

*. . . I don't know if Curtis Rensworth was always
evil, I only know that's how he ended up. . . .*

As Carter and Bruce pondered about the whereabouts of one Curtis Rensworth, the man in question sat not two miles away from Rose Brier in the
White Horse Tavern. A half-empty bottle of whiskey in
front of him, he stared bleary-eyed at the few silent pa-
trons who sat in the dim-lit, dark-paneled room. It was
barely past noon, but Rensworth was well on his way to
being more than drunk. Both paws surrounded his glass,
smudged to opaque from his greasy fingers. For long
moments his mind had been blessedly blank, his body
pleasantly numb from the drink. But his knuckles grew
white as he clenched the glass tightly when he thought
about the reason he was lingering in the tavern. Margaret Johnsbury.

He was consumed with rage. Why was Margaret ignoring him? For what purpose? He'd heard the ridiculous rumors that she and her manipulative husband had
had a reconciliation. It was preposterous. Margaret
loved him, not her low-bred husband. At least he
thought the lying bitch loved him.

Everything had been going so beautifully . . . until
the Johnsburys' party. After a month with no word and
when she'd failed to show up at their preplanned meeting, he'd been bold enough to show up at their party.

Although he knew she would be there, he was still surprised. For if she had been at Rose Brier all along, why had she failed to meet him? He regretted his actions toward her afterwards, for her husband had beat him unmercilessly, but he'd been confused by her reaction to him. She'd acted . . . repulsed by his attentions. Margaret may not have been the most passionate of lovers, but she at least was accommodating, submitting to his more base fantasies. Seeing her again brought back memories of the last time they'd been together, which made her rejection all the more maddening.

He remembered how angry his darling had been when she came to him with the news that her grandfather had demanded she make amends with Carter else lose her inheritance and trust.

"What else can I do, but go to Rose Brier," Margaret had whined. "I have to have that money. God knows Carter alone can't finance me. Is it my fault I have expensive tastes?"

Margaret had paced madly around her New York brownstone bedroom, decorated in opulent red velvet and looking more like a bordello than a lady's bedroom. Pausing and crossing her arms around her generous breasts, she had stamped her foot and pouted prettily, allowing her eyes to glitter with tears.

"There's nothing we can do. But we mustn't let this ruin our plans for Carter. It will be difficult, darling, but we must plan to meet. I should be able to get away. Oh, why does Grandpapa have to be so stubborn. I just don't know why he thinks it is so important that Carter and I keep up appearances. I was quite cross with him, Curtis."

"Goddammit, Margaret. Do you always have to bend to that old man's wishes? He has ruined our lives, forced us apart. Can't you for once refuse him?"

Margaret had looked quite shocked at Curtis' angry words.

"My darling," she soothed. "You can't mean that. Grandpapa has always been fair to me. Certainly you can understand his wanting his granddaughter to live comfortably. As much as I love you, darling, we both know that until I have my hands on that trust and inheritance, I cannot afford to keep us both living this way." She swept a chubby arm around her bedroom to emphasize her words.

"There is some good that will come of this," she said, drawing Curtis' head against her breasts. "It will be easier to get the information about Carter's shipments."

"That's true."

"And I'm sure I'll be able to get away. Carter ignores me most of the time I'm not ignoring him. I just have to put on a happy face." Margaret shuddered. "I can't tell you how the thought of being near Carter repulses me. He's so . . . robust, so base."

And Curtis, consoling her, soothing her, had told her he understood. But now, goddammit, she wasn't returning his letters, she was ignoring him, and at the party—he shook with rage at the memory—she'd actually pretended not to know him, pretended not to want him! He was being driven mad by the woman.

She had told them they would continue their affair while she was at Rose Brier, that she'd find a way to see him.

In the back of his mind, Curtis knew his letters were getting more and more desperate, that he himself was getting more and more desperate. He was running out of money fast and his creditors suddenly were not nearly as polite as they had been when Margaret had been feeding them a portion of his debt. He'd put too much time and too much effort to back down now. They'd been so close to ruining Carter Johnsbury. So close. Once ruined, Margaret's grandfather would quit his ridiculous attachment to the man. Without money, what in God's name could Carter offer Margaret? When

Carter was penniless, Margaret had assured Curtis that she could convince her grandfather that the marriage should end. Now he wasn't so sure that it was money alone that was driving the old man in his quest to keep Carter and Margaret together.

It certainly was more than money that drove Curtis to want to ruin Carter. It was also revenge against the man who'd ruined his life—Carter Johnsbury. He'd known Margaret years before Johnsbury came onto the scene. The two young teenagers had spent many nights, groaning and sweating wherever the two could find a private place. Curtis had simply been biding his time until she was old enough for him to openly court her. But her grandfather, damn him, had other plans for his precious granddaughter.

Her beautiful face tear-stained, Margaret had told him her grandfather was forcing her to marry Carter Johnsbury, a young man with few connections but a nice inheritance and a mind for business. Curtis had always suspected her grandfather had arranged the marriage to atone for his own gambling sins. Although he had won Rose Brier fairly, Curtis believed the soft-hearted old man had never felt right about accepting that estate as a gambling debt and so was, in a way, returning it to its rightful owner.

Even then, Curtis had relied heavily on Margaret for funds. His own father had squandered a vast cache of money on bad investments and later on gambling debts. By the time Curtis was old enough to tap into his trust fund, it had been all but emptied by his desperate father. Margaret had bought him presents, clothes, and had funded his little jaunts with no one the wiser. They continued their relationship throughout her courtship with Johnsbury. The thought of Margaret sleeping with Johnsbury tore at him, but not as much as the thought of Johnsbury using her money to help his own causes. It all should have been his! Margaret had pouted and

cried and told Curtis that marriage to him was impossible, that her grandfather had insisted she marry into
money—why, when she had plenty of cash of her own,
Curtis could not understand.

The two had convinced themselves they were in love,
and perhaps in some way it was true. They vowed one
day shortly before Margaret's wedding that someday
they would be together, and they vowed they would continue their relationship. And so they had. Curtis was
aware that Margaret slept with other men and it did not
concern him, for he knew she only did it for practical,
not personal reasons. He did the same. He only cared
that she did not sleep with her husband. Every time
Curtis drove into her, he was filled with a deep sense of
satisfaction that he was enjoying at least one thing that
Carter Johnsbury was not.

Curtis took a long drink of whiskey, loving the familiar burn as it made its way down his throat. He barely
had enough cash to pay his bar tab, something that
made him furious. He should be living at Rose Brier. He
should be a wealthy man. He clenched his hand so
tightly that he spilled a bit of the amber whiskey still in
the glass. Goddamn Carter Johnsbury to hell! And goddamn Margaret Johnsbury! She'd not even contacted
him after the fire, and he'd done it for her. Surely she
would know that. He'd come closer to getting caught
than he wanted to think about. With barely any cash, he
hadn't been able to afford to hire even the cheapest
thug to carry out the arson, so he'd had to do it himself.
Now he could do little more without the dates and shipments that Margaret had been providing him, except,
perhaps, to torch another of Johnsbury's holdings. He'd
told himself that was too risky by far.

But the alcohol was making him bold, and his befud-
dled mind imagined Rose Brier burning. A smile
crossed his hard lips at the thought of it. How fitting, he
thought gleefully. Maybe he could plan it so not only

Rose Brier would burn, but Carter and Margaret, too. Curtis had always believed the quickest way to solve their problem was to have killed Carter outright, but Margaret had always balked. Now, the thought of killing both seemed wonderfully appealing. They would clutch each other in fear, coughing at the smoke, cringing from the flames. It would be beautiful. He shook his head to clear his mind. What was he thinking? He could not kill his Margaret. Surely she had some explanation for spurning him. Surely. Johnsbury must be holding something over her head that she was remaining there. Could Johnsbury know about their plans? Could he have somehow found out? Rensworth's ego would not permit him to believe that Margaret had jilted him. It simply could not happen. She loved him. How many times had she told him that.

Drunken tears filled his eyes as he thought of his beloved, his Margaret. He must see her, he fumed, he must. Then she could explain, for there must be an explanation to all this. He wiped the tears away with the heel of his hand, suddenly embarrassingly aware he was crying in the middle of a tavern. He had to see her. Since the notes were not working, he had to take the chance to visit her in person. He still winced when he thought about the beating Johnsbury had given him, but he would simply have to take a chance.

~ Chapter 18 ~

. . . Even the sun has trouble in the wintertime melting the ice. But, eventually, it begins to thaw. . . .

"Aunt Maggie! Aunt Maggie! Come quick!" Reggie bounded up the stairs and flew into Maggie's room just as she was giving herself a final adjustment. Even after all these months, wearing these ridiculous long dresses were uncomfortable and she longed for her jeans and a T-shirt. Maggie could barely breathe in the thing that the seamstress had assured her was meant for more strenuous activities such as tennis, croquet, and badminton. Maggie's frown quickly turned into a beaming smile as her nephew tumbled into the room like a puppy. Certainly, if he'd had a tail, it would have been wagging wildly.

"Whoa! What's up, squirt?" Reggie gave her a grin, liking the new nickname. He liked everything about his Aunt Maggie. She was pretty, she smelled nice, and she knew how to play pretend better than anyone he knew. He knew his mother did not like for him to spend so much time with his aunt, and that worried him. But Reggie was already an independent-minded little boy, so he continued to be Maggie's shadow.

When the Johnsburys first arrived, Maggie's heart nearly broke at the reserved and shy little hello Reggie had thrown her way. She had missed him terribly, but it appeared he'd all but forgotten her. After giving

Charles, Patricia, and Kathryn polite hellos, she got down on her knees and wooed Reggie with funny faces until the little boy was giggling with delight. Patricia had watched with disgust, Charles with wry amusement, and Kathryn with an intensity that made Maggie decidedly uncomfortable. But Maggie did not care. She had her Reggie back and someday hoped to win Lily over as well when she was a bit older.

In the week since Carter's family arrived, the house had been in a turmoil. Strange servants and visitors were constantly afoot transforming Rose Brier into an indoor garden. It was all a bit much for Maggie's tastes, who preferred the house's simple elegance, but she had to admit that the ballroom oozed wealth when the workers were through. Ten new sparkling chandeliers hung from the molded ceiling, a water fountain complete with a Cupid spouting water graced one corner, and urns which would be filled to brimming with floral bouquets for the night of the ball were just some of the changes that had turned the sparse room into something out of Rome or Greece. Outside, caretakers worked nonstop digging a horseshoe pit, repairing two tennis courts, stringing a badminton net, as well as trimming shrubbery, planting decorative flowers, and placing marble benches in strategic places.

For the first time, Maggie realized Rose Brier's estate consisted of several acres. She had limited her wanderings to the house and the immediate lawn surrounding it as well as the beach. But during the week before the party, she discovered the estate contained acres of land crisscrossed with horse trails and smaller paths. She had not returned to the scene of Margaret's fated fall from her horse, and had not realized that the field in which she first walked beside Carter was part of Rose Brier.

She and Reggie spent hours traipsing about the woods, much to the bafflement of everyone else in the house—except perhaps Carter. Nothing she did sur-

prised him, it seemed. It was almost as if he expected
her to do the unexpected—almost as if he welcomed it.
Maggie shrugged when she thought of Carter's behavior
during the past week. He had seemed warmer, almost
solicitous in front of his family. Maggie could not help
but recall his treatment of her the first time the Johnsburys had come for a visit. He had been downright rude.
Granted, the two of them had been through the wringer
in the last months and had forged a sort of truce that
day in the parlor, but Maggie felt sure there was something deeper behind his behavior.

Despite being polite and casting intense looks her
way during dinner, Carter continued to exclude Maggie
from family events—something that hurt more than she
wanted to admit. The lot of them went sailing several
times on Carter's graceful sloop, happily bringing along
a picnic lunch. They'd come back windblown and relaxed, Reggie almost always asleep in Carter's arms.
Maggie would watch with a longing that was painful as
they marched tiredly up the last stairs from the beach. It
was during these times when Maggie almost longed for
a time when she was no longer at Rose Brier. Perhaps
when she left Rose Brier in January and was living on
her own, that terrible pain of being left out, of being a
castoff in her own home, would leave.

"Aunt Maggie." Reggie was tugging on her dress, obviously impatient for their day to begin. "People are
here."

"Oh, my God!" she said in mock horror. "Not people.
Here? Let's hide!"

Reggie giggled helplessly, despite his continued impatience. In a rather chastising tone, he said, "Aunt Maggie, you know who I'm talking about. Party people.
They're here."

That imaginary hand that squeezed her stomach at
times like this was back with a vengeance. Maggie had
never been nervous at social occasions, had always

looked forward to meeting new people. She'd always
loved a good party. But in this world, Maggie found
herself dreading anything remotely social. She wished
she could hide for the entire weekend.

"Are you sure we shouldn't hide?"

As if sensing that his aunt truly was a bit frightened,
Reggie solemnly took her hand. "C'mon. Everyone is
waiting."

"Everyone?"

"You know. Mother, Father, Uncle Carter, Grandmother. And Lily."

"Oh, Lily, too? Then I guess I have to go too."

Maggie walked down the stairs and spied them on the
front steps in a kind of informal reception line. It was
clear that whoever they were greeting were old friends,
for they were chatting amiably. Before she got to the
door, Maggie bent down and tucked Reggie's shirt in as
the little boy squirmed impatiently. "Hold on, squirt. By
the way, did you come to get me on your own, or did
someone tell you to come get me?" Maggie did not
know why the answer mattered so much, but it did.

"I came got you," Reggie said proudly. "I noticed you
wasn't here and came got you."

"Weren't here," Maggie corrected automatically.

Maggie hid her disappointment. She had desperately
hoped Carter had sent the little boy for her. "That was
very thoughtful, squirt." Reggie grinned and held up his
hand for holding, and led her to the small group on the
steps. Maggie tried to hesitate, but Reggie would have
none of it, dragging her, it seemed to Maggie, toward
her doom.

At the sight of Maggie being towed reluctantly by
Reggie, Carter's stomach clenched tightly. He had not
told his mother or brother of her apparent betrayal, but
he could tell they noticed that all was not well between
Carter and his wife. He knew that suited them just fine.
More than once his mother had tried to steer their con-

versation to a more personal level, and each time Carter
had successfully managed to deflect any discussion
about Maggie. He knew he was not fooling the old
woman, but Carter was in no mood to discuss his own
confusion. His talk with Bruce lay heavy on his mind.
Was he being a fool?

Since his family had arrived, he had devoted himself
to making them happy, and that meant excluding Maggie from almost everything they did. They had made
very clear what they thought of a reconciliation, and had
not been shy giving Carter their opinion of his errant
wife. For their sake, he had kept away from Maggie
except at mealtimes. He had not been immune to her
hurt; it bothered him like hell. The last time they had
come back from a day sailing on Narragansett Bay, he
had seen Maggie looking out her window and guilt as-
sailed him. But he had quickly squelched any tender
feelings by forcing himself to think about what Bruce
had said, forcing himself to remember how he had been
taken in by her charms when they'd first met.

There she stood, a bit apart from everyone else, back
stiff, chin high, looking so lovely in her cream-colored
gown that Carter found himself staring.

"Ah, Mrs. Johnsbury. It's been a long time." What a
neutral thing to say, Maggie thought, looking at the
young man before her. He was tall, slight and blond,
with unruly bangs he was constantly pushing aside. Next
to him was a woman who could have been his twin, but
turned out to be his young bride.

Maggie smiled and darted a quick look toward
Carter, hoping he'd come to her rescue. To her great
relief, he said, "See, Maggie, even George and Celia are
surprised to see you here." George and Celia. George
and Celia. Maggie was not sure whether she should continue to pretend amnesia or pretend to know these people. Certainly amnesia would be the simpler solution for
her since she did not know anyone. But explaining her

amnesia to all of the two hundred people expected to attend the weekend would be so tiresome, Maggie thought suddenly.

"Yes. George, Celia, it has been a long time." She could almost see Carter's relief. What in God's name had he expected her to do? she thought. Perhaps Margaret did not like the couple. George, his cheeks tinged slightly red, turned away to talk to Charles, leaving Maggie staring fretfully at Celia, who looked like a frightened blond deer.

"How long have you and George been married now?" Certainly that was a safe question, Maggie thought.

"Just a bit over a year. I'm sorry you could not attend the wedding," she said, blushing bright red.

Maggie clenched her teeth together, knowing there was some meaning behind that blush. She knew the entire weekend would be filled with awkward moments like this unless she got someone to stand by her side and educate her before she put her foot in her mouth without knowing it. It would have to be Carter, she thought, with a bit of dread. He would either have to help her or she would hide away in her room, something she wanted to avoid. Since her "dark month" Maggie had avoided her room as much as possible and had even considered moving to another. A weekend of seclusion, more than likely feeling sorry for herself, could be devastating, she knew. But it would be her only choice if Carter refused to assist her.

Maggie smiled blankly at Celia and nicely excused herself.

"Carter, before any more guests arrive, could I speak to you, please?"

Carter followed Maggie into the house. "Yes?"

"I was making small talk with Celia—who, by the way, I have never met," she said, throwing him a challenging look, "and I apparently said something wrong. I asked

her how long she'd been married and she turned as red
as a lobster."

Carter sighed. He'd known something like this would
happen, he just did not think it would happen so
quickly. "About one month before the wedding, Celia
found George in a slightly compromising position. With
you. You were just having fun, you said, and admitted
that poor George was innocent of any wrongdoing. You
were drunk. It was a minor incident, but for about a day
the wedding plans were in doubt."

"Oh God." Maggie was mortified by the story, but
pleased that Carter was filling her in on the past.
"Carter, what am I going to do? Have I insulted the
entire population of Newport?"

"No. Just our friends," Carter said dryly.

"This isn't funny." But she started to laugh, then
turned serious, wondering aloud, "I don't know why you
didn't throw me out."

"I didn't have to throw you out. You left, thank God.
But now you're back."

Noting Carter's frown, Maggie said, "You don't seem
very happy about the prospect."

"Why should I be?" Carter challenged.

"I guess you shouldn't be." Maggie hugged her arms
about herself. *If I hadn't promised that old man I'd stay
until January, I'd be gone,* Maggie thought. She scowled
at the happy crowd just outside the door and was almost
overcome with self-pity.

Carter cringed at her hurt tone. "You didn't drag me
in here to talk about the past, Margaret, so what's on
your mind?"

Maggie looked at Carter, her eyes scanning his face.
"Carter, I need help. It becomes more and more apparent every time I'm in a social situation that I am carrying an enormous amount of baggage. I feel like that
ghost in *A Christmas Carol,* you know, Scrooge's part-
ner."

"Jacob Marley?"

"Yes, that's the one. He carried around those big chains, weighing him down. That's how I feel. Like I'm carrying around this huge weight, except it's someone else's sins I'm paying for. Do you understand?"

"You said you needed my help," he said noncommittally.

Maggie gave him a little smile, noting he did not answer her question. "I just want you to stay close by, to tell me about the people at the picnic. I want you to be honest and tell me whether there is anything horrible I did to them so I can stand clear or at least not say anything that will make them uncomfortable."

"Is all this really necessary, Margaret?"

"It's either that or I embarrass our guests. Or I could just stay out of the way."

"Perhaps that would be best." Carter did not mean to be cruel, but he did believe Margaret would make too many people uneasy. These people were his friends and they were coming to his home to enjoy themselves. The last thing any of them needed was a reminder of the unpleasant past.

Maggie looked up at Carter, stunned. How could he say that? How could he? She'd been such a fool, pretending she had seen a new warmth in this iceman. Anger boiled up inside her and threatened to overflow. Every smidgen of self-pity flew away as if carried by a stiff breeze to be replaced with red-hot rage.

"You would like that, to lock me away out of sight. No way. This is my house too. They may not be my friends, but they're my guests as much as they are yours. How dare you tell me . . ." Maggie was so mad she could hardly talk. "I hope I do embarrass every mealy-mouthed, self-absorbed, two-faced person in this crowd. Including your snobby little family. The only person worth a salt is Reggie. He's the only honest one among you. To hell with your silly friends. To hell with you, Carter Johnsbury."

Maggie was so mad she did not realize she had raised her voice, or that she had attracted to the door the very people she was denouncing. Seeing Carter's eyes go to the door, she turned to see them with their shocked looks and censuring expressions. Maggie felt as if she were suffocating. She had not intended to blow up like that and was already cooling down and regretting her words.

His voice hard, his eyes gray steel, Carter said, "I think you owe our guests an apology."

Maggie looked at him, pain naked in her brown eyes. Even knowing how he felt about her, she was disappointed in his reaction.

"No, Carter. I think they—and you—owe me one," she said quietly. Holding her head high, Maggie gently pushed her way through the gaping audience. She had to get outside. Had to. Reggie apparently made to follow, for she heard Patricia admonish the little boy to remain where he was. Once past the drive, Maggie picked up her skirts and ran to the stairs leading to the beach. Several people strolled up and down the sandy stretch, a few swam, laughing and splashing, wearing their charmingly old-fashioned swimsuits that covered them from head to toe. Maggie wanted to cry, but couldn't with so many people around. She sat on the bottom step, swallowing painfully, with unshed tears blinding her. Why was she always crying? Ugh!

Carter was left in the foyer facing a silent and uncomfortable audience. "Son of a bitch," he said under his breath, turning away.

Kathryn excused herself from the gawking crowd, which hastily retreated to the porch, and walked toward her oldest son, who was clearly torn about what to do.

"I couldn't help but notice that you don't look like a

man in love. You look miserable, Carter. What has happened?"

Carter was still unwilling to share with anyone other than Bruce the story of the ultimatum and Margaret's possible betrayal. He was still too torn himself about what Margaret was. He knew, without a doubt, what his family's immediate and irrevocable conclusion would be. Carter looked up at the ceiling, high above his head as if searching for an answer.

"Something happened—and I do not want to get into what—that made me doubt Margaret's sincerity since the last time we spoke." He saw his mother's nostrils pinch and her mouth press into a frown. "But since then, I have seen more and more evidence that I have judged her too harshly. I have decided to give her another chance, to prove that she is what she says she is."

"And just what is that?"

"A woman who has been falsely accused." Carter found that a huge burden lifted as he said the words. Although a tiny bit of doubt continued to plague him, he realized he was finding it more and more difficult to believe Margaret was lying.

Kathryn could not help herself. She rolled her eyes in disbelief. "Oh, Carter." Her voice was tinged with regret, but also held a large dose of impatience over what she perceived as her oldest son's obtuseness.

Carter gave his mother a crooked grin. "Mother, you do not know the whole story. You haven't been here. I don't expect you to understand. But I have come to believe that the accident last spring did indeed wipe Margaret's memory away. She has been unfailingly consistent. For a while, I let my anger allow me to ignore that. And I hurt her badly."

Kathryn let out an uncharacteristic snort. Again, Carter grinned.

"Mother. Just keep an open mind. Now, if you'll ex-

cuse me, I am going to find my wife. I have a good idea
where she'll be."

When Maggie heard footsteps on the stairs several minutes later, she picked up a handful of sand and pretended to be fascinated by the way it slipped between
her fingers. The closer the footsteps got, the more fasci-
nating the sand got. And when Carter sat down beside
her, it was as if she had never before seen this gritty,
pale pink stuff. They sat in silence for several moments
as Maggie continued to pick up sand.

"I don't think you'll get an apology from my family.
And certainly not from our guests." Carter looked at
Maggie, her head bent gracefully, exposing the nape of
her neck as she studied the sand. "But you will get one
from me."

Carter brought a hand up to rest lightly on the back
of her neck, where a few loose curls caressed his fingers.
Maggie brushed the sand from her palm in a businesslike gesture and looked up at her husband. If her heart
were made of wax, it would have been a puddle, it
melted so fast. She simply could not maintain her anger,
dammit, not while looking at his handsome face, not
when those gray eyes were so filled with remorse.

"So. Apologize."

He smiled, causing her to catch her breath. "I apologize." He leaned forward and brushed her lips with his,
and she was so surprised with the gesture, she jerked
away.

"Sorry," Carter said, pulling away, but he clearly
thought Maggie had rejected his kiss.

"No. Don't be." And Maggie leaned forward and
drew him toward her with a gentle hand on his beard-
roughened cheek. She pressed her soft mouth against
his, then pulled back slowly, keeping her hand on his
face. With a small groan, Carter pulled her to him for a
deeper kiss and her arms wrapped around his neck.

"Aw, Jesus." That expletive came from Charles who was marching down the stairs, clearly disgusted with the display before him.

"Weren't the two of you just at each other's throats?" Maggie looked up at Charles and smiled. Carter scowled deeply.

"More of your guests are arriving by the minute, Carter. Perhaps you would be kind enough to be present to host your own party. If you can drag yourself away." Charles gave Margaret a curious look as if trying to figure out what it was about her that so clearly attracted his brother.

Carter stood and held out his hand to Maggie to help her up. "Are you coming?" When she hesitated, he bent and grabbed her hand. "You're coming."

As much as she'd fought to stay and welcome the guests, Maggie suddenly wished to stay right where she was. When she pulled back, Carter said, "Oh, no you don't. You were right. You are my wife. This is your house, and these are your guests as much as they are mine. You will stand by me and you will be nice."

Smiling, Maggie said, "Well, I will stand by you. But I cannot promise I'll be nice to people who aren't nice to me."

The rest of the day was a blur to Maggie, but thankfully, it was a pleasant blur. Everyone seemed to be in high spirits; a summer kind of casualness permeated their demeanors, making them more forgiving, more accepting of the woman standing next to Carter. No one was overly warm when greeting Maggie, but she did not mind. After a while, so many were about, they had abandoned any notion of keeping even an informal reception line and found themselves meandering about. Carter never left Maggie's side, and she found herself giving him quizzical looks. She could not help wondering why he was being so nice, considering how he had been in the past few weeks. His arm was constantly

about her waist, caressing the small of her back. And
Maggie loved the delicious feeling when he whispered
close to her ear about some awful thing Margaret had
done to this one or to that one. It was almost as if they
were talking about a third person. Maggie had always
thought of and talked about Margaret as if she were a
separate person. But Carter never had. It was heady,
indeed, to hear him talk about one of Margaret's misdeeds with laughter tingeing his voice, as if talking
about someone from his past.

"Ah, you'd better steer clear of this one," he whispered, nodding to a woman who Maggie thought resembled a vulture.

Trying to squelch a smile, Maggie listened intently as
Carter relayed one of Margaret's sins.

"We were first married when Mrs. Appleberry invited
us to her home. She's always been intensely proud of
her chef, something you knew, of course. You'd taken
one bite of her cheese soufflé and extracted a long bit of
hair from your mouth with much drama. After that, at
every course, you examined the food with exaggerated
care, obviously looking for more hairs. Every time Mrs.
Appleberry looked over at you, you were peering into
your fork as if the food on it were still alive."

"Did she ever invite us back?" Maggie asked, smiling
into Carter's face.

"Never."

It was as if they were conspirators in a spy game that
only they knew. They were having such fun, they did not
notice that people were giving them strange looks and
doing a bit of their own whispering. Many had never
seen Carter standing so close for so long with his es-
tranged wife. And to see him look down at her with a
smile, his eyes filled with admiration and . . . could it
be . . . love? That was the grand debate of the day.
Was Carter Johnsbury in love with his conniving little
wife? The poor bastard, if it were so.

Charles was getting damned sick of fending off questions about his big brother. When he'd first arrived at Rose Brier a week ago, he'd been greatly relieved to see Carter acting rather coolly toward Margaret, quieting any fears he'd had since the fire. He shook his head in disbelief when he spied Carter laughing uproariously, his arm supporting Maggie, who was doubled over, shaking with mirth.

"Damn fool," he said aloud, not knowing anyone was nearby.

"I'm not so sure." Kathryn Johnsbury was taking in the unbelievable scene herself. And she was not frowning.

"You know, Charlie, I haven't seen your brother this happy in a long time."

"Bah."

"Just look at him. Look at him look at her."

"He's always been a fool for Margaret. He's a sick man."

"Then look at her, looking at him."

Charles did then and what he saw shocked him. If he'd had a woman of Margaret's beauty look at him that way, he would have been hard pressed not to pick her up and carry her to the nearest bed.

"I'll be damned," he said, the awe apparent in his voice.

"Yes. I was surprised too. I was so intent on watching Carter, I forgot to watch her." Kathryn shook her head as she watched the pair. "Charlie, that's a woman deeply in love."

Charles watched more closely, watched how Carter's hand rarely strayed from Margaret's back, watched how she put a small hand on his shoulder to draw him down so she could say something in his ear. She looked up at his brother, her heart on her sleeve.

"It's got to be an act."

"We'll see, Charlie. We'll see. I'm not convinced yet either. Let's watch her, you and me, eh?"

Charles and Kathryn were not the only eyes fixed on Maggie and Carter. Curtis Rensworth, his rage building every time his pretty Margaret smiled into that devil's face, watched as well. He did not plan on simply watching much longer.

~ *Chapter 19* ~

*. . . Everything was finally getting better. I began
to feel as if I belonged here, and was not some alien
visitor from another time. . . .*

For the first time in months, Maggie woke up with a
smile on her face, her spirits soaring with renewed
hope. Like a flower too long without sunlight, Maggie
blossomed under Carter's warm gaze the day before.
She was a bit put out that one man giving her some
attention and a few heated kisses could make such a
vast difference in her outlook on the future. She no
longer thought it inevitable that she leave Rose Brier in
January. She stopped questioning why Carter had made
such an abrupt change and was simply thankful that the
change had occurred. There was time enough to discover what had brought it about. Maggie, her hair sleep-
tousled, her skin warm and glowing from a good rest,
brought her knees up and lay her head on them, allowing herself just a few moments of unabated happiness.

Since most of the guests had arrived the day before,
they had all headed toward the beach, where workers
had been preparing a New England clambake with lobster, quahogs, corn on the cob, and chowder. A huge
pile of logs had been placed on the beach for a bonfire
to be set later in the evening. A more perfect day could
not have been imagined, Maggie thought. Carter was
utterly charming and appeared utterly charmed by his

wife, many would note. Although many of Carter's friends felt obviously awkward with Maggie by his side, there was none of the coldness and rejection she had suffered at other gatherings. When the bonfire had been lit, to great cheering from the happy crowd, Carter led her into the shadows, making Maggie almost swoon from his kisses. He said nothing, simply held her and kissed her, molding her body tightly against his, allowing her to feel his desire. Maggie, too, was silent except for little pleasure sounds that drove Carter insane. She was afraid of breaking this magical spell that had somehow been cast, and she sensed that Carter felt the same way, so neither broached the subject that would have dampened their moods: her leaving.

When it was time to retire, Carter led her to her room and kissed her gently good night. Maggie was vaguely disappointed that he had not invited her to share his bed, as she had become certain he would. But she sensed Carter had more issues to resolve in his own mind before carrying their relationship to the next level. His kisses, while enjoyable, were slightly reserved, as if Carter were holding himself back, still wary, still cautious. Looking down at Maggie, her cheeks rosy from the fire, her eyes warm and trusting, Carter almost threw away his resolve to move slowly. But damned if it was not getting more and more difficult to imagine that this warm, loving woman she appeared to be was somehow a fraud. How could this impish angel standing before him be the evil bitch he and others believed her to be?

"More guests will be arriving tomorrow and some will be staying here. We're almost out of bedrooms," he'd said in a low rumble of a voice. "So you may be forced to relinquish your room. Any suggestions on where we should put you?" He stood close to her, one finger caressing her bottom lip. He playfully pulled her lip down, allowing it to snap back with a popping sound when Maggie pretended to mull the question over.

"I could sleep on the couch in the library," she'd said, in mock innocence.

"That would never do. What if one of our guests was wandering about in the night and discovered you in your night clothes? I think you'd better stay in my room tomorrow night. I'll sleep on the couch."

She'd given him a little punch on the arm, then pulled him toward her for a hard, quick kiss. "Good night, you." She'd quickly turned and entered her room, shutting the door behind her. But she'd heard his muffled, "Good night, Maggie." Maggie hugged her knees and squeezed her eyes shut in the pleasure of the memory.

Within minutes she was washed, dressed, and out the door. The house was quiet, for the sun had yet to make an appearance. Maggie wondered why she should feel so awake, for she had only gotten four hours of sleep. She walked outside, her bare feet and the bottom of her dress getting soaked in the early-morning dew. The eastern horizon was just turning pinky-orange, announcing to the world that the sun would soon be making an appearance. Birds had already begun a cacophony, and all but a few crickets had stopped their nighttime mating calls.

Maggie decided to forgo the beach for now and headed for the tennis courts. She'd been an avid player in the 1990s and was curious about what the racquet and balls were like. She would have to practice a bit to get used to hitting the ball from her new, smaller perspective, she thought, and so headed to the courts hoping to get in a few serves. Maggie picked up a racquet leaning against a bench and was alarmed at how heavy it seemed and how small the head was. Used to a light graphite racket with an oversized head, Maggie eyed this small, heavy wooden thing in her hand with wariness. The ball, made of rubber covered by white felt, was surprisingly like modern balls, although it seemed a bit more flimsy in her hands.

Not one to give up before even trying, Maggie went to the service line and attempted to serve. Whack! The ball skidded into the net and the racquet vibrated uncomfortably in her hand. Several balls later, Maggie was getting frustrated, for few had found their way into the proper part of the court. After using up her initial supply of balls, Maggie went about the task of gathering up the errant spheres so she could continue practicing her loathsome serve. Reaching for a ball blindly that had rolled under a nearby bush, Maggie's hand came in contact with a man's shoe. Maggie's head shot up and her heart literally stopped.

"I didn't know you played tennis, Margaret." Curtis Rensworth walked out from behind the bush, bent down and, grabbing both her arms in a steely grip, roughly lifted her up.

"Why the hell haven't you answered my letters?" His thin mouth was pulled back into a feral snarl as he shook her.

Maggie would never know whether it was a divine message or her own cool head that saved her. But she forced herself not to panic, not to struggle, although every instinct told her that she should. Instead, she beamed a smile up at Rensworth, relaxed and gave him a mighty hug.

"Oh, Curtis. Thank God! You have no idea what I've been through. No idea." Well, that was true, her panicked mind thought. Tears filled Maggie's eyes, real tears of terror, but she used them to her advantage, gazing up at Rensworth with what for all the world looked like tears of happiness.

Curtis' arms automatically went around his love, his face almost comically confused.

"I've been almost mad thinking about you and that bastard," Curtis said harshly. "I saw the two of you yesterday. You seemed to be enjoying yourself quite well." His arms tightened convulsively and painfully around her.

Maggie gave him a coquettish smile, hoping he didn't notice how her lips trembled. "Oh, wasn't I good, though? I have most of them completely fooled. Grandfather is so pleased with me."

Maggie prayed Margaret had told her lover about the ultimatum and she smiled with relief when Rensworth's face broke into a leering grin.

"So it was just an act." Rensworth seemed momentarily appeased. "But why didn't you answer my notes? Why did you fail to meet me? And why did you reject me and force me to almost rape you?" His grip tightened, bruising her arms, as his temper again rose.

Maggie blinked her eyes rapidly, anticipating a blow. When none came, she regained some of her confidence.

"What was I to do, Curtis? Welcome you with open arms and risk losing my inheritance? It almost killed me to treat you so harshly. You've no idea the tears I've cried over you." Maggie would have laughed at her performance had she not been so terrified and sickened by his touch. "I couldn't get away and I was so afraid any note I sent would be intercepted. I've been like a prisoner in my own home. Carter is suspicious of everything I do. My heart broke every time I received a note, knowing I could not see you."

Rensworth narrowed his eyes at her. "You could have contacted me. There were ways. You've been ignoring me. And after the fire, after I put my life on the line for you, nothing! Not even a note. I am not stupid, dear Margaret." He gripped her jaw tightly, reminding Maggie of the last time he had nearly forced her. Shaking her head, his grip steely, he said, "I could have died for you and you ignored me."

"The fire?" Maggie asked in confusion, trying to pull her head from his grip.

"Yes. The fire," he said mockingly, dropping his hand. "You knew I set it, you knew and still you ignored me. Don't try to tell me you didn't know it was me. I had to do it myself, of course. I have no money since you abandoned me. Do you know how close I was to getting caught? And I did it for you. For us! And you have done nothing!" Rensworth was so angry, spittle flew from his mouth, hitting Maggie's face. His tirade continued, convincing Maggie that Rensworth was wrong in the head—and that frightened her even more. "I have sacrificed everything for you. I've waited on the sidelines while you spent your money and lived like a queen, forcing me to beg for every dime you threw my way. This should be mine! You promised we'd be together by now. Do you have any idea what it's been like to see you simpering at that smug rich bastard who is living in MY HOUSE?"

Keep calm, Maggie told herself, fighting back the urge to run. She knew Rensworth would catch her, and knowing what he would do when he did was enough to stop her. Think, think.

"My poor darling. How lonely you've been. How hurt. And to think you did all that for me. I have been a wretch and didn't even realize it. I won't even ask your forgiveness." Maggie swallowed painfully, praying he would believe her. "I was so miserable without you, I didn't stop to think how this was all affecting you. I've been so selfish, darling. I had no idea your funds were so low. My poor, poor darling." Maggie forced herself to caress his face in a soothing gesture and tried to suppress a shudder of revulsion.

Rensworth grabbed her hand and pressed it to his moist lips. He so wanted to believe her. His darling. "No. No. I've been selfish, too. I've imagined you here, in the lap of luxury, without a care except to please that bastard. . . . Tell me, are you sleeping with him? I'd understand, believe me."

"No, Curtis." Maggie was glad she was able to answer

honestly, for this acting job was getting more and more difficult.

"Good," he said fiercely, a frightening glint coming into his eyes. He pulled her against him, bringing his mouth down hard onto hers and thrusting his rough tongue into her mouth. With all her willpower, Maggie fought the gag that threatened to expose her, and suffered the kiss. But when he pressed his swollen member against her, Maggie pulled away.

"No, we mustn't. We'll be seen," Maggie said, trying not to let panic into her voice.

"Ridiculous, no one is about this early." And Rensworth forced his tongue into her mouth once again, swirling it about obscenely as he rubbed himself against her, reminding Maggie of a rutting dog. Maggie could have cried in relief when they heard distant voices and Rensworth pulled away in fright.

"I must meet you again. Tomorrow. Bring money and the list."

"It isn't safe now. The party. There are too many people."

"No, it's perfect. He won't miss you. We will meet tomorrow. Go for a walk on the beach heading north at noon. I'll be waiting for you at the rocks. We'll be hidden there. Don't forget. Bring the money and the list. We've not finished the job yet, my darling."

The voices were louder, so Rensworth gave her another awkward kiss, missing her mouth when Maggie moved her head slightly, and disappeared into the brush. With a sob of relief, Maggie began running for the house, passing the two caretakers who unwittingly had saved her. Maggie ran directly into the kitchen, ignoring the servants there, and mixed a strong solution of water, vinegar, and salt. She rinsed the noxious solution over and over again in her mouth in an attempt to wash every trace of the vile animal from her lips. She rubbed her lips until they hurt in a futile attempt to erase the memory of those ghastly kisses.

Tears still coursing down her face, Maggie ran from the kitchen with one thought: Carter. Picking her skirts up, she ran towards his room like a starving man running to a table full of food.

Carter was still getting dressed when he heard the sounds of a sobbing woman coming down the hall and opened the door to investigate. Maggie flew into his arms, crying uncontrollably. He closed the door before curious onlookers had a chance to see what was amiss.

"What's wrong, Maggie? What's wrong?"

Maggie found herself hyperventilating and unable to speak. Her poise in front of Rensworth had taken its toll and now Maggie was near hysteria, reliving not only the horror of his recent unwanted touches, but also the night of the ball. "Calm down. Take deep breaths."

Maggie did as he asked, willing herself to calm enough to bite out two words. "C-C-Curtis R-R-Rensworth." She sagged against him, having finally spoken the words. Carter's breathing stilled and his body tensed.

"He's here?" Maggie nodded. "Did he hurt you?"

"N-N-No. N-Not really."

Carter breathed harshly through his nose. He should have killed the bastard when he had the chance, he thought. Carter walked Maggie over to the bed where he sat her down. Sitting beside her, he cradled her head against his chest and waited until she was breathing normally before speaking.

"Tell me what happened."

"I was at the t-tennis court. He was there. He . . . oh, God, Carter, he told me he set the fire. That he did it for me."

Carter was stunned. Never would he have imagined Rensworth would be capable of that type of deviousness.

"The Pawtucket fire? Rensworth? What did he say?"

Maggie took a deep, fortifying breath. "He said he set the fire. He was angry with me for not responding to his letters. He couldn't understand why I continued to ignore him even after the fire."

"What did you tell him?"

"I told him I couldn't get away. You had been watching me." Maggie had been staring blindly in front of her, reliving the horror of the encounter with Rensworth. But when she looked at Carter, expecting to see compassion, she saw that horrible coldness.

"Carter, you don't understand. I was trying to fool him. I was trying to get away. He was so angry with me. Carter, I lied to Rensworth, not to you."

"Damn." Carter cursed under his breath. He did not know what to believe.

"Carter. Look at me." Maggie got up from the bed, her heart beating madly with fear over what she saw in Carter's eyes. She kneeled in front of him, a small hand on each of his knees, forcing him to look at her. "I came up here to tell you Rensworth is here. That he is behind the fire and the notes to me. Don't you dare believe that I am lying to you now." Maggie's eyes filled with tears. "I'm afraid of him. He seemed unbalanced. I did what I had to do to get away from him. Please, Carter, I need your help."

Carter gazed at her, his expression unreadable. He was loath to believe her words, a fool to be pulled in by those watery eyes. His stomach clenched when he thought of Maggie willingly going to see Rensworth, then spilling some grand tale to cover her own actions.

Maggie read the doubt in his eyes and it almost killed her. She stood. "Fine, Carter, don't believe me," she said, her voice resigned. "I really don't care." After yesterday's tenderness, she thought Carter was finally warming toward her. She had been horribly wrong.

What a fool I am, she thought bitterly, to run up here crying and think Carter would save me.

"I never said I didn't believe you."

"You never said you did."

"Jesus, Maggie. Don't you realize how difficult it is to believe anything you say?"

She stunned him by softly saying, "I know."

Carter heaved a sigh through tightened lips. "Tell me what else he said."

In a monotone, Maggie reported the entire conversation, leaving out the times when Rensworth had forced himself upon her. In Carter's frame of mind, she suspected he would believe she was a willing participant.

"He wants me to meet him tomorrow on the beach. He wants me to bring money. He also mentioned a list twice. He demanded I bring 'the list' but I haven't the foggiest idea what he's talking about."

Carter creased his brow in concentration, trying to decide what to do. Should he confront Rensworth or wait until he caught him in the act of doing something illegal? He lifted his head when he heard Maggie's sharp intake of breath.

"What is it?"

"The list!" Maggie said triumphantly. "I think I know what he was talking about." Maggie grabbed Carter's hand and dragged him out of his room, down the hall, and into her room. Dropping his hand, she rushed over to her secretary, opened it, and lifted up a piece of paper as if it were some grand prize.

"I don't know what it is, but it was the only thing in Margaret's desk. I discovered it that day I was looking for the address for the New York house. Could this be it?" she asked, handing over the paper to Carter.

Carter could not believe what he held in his hand. Such a rage rushed through him, he unknowingly clenched his fist, crumpling one side of the sheet. Maggie watched his reaction, her eyes growing huge, as she saw Carter go almost white, his jaw flexing, his eyes burning with fury.

"Carter. What is it?" Maggie felt the same dread that washed over her when Carter had come home after just seeing her grandfather.

"Do you know what I have in my hand, my dear?" he said with such odd calm, it made Maggie shiver.

"No, Carter, I don't."

He looked at her, taking in the concern—and innocence—in her eyes. He put a hand to his head, stunned by what he had just realized. If the woman before him had indeed written this list, the last thing she would have done was lead him to it. Closing his eyes, he tried to think, tried to fathom what this revelation meant. Not even Margaret was bold enough to present him with this damning list and then pretend innocence. Unless she believed in her heart that she was innocent. But the list, the dates and locations of the sabotaged deliveries, were in Margaret's handwriting.

"Carter?" Maggie, relieved to see that awful coldness leave his eyes, reached out and touched his arm. "Please don't shut me out."

"Do you have a pen and paper?"

Startled by his abrupt change, Maggie gave him a curious look, then produced the items.

"Write the following: Danbury, Jan. 12, 8:30 a.m."

Confused, Maggie hesitated.

"Please do as I say." It was an order.

Maggie wrote the words, grimacing as she noticed the splotches that appeared at the beginning and end of each word. She had yet to master using a pen and ink and once again found herself longing for a ballpoint pen. Carter continued his dictation, and Maggie continued to messily write down what he said.

When they were finished, Carter perused her sloppy penmanship. Holding the two sheets in his hand, with an incredulous look on his face, Carter came to the unbelievable conclusion that two different people had written these words. He'd recognized Margaret's elegant cursive immediately. But the new version he held in his hand was almost illegible, filled with splotches and messy, rounded letters.

"I haven't been able to master using the damn pen and ink yet," Maggie said, wrongly interpreting his expression.

Carter put the two pieces of paper down and stared at her, a long and penetrating stare that made Maggie decidedly uncomfortable. It was as if he were trying to stare into her soul.

Creasing her brows in irritation, she said in a low voice, "What are you looking at?"

Shaking his head a bit, he said, "I'm not sure." An odd smile flitted across his face.

Sighing in frustration, Maggie said, "Well, could you at least tell me what that list is and why you reacted to it the way you did."

Carter obliged. "Last winter, several of our suppliers suffered grievous losses. Shipments were stolen, lost, or burned. At first I thought the losses were unfortunate coincidences, since it seemed every shipment was bound for one of my factories. After a time, it became very clear that the losses were no coincidence, that we were being systematically sabotaged. My brother and I were at a loss as to who was behind this. Who held such a grudge and had the means to pull off a sophisticated scheme like this? Now I know. It was you."

"Me?" Maggie squeaked. She would have immediately announced her innocence had it not been for the warm expression on Carter's face. "I don't understand."

"Neither do I," Carter said honestly. "This is a list of transports, times, dates, when those shipments were made. It is in your handwriting. Or at least what your handwriting used to be."

Realization dawned on Maggie's face. "Margaret,"

she said, without realizing she was again talking about "herself" in the third person. "That evil, conniving bitch. With all I knew about her, I never would have thought she was this devious. What a rotten thing to do. To try to hurt your own husband."

"You are Margaret," Carter said, still using his head when he knew he should listen to his heart.

"Carter. I know I'm Margaret," she said. "But Margaret is not me." She pursed her lips, knowing that what she'd just said made no sense. "What I mean is . . ."

Carter interrupted. "I know what you mean."

"You do?" Maggie clearly was doubtful, but allowed a bit of hope show. Carter was frighteningly relieved that the handwriting had been so markedly different. It was another bit of evidence that fit nicely into place. Oh, God, dare he hope? Just the thought of giving away his heart again made him ache. He looked at her, so lovely, her eyes shining with an emotion that Carter believed could not be feigned.

"I'm not entirely convinced," he warned, but his voice lacked conviction, even to his own ears. "Come here."

Maggie walked over to him, a shy smile on her lips. "Do you really think a kiss will help prove my innocence?"

"It might help. I cannot guarantee anything."

Maggie placed her hands on her husband's shoulders and lifted her face up. Carter brushed his lips against her, telling himself that in this, at least, he should maintain some control. But the moment his lips met hers, Maggie leaned against him, offering herself with abandon. He opened his mouth and urged her to do the same so that he might stroke her tongue with his. With a small moan, Maggie let her tongue dance against his.

Carter drew his head abruptly back. "What in God's name have you been eating?"

Blushing, Maggie stepped back. She hadn't wanted to tell Carter that Rensworth had forced kisses upon her—

and that she had pretended to accept his kisses to dupe him. She wanted to forget Rensworth's wet kisses and rancid breath.

"I rinsed my mouth out with, um, vinegar, salt, and water after I saw Rensworth."

"He kissed you."

Maggie shuddered with revulsion and nodded her head. Carter looked at her closer, and his eyes narrowed when he noticed the beginnings of a bruise under her jaw.

"You said he didn't hurt you. By God I'll kill the bastard." His fierce expression was at odds with the gentle way he touched her bruised jaw. He drew Maggie against him, holding her, trying to draw her pain into him. He stroked her hair, loving its softness. He drew back, and taking a finger, he tilted Maggie's chin up so that she was looking into his eyes.

"He won't ever hurt you again, Maggie. I promise."

It was a promise he could not keep.

~ *Chapter 20* ~

*. . . So we put together this plan to get Rens-
worth. . . .*

Curtis Rensworth was happier than he had been in
months, perhaps even years. His Margaret had not
betrayed him as he feared. She had responded so
sweetly to his kisses, so different from the last time he
had seen her. He ached with his need and vowed he
would make love with her at their next meeting. Margaret had always loved trysts that had an element of danger. If those damned people had not come along, he
knew they would have dropped all caution and made
love there on the ground by the tennis court. Just thinking of her left him hard and he closed his eyes and
rubbed himself to relieve some of the strain. He could
wait, he told himself. To be with his beautiful Margaret,
he could wait forever.

She would be bringing money with her, and that
thought made him almost giddy. He could buy some
new clothes, he thought happily, looking down at disgust
at the clothes he now wore. They were from last season,
starting to get a bit frayed and shiny from overuse.
Rensworth had always prided himself on dressing im-
peccably. He would pay off his gambling debts—or
enough to let him back at the gaming tables he so loved.
He let his imagination drift, picturing Margaret and him
once again in New York, arm in arm, attending the op-

era or visiting some of their acquaintances they had
been ignoring for far too long. He rubbed his hands
together in unabashed glee. No longer would he have to
avoid the gazes of people he owed money to. He would
regain his place in society, he would be respected once
again. That he had never been respected and only admitted into his small bit of society because of his family
name did not cross Rensworth's mind. His nightmare
was coming to an end. Thanks to Margaret.

Surely she was sincere. He clenched his fists when he
thought of what he'd do to her if he found out she was
playing him for a fool. She would pay, he thought,
grinding his teeth together in rage. He shook his head,
and let out a small laugh, passing his hand over his forehead, which was wet with a fine sheen of sweat. What
was he thinking? Margaret loved him. Didn't she? In
the back of his mind, Rensworth was a bit worried about
his confusion, about his inability to keep a single train of
thought. He put it down to being upset about not having
money, about not having Margaret. Who would not be
confused, he thought, thinking about the way Margaret
had greeted him in the spring with revulsion and the
way she had just melted in his arms. She loved him, he
thought with the smile of a simpleton. But his expression grew hard and ruthless and frighteningly intelligent
just moments later. God help her if she didn't.

Carter had gathered Charles and Bruce into the library.
Maggie stood by his side, a hand on his shoulder. Only
the tightness of her grip told Carter just how nervous
she was about this meeting. She knew how Charles and
Bruce felt about her and she feared they could somehow convince Carter he was wrong. Walking in the
room, Charles had simply raised a curious eyebrow
when seeing Maggie standing by his older brother. But
Bruce had not hid the hostility he felt when he saw the
beautiful woman who had obviously managed to manip-

ulate a man he greatly admired but was quickly beginning to think was the biggest of fools. The two sat in
matching chairs Carter had positioned in front of his
desk.

Where to begin, Carter thought, looking at the two
men whose opinions meant the most to him. At Bruce's
deep scowl, he felt Maggie's grip tighten suddenly, then
relax, and he could almost feel her willing herself to
remain calm.

Carter decided to be blunt and to the point. "Curtis
Rensworth is not only behind the notes to Margaret, but
also behind the sabotage, including the fire. And, as of a
few hours ago, Rensworth was here, at Rose Brier."

Charles stood immediately. "What? How do you
know this," he demanded, casting a hostile look at Maggie.

Carter almost grimaced from the amount of pressure
Maggie was putting on his shoulder. He lifted up one
hand and laid it upon hers, a gesture that was not lost
on either man staring at Carter. Maggie, not realizing
what she was doing until she felt her husband's warm
hand on hers, instantly relaxed.

"Let me start at the beginning. Bruce, you already
know about the ultimatum Maggie's grandfather gave
her. But Charles does not, so if you'll bear with me a
moment . . ." Charles listened, his expression going
from curious to angry when Carter described the meeting he'd had with Maggie's grandfather.

"I hated her, Charles. If I had been a different man, I
might have killed her. Instead I ignored her, and almost
got my wish." At Charles' confusion, Carter explained
how Maggie had come so close to death and only a few
weeks ago had been just a few days away from closing
her eyes forever. Maggie's eyes filled with tears, remembering her anguish, but she blinked them away.

"It wasn't until Maggie's grandfather came to visit her
that I began to have doubts. They met in the main par-

lor, I was in here. As you know, sound travels quite nicely between the two rooms and I heard every word." Maggie turned to Carter in shock, but remained silent. "She didn't know her grandfather, Charles. You know Margaret doted on her grandfather. I thought she, for some reason, was trying to fool the old man until she announced she wanted a divorce. She wanted to leave me, and give me Rose Brier as part of the settlement. She threw her inheritance and her trust fund in the old man's face! Even then, I thought she might be playing some game, but I no longer believe that."

Charles looked from Carter to Maggie as if trying to weigh what his brother was saying. Bruce sat with his arms crossed in front of him, his legs straight out, in a stance that clearly said he had yet to be convinced. But when Carter had described Maggie's illness, his eyes had wandered over to the woman he had once respected and liked . . . and, if he were honest, even pined for.

"I began watching her, testing her. But Maggie never failed to be . . . Maggie." A small smile touched Carter's lips.

"And today the final puzzle piece fit into place." Almost relishing the suspense he was putting the two men through, Carter leaned back to give Maggie a reassuring smile. His throat closed and he had difficulty swallowing when he saw the look in Maggie's eyes. Those damn eyes, always so expressive, always so naked. Couldn't this woman learn to hide her feelings? And now those eyes that Carter could not drag his gaze away from were so full of love, so full of promise, that Carter almost felt like abandoning the library and carrying her up to his bed.

"Carter, would you mind continuing?" Charles asked, his voice laced with reluctant humor.

Almost startled, Carter looked back at his brother and friend, and smiled. "Er, yes."

"The coupe de grâce?"

"Yes. This morning Maggie went for a walk and saw Rensworth. He insisted that she give him money and said something about a list. At first Maggie didn't know what he was talking about, then remembered seeing a list of sorts in the secretary in her room. It was a list of our shipments, times, dates, names. And it was in Margaret's handwriting."

Charles' hands grew into fists and he cast Maggie a murderous look. "If that's so, then why is she standing there? Why isn't she in jail? By God, Carter, explain yourself."

Carter clenched his jaw in an effort to keep his temper in check.

"Take a look at these." He passed two lists to the men—one written by Margaret months ago, and one written by Maggie just hours ago.

After both men had looked them over, Carter explained.

"One list is clearly written by Margaret. I recognize her handwriting. It was the one thing about her that was elegant. The second list was written today, by Maggie."

Carter's obvious use of two names to describe the same woman was not lost on either man.

"Anyone could fake their handwriting." Bruce flung the paper with disgust onto Carter's desk.

"I have to agree with Bruce, Carter."

Carter let out a heavy sigh and glanced up at Maggie. Her face was stricken. Clearly she felt betrayed by Bruce's judgment, and Carter wanted nothing more than to take her in his arms and comfort her. But once again, his little spitfire of a wife surprised him.

"Charles, I can understand you not believing me. After all, we've only seen each other a few times. Although I would hope you'd have more faith and trust in your brother than this. But, Bruce, you know me." Maggie tried to keep the tears out of her voice. Now was no time for tears.

"I don't know you, Ma'am."

Carter let out a noise of impatience. "She led me to the list, gentlemen. How do your suspicious minds explain that? Certainly not even Margaret is stupid enough to lead me to the list that would certainly damn her."

Both men were silent.

"Oh, this is ridiculous, Carter. They'll never believe me. Or you, apparently." Maggie crossed her arms in disgust.

Carter studied the two men over steepled fingers. "Maggie, would you leave us alone now?" Maggie was about to argue, then realized that her leaving was probably best, although she was curious to find out what the men would say once she was out of the room. More than curious.

When she agreed to go so readily, Carter immediately became suspicious.

"And I don't want to find you in the parlor with your ear pressed up against the wall."

A guilty flush spread across Maggie's face and she smiled at her husband's perception.

"Oh, all right." He grinned at her as she left, a grin that disappeared when he turned back to Bruce and Charles.

Once Maggie had left the room, Bruce stood up from the chair as if it were on fire. He paced madly, stopping to say something several times, then changing his mind and continuing with his pacing.

"You're wearing a hole in the carpet, Bruce."

"A hole. Do you mean like the one in your head?"

Carter stood up as well, and Bruce knew then he had crossed a line. He immediately shut his mouth, reminding himself bitterly that if he said what he really felt it could mean his job.

As if reading his mind, Carter said, "Bruce, you know I like you to speak freely to me. You are a friend, one I have relied on to keep a level head. But this time you are simply wrong. Maggie has changed. Let's for a moment, though, suppose she is guilty. Please explain to me why she would lead me to that list."

"To throw you off, of course," Charles supplied, but he was clearly saying that for argument's sake.

"To throw me off what? We had no inkling Rensworth was involved in the crimes. And certainly no inkling Maggie was."

Charles sighed. "If you remember, Carter, I did raise that suspicion."

"Yes, and it turned out you were right. Margaret was involved. But Maggie is innocent."

Flabbergasted, Bruce yelled, "You're talkin' about the same woman, dammit! Maggie, Margaret, it's the same female, the same lies."

"Bruce, think back to the accident. Even you noted that she had changed. Maggie did not know about her grandfather's ultimatum because it had been made before her accident. Maggie did not know Rensworth. My God, she was nearly raped by the bastard. Rensworth was Margaret's lover. Don't you see a pattern here? Even the handwriting. I'll give you that it could have been faked, but I watched her write the damned thing. She didn't even know the right way to hold a pen or when to dip for more ink. I've thought about this long and hard, I've watched her like a hawk, waiting for her to make a mistake, to revert back to the woman she was before the accident. But she hasn't."

Carter could see he was finally getting through to the two men.

"So, you truly think she has amnesia?" Charles asked.

"Yes. I do."

"Isn't that supposed to be a temporary condition?"

Carter looked up at his brother sharply. Temporary. He sat down heavily in his chair. "God, I hope not. The doctor did say that there have been cases of permanent

memory loss." But he'd also said such cases were rare.
Carter's stomach clenched at the thought.

All three men seemed to understand the implications
should Maggie's memory return. Margaret would be
back, and she would be guilty of sabotage. And she
would not love Carter. Why hadn't he thought of that
before giving away his heart again? He closed his eyes
so the pain he was feeling would be hidden from the
other men.

"I'll deal with that when and if the time comes."

"Jesus, Mary, and Joseph, what a mess," Bruce said,
his brogue becoming heavy, exposing just how upset he
was.

"You could say that," Charles said dryly. For his part,
he was close to being convinced. After observing Margaret all day yesterday looking up at Carter as if the sun
rose and set just for him, he was almost willing to throw
away his remaining doubts. Seeing the pain in his
brother's eyes when he realized Margaret's memory
could return ripped at his heart. If there was a God and
if He was merciful, He would give Carter this tiny bit of
happiness. He would have to.

"I don't know about you, Bruce, but I'm damn close
to apologizing to the lady," Charles said. Carter gave his
brother a grateful smile.

Bruce, all bluster, and still smarting from the hurt
she'd unknowingly dealt him, mumbled something under his breath about soft-hearted weaklings. But it was
clear he, too, had been swayed. He'd protect his own
heart a bit longer, thank you very much, but he knew it
was a losing battle. Mrs. Johnsbury, Maggie, was someone a person simply could not remain angry with, he
thought with disgust. His lips were still frowning, but his
Irish eyes were smiling.

"I've got to know you believe her before we discuss
what you're really in here for."

"Goddammit, Carter, you've had weeks to come to

grips with all this. We're getting this all at once. You're asking too much. Let's just say we're close, but still a bit wary. Agreed, Bruce?"

Bruce grunted his agreement.

Not satisfied, but knowing he was asking a lot of the two men, Carter acquiesced.

"Here's the question. Do we get Rensworth tomorrow as he is meeting with Maggie, or do we wait and catch him red-handed?"

"Certainly you're not going to let Mrs. Johnsbury meet with that bastard," Bruce burst out, revealing more about his feelings towards Maggie's sincerity than he'd meant.

"I wasn't sure myself, but Maggie convinced me she must. She's to meet him on the beach. It's too wide open for us to hide and then ambush him."

"You sound like you've already made up your mind what to do," Charles said. "You want to catch him in the act."

"I would prefer to, yes. Maggie will give him a list—fake of course—and some cash. But it won't nearly be enough for Rensworth to hire thugs to do his handiwork. He'll have to do it on his own. And we'll be there with the law when he does."

"What if you're wrong. What if he scrapes up enough cash to hire someone. What if he finds someone desperate enough for money that he'll do the job for next to nothing?" Charles asked, but he clearly liked the thought of catching the scoundrel in the act.

"Maggie has thought of that. She believes she can convince Rensworth to do the deed himself, for her."

Bruce had taken up his pacing again. "What if something goes wrong? What if Rensworth don't believe her?"

"We'll be there watching from above," Carter answered. "If something should go wrong, we'll move in. Or at least fluster Rensworth enough that he allows her to go. Bruce should be the one to call for her, shout that she's needed at the party and walk toward them. That way, Rensworth won't panic."

"Maggie's willing to do this?" Charles asked, allowing some doubt about her motives to creep into his voice.

Carter swiped a hand through his hair. "She's afraid of Rensworth. He hurt her this morning and she's terrified about seeing him again. At first I was completely against her delivering the list and money. But dammit, she's right. She must deliver it in order for us to catch him, in order for us to end this once and for all. I will not let anything happen to her."

"All right, then," Charles said, clapping his hands together, unable to hide his youthful enthusiasm for his involvement in this adventure. "We've got a plan!"

Once the two men left the library, Carter immediately went to find Maggie. Their discussion about amnesia had shaken him to the core. He needed to see her, needed to hold her, before she was taken from him. He found her in her room with Stella, who was putting the final touches on her hair.

"Lovely," Carter said, gazing warmly at Maggie. She was dressed in a peach-colored dress with a sweetheart neckline and fitted waist that emphasized her trim figure.

"I feel a bit . . . exposed," Maggie said, staring down at her cleavage. "But everyone else is wearing dresses like this, I guess."

Carter gave Stella a nod and she disappeared from the room. "You look beautiful, Maggie."

Maggie looked up, hearing something in Carter's voice that she had never heard. There was something in his eyes, a sadness, as if his heart were breaking as he looked at her. Maggie stood up to greet him and he pulled her into his arms, laying his cheek against her hair in a fierce gesture. Maggie gladly went into his arms, but she sensed something was wrong.

"You couldn't convince them, could you," she said, pulling away so she could look at his face.

"Well, they are not completely convinced. But they are very, very close."

Maggie smiled, her eyes crinkling at the corners. Instead of smiling back, Carter looked more sad. Maggie did not want to know what was bringing that look of longing into Carter's eyes; it could only be bad news, and she was far too happy to hear such news. She clung to him, burying her head against his chest in an attempt to move even closer. He smelled so good, like the outdoors on a fall day. Carter wrapped his arms around her, holding her against him. "I . . ." Fear gripped him as he started to speak. Would this tender scene someday come back to haunt him? Would Margaret throw it in his face when she regained her memory?

"Oh, Maggie." He pulled away, putting a large hand on either side of her lovely face. He noticed unshed tears in her eyes. She feels so much, he thought, and so do I. Taking his thumb to gently brush away the tears, he bent his head for a soft kiss. "I love you, Maggie," he said against her trembling lips.

Maggie breathed in sharply. Surely all her dreams could not come true like this. Surely her angels were playing with her again. "Oh, Carter. Really?"

"Yes."

Maggie let out a shaky breath and for the first time since she'd come to this place, she was crying tears of joy. "I know how hard it was for you to say that, Carter."

He smiled, feeling an odd aching in his throat. "Not so hard."

Maggie hugged him tightly, smiling as tears coursed down her face. Then she remembered his face when he had come in, how sad he had looked. Certainly he could not be sad about loving her.

"There's more, isn't there?"

Ah, his perceptive Maggie girl. But he dared not remind her that her memory could return, ending this small slice of paradise they had managed to find.

He brought his lips to hers, kissing her deeply, desperately showing her all the love he had for her in a single kiss. "No, Maggie."

"Then let me hear it again."

He grinned down at her, loving her more than he thought possible.

"I love you, Maggie girl. With all my heart."

Maggie put her head against his chest again and sighed happily.

"Can I say it too? You once told me you never wanted to hear me say it."

"I never!"

"You did, too, and you certainly remember. You broke my heart, you know."

Carter brought his thumb up to her soft lips to erase the frown that had formed there. "I thought you'd broken my heart, too."

"But I didn't."

"No. I was just a blind fool."

"Yes, you were. But I can understand you coming to the conclusion you did. It must have been awful."

"It was," he said, nipping her mouth with his.

"Well. Can I say it?"

"Please do."

"Maybe later," and she began laughing her head off as if she'd just told the funniest of jokes.

"Say it, woman." He gave her his most cross look.

"Ooo. You don't intimidate me, you brute."

He brought his head down and ravaged her mouth with a kiss that left her weak-kneed and clinging to him.

His hands went to the small of her back and pressed her to him so she could feel how much he wanted her.

"Unfair tactics," she managed to mumble. "You know I love you." They would have proved their love for each other then and there if a timid knock had not sounded on the door. Muttering a curse under his breath, Carter swept the door open, startling Stella who was just about to give the door another knock.

"I'm sorry, sir," Stella said, her gray pallor turning a beet red. "But the horseshoe contest is about to begin and your brother requested your presence."

"He did, did he?"

"Yes, sir."

"Tell him . . ."

Maggie interrupted her husband. "Tell him we'll be right down." Once Stella disappeared, she turned to Carter. "If we don't go down then everyone will know what we've been doing."

"So? We're married."

"But nobody even thinks we like each other."

"Well, they're about to find out differently, madam, for I'm afraid I'm going to be sorely tempted to kiss you repeatedly in front of the gawking crowd."

"Only tempted?" Maggie said impishly.

Carter growled deep in his throat and pulled her against him once more. After a long few minutes, Maggie said breathlessly, "If we don't go down now, I'm afraid our guests won't see us all evening."

With a sigh, Carter let his wife go. As it was, it would be several minutes before he would be able to decently go into public.

Charles managed to pull Patricia aside before seeing Carter and Maggie again so that he could explain the situation. As he suspected, Patricia stubbornly refused to believe Margaret Johnsbury could be anything but what she had always been—a conniving bitch.

"Open your eyes, Patricia. If you don't believe me, then watch the two of them together. I've never seen two people more in love."

"Two fools, rather," Patricia said. She would never forgive that woman. Never.

Charles shook his head, suddenly jealous of his brother for having such a devoted wife. He never thought he'd see the day when he wished for a wife like his brother's. He loved Patricia, and she loved him. But he could barely recall an all-consuming, desperate love like he saw between Carter and Margaret. And he wished that just once Patricia would look at him with near worship and her heart on her sleeve, like he'd seen Maggie look at Carter. He gazed at his wife, her face a stony mask, and he could tell she was angry with him. Her unlined face, perfectly noble, coolly beautiful, a face he loved still. Charles gave his wife a quick kiss.

"Charles!" she said, acting surprised and embarrassed by his spontaneous show of affection. But he saw her lips curve up just slightly, and her eyes were shining a bit too brightly. He kissed her again, this time on her neck, and she dissolved into giggles while trying to maintain some sort of dignity.

"Oh, you, stop," she said, but clearly she was enjoying her husband's bit of play. When was the last time he had acted this way? she thought. When they were still courting. What had happened to them? They were only twenty-five and twenty-two years old. When did they become an old married couple?

"You know, Patricia, you pretend to be this paragon, but I know better, don't I?"

Patricia looked at her husband and tilted her head, giving him the full force of her charm. "Yes. You do." And she turned back, apparently deeply absorbed with the current horseshoe contest.

"I love you, Patty."

Patricia turned to him then, smiling, her heart on her sleeve. Just where it belonged.

She was not smiling a few minutes later as she stood stiff-backed and oh-so-proper next to Margaret Johnsbury as they watched their husbands face off in horseshoes. They stood on a sun-dappled incline, looking down on the horseshoe pit, which was surrounded by cigar-smoking men.

Maggie clearly sensed that Patricia wished she was standing anywhere but where she stood, but Maggie stubbornly refused to leave. And she knew that Patricia had far too good manners to walk away. When she walked to the horseshoe area on Carter's arm, she was completely oblivious to anything but the beautiful summer day, and the feel of Carter's muscles beneath her hand. She was in her own little fog, which cleared suddenly when she finally noticed who she was standing next to while Charles and Carter exchanged brotherly insults about each's ability in horseshoes. Once they left to begin the match, a terrible silence grew between the two women. Maggie searched for something to say, then wondered why she should be the one to precipitate conversation. "Because you're the hostess," she told herself.

"Beautiful day."

"Yes. Quite."

Horseshoes clinked against posts, men's shouts rang out.

"I hope the weather holds."

"Yes."

In the distance, the squeal of playing children could be heard; a breeze kicked up the leaves in the trees overhead.

"The sun can be a bit brutal this time of year."

"Mmmm."

Someone apparently got a ringer, for the men were

practically deliriously happy. Money was exchanging hands as bets were laid as to which of the Johnsbury boys would win.

"But we'll be praying for the sun come winter."

Patricia actually turned her head imperceptibly to give Maggie a quick look of irritated disbelief before responding between closed teeth.

"True."

Maggie sighed. A seagull flew overhead, late summer bees buzzed lazily nearby searching for the last bit of pollen.

"I love him, you know."

Maggie did not think Patricia could stand any stiffer than she already was. She was wrong. She waited for a response, any response, but heard nothing. Better go back to the weather, she told herself.

"I hope it's cool tonight for the ball."

"I don't believe you."

"No. I really do hope it's cool," Maggie said, purposely misunderstanding what Patricia was talking about. Was that an unwilling smile quirking on Patricia's lips?

"Don't be obtuse," Patricia said.

"I won't if you don't," Maggie shot back.

Patricia might not like the brunette standing next to her, but she had to admire her at that moment. She turned toward the woman who she believed had caused her entire family so much pain.

"I'm not as easy to convince as the men, you know. I still see through your pretty exterior."

"No, Patricia. You cannot see me. You don't know who I am. If you can't trust me, trust Carter. Trust Charles."

Patricia turned away, unwilling to discuss the matter any further. And she vowed she would whack the woman standing next to her over the head with her fan if she dared make another comment about the weather.

～ *Chapter 21* ～

*. . . We were both so happy, Steve. I hope you un-
derstand. . . .*

As Maggie stood before the full-length mirror she
could not help but remember the last time she'd
stood looking at her gowned image before descending
the stairs to a throng of people below. She had been
scared silly that night, a stranger to everyone in that
room, including her husband. How different tonight
would be, she thought. She would face the crowd with
her husband beside her—a husband who loved her.
Maggie smiled at her reflection, biting her lip upon seeing the impossibly happy woman reflected before her.
She wrapped her arms around herself to keep from
bursting from happiness. Stella rustling in the back-
ground, fussing with her dress, brought Maggie back
from her reverie.

"You're too thin, Ma'am," Stella said sternly. She had
been shocked when she'd first seen Maggie after returning from her holiday and had since taken every opportunity to point out to her mistress that she needed to
gain some weight. "The dress just hangs on you."

"Oh, it does not," Maggie said, but tugged at the ex-
cess material at her fitted waist with a frown. "Well, not
that much. And I'm gaining weight every day."

Maggie knew that Stella had been hurt that she had
been sent away on a so-called vacation just so Maggie

could slip into despair. It was her job to protect her
mistress, no matter how she felt toward her personally.
As if Carter was the barometer from which all the servants measured their feelings toward Mrs. Johnsbury,
the household staff, including Stella, had been markedly
warmer to her in the past two days than in the previous
weeks. When Stella had become part of the Rose Brier
crowd, Maggie did not know.

"You're skinny as a rail," Stella grumbled affection-
ately as she tugged once again on the shoulders of her
gown in a vain attempt to keep them in the proper
place. The dress was supposed to cling to the very tops
of her shoulders but kept slipping off and down her
arm.

"I'm going to have to pin it to your chemise," Stella
said with disapproval.

"Hurry, Stella, Carter will be here any minute."

"He is here," a deep voice rumbled. Carter's heart
made a mighty leap when he saw the smile that spread
across Maggie's lips. He leaned against the doorjamb
and watched as Stella worked fussily to correct some
problem with his wife's gown. What that problem was,
he could not fathom, for she looked gorgeous in the
white creation that bared most of her shoulders and a
tempting amount of her creamy chest.

Once her gown was firmly pinned, Stella eyed Maggie's hair critically and began making inconsequential
adjustments.

"Enough. She's perfect."

Not wanting to accept an impatient man's opinion,
Maggie looked at Stella for reassurance. After putting a
wayward curl back into the mass of curls piled softly, but
firmly, atop her head, Stella stepped back eyeing her
mistress. With a satisfied nod, she agreed with Mr.
Johnsbury. "Perfect."

After Stella left the couple alone, Carter crossed over

to Maggie and gave her a soft kiss. "You do look beautiful, Mrs. Johnsbury."

"So do you." He laughed at being called "beautiful" and bent his head for another kiss. And another.

"Do we really have to be present at our own ball?" Maggie asked between kisses that were becoming longer and bolder and more distracting every minute.

"No." She could feel Carter smiling against her mouth and leaned back to look at him.

"You know, Carter, you really are beautiful when you smile. I love it when you smile. You don't do it enough."

Carter sobered slightly. "Up until recently, I did not have much reason to smile, Maggie."

"And now you do?"

The smile was back.

"Oh, God, yes." He pulled her to him, wanting to hold her close forever. He did not truly want to attend his own ball. He simply wanted to be with his wife, to make love to her, to hold her, to talk to her. He wanted to relish every moment as if it were their last. For the grim reality was, it could be their last, he thought with anguish. Her amnesia could disappear suddenly and without warning. If his heart broke when it happened, then that was something he would have to face. But until that time, he would love her with all his being.

Maggie's finely arched brows drew together in concern. Here was that same sadness, that same . . . desperation she'd felt before in Carter's embrace.

After several moments, Carter relaxed his hold and looked down at Maggie's worried face. "What's wrong?"

Not wanting to say anything that would ruin the evening, Maggie smiled and shook her head. "How could anything be wrong?" she asked, giving him another kiss.

"Well, Mother, he's completely gone again." Charles stood by Kathryn as they waited for Patricia to return from putting the little ones to bed. "And he's got me half convinced he's doing the right thing. More than half convinced."

He told his mother about the day's revelations, about their plans, and was surprised at his mother's calm acceptance of the news.

"You don't seem surprised."

"I'm not. But, like you, I'm not totally convinced. And, like you, I am concerned that her condition—if she does indeed have amnesia—is temporary. Your brother has not had an easy time of it, you know, Charles."

"I know, Mother."

"I'm not sure you do. Carter loves Reginald and Lily, but I think a little bit of him dies whenever he sees you all together as a family. He wants so much, but he's kept that need hidden for so long. And now, I almost think he'd be willing to believe anything, even that Margaret loves him. I'm so afraid for him."

"Two days ago, I would have agreed with you. I would have done everything in my power to convince Carter he was crazy. But they seem so damned happy together, so much in love. They're so intense you can almost see the sparks flying between them. You should have seen them in the library. She kept her hand on his shoulder the entire time, as if he were some kind of a lifeline. And when he looked at her, my God, Mother, it was as if he were devouring her with his eyes." Charles shook his head at the memory. He tried to remember Margaret during their early courtship. He remembered thinking his big brother had found himself a beautiful bride. But, for the life of him, he could never recall having liked her. He liked her today, but he could not put his finger on why.

"Talking about them again?" Patricia gave them both a look of irritation. "Aren't you getting bored by all this?"

"Bored? My dear, this is the most excitement we've had in years," Kathryn said, arching one eyebrow. She understood her daughter-in-law's animosity toward Margaret but was getting a bit impatient with the blatant hostility Patricia was showing toward her. After all, if she could give the woman the benefit of the doubt, certainly Patricia could.

The objects of their conversation stopped all discussion as Maggie and Carter walked toward the little group that had gathered near the top of the curving staircase. Maggie, feeling more confident than she had in months, greeted her in-laws with warmth and refused to allow their rather cool responses to get her down. Carter gave her arm a little squeeze of comfort after noting their polite "good evenings." He had the very distinct feeling that they had all been talking about him before they walked up to the group, for they all had slightly guilty looks on their faces.

"Don't let us interrupt your conversation," Carter said, clearly baiting his family. His mother chose to ignore her son's insolence and held up her arm to be taken by her eldest son's free arm. The gesture, a sort of acknowledgment that she would—and should—share her son with his wife was quite telling to Carter. Maggie did not catch the significance of his mother walking on equal footing with her. But everyone else would, Carter knew, including Charles and Patricia. Charles gave his mother a smile, but Kathryn pretended nothing out of the ordinary was happening.

Patricia knew, however, that her resistance to her sister-in-law was beginning to wear down. She begrudgingly admitted to herself that Margaret was quite charming and quite beautiful and she had apparently made Carter happy. Patricia could not remember the last time she had seen her brother-in-law looking so relaxed, so content. At least she could give the conniving little bitch that much credit, she forced herself to think

uncharitably. She could not stop the startling wave of
guilt that washed over her at her malicious thoughts.
She's getting to me, too, Patricia thought with disgust. It
was almost a badge of honor to her to remain the last in
resistance, the last to fall for what simply had to be
false.

"We should be getting downstairs," Kathryn said,
drawing her son toward the stairs. "I'm sure we are all
in for an interesting evening."

Kathyrn's prediction was not wrong, Maggie thought
much later, as she waited for Carter to come to his
room. He had said he would just be a moment or two
talking to his brother about Rensworth and their plan.
The few minutes alone gave Maggie a chance to recall
the evening in which Carter had publicly declared in
both actions and words that all was well between Mr.
and Mrs. Johnsbury.

Maggie lay her head down on the pillow, for she was
exhausted from the long and eventful day. The ball had
been the stuff of fantasies. Carter, dashing and atten-
tive, stood by her side nearly the entire night. Each time
they danced, Maggie felt as if she were floating on air.
She loved the feel of his firm hand at the small of her
back, loved looking at her small hand being swallowed
up by his large one. She felt protected and loved and
beautiful. But perhaps the event that warmed her heart
the most had nothing to do with Carter. It was toward
the end of the evening and Carter had asked his mother
to dance with him, when Charles approached her.

"Would you care to dance, Margaret?" he asked as if
it were something he did every day. Maggie looked up
at him, beaming him a smile, making Charles know,
without a doubt, why his big brother was so utterly captivated by the winsome beauty before him.

They danced for several minutes in comfortable silence before Charles said simply, "I believe you."

Maggie brought her head up, her eyes shining with emotion. "Thank you."

They said not another word for the rest of the dance, but Maggie's heart soared. Charles believed her. Maggie thanked her angels and God for giving her the fortitude to get to this point. She did not care if every other person in that ballroom never spoke a word to her again. Carter loved her. Charles believed her. It was enough to keep her happy for a long, long time.

When Maggie looked ready to drop from exhaustion, Carter urged her to go to his room. "I have ulterior motives, you know, for wanting you well rested by the time I get up there."

Maggie innocently brushed up against him causing him to breathe in harshly through his nose. Throwing a painful smile at his wife, who looked up at him with an utterly blank look on her lovely face, he whispered, "I will make you pay for that, you little temptress."

"Promise?" Carter let out a little growl and prayed no one looked below his waistline.

After saying good night to most of the people remaining in the room, she dragged herself up the staircase, weary beyond belief. It had been an interminably long day. Was it only that morning that she had met Rensworth? It seemed more like weeks. She did not want to think about tomorrow, for she was more frightened than she'd ever admit to Carter about meeting with the man. Had Carter suspected just the thought of seeing Rensworth again made her want to vomit from nerves, he would never allow her to meet with him. But Maggie was convinced it was the only way to catch him in the act. Maggie believed with little doubt that she would be in no danger from Rensworth. After all, Carter, Charles, and Bruce would be nearby to lend assistance should Rensworth get out of hand. And the plan to have Bruce act as if he were simply looking for Maggie, if he began pawing at her, seemed to be perfect.

Maggie tried to force her thoughts away from Rensworth to concentrate on the passion that had been promised for later this evening. She was picturing Carter naked, his great muscular body hovering over her, when she fell asleep.

As Maggie succumbed to a wonderful dream, Carter was in the library with his brother, once again going over tomorrow's plans. Although he was impatient to make love to Maggie, and his thoughts continuously strayed to the beauty in his bed, he knew he could not relax completely until he felt confident they were doing the right thing by allowing Maggie to see Rensworth.

"It has to be Bruce who interrupts them should Rensworth get out of hand," Charles argued. "If it is you or I, he'll panic. He'll think of Bruce as an annoyance, not a threat."

"You're right. I just want to make sure she doesn't get hurt."

"She won't, Carter. We'll all be there."

"We'll be too damn far away," Carter said, clenching his fist, his mind seeing Rensworth mauling Maggie while she struggled.

Charles sighed. He could imagine what Carter was going through. He would be the same if it were Patricia they were offering up as bait.

"Rensworth will have nowhere to go, Carter, you know that. I will be south of them, Bruce and you will be north. The bay is to the west and the bluffs to the east. There is nowhere for him to go."

"You're right." He was beginning to sound like a broken record, he knew. Why couldn't he shake the feeling that something was going to happen. Was it just his lingering concern about Maggie's amnesia plaguing him? he wondered.

"Damn." He hadn't realized he'd said the word aloud until he heard Charles chuckle.

"What's so goddamn funny, little brother?"

"You. My God, Carter, you're pacing like a caged tiger. You're insane with worry."

"And you find that funny?"

"No, I find it gratifying. It's about time you had some-one to worry about. The fact that it's your wife makes it even more funny."

Carter glared at his brother. And Charles laughed again, clapping his brother on his back.

"I'm happy for you, you idiot."

Finally Carter smiled. "Oh."

"Listen. Everything will be fine, Carter. Stop worry-ing. Now, go up to your wife. And do try to get some sleep, tomorrow's a big day."

Carter gave his brother a withering look that turned into a crooked smile and headed up to make love to his wife.

When Carter entered his room, his gaze went immedi-ately to the sleeping form of his wife and he gave a frustrated little sigh. Her hair lay tousled on the pillow, her cheeks flushed from sleep. Carter quietly got un-dressed, peeling his clothes off his taut body that wanted anything but to simply sleep next to this half-naked woman beside him. He lifted the covers up gently, then, smiling devilishly, plopped the full weight of his body on the bed making the frame groan beneath him. Maggie, her back turned from Carter, could not help but smile, but continued feigning sleep. Letting out a sleepy mum-ble, she brought the covers about her more snugly and pretended to slip into oblivion.

Scowling at her sleeping form, Carter pulled the blan-kets roughly from Maggie's back, muttering something about people in comas who hog covers. Maggie could no longer keep up the pretense and threw herself onto Carter with a laugh, then caught her breath when she realized her husband was very, very naked.

Frowning down at him, she said, "Carter, there's something very wrong here."

Trying not to smile, Carter inquired as to what could be possibly wrong. "There's only one of us naked." And she sat up, straddling Carter's big body, and flung her nightgown off with a flourish. "There. That's much better."

Carter, his eyes gleaming with lust and admiration at her lack of inhibition, brought his hands to the sides of Maggie's knees, bringing them in a slow caress up her body, grazing the sides of her breasts, and up to her neck where he buried his hands in her hair. He dragged her down for a long, drugging kiss, thrusting his tongue into her mouth for slow exploration. Maggie lay full length upon his body, her toes just reaching midcalf, loving the feel of this man beneath her. Carter ended the kiss letting out a shaky breath.

"Lord, woman, you feel good." He caressed the side of her face, suddenly becoming serious, his eyes searching Maggie's. "Do you know how long I've wanted this?"

Maggie felt sure he meant more than making love and gave him a tender smile. My God, Carter thought, this is the first time I have made love with a woman. The first time. For he knew, that until now, he had never fully loved, never allowed himself this most glorious of feelings. He smiled a smile that was so bright, it almost hurt Maggie as she gazed down at this man she loved so.

"You've got me, Carter. Forever. It's real." She sensed he needed this reassurance, needed to believe this unexpected happiness would not be snatched away from him again. But a shadow still remained in his gray eyes, and Maggie's brown ones filled with distress.

"Please, Carter, tell me you believe in me. If you don't, I can't do this. I love you too much, it hurts too much. If you're not completely sure I love you or that you love me, tell me now. Please."

Shocked that Maggie would come to such an erroneous conclusion, Carter quickly brought her head down for another fierce kiss.

"Never doubt that I love you, Maggie. Never." But he did not tell her about his fears that she would be lost to him forever should her memory return.

Crossing her arms on his beefy chest, she gave him one of her smiles, the kind that slowed his heart. The shadow was gone, and Maggie told herself she must have imagined it. She had become cautious of happiness in the last few months.

Giving him an impish grin, Maggie proceeded to kiss Carter's chest. She heard his rumble of laughter at her little kisses sprinkled playfully on his abdomen, slowly trailing downward. But when she moved even lower, his breathing became shallow. Certainly she would not . . . Oh, God, he thought, swallowing thickly, squeezing his eyes shut at the pleasure . . . she would. Scarcely able to breathe, Carter ventured a look down at his beautiful wife who was making him mad with her mouth and tongue. Sitting up, unable to endure any more, he grabbed her beneath her arms and dragged her upward so that he might kiss that wonderful mouth.

Maggie could not get enough of this man. She moved her hands over his chest, his neck, his hair. She caressed his face as they became lost in another endless kiss. She squirmed against him in pleasure when his hands smoothed over her round buttocks and gasped aloud when his mouth found her breast. Never before had she felt such fire, such burning need.

"Please, Carter. I want . . . oh, please."

With a low growl, Carter joined them together as they lay pressed together, side by side, wrapped around each other in an almost desperate embrace. He moved his hand between them, as he thrust into her, making Maggie screech with delight. Their mouths became fused, lost in a warm, sensuous melding of tongues. Maggie moved against Carter, frenzied by his touch, raking her hands up and down his muscled back. It could not be this good, she thought crazily, nothing could be this good. When the sizzling warmth spread throughout her body, making even her toes curl in pleasure, Carter drove into her, lost in his own release, spilling himself, and letting out a deep sound of male satisfaction.

Still clutching each other, Maggie felt Carter's body shake with laughter.

"What's so funny," she said, with laughter in her own voice.

"Oh, my God, Maggie. If we are that way together every time, I'm afraid this old body will not be able to take it." He shook his head, amazed that he had reached some unimaginable peak of fulfillment.

"You're not old, Carter," Maggie said, passion already lighting up her eyes. "And I mean to prove it to you."

~ *Chapter 22* ~

> *. . . Carter was beside himself with worry for me, but our plan was perfect. . . .*

Curtis Rensworth sat uncomfortably on a rock waiting for his Margaret to appear. He felt ridiculously nervous and he again checked to make sure his suit was still free of sand. He'd donned his best suit for this rendezvous, even though he was quite sure he would be taking it off before his meeting with Margaret was complete, something he looked forward to with relish. How long had it been since he'd made love to her? He could not even remember. If she had not been so utterly convincing the night of the old hag's birthday, he would not have had to resort to violence and they could have made love. Instead, it had turned into something ugly, something he blamed Margaret for entirely.

After seeing her yesterday, after feeling her come so willingly into his arms, he was convinced that everything would turn out the way they had always planned. Once he had Margaret, once he had money, all would be well. He did not like this feeling of being out of control, and a part of him realized how close he had come to losing himself completely. Rensworth knew he was thought quite charming by many of his contemporaries, and he was brutally aware of the pulling back, the distancing in the past several months by people he believed to be his friends. All doors had been closed to him when it became apparent he could no longer pay his bills or his gambling debts.

He needed Margaret. Needed her. Why couldn't she have realized that? Why couldn't she have returned just one goddamn letter? Rensworth clenched his fists so tightly, his long nails bit into his palm painfully. He took a deep shuddering breath and wiped a shaking hand across his slick forehead. It was godawful hot today and would have been unbearable if not for a brisk wind. God, he needed a drink. He had thought himself rather responsible when he did not bring with him the half-empty whiskey bottle that sat on the bureau in his cheap rented room. But now he cursed himself. A few sips would not have dulled his senses so much, he thought now. Glancing up at the sun, which was high in a cloudless sky, Rensworth felt an odd rage come over him. "Where the hell is that bitch!" he swore. He'd told her to meet him at noon. Surely it was well past that now! He glanced down the beach for what seemed like the hundredth time and his rage disappeared almost instantaneously. There in the distance, a slim lone woman walked along the beach toward him. Margaret. She was coming to him. Thank God.

Carter, on his belly next to Bruce, clutched the grass at the edge of the bluff so tightly, it began to tear at its tough roots. His eyes shifted from Margaret, who walked so confidently down the beach away from him, to Rensworth, who was half-hidden. Rensworth stood by a large outcropping of boulders that appeared to have been strewn there by a giant's hand, separating the beach into two portions. Charles was on the other side of the rocks in case Rensworth dragged Maggie in that direction. The muscles in Carter's neck and stomach began to ache from the tension. He relaxed slightly when he noticed a young couple drag their sailing dory onto the beach not far from where Maggie would meet

up with Rensworth. Surely the appearance of people
would stop Rensworth from doing her any violence.
Other than Maggie, the couple, and a young woman and
a toddler playing directly below Carter in the surf, the
beach was nearly deserted.

"That's good," Carter said, jerking his head toward
the young couple.

"Rensworth won't try anything in such a public place,
Carter. Stop worrying. But you're right. Their being on
the beach can only help Margaret," Bruce said. He felt
sorry for Carter. He could tell remaining on the bluff, so
far away from Rensworth, was taking almost more control than the man had.

"Son of a bitch." Bruce jerked his head back to look
at Maggie at Carter's harsh whisper. Rensworth was
hugging Maggie familiarly. Carter's breath was coming
out in harsh gasps as if he had been running.

"Calm down, Cart. Maggie's playing this just right.
Rensworth has got to believe she wants to see him."

Carter swallowed. He was clenching his jaw so tightly,
a part of him feared he would shatter his teeth. Rensworth and Maggie appeared to be talking calmly. Carter
watched with loathing as Rensworth's hand caressed his
wife's arms. He stiffened with a jerk when he pulled her
into an embrace and kissed her. "I can't stand this. We
should have thought of another way."

Bruce put a reassuring hand on Carter's shoulder.
"You know it was the only way, man. We've got to give
her a chance." Bruce was still looking at Carter when he
saw his friend's face contort.

"Jesus Christ. No!"

The two men watched helplessly as they ran toward
the stairs that led to the beach. Rensworth had suddenly
become vicious, slapping Maggie across the face and
tearing her dress. Maggie tried to run from Rensworth
but he dragged her back to him. The young couple who
had been strolling casually down the beach were

shocked into immobility and simply stared as Maggie
struggled with Rensworth. As if in slow motion, the couple turned in unison hearing the shouts of two men who
were running full speed toward them. But by the time
they realized the men were shouting something about a
boat—their boat—it was too late. Rensworth had already thrown a struggling Maggie into the couple's little
dory and was shoving the craft into the water.

Carter watched in horror as Maggie attempted to escape the sailboat only to be brutally backhanded by
Rensworth, who immediately climbed aboard and
lashed her hands to a cleat. Carter, a few steps ahead of
Bruce, shedding his clothes as he ran, brushed past the
gaping young couple and flew into the water in a desperate attempt to stop the boat which Rensworth had
already expertly got under sail. The brisk wind filled the
sail instantaneously, pushing the boat away from the
sandy beach, away from Carter. Charles and Bruce
joined him in the surf moments later, but it was clear to
both men that they would never be able to outswim the
boat.

Carter swam until his arms ached, until he knew it
was a futile exercise. Helplessly he tread water, his eyes
boring into the sailboat that was slipping farther and
farther away. His head was filled with Maggie's screams
as she pleaded and begged for help. And he could do
nothing. He would hear those screams in his head for a
long, long time.

Rensworth was silent as he steered the little boat out
onto the bay. He clutched the tiller tightly; his only
movement was a slight adjustment to the sail so it would
continue racing with the wind. Maggie struggled with
her bindings, not caring that the skin beneath the rough
hemp was tearing, until Rensworth slapped her yet
again. Her throat was raw from screaming and her face
hurt in the places Rensworth had struck her. She could

tell one eye and both lips were swollen, and her nose hurt so much, her entire head ached. She prayed it was not broken. She prayed that Carter would come for her soon. She prayed Rensworth would fall off the boat and drown. Slowly.

"What now?" Maggie said, trying to sound tough.

Rensworth simply jerked his head toward her and sneered. Maggie rolled her eyes.

"You must have some plan." Mustn't he? No, Maggie thought, he probably did not and from the irritated look on his face, she was sure he did not. In his wildest imaginings he probably had not thought he would be sailing in this little boat with a kidnapped woman aboard. Then I'll have to give him a plan, Maggie thought.

"I hope you're not kidnapping me for ransom, Curtis. Carter would probably be only able to dig up a few thousand dollars or so on short notice. And I'm sure that would not be enough to keep you happy. And it's dangerous. Carter is smart, and you'd probably get caught. So if you're thinking of hiding me someplace and then demanding a ransom, I'd think again. It won't work."

Rensworth said not a word, but Maggie saw his eyes shift as he thought about what she was saying. She knew that few kidnappings were successful. It seemed the culprits were always getting caught. And that's what she hoped for Rensworth. That he would get caught. By Carter. Maggie could have smiled just thinking about what Carter would do to Rensworth when he caught him.

"Where are you taking me? You don't know, do you?" Maggie's confidence had grown with Rensworth's silence. It was a mistake. He lashed out, slapping her yet again. Maggie, still tied to the cleat, could not move out of the way and her head snapped back.

"Shut up, bitch!"

Tears of pain and anger formed in her eyes, and she turned her head away, refusing to let Rensworth see that he had hurt her.

But Rensworth saw the tears and smiled maliciously. He wanted to kill the bitch, and had planned to, until she had given him a better idea. Kidnapping was perfect. He could still have the pleasure of killing her, but would also be able to hurt Carter, too. He'd demand, say, twenty thousand dollars from the bastard. That ought to set him back. Rensworth was so happy, he almost started to giggle.

Carter dragged himself out of the surf, his wet pants weighing him down, and fell to his knees coughing and gasping for air. Bruce and Charles collapsed next to him, each swearing under their breaths in rage at the events that had just transpired.

Carter looked up at his brother, his eyes tortured. "If anything happens to her . . ."

"We'll get her back, Carter," Charles said, interrupting him.

Carter shook his head, drops of water spraying off his hair as his hands dug into the sand. "If anything happens to her, I'll kill him. I swear to God, I'll kill him."

"And I'll help you, Cart," Bruce said. "But right now, we've got to get going. We've got to get aboard the *Misty Sea* and go after them."

With that rallying cry, the three men began running toward several rowboats stashed up against the beach that were used to row out to sailboats moored in the deeper water two hundred yards from shore. They had just gotten to the boats when Carter let out a groan.

"The Salisburys have *Misty Sea*. They wanted to go for a sail today. Jesus, what else can go wrong!" Carter spat.

"I can still see 'em, Carter. We'll just use another boat. How about the Elders' sloop?" Bruce said, eyeing the sailboats that bobbed in the waters offshore. Several guests had sailed to the Johnsburys' party.

"We might as well row as take that tub," Charles said. "The *Madeline* would be better. Bruce, run up and get John Peters and tell him we need him and his boat. Nobody sails the *Madeline* like he does."

Bruce seemed to take a maddeningly long time to find John Peters. Carter and Charles stood by the rowboat at the ready, their eyes peeled on the small sailboat that was getting more and more difficult to differentiate from tens of other small boats on the bay. It was a fine day for sailing and it seemed that all of Rhode Island was out on the bay enjoying one of summer's last weekends.

As the sound of footsteps running down the wooden steps hit Carter's ears, he said with despair, "I've lost them. I don't know which is Maggie." His eyes searched the bay frantically, willing himself to pick out one particular sail among the many that dotted the bay. They had lost too much time getting Peters.

"We'll find them, Carter." Charles said it with such confidence, Carter's spirits were lifted. He had been torturing himself, blaming himself for this predicament. He never should have allowed Maggie to meet with Rensworth. He should have captured Rensworth then and there and to hell with their grandiose scheme of catching him red-handed. Maggie would be safe, she'd be in his arms. He tormented himself with images of Rensworth slapping her, kissing her as she struggled in his arms, forcing her. . . . He felt he would go insane if he did not find her. Oh, God, Maggie, he thought, I'm so sorry. So goddamn sorry.

I'm sorry, Carter, Maggie thought as her eyes bleakly searched the waters behind them. If only she had kept her head, if only she had let Rensworth do what he wanted. Surely Bruce would have been there any minute

to interrupt them. But the memory of the last night's
passion, the magic of Carter's lovemaking was too fresh
in Maggie's mind. When Rensworth thrust his tongue
into her mouth, she could not help herself. She gagged
and shoved him away. Covering her mouth as she
heaved, Maggie knew then the game was up. She had
failed.

She looked down at her raw wrists and saw that she
was shivering despite the warm sun. Closing her eyes,
she tried to stop the fear that had begun to strangle her.
Her face hurt horribly and one eye was nearly swollen
shut. She was on a boat with a madman heading for
God-knew-where. And when they got to wherever they
were going, Maggie was convinced Rensworth would at
the least rape her, and at the most beat her to death.
Tears seeped between her tightly closed eyes and Maggie stifled a sob that threatened to erupt. The entire day
had taken on a feeling of unreality. This cannot be happening, Maggie thought, over and over. Gone was the
odd bravado she'd felt after she got over the hysteria of
being shoved into the boat and seeing Carter vainly try
to swim after her. She would never forget that look of
horror on Carter's face when he realized he would not
be able to reach the boat in time.

Maggie's tortuous thoughts were interrupted by the
telltale scraping sound of the boat hitting bottom. Looking up toward the bow, Maggie saw that they had
beached on a small island. Rensworth silently and effi-
ciently took down the sail that flapped noisily in the
wind, then jumped to shore, dragging the small boat
behind him with Maggie still aboard. He stared at her,
then at the woods that bordered the small rocky beach,
as if trying to figure out what to do. He apparently decided, for he began untying Maggie's hands. Maggie unconsciously moved away from Rensworth to avoid
coming close to him, and she shuddered as his fingers
touched the skin on her arms as he worked to loosen the

knot. He began mumbling something under his breath when he noted her revulsion, working quickly to loosen her binds. When she was freed, Maggie automatically rubbed her sore wrists, giving Rensworth an accusatory look. But she said nothing, afraid he would hit her again if she did. While not as big as Carter, Rensworth was strong—and vicious. She did not want to do anything that would spark his rage.

"Put your wrists together."

Maggie pulled back automatically. "You don't have to tie me again, Curtis. There's nowhere for me to go."

Rensworth brought his hand back to strike her and Maggie cringed, anticipating the blow. When none came, she peeked up at him cautiously and was even more terrified to see an evil grin spread across his face. He is enjoying himself, she thought, fighting down a feeling of panic. Ashamed, but knowing she could do nothing else, Maggie put her wrists together meekly, flinching as he tied the rope cruelly tight around her wrists.

He jerked the rope, causing Maggie to stumble awkwardly out of the boat and onto the ground, hitting the rocky beach hard with her knees and elbows.

"Get up," Rensworth snarled, jerking on the rope. Maggie's skirt was wet at the bottom and clung to her ankles making walking difficult. Her thin slipper-like shoes, perfect for walking on a sandy beach, gave her little protection from the jutting stones and rocks that made up the island's shore. Rensworth, dragging the boat with one hand and holding the rope tightly with the other, led her toward the thick woods that bordered the beach. After pulling the boat far enough so that it was hidden, he led Maggie straight into the dark woods, allowing branches to snap back into her face. After struggling through briers and brush for about twenty yards, Rensworth stopped before a large oak tree. Untying her wrists yet again, he made Maggie sit at the base of the tree.

Rensworth could not believe the woman before him was Margaret. He could not believe she had betrayed him. He would make her pay, he would leave her out here to rot while her bastard of a husband searched in vain. Narragansett Bay was dotted with numerous small uninhabited islands, and this was simply one of them. Perhaps one day, some sailor would stumble upon her bones, bleached by the sun, and the great mystery of Margaret Johnsbury would be solved. But it would be a long time before her remains were found, he thought with relish.

He pulled his sweat-soaked shirt away from his body, and noted with satisfaction that Margaret was shivering. From fear, no doubt. That thought gave Rensworth immense satisfaction. He knelt down before her, noting her swollen, bruised face. He reached out and squeezed one breast as she ineffectually tried to bat his hand away. She let out a little mewling sound as he thrust his hand down her dress to feel her naked breast and she began to struggle in earnest.

"Please, Curtis, don't hurt me. Please. I'll get you money, all the money you want. Please."

To her amazement, he stopped his assault.

"How?"

"Let me go. My grandfather will give me all I need."

Rensworth laughed. "I'm not letting you go, Margaret."

"But . . ."

"You want to know what my plans are?" he asked in a conversational tone that somehow was more frightening than his anger. He began tying one end of the rough rope to one of her wrists.

"Let me tell you what will happen, my dear. I am going to leave you here, all by yourself, tied to this tree without food or water or cover. I am going to sail back to Newport and demand a cash ransom from your adoring husband. And once he pays me, which I am certain he will, I am going to leave on an extended trip. And the best part of my plan, my dear, is that I am not going to tell your dear husband where you are." He stopped his story to let out an odd little laugh.

As he told her this horrific plan, he completed tying Maggie to the tree. Her arms were pulled painfully back and tied together around the tree. A stretch of rope of about six inches connected her wrists so that her arms were bent at an awkward—and painful—angle. The rope was stretched so tightly, it offered almost no slack, no respite from the pain in her arms.

Finished tying her, Rensworth squatted in front of her once again, tilting his head to take in his handiwork.

"How long do you think it will take you to die, Margaret, dear? Certainly no one will find you, but there is that chance. Why don't we both dwell on the tiny chance that someone will come by and save you." Again that odd laugh.

"You know, my dear," Rensworth said, roughly touching her face, "you don't look so beautiful right now. In fact, you look downright ugly." His expression became harsh as he squeezed her face and pushed her head back into the tree. Maggie cried out from the pain, but kept her eyes hard on Rensworth. She must not let him know how very frightened she was for he seemed to thrive on terrorizing her.

Rensworth stood abruptly, arching backward to stretch his back. Maggie looked up at him and noticed a subtle change in his expression as he looked down at her, as if he were suddenly aware of what he had done, and was frightened by it. Bending at the waist, he tilted her head up so that she was staring at those clear blue eyes.

"Where are you, Margaret? Are you in there somewhere? Do you still love me?" He blinked his eyes and straightened. Without another word, Curtis Rensworth began fighting his way through the brush back to the beach where he'd hidden the little boat. Maggie would never see him again.

Rose Brier was lit as if there were a great ball being held behind its graceful façade. But inside, there was no laughter, no music, nothing but an overwhelming sense of doom. The men had returned without Maggie after futilely continuing their search past dark. Charles and Bruce had to force Carter to give up the search, to convince him that it would be better for everyone to try to get a good night's sleep and resume the search at first light. Eventually, he had relented, but he had felt himself torn to pieces when he trudged alone up those wooden steps that led from the beach.

Kathryn, who knew only sketchy details of what had happened earlier in the day, had taken one look at the morose expressions on the men's faces and knew they had failed to find her. Her heart ached for her son, for his face was etched with worry and grief. She held him to her, offering no words of comfort, for she knew nothing she said would give solace. The last time she had seen Carter so distraught was the day his father died.

Bruce, Charles, John Peters, and Carter sat glumly in the library having gone over a search plan for the morrow. Although most of the guests had left, several men had stayed, offering their sailboats and services to try to find Carter Johnsbury's kidnapped wife. One had made the mistake of casually saying within earshot of Carter that he would help with the search even though he was certain Mrs. Johnsbury had gone with Rensworth voluntarily. Carter had erupted from his chair with a low growl and flung himself at the surprised young man but had been thwarted by Charles and Bruce, who held him back with some difficulty. The man apologized pro-

fusely, stuttering and stammering, but Carter had
thrown him out and rejected his offer of help.

Now, several hours later, with dawn only a few hours
away, the four exhausted men sat silently.

"We should try to get some sleep," Charles said, directing his comment to his brother.

"I'm with you," Bruce agreed, with false heartiness.

"You go ahead. I cannot sleep knowing she's out
there with . . ." Carter clenched his fists, unable to say
the scoundrel's name. Charles nodded to the two other
men for them to leave. When they had gone, he went
over to his brother and placed a hand on his arm.

"Carter, you can't drive yourself like this. It won't do
Maggie any good for you to go crazy with worry."

"What the Christ am I supposed to do?!" he yelled.
"I can't look for her. I can't just sit here. I've never felt
so goddamn helpless in my life. She's out there. With
him! God knows what he's . . ." Carter began breathing heavily, and he closed his eyes in an attempt to shut
off the horrible images that kept erupting before him.

"You've got to stop doing this to yourself, Carter!
You've got to stop imagining the worst. You're making
yourself insane."

Carter took a deep, fortifying breath. "I know,
Charles. I know it doesn't do any good. I just can't seem
to help it. I love her so much. If anything happens to
her . . ." Carter's throat closed with emotion and he
could say no more.

"We'll find her, Cart. We'll find her." But Charles
knew he'd best be prepared to help his brother, to be
there for him, if they did not.

~ *Chapter 23* ~

. . . It was awful, tied to that tree. I don't know if I was more afraid that Rensworth was not coming back, or that he would. . . .

Maggie awoke with a start and immediately became aware that her entire body ached, except for her arms, which were numb from being tied. For hours after Rensworth had left, Maggie struggled with the ropes, trying in vain to wriggle her wrists and loosen the ties. She had screamed for help, praying someone would sail by the island, until her voice was nothing more than a harsh croak. Exhausted, she finally stopped and fell into a fitful sleep, waking often during the night as small woodland animals rustled nearby.

"Okay," she croaked aloud, needing to hear her voice, needing to sound rational to her own ears. "You've been left here to die. But you're not going to die, are you? You have already fought death, remember? You beat it. You, Maggie Johnsbury, are going to live. You just have to figure out how to do it." She again began to struggle with the thick rope that held her wrists, gritting her teeth against the pain, but was quickly frustrated.

"There's got to be another way," she said, and began looking around her for anything that could be remotely used to cut the rope. That's when she spotted a rock about the size of her fist that appeared to have a fairly sharp edge lying next to her left foot. Putting her foot atop the rock, she dragged it as far as her knee. "Not good enough, Maggie girl." Contorting her body, she managed to kick the rock to her hip and began wriggling frantically to shove the rock closer to the tree. Inch by inch, the rock moved closer, until finally it rested at the base of the thick oak. Letting herself smile at the image of herself writhing and squirming to get the rock to its proper place, Maggie rested her head against the tree and caught her breath.

She looked down at the gray rock as if it were her savior, her best friend, her confidant. She frowned a bit, noticing that what had looked like a sharp edge, was more smooth than it appeared. Scooting around the tree so that one tied wrist was even with the rock, Maggie tried to bring her arms down the trunk so she could rub the rope against the rock. The farther down the trunk she pushed her arms, the tighter the rope became, until, by the time her wrist was even with the rock, the pain was almost unbearable. Her neck was pressed forward so that her chin rested on her chest and her arms were stretched nearly past endurance. All this, and the rope barely grazed the smooth rock. "Damn." Maggie choked back tears of frustration, determined not to panic.

Then it came to her. "What an idiot I am!" she said, embarrassed that she did not think of this solution more quickly. Instead of scooting down, making her bindings tighter, she should stand up to make them looser. Maggie struggled to sit up, then to stand. She brought her feet up underneath her and pushed up, wriggling to a standing position. "There!" she said with satisfaction. Her arms were no longer pulled so tightly and she found she could walk around the trunk fairly easily, only scraping her back and arms a little bit. What she saw was not very encouraging. Woods spread out in all directions, so thick that if she did not know which direction the bay was, she would not be able to tell.

But standing gave her enough room to move her arms a bit and loosened the rope enough so that it no longer pulled painfully tight. She also found that she could rub her wrists against the tree trunk, perhaps fraying the rope enough to get free. She tried to ignore her hunger and thirst and concentrate on the rope. She visualized it in her head, pictured it fraying bit by bit as she rubbed frantically. It seemed she'd been moving her right arm up and down for hours when she finally allowed herself to stop. Her wrist was slick against the rope, from either blood or sweat, Maggie could not tell. She tried once again to pull her hand free, hoping she would be able to slip her hand through, but the rope was simply tied too tightly. Stifling a sob, Maggie worked her way down into a sitting position once again. She was so very thirsty, she thought, as she licked her dried lips. The sky was an unrelenting blue, the sun brutally hot. Her dress clung to her uncomfortably and she realized to her disgust that she had to relieve herself. Allowing her painful bladder to empty, she swallowed her shame and distaste, telling herself she had no other choice, and realizing she might be forced to give in to even more unpleasant bodily functions if she could not free herself.

For the first time since Rensworth left her almost twenty-four hours ago, Maggie felt despair grip her heart. She'd rubbed her arm against the tree for hours, it seemed, and she could not even tell if she had made any progress.

"Please come find me, Carter. Please," she whispered, allowing precious wet tears to fall from her face.

Carter stared hollow-eyed onto the dark bay. Three days. Three days of searching, of asking fishermen and innkeepers and sailors up and down Narragansett Bay if they remembered seeing Rensworth and Maggie. It seemed as if they had simply disappeared off the face of the earth. Newport's police force had canvassed the town, Carter's friends had expanded the search up and down the bay, but there was so much ground to cover, so many places they could have gone. Newspapers ran the story of the kidnapping on their front pages. But no one had seen them or the little dory Rensworth stole. Carter had slept and ate only enough to give him the energy to continue searching. He could not get Maggie's screams out of his head. He brought his hands up to his head, as if to shut them out. For the past two days, he had refused to think the worst—that Rensworth had killed her and had gone into hiding. What else could explain their inability to locate them? A single man on the run would be difficult to find, but a beautiful woman, disheveled and held against her will—that was something else entirely. The bay he loved so much, that soothed him, looked menacing and evil. And he bitterly realized that Rensworth had taken two things he loved: Maggie and Rose Brier. For Rose Brier was nothing without his Maggie to give it light and warmth. He shook his head to rid himself of such calamitous thoughts. He must believe her alive. He must keep hoping, even though everyone around him had given up. He saw it in their pitying looks, their eyes as they took in his haggard appearance. They continued searching for Carter's sake, not for Maggie's, for few believed the outcome of their search would be happy. Too much time was passing. Carter pushed back an overpowering panic that seized him, clenching his fists to fight the doubts that flooded his soul.

"Carter! Carter!" The urgency in Bruce's voice stopped Carter's heart. Someone had been found. Oh, thank you, God, thank you, Jesus and Mary. He ran toward Bruce whose face was lit by excitement.

"Maggie! You've found her!"

Hating to disappoint Carter, Bruce quickly shook his head. "No, but the next best thing. Rensworth at this very minute is at the White Horse Tavern getting lit. Old

Joe Miller saw Rensworth there and remembered us asking about him. He stopped by on his way home to tell us. I gave the old gent a kiss, I was so happy. C'mon, man. Let's go get the bastard."

Carter needed no convincing. He had Bruce get Charles and he ran to the stables to ready three mounts. Within ten minutes the three men were galloping down the drive at breakneck speed heading toward the downtown.

Rensworth felt wonderful. He was full of good food, wearing a fine new suit, and warmed by liquor. He did not stop to think of Margaret, still tied to that tree, probably dying of thirst and hunger, as he shoveled yet another mouthful of honeyed ham into his mouth. There had been moments when he had confusedly thought about Margaret and a sense of regret washed over him. But, Margaret was getting what she deserved, wasn't she? She had betrayed him, played him for a fool. And he loved her. She deserved to pay. It was as simple as that. So when those rare moments came, when he remembered leaving her there, when he thought of her wrists, already bloodied from the bindings, he forced those thoughts away. He reminded himself that she deserved to be punished. Deserved whatever happened to her. And he deserved everything she had tried to deny him. It was his right after all the sacrifices he'd made for her, after everything he'd done for her.

Taking a long sip from his whiskey, top-shelf stuff this time, he allowed himself a satisfied smile. The money Margaret had given him was already running short, but there was more where that came from. He had just finished composing his ransom note to her bastard husband and was reading it over, laughing aloud at the part where he'd written that Margaret would be safely returned, when the front door to the tavern crashed in. Rensworth nearly peed in his pants at the sight of

Carter Johnsbury searching the room with those steely gray eyes and nearly squealed when those eyes found their prey. Rensworth's sense of self-preservation hurtled him to the tavern's back door. With Carter in pursuit, shouting at him to stop, Rensworth ran blindly ahead, so filled with fear he let out a pathetic sob.

Carter exploded through the back door just steps behind Rensworth but stopped dead. He would never forget the sound that came from Rensworth as he was trampled by the speeding carriage. It was inhuman, a sound that brought passersby to a standstill, the stuff of nightmares. Rensworth was dragged several feet before the carriage driver managed to bring his frightened team to a halt. Leaping down, the poor driver stared at the gawking crowd in horror.

"He just ran out in front of me. I didn't have a chance," he said, although no one there cast any blame in his direction. But the driver felt the need to explain after taking in the look of raw despair on the face of the young man who was first on the scene. The despair on Carter's face was not for Rensworth, but for Maggie. For Rensworth was the only person on this earth who knew where his wife was—and whether she was alive.

Carter swallowed the bile that came to his throat when he reached Rensworth, for he had been torn almost in two. "Be alive, be alive," Carter prayed over and over. Impossibly, Rensworth was indeed alive. Barely.

Gripping the injured man's shoulders, Carter said, "Where is she, Rensworth? Tell me. For God's sake, tell me. You're a dying man. You've got to tell me." And for himself he prayed aloud, "Oh God, make him tell me."

But whether Rensworth even understood his words, Carter would never know. He let out a bloody gurgle and his lips formed a small smile as he looked up at Carter's grief-ravaged face. And then he died.

Carter shook the dead man, willing him to come back

to life and tell him where his Maggie was. "Tell me! Tell me where she is!" he shouted. Carter shook him until Rensworth's head flopped obscenely against the cobble-stone street. "Nooo!" And his scream of denial, many would say later, was almost as horrible, as haunting, as the screams of the dead man when he was struck by the carriage.

The three men arrived at Rose Brier just as the east was beginning to brighten despite heavily overcast skies. Kathryn met them at the door, her eyes questioning, but one look at Carter's face and she knew something was horribly, horribly wrong. Her heart constricted with fear and she quickly looked at Charles, silently asking him with her eyes what had happened. Her youngest son shook his head, and as he passed, he whispered he would explain all in a few minutes.

Without a word, Carter headed to the library, thrusting one hand behind him to stop anyone who might want to follow.

When the door closed, Charles took his mother aside.

"Rensworth's dead and there's no sign of Maggie," Charles explained, his voice gruff from exhaustion and emotion. He explained how they'd found Rensworth and how he died before telling Carter where Maggie was.

"We went to his room, hoping to find something that would tell us where she was. There was no sign of her and no one at the rooming house had seen a woman with Rensworth. We found this where Rensworth was sitting. It's a ransom note and says he planned to return Maggie, but I'm not so sure."

"Why?" Kathryn shifted her worried gaze from the note to her youngest son's weary face.

"Rensworth had been staying at the rooming house for nearly three days. He rarely left his room, except to buy a suit of clothes and some liquor. That means he probably didn't go to wherever he is keeping Maggie. And that means she's likely been without food or water. If she's alive." Charles brushed his hand through his hair. "It doesn't look good for her, Mother, and Carter knows it. Even if Maggie is alive somewhere, we have no idea where to look. And, frankly, time is running out." His gray eyes filled with tears. "It'll kill him, Ma. He loves her so. He's already half dead inside." Charles let out a shaky breath. "You should have seen him when Rensworth died. Carter's eyes were so odd. I've seen that look before, an innocent man they'd sent to the gallows. Two days later, they found evidence that would have cleared him. I'll never forget his eyes as they brought him out. That was the look in Carter's eyes. I never thought I'd see another man look like that. Those eyes. They were dead, nothing in them. So goddamn dead."

Charles, tired beyond belief and grieving for his brother, let out a sob and hugged his mother to him. "We can't give up," she found herself saying. "Not while there's still hope."

Maggie slumped against the tree. She feebly tried to rub her right hand against the rough bark, but she had so little energy left. Her hair fell in greasy strings across her face, which was still bruised from Rensworth's blows. Her thirst had become an obsession, it was all she could think about, and she cried each time she emptied her bladder, to see that wasted water soak into the ground. She had lost track of how long she'd been tied to the tree, and thought only of her thirst. Her tongue felt thick in her mouth, her lips were cracked, her skin gritty from her salty sweat. Closing her eyes, she visualized a cool, clean spring of bubbling water. So real was the image that for a moment she thought she had conjured up water out of thin air when the first drops of rain fell on her. But as the rain came faster, Maggie

lifted her head and let out an odd little noise that would
have been a scream of joy if she had had the energy to
produce it. Tilting her head back as far as she could,
Maggie's mouth was soon blessedly wet. She swallowed
rain that was sweeter than anything that had ever
touched her tongue before.

"Rain, rain, rain," she chanted joyfully, as she tilted
her head to the sky. She kicked off her shoes so that
they could fill with precious liquid she might drink later.
How wonderful was this rain, she thought, taking a
stockinged foot and digging a hole near the base of the
tree so it, too, would fill with rain. In heavy sheets it fell,
until Maggie was drenched. Still she lifted her face, her
tongue darting out to catch the precious rivulets that
poured down her face.

To her joy, one slipper had already filled with water.
She moved it slowly with her foot, careful not to let too
much spill, so that the slipper rested by the base of the
tree. Squirming down, she stretched her arms, her back
and her neck painfully so that she could reach the wa-
ter-filled shoe. With a little shout of triumph, Maggie
slurped up a mouthful. "Oh, so good," she murmured
aloud, smiling widely. Bending down again, she managed another long draw, stopping only when she realized she was beginning to feel a bit queasy. The last
thing she wanted, she thought, was to vomit up this precious gift.

Three hours later, rejuvenated from the water, Maggie felt good enough to actually grumble at the rain that
fell unceasingly. With two slippers filled to the brim with
the water, she felt she could last a few more days. And
surely someone would find her. Surely Carter would find
her. As if possessed of magical powers, the water had
strengthened Maggie's body and mind. Standing with
renewed energy, she once again began rubbing her arm
against the tree. "I must be making headway," she said
aloud, as she ignored the aching in her arm. She could

only move her arm a few inches at a time, but felt certain the rope was beginning to weaken. She just prayed the rope would weaken before she did.

All day, Maggie worked, turning her mind from her obsession with water to an obsession with the rope. Resting periodically, and drinking from her slippers, Maggie moved her right arm up and down, up and down, until darkness began to fall once again.

"No!" she shouted at the shadows as if her mere shouts would hold the night at bay. In a frenzy of motion, she moved her arm violently, tearing her flesh and ripping the fabric on her dress. She let out an animal-like sound, a chant of sorts, in the rhythm of her arm, ignoring the pain, ignoring her weariness. The chant turned into a scream of frustration as she began to tire—a scream that turned into triumph when she felt the rope snap away from her wrist.

"Yes! Yes! Oooh, I'm free." Maggie stared at her arms for several minutes, relishing being free. She skipped away from the tree, hooting and dancing like a pagan fairy. She worked the knot that still kept the rope attached to her left hand and flung it from her when she was finally free of that as well. Drinking the last of the water from her slipper, Maggie followed the path that Rensworth had taken through the thick brush when he'd left her all those days ago. Wiping the rain from her eyes, Maggie squinted through the branches and leaves trying to see the shore. Her dress catching and tearing in the brambles, she gave a mighty yank and fell—onto the rocky sand of the island's small beach. Picking herself up, Maggie ran to the water's edge, too happy to care that it was too dark and too stormy for anyone to be out on the bay. But when the joy of being free began to dissipate, Maggie crossed her arms and shivered. She realized with dread that she would have to spend yet another night on this dratted island. Tears of frustration fell down her face as she hugged herself to keep warm.

"I want to go home," she said pitifully. "I want to go home."

Carter's face, his warm gray eyes, appeared in her mind, giving her some comfort. She tried to console herself that tomorrow someone would sail by, that tomorrow she would be in Carter's arms. But tonight, it was dark and cold and Maggie wanted nothing more than to be beside her husband in his huge soft bed, being held. She looked back at the woods, which looked impossibly dark and forbidding, and decided she would stay on the beach despite the cover from the storm the woods would afford her. Clearing the stones away from a portion of the beach, Maggie curled up on the soft wet sand and decided to try to sleep. It was not long before exhaustion overtook her and she was sound asleep, her head cradled on her arms.

She awoke the next morning with a groan. It was still raining and the wind was strong and steady, lashing stinging drops against her face. Her water-blurred eyes searched the choppy bay in vain. Visibility was so poor that Maggie could not make out the distant shore, a distance much too far to try to swim in these seas, she knew. She shivered uncontrollably and decided to try to find some shelter from the storm that battered the little island. Finding an outcropping of rocks that shielded her from most of the wind, if not the rain, Maggie huddled, hugging herself to keep warm most of the day while her eyes searched endlessly for boats. She felt weak from hunger and was beginning to feel feverish. "Oh great," she mumbled to herself, "I survive days of being tied up without water only to die of the flu once I'm free." Shivering so much her teeth rattled, Maggie forced herself to relax and think about other things than how cold and sick she was. But with the wind driving rain onto her, even Maggie's will began to weaken. Pushing her head against the rock, Maggie tried to sleep to pass time, but could not. "I'm s-s-so c-c-cold," she said. "I-I-m n-never gonna c-c-complain 'bout the heat ag-g-gain." And despite herself, she smiled, remembering her strained conversation with Patricia. *If I can still smile*, Maggie thought, *I must be okay*.

"Dammit, we should be doing something. Two days and we've been stuck in here. Two days!" Carter ranted at Charles.

He walked over to the windows where rain was lashing up against the glass and raised one arm over his head as he leaned against the pane. Water fell in steady sheets blurring the view to outside. He knew it would be foolhardy to be out on the bay during such a storm. They'd spend so much time trying to weather the storm, any search would be fruitless. But it drove him insane to be warm inside Rose Brier when Maggie could be outside. Tears flooded his eyes as he thought of Maggie out there. "It's so cold," he said softly. "She's going to be so cold."

"We don't know that, Carter," Charles said. Despite himself, he was getting weary of trying to lift his brother's spirits when he felt in his heart they had lost this fight. It had been five days. If Maggie were alive, someone would have found her by now, he was certain.

"I goddamn do know she's cold," Carter shouted, his voice cracking with emotion. Charles' heart almost broke when he saw his big brother collapse to his knees, his body wracked with sobs. His head on the carpet, his hands clenched in fists by his head, Carter shouted his frustration and grief. "She's alive! Don't you goddamn forget it! She's alive!"

Bruce, drawn by the shouting, quickly entered the library but stopped short at the sight of Carter kneeling on the floor.

"Aw, Jesus," he mumbled to himself, as he cast a pained look to Charles. The two men let Carter spend his grief. After a while, Carter sat on the floor leaning against the wall, his face still wet from tears, and gave his brother and friend a crooked half-embarrassed smile that quickly disappeared.

"I know she's probably dead," he said, and swallowed heavily. Fresh tears coursed down his face. He looked up at the ceiling as if willing himself not to lose control again. Using the heels of his hands to wipe his face, Carter stood and walked unsteadily to his desk and sat down heavily. "I'm not going to stop looking for her. You two, you can do what you want. But I'm not going to stop. I'm going to look until I find her."

Each silently acknowledged that they were no longer looking for a living woman. They were looking for a body.

~ *Chapter 24* ~

. . . I have never been more exhausted in my life, or more alive. . . .

Maggie lifted her head slowly, closing her eyes as the world spun crazily. "Thirsty," she said aloud, smacking her lips and swallowing. She opened her eyes again and squinted. Sun! Moving slowly, for she was overwhelmed by dizziness, Maggie straightened and looked around her. It was as if the storm had never happened. The bay was smooth and impossibly blue, the sun warm against her face. "Today is the day I go home," Maggie said aloud with joy. She stood unsteadily, shielding her eyes from the sun with one hand, her eyes searching the waters around her. Voices! She could hear voices.

Moving gingerly around the rock formation, she eyed the beach expectantly. There, not twenty yards from the beach, were two men tonging for oysters from their boat. Tears of joy fell from Maggie's eyes as she walked drunkenly toward them. When she was even with the men, she let out a thin croaking sound that could hardly have been described as a shout. The men kept working, oblivious to the frantic young woman standing on the shore. Swallowing and clearing her throat, Maggie let out a surprisingly clear "Help!" as she waved her arms to get the men's attention.

Out on the boat, Carl Wilcox jerked his head up at

what sounded like a woman shouting. "Hey, Spinner, get a load of the woman on shore."

Spinner, a thin man with arms of steel, stopped his raking to see what had interested his brother-in-law enough to stop working.

"Well, I'll be damned. It's a girl! What's she saying?"

"Can't tell. But looks to me like she got herself stranded. Looks like she's trying to get our attention."

"Well. She's got it," Spinner said, with his Yankee sensibility.

In unison, the two men brought up their tongs, lifting them hand over hand. Spinner manned the oars and began pulling the boat to shore. When Maggie noticed the two men had seen her, she jumped up in pure joy. The sudden movement had her head swimming and the next thing she knew, she was hitting the beach in a dead faint.

"Oh, shit," Carl said, causing Spinner to turn his head as he rowed. "Yep," he agreed when he saw the crumpled figure on shore.

The boat scraped the bottom and the two men got out, gingerly making their way over to the fallen lady. Bending down, Carl shook the woman, taking in her yellowing bruises, the raw wounds on both wrists, and her disheveled appearance.

"Holy! Do you know who we got here?" Carl said, clearly amazed at what he was looking at. "We got here a genuine kidnap victim."

At Spinner's blank stare, Carl said, "You know, the one in the paper a few days back."

"No kiddin'," Spinner said, taking a closer look at the woman, who was beginning to moan. "Thought she'd be dead by now."

"Looks pretty close to it now, don't she?" Carl said in his blunt manner.

"Not dead," Maggie said, opening her eyes.

"Not yet," Carl said, but he was smiling at the woman, his tan face wrinkling.

Maggie struggled to get up to prove to these two men that she had no intention of dying.

"Looks pretty healthy to me," Spinner said diplomatically. "What's your name, miss?"

"Maggie. Maggie Johnsbury."

"Dint I tell you, Spin? It's her! It's the missing girl. I'll be damned!" he said, as if he'd just discovered a pearl in an oyster. "I'm Carl Wilcox and this here's Spinner Crabbs." He smiled a gap-toothed smile, clearly overjoyed. "There's been an awful lot of people looking for you, Ma'am."

"Well, you found me. Or I found you." Maggie felt so groggy. "Could you take me home?"

The two men helped Maggie onto their boat while she tried to clear her head. She felt so light-headed that she was afraid she was about to faint again, until she found herself seated securely in the small boat.

"Do you have any water?" she croaked.

"Naw," Carl said, wrinkling his nose. "But got some whiskey. Probably do you a world more good. I know it does me." He opened up a jug with a "thunk" and helped her take a sip. Maggie gasped and choked, much to the two men's delight. It was nasty-tasting stuff, but it was wet and it warmed her insides. She took another little sip before passing the jug back.

"Grow hair on your chest, it will," Carl said, cackling with glee.

"Lift the sail, Spinner. Let's get this gal home."

The two men talked nonstop, so excited were they. Maggie idly thought the two men hadn't had such fun in years. They told her about the newspaper articles, about the search, about all the people who had been looking for her. And then they talked about how they planned to tell everyone they had found her and were already recounting what had happened just minutes ago. Maggie asked about Rensworth, but neither man had heard anything. All Maggie could think was, *I'm going home. I'm going home.* She repeated the sentence a thousand times during the hour-long sail down the bay toward Newport. She looked down at herself, at her tattered, filthy dress, at her wounded wrists and grungy feet, and grimaced. Then giggled. The whiskey, while she'd had only a tiny bit, was making her even more light-headed than she had been, she realized.

"You tell us which house, Ma'am," Carl said.

Maggie looked up at the bluff, seeing the Brownings' mansion set back from the beach and knew they were close. "There!" she said, pointing to Rose Brier huddled atop the bluff. It had never looked more lovely and Maggie's eyes filled with tears once again. "I'm home," she said softly and with wonder. It seemed like years since she'd taken that fateful walk down the beach toward Curtis Rensworth. She looked at the wooden steps that led up to the house and thought that the path to heaven could not have been more beautiful.

Mrs. Brimble had just yelled at a maid for the third time that morning for missing a speck of dust. What has come over me, she thought, wiping her hands on her dress. The same thing that has come over everyone in this household, she thought sadly. Mr. Johnsbury had locked himself in the library early that morning with his brother and Bruce. The three were devising a systematic search that would encompass all of Narragansett Bay and its surrounding towns. It was not the plan for a search that was so unsettling to those at Rose Brier. It was the lack of urgency. For that could mean only one thing; they did not expect to find Mrs. Johnsbury alive. Poor, poor Mr. Johnsbury, Mrs. Brimble thought, shaking her head. Although she rarely let her emotions show, Mrs. Brimble was heartbroken over the disappearance of Mrs. Johnsbury. She was a kind woman who knew well how to run a household, Mrs. Brimble thought. She made Mr. Johnsbury happy, and any fool could see she loved him with all her heart.

Mrs. Brimble's thoughts were interrupted by a banging at the front door. Whoever it was, she thought angrily, they certainly did not know how to knock properly or that this was a household in a kind of mourning. Marching to the door, Mrs. Brimble swung it open, ready to give whoever stood on the other side her most stern look. But all she could do was gasp and place one trembling hand over her mouth. Two scruffy-looking men wearing working clothes and reeking of fish stood at the door. The younger one, gangly, but apparently strong, held Mrs. Johnsbury in his arms. Her eyes were closed, but the small hand that clutched the thin man's shirt proved that she was alive.

"This lady says she belongs to you," said the wrinkled older man. "I'm Carl Wilcox. He's Spinner Crabbs. That's Maggie Johnsbury in his arms."

Mrs. Brimble could only squeak, her eyes wide above her hand. She turned and ran to the library, completely forgetting to escort the two men with Maggie into the house, completely forgetting that she never, ever ran anywhere.

Carter was standing behind his desk, a chart of Narragansett Bay in front of him, when Mrs. Brimble stormed into the room, her finger pointing to the foyer behind her, her mouth opening and closing with no sound coming out. Carter came out from behind the desk, knowing something must be terribly wrong for Mrs. Brimble to act so flustered.

"Two men. Mrs. Johnsbury." To her utter frustration—and the men's in the library—it was all she could spit out. Carter stopped dead. Then he straightened, mentally preparing himself for whatever awaited him outside that door. He glanced back at Bruce and his brother. "Wait here."

Carter's heart gave a lurch when he saw a thin man with soulful brown eyes holding Maggie, drooping, in his arms. *She's dead,* he thought, as he walked steadily toward the two men who fidgeted on the doorstep. His chest felt as if a heavy weight had been placed upon it as he took in her battered face, tangled hair, and her ragged dress, torn and filthy. He closed his eyes, willing the image of her bruised body to disappear. Please God, I cannot live without her, he thought in desperate prayer. His eyes shot open when he heard a thin moan and his heart soared when he saw her lift her head and smile at him the most beautiful of smiles.

"Home," she whispered, before slumping back on the man's arm. With a cry of joy, Carter lifted Maggie from the man's grasp, giving him a look of immense gratitude.

"She's alive!" he shouted back into the house, holding his frail Maggie in his arms. "Oh, my God, she's alive," he said to himself, holding her to him, burying his head against her neck. He ran up the stairs, taking them two at a time, clutching Maggie to him. "Get Dr. Armstrong, and be quick!" he shouted, his heart beating wildly, with joy and with fear, for he did not believe Maggie was out of danger yet. He put her gently onto his bed and began his own examination as tears fell unbidden. Yellowing bruises marred her beautiful face and neck and he cried aloud when he saw her injured wrists.

"Oh, Maggie, I'm so sorry," he said raggedly, holding her hand in his and bringing it to his lips.

"Don't cry, Carter." Carter looked up through his tears to see Maggie's worried face. She's worried about me, he thought with awe.

He crushed her hand against his mouth and dragged it across his bearded cheek, needing her caress, needing to touch her, to make sure this was not some cruel dream.

"Oh, God, Maggie, I cannot believe you're here.

You've no idea how much I love you. You cannot know how much. I didn't think I'd ever see you again."

"I know, Carter. I love you, too." She sounded so tired, her words were no more than whispers. He brushed her scraggly hair back from her forehead with tenderness as she closed her eyes once again. He gave her a little shake, fearing every time she closed her eyes, he was losing her. She opened her eyes, blinking to focus. Maggie had never felt so tired in all her life. Why wasn't Carter letting her sleep, for God's sake? Then she realized: *He's afraid.*

"I'm okay, Carter. Really. I'm just very tired." Though she tried to sound strong, healthy, her words came out slightly slurred and were mere whispers.

Giving her an intense look, he let her close her eyes, but did not relinquish her hand. He felt he would never let her go. Behind him, Charles, Patricia, and his mother entered the room. He turned, his eyes bright. "She's okay. Just tired." His smile warmed Kathryn's heart and she clutched her hands in front of her with happiness.

"Jesus, that bastard!" Charles said, when he saw the bruises and her ravaged wrists. "If he weren't already dead, I'd kill him."

"And I'd help," Patricia said, surprising everyone in the room with her fierce statement. "Well I would," she said, noting their looks of disbelief.

"We should get that dress off her, Carter," his mother said kindly. She knew they might find more bruises underneath that tattered dress. God only knew what Rensworth had done to her before deserting her. Once Patricia and Charles left the room, Kathryn and Carter removed the soiled dress. Carter searched his wife's body for more bruises and nearly cried with relief when he saw nothing except some small scrapes on her back. Perhaps Rensworth had not raped her. They bathed her gently, waking a groggy Maggie more than once. It felt so good to be clean, she'd thought she would never be clean again.

By the time Dr. Armstrong appeared, Maggie was washed and dressed in a soft cotton nightgown. Dr. Armstrong was well aware of the trauma the young woman had just been through, but he was still shocked at the bruises he saw on her sleeping face. Keeping his expression bland and professional, he gently touched Maggie's face to see if Rensworth had broken any bones.

Maggie awoke in a panic at Dr. Armstrong's first touch, knowing instinctively that it was not Carter. Pushing away from him with a small scream, Maggie lunged to get out of the bed before realizing what was happening.

"It's okay, Maggie. Shhh. Shhh. It's just Dr. Armstrong," Carter said, his throat constricting painfully as he held her and rocked back and forth. The fear he'd seen in Maggie's face tore at him. After a few moments, Maggie, embarrassed by her reaction, pushed away and peeked around Carter's strong arm.

"Sorry, Doc." Dr. Armstrong smiled down at Maggie with understanding.

"Here we are again, Mrs. Johnsbury," with mock sternness. "I want you to promise me this will be the last visit for a while." Maggie rewarded him with a small smile.

"I'm going to check your face for broken bones," he said, as he gently moved both hands along her jaw. Maggie winced as he touched a bruise that had not quite healed along her jaw and again when he touched her nose.

"Is it broken?" she asked worriedly.

"It does not appear to be, no."

Maggie cast a glance at Carter, who hovered behind the doctor as if ready to come to her rescue at any moment. "I must look awful," she said to her husband.

"You're the most beautiful sight I've ever seen," Carter said honestly. But Maggie's snort of disbelief caused a broad smile to spread on Carter's face.

"Lose any teeth?" the doctor asked.

"No. Just loosened a couple, but they seem better now," Maggie said, moving her tongue to test her damaged molars.

His exam continued at her wrists. "Rope?" At Maggie's nod, a frown formed on Dr. Armstrong's kind mouth. He'd never seen such heinous injuries to a woman. "I'm going to have to clean these wounds. It may hurt."

Dr. Armstrong spent several minutes cleaning the raw wounds on her wrists and Carter winced more than Maggie. The right was much worse than the left, the doctor noted, his frown deepening. After wrapping her wrists, he straightened.

"You're dehydrated and half starved. And you never fully recovered physically from the last time I was here. But I don't see any permanent physical damage, Mrs. Johnsbury."

Dr. Armstrong then turned to Carter. "I need to speak with Mrs. Johnsbury alone for a few minutes, Mr. Johnsbury."

"No." Carter clenched his fist and looked quickly over to Maggie who lay watching the two men with interest.

Dr. Armstrong drew Carter away from the bed to speak to him privately, taking his arm with a strength that surprised Carter. "Mr. Johnsbury, there are things a woman feels more comfortable discussing with a doctor than her husband. She may have been . . . injured in other ways that are not as clearly evident."

"You mean he may have raped her."

Raising an eyebrow at the man's bluntness, he nodded his head with a quick jerk. "I'm aware of that, Doctor, and also aware that Maggie needs me by her side. If she was raped, she needs to know that I love her. I spent five days, Doctor, looking for her. I will not leave her side. She needs me."

Heaving a little sigh at the man's stubbornness, but understanding his reasons completely, Dr. Armstrong turned back to a curious Maggie.

"What was that all about?" she asked, scowling at the two men.

Before Dr. Armstrong could say a thing, Carter interjected, somehow knowing that they should not dance around the question. "Did Rensworth force you, Maggie?"

Maggie creased her forehead. "Do you mean did he rape me?" she asked, shocking the two men in front of her. Smiling gently at their nineteenth-century sensibilities, Maggie shook her head. "No, he did not. I think he intended to, but for some reason he didn't."

"Thank God," Carter said, taking her hand.

"Speaking of Rensworth. Has he been caught?" Maggie asked, an overwhelming sense of fear strangling her.

Carter immediately knelt by her bed and squeezed her hand. "Rensworth is dead, Maggie. He was run over by a carriage while running away from me. He died before he could tell us where you were." Carter closed his eyes against the memory of that horrible night. The guilt he'd felt for Rensworth's death had raged at him. He was not sorry the man was dead, but for two long days he tormented himself with belief that had he not rushed at the man, Rensworth would have told him where he had hidden Maggie.

"Dead?" Relief flooded Maggie. Rensworth was dead. She did not feel even a smidgen of guilt at being so happy.

After Dr. Armstrong left, having made sure she drank a small amount of water and leaving behind detailed instructions about how much water and food to give her, Maggie gazed at her husband.

"You look tired," she said, taking in the deep circles under his eyes and his unusually pale complexion.

Carter was holding her hand again, half on the bed, one hand stroking her forehead. "I was so worried, Maggie. I thought you were lost to me."

"So did I," she said, her eyes filling with tears. "You'd think with how dehydrated I am, I wouldn't have any water left for silly tears," she said, wiping the drops away.

"Oh, Carter, I'm so glad to be home. You've no idea. Come in bed with me, Carter, and hold me. I dreamt of this, laying in your bed, warm, with you holding me. It kept me going."

Fully clothed, Carter drew back the covers and pulled his wife to him, wrapping his body protectively around hers until she fell asleep.

Downstairs in the library, Carter's family huddled together, united in their worry for Maggie and Carter. Kathryn, a glass of sherry forgotten in her hand, stared at the dying fire in the hearth. She could not forget the bruises on her daughter-in-law's face and body, nor the horrid wounds on her wrists. To survive such an ordeal took more courage and more character than many women possessed. Certainly more than Margaret Johnsbury ever possessed. She had cried tears of joy for her son, knowing that had Margaret died, he would have been forever changed. But she also found herself shedding tears for Margaret . . . Maggie . . . the woman who fought so valiantly to return to her husband's side. The husband she so obviously loved.

"Do you all remember my birthday visit?" she asked Charles and Patricia, who sat together on the leather sofa. "Do you remember when she came down the stairs looking scared to death? She asked Carter to introduce her. We all thought she was being rather manipulative."

Patricia's face flushed at the memory of her holding

her Lily away from Margaret, of her forbidding Reginald to see his Aunt Maggie, whom he so clearly adored.

"I know it seems in hindsight that we are all rather cruel, Mother," Charles said blandly. "But we all thought we were dealing with the old Margaret. Even Carter wasn't taken in by her in the beginning."

Kathryn seemed a bit reflective. "I'm not so sure. I remember getting rather disturbed by his solicitous attitude toward her. It was quite disconcerting at the time—even for Carter. He fought it. We all saw it. But she won."

"What are you saying, Mother."

Kathryn gave her son a small smile. "I'm saying that we were all wrong. I'm saying that perhaps we should apologize to Maggie." She said Maggie's name very clearly, enunciating the syllables succinctly. They looked at each other, each feeling their own guilt over their treatment of the woman upstairs.

At the sound of the library door opening, all heads turned expectantly, seeing Carter enter.

"She's sleeping," he said, throwing himself down in his chair. His hair was rumpled, his shirt partially unbuttoned and uncharacteristically wrinkled, and his face was marred by deep circles from lack of sleep. But his family had never seen Carter happier.

"Are the two men who found her gone?"

Charles chuckled. Carl and Spinner had made their excuses, claiming they had to get back to work and good-naturedly grumbling about how the detour of rescuing Mrs. Johnsbury had cost them a day's wages. Charles had happily handed each man a generous sum of money, enough that both were left speechless, a state which Charles believed was rare indeed for those two.

"They're gone," Charles said, and informed Carter about the reward. He grunted his approval, too tired for a more human response.

Kathryn straightened, drawing the attention of her eldest son. "When Maggie is up to it," she said, noting the satisfied gleam in her son's eye at the name she used, "the three of us would like to apologize to your wife. We have been dreadful."

"Not that we didn't have some reason to be," Charles interjected, unwilling to take complete blame.

Carter threw his brother an understanding look. "Maggie understands. I don't think a formal apology is necessary and she'll likely find it downright embarrassing. Just let her know she's welcome. She's part of the family. She needs that more than anything right now."

Maggie's recovery was nothing short of remarkable. Once she had rehydrated her parched body and eaten a few good meals, she was almost back to normal, albeit a bit weak. Carter rarely left her side and Maggie was beginning to get a bit disconcerted by the way he seemed to never want her out of his sight. Her third night back at Rose Brier, Carter lay next to her in bed and held her tightly to him. They had been laying there silently, needing simply to hold one another, when Maggie became aware of a sudden change in Carter.

"I'm not letting you go," Carter said fiercely, tightening his hold on her. "No matter what, Maggie, I'm not letting you go!"

Again, Maggie sensed a fear that transcended what he'd felt about her disappearance. Turning, Maggie put a hand on the side of one cheek.

"What's wrong, Carter? Something has been bothering you for a while, from even before Rensworth. Tell me. I'm back, I'm safe, but you still look like you're afraid I'm going to disappear right in front of you."

Swallowing heavily, Carter gritted out, "You still could."

"I don't understand."

"The amnesia, Maggie," Carter said, his voice tinged

with bleakness. "No matter that your memory has not returned, it still could. And I would lose you. This time for good."

So that was it, Maggie thought. She brought her arms around his neck, ignoring the pain in her wrists and kissed him soundly. She decided then and there that she would have to try to convince him of the truth, even though it was far more bizarre than the fiction she'd been forced to create.

Maggie gave him her most stern look. "Do you love me, Carter?"

"You know I do."

"Do you trust me? Completely?"

Carter tensed. "Of course."

"Do you believe I would ever lie to you?"

"Well . . ." Maggie elbowed him sharply.

"No, Maggie, I don't believe you would lie."

Maggie let out a huge sigh, gathering the resolve to tell Carter the full truth.

"That's good, Carter. Because I've been lying to you, in a way, for a long time." At his startled look, Maggie laid a gentling hand upon his face. "Trust me, Carter," she said, all the love she had for him shining in her eyes.

"Now. Do you remember that story I told you when I first awoke from the horse accident? The one about Margaret dying and me coming into her body?"

She felt Carter stiffen slightly.

Propping herself up on one elbow, Maggie gazed down at her husband, willing him to believe her, for it was the only way he could live in peace.

"As crazy as that seems, it was the truth, Carter. It was the truth." Carter made a sound of denial, but Maggie interrupted him.

"Think, Carter. Think. Even amnesia cannot produce a complete personality change. I was given a second chance at life. And now, I believe, you were too. We were both dead, in a way, me physically and you emotionally. God gave us another chance to live, and we've got to take it. I know it sounds impossible, Carter, that's why I went along with the amnesia tale. It seemed so much more believable, so much more plausible. But it was a lie. A lie." Carter turned on his back and looked up at the ceiling trying to process everything she said. It could not be true. It was impossible. But . . .

He looked back at his Maggie, his gray eyes searching her clear brown ones. So honest, so open, so filled with love. Maggie gave him a look that told him she knew her story was impossible. Impossibly true. He shook his head, and Maggie let out a sigh of disappointment. Then he surprised her.

"All right, Maggie Johnsbury," he said, giving her a gentle kiss. "Tell me who you really are."

~ *Epilogue* ~

S teve leaned forward, Susan's last letter still dangling in one trembling hand. His eyes burned from reading all night and a glance at his watch told him it was two in the morning.

"Leave it to you, Susan, to not even die like the rest of us," he said aloud, smiling. Gathering up the precious letters, he lifted them to his lips, and breathed deep trying to get an essence of his wife. God, I miss you, Sue, he thought. But the papers smelled only of leather and must. Laughing at his own foolishness, he put the letters in a neat stack and tucked them back into the leather folder. Knowing that she had lived did not ease his pain, but somehow it felt right. Susan was too full of life to have died. Too full of love.

Glancing over at a dusty picture that sat on the nearby endtable, he picked it up and wiped it on his shirt. Susan looked back at him, her long wispy blonde hair falling straight down her back, her blue, blue eyes smiling at him through bangs that she was always tossing away. He could not imagine this petite dark-haired woman she had become, whom she had described in her letters. But he had an overwhelming desire to find out as much about her as he could. Resolving to drive over to Newport the next day, Steve fell asleep on the couch, still unwilling to lay alone in the bed he had shared with his wife.

He stood in the inn's foyer feeling an overwhelming sense of déjà vu, although he had never stepped foot in the grand old building before. The main parlor would be to his left, he thought, glancing at a closed door. A small sign told him the room was now the inn's office. The library doors, painted white, were opened, showing a portion of a large, lavishly furnished sitting room for guests. Along one wall was a long table with fruits and danish set up for a sumptuous continental breakfast. As he stood waiting for someone to approach him, a couple jogged down the sweeping staircase, tennis racquets in hand, chattering happily.

The office door opened, revealing a young woman with frizzled red-gold hair clipped back carelessly by a barrette. She wore tan pants and a matching linen blazer with a simple white T-shirt underneath, epitomizing Newport's casual elegance.

"Mabel Gibbons? We spoke on the phone. I'm Steven Butler."

"Oh, yes. I remember. You were interested in the history of the Sea Rose Inn. I gathered some articles and a couple of brochures together. They're in my office." She led Steve into the room decorated in comfortable and welcoming pastels and earth tones. The floor was carpeted, a soapstone woodstove sat cold in the marble fireplace.

"May I ask why you're interested? As far as I know, this inn has only minor historical significance. It's a nice example of New England shingle architecture and remained a single-family residence longer than a lot of these old houses, but no one ever famous stayed here. I know it used to be called Rose Brier, but we changed the name."

Steven smiled. This house was witness to one of the most remarkable stories imaginable and no one would ever know it. He said simply, "I'm . . . related to someone who used to own the house. Johnsbury."

"Really? The Johnsburys? Then we're cousins of sorts. My great-great grandfather owned this old place. It was out of the family for about twenty years and went on the auction block and my father snagged it for almost nothing. It was a mess, but he restored it and we've had it ever since. That's the whole story. Sorry, no ghosts, no deep, dark secrets." Mabel's bright smile faltered when she saw the expression on the man's face change. His polite interest in her turned into such burning intensity, she felt uncomfortable.

Steven was aware he was frightening the young woman, but he could not believe he was standing there chitchatting with Susan's great-great-granddaughter. He had to force himself from blurting out, "I was married to your ancestor!" His skin prickled with the discovery. Although this red-mopped little thing looked nothing like Susan, he was reminded of her just the same when she smiled. She was not smiling at the moment, however. She was looking at him as if he were somehow dangerous.

Steven forced himself to smile casually. "I'm sorry, I always get a bit intense when I research," he said lamely. Mabel instantly brightened.

She loved working in the old inn, loved the elegance of the place, even though it did not have the colorful history of some of Newport's more lavish residences. She didn't care. This house held her history. "Oh, don't worry. I'm flattered by your interest."

For a guilty moment, Steven thought she had noticed his attraction to her. He did not want to be attracted to anyone so soon after Susan's death, and certainly not Susan's great-great-granddaughter! Then he realized she had been talking about his interest in the inn.

"You said you had some brochures," he said quickly to cover his discomfort. Steve flipped rapidly through the papers she'd given him, quickly discerning there were no pictures included.

"Are there any portraits or photographs of the Johnsburys?" Steve asked.

Mabel frowned. "I'm sure my mother and aunts and uncles have some, but they are scattered about. There's nothing here. We never thought anyone would be all that interested. No! Wait. I can't believe I forgot. In the library is a gorgeous portrait of Margaret Johnsbury, my great-great-grandmother. She lived in the house until it was sold." She began walking Steve to the library. "The portrait was painted in 1896 of her and her son, my great-grandfather. He's the hero of the family. When he was twenty-two he was on the *Californian.* You know, the ship that spotted the *Titanic*'s distress signal? My grandmother told me he's the one who spotted the signal. They say he saved hundreds of lives. I wonder what would have happened if he hadn't been aboard?"

When they reached the library, Steve was again overwhelmed by its familiarity, for Susan had described her favorite room in loving detail. He walked directly to the portrait, his eyes eager to see something of Susan there. He gazed at the young woman, sparkling brown eyes, curling brown hair—a beautiful young woman that looked strikingly like the woman standing next to him. But so unlike Susan, he thought with disappointment. Then he looked again at the woman in the portrait's eyes. Even though they were brown, not blue like Susan's, he could see the artist had captured a vitality, a mischievousness so like Susan's. It was her, after all, he thought, shaking his head at the impossibility of it all. The little boy must have looked like his father. His hair, wavy and black, his eyes startlingly gray and intelligent. He stood beside his mother, holding her hand in an almost protective way.

"I've always wondered if the artist took any license," Mabel said, tilting her head up to study the painting

she'd looked at a thousand times. "I mean, it's hard to
believe that two people could be so perfect, you know?"

Steve felt his throat constrict, realizing he was looking
at Susan. His eyes filled with tears a moment later.

"What is the boy's name?" he asked, his voice taut
and husky.

Mabel looked at him suddenly, sharply, as if knowing
the answer to his question meant something significant.

"Steven," she said. "His name was Steven."